# THE ILLU...
# MER... BROWNE

# THE ILLUMINATION OF MERTON BROWNE

j. m. shaw

SCEPTRE

First published in Great Britain in 2007 by Sceptre
An imprint of Hodder & Stoughton
An Hachette Livre UK company

First published in paperback in 2008

1

From 'Ode with a Lament' translated by WS Merwin 'Poetry' translated by
Alastair Reid from *Pablo Neruda: Selected Poems*, published by Jonathan Cape.
Reprinted by permission of the Random House Group Ltd.

From 'The Love Song of J. Alfred Prufrock' and 'The Waste Land' by T.S. Eliot,
published by Faber and Faber.
Reprinted by permission of Faber and Faber Ltd.

A CIP catalogue record for this title is available from the British Library

ISBN 978 0 340 93364 0

Typeset in Sabon MT by Palimpsest Book Production Limited,
Grangemouth, Stirlingshire

Printed and bound by Clays Ltd, St Ives plc

Hodder & Stoughton policy is to use papers that are natural, renewable and
recyclable products and made from wood grown in sustainable forests.
The logging and manufacturing processes are expected to conform to the
environmental regulations of the country of origin.

Hodder & Stoughton Ltd
338 Euston Road
London NW1 3BH

www.hodder.co.uk

To Caroline, I. M. C. S

# 1

I don't know who my father is, and to tell you the truth I don't give a shit. As soon as he'd shot his load, setting me afloat in my mother's brown velvety womb, he scorched his tackle under the hot tap, grabbed his coat, and scarpered. I used to wonder what kind of man provided the single triumphant sperm – what thoughts gripped his heart as he grunted and the condom burst. But I've seen other people's fathers, and I reckon I'm doing all right without one.

Of course my mother claims she knows exactly who he was, but I bet she can't remember for sure. I don't use his name, and there's no reason I should take hers either. I'm free to choose my own, if you think about it. But my first name is Merton. At school I was Merton Browne, after my mother. Since my father was called McNeill – according to Mum's cagey account – I might really be Merton McNeill, which isn't bad. Or I could try something else. It doesn't matter.

I wanted to write down everything that happened, right from the start, so that I could get it straight in my head. But the fact is, I hardly remember anything before I was nine.

My first real memory is hiding in the boiler cupboard with a torch, reading a Tintin book, *Destination Moon*. If I lifted the corner of the carpet, I could see the light of the TV in the sitting-room, glowing through the floorboards. The news was on, and Mum was quiet, probably smoking in her dressing-gown, feet up on the sofa. Tuck Martin was with her. I could hear his deep voice.

I wasn't reading, exactly. I was just looking at Tintin and Snowy in their spacesuits. But when Tuck started to raise his voice, I decided to disappear. I turned off the torch and closed my eyes, and immediately the cupboard became a space capsule, sealed and pressurised. In a moment I was shot up, miles into the sky, the little ship trembling as it left the atmosphere, until suddenly everything was silent, because you can't hear anything in space. All around were the stars, and far below, shining more than all of them, the big blue world.

But there was interference on the radio. Tuck was shouting at Mum. She replied in a soothing voice, and I imagined the smoke escaping from her mouth. Then Tuck hit the kitchen table – the sound shook the walls and my heart jumped; Mum's voice began to rise. I could hear her getting up from the sofa. She was angry now, yelling back at him. There was a thump; she started screaming like she was hurt. My stomach contracted, and after that I started falling, down and down, a thousand feet a second, back on to the ground.

There was silence on Earth when I landed: the screaming had stopped. I waited for ages in the darkness. Even the TV was quiet, and I thought probably Tuck had smashed it. I could have stayed upstairs all night. Nobody was going to look for me. But I needed to see for myself; I wanted to find out what they had done. It was so quiet, I remember wondering if they had killed each other, or if Tuck had gone away. So I opened the hatch, looked out over the landing, and crept downstairs.

'Diana, love, I'm *sorry*. Don't be mad, sweetie.'

Tuck was leaning over Mum, gazing into her hair, while she lay on the sofa with her back to him. I was at the door. They hadn't seen me yet.

'Piss off, why don't you?' She had a clump of kitchen paper pressed against her face.

'I *said* I'm sorry, like. I'll make amends.'

'Animal!' Mum said. 'Don't you come near me.'

Tuck got up from the sofa and wandered away, his big head hanging forward. Mum rolled over and got to her feet. Her mouth and nose were bleeding. She passed me without a word, putting a hand out to the banisters, and felt her way upstairs. The bathroom door slammed, and I heard the water drumming in the bath.

Back in the boiler cupboard, everything was quiet. I leaned against the wall, reading *Destination Moon*. I could remember everything: names, dialogue, the way the rocket controls were laid out. I didn't need to read the book – I could practically say it by heart. I started preparing to escape – to fly into space again – and, as I checked everything over, I began to feel calm.

But I was too late. Tuck came up and sat on the landing. He started pleading with Mum through the bathroom door. 'Don't be dippy, Diana, love. Let me in. You know I didn't mean it.' Then, opening the cupboard door, he tried to enlist my support. 'Put in a word for uncle Tuck, won't you? I'll let you stay up, scamp. I'll give you a tenner.'

'This is the launching zone,' I said. 'Clear the area.'

'Now, listen, you . . .'

But I backed away deeper into the cupboard.

'Take-off in two minutes.'

'Freak!' Tuck said. And he slammed the door.

In the darkness, I hid my book in the angle of the roof. I was stranded on Earth for the night, the worst place to be. Tuck settled down on the stairs, resting his head against the wall. I could see him through the crack in the cupboard door, lighting a reefer. He took a drag, keeping the smoke deep in his lungs, and he was smiling, shaking his head. The smell of grass started to fill the cupboard, and I sucked it in, inhaling until my head grew light and my thoughts started to race about – up into space, far away, until the world disappeared.

The bolt on the bathroom door shot back, and I shuffled across the cupboard to look through the crack. Mum appeared in a bathrobe, her face blotchy and red. Tuck offered her his joint, but she ignored him, gliding towards the bedroom. All the same, when she had gone, he pulled my door open.

'Come on, professor,' he grinned. 'Your mum's back in the land of the living. Let's get some tea.'

Tuck and I cleared up the sitting-room. The goldfish were dead, stranded on the wet carpet next to Tuck's record collection. He scooped them into the bin. Then he dimmed the lights and put Marvin Gaye on the turntable. Soon the place smelt of dope and joss-sticks, and I lay down on the sofa.

I woke when Mum picked me up. She was squeezing me, murmuring smoke into my hair. Then Tuck turned the volume up, my mother dropped me back on the styrofoam, and they started dancing, until Tuck gave her a long, bruised snog.

Later she made fried eggs and toast, and we had tea, the three of us, sitting at the kitchen table – 'Like a proper fucking family,' Tuck said. Tuck and Mum kissed again, and she said she loved him. Then he rolled her a brand-new joint, and they went upstairs.

I remember other things, but they happened later, after my eleventh birthday.

I was awake and it was very early – not even six. There was so much adrenaline inside me I couldn't lie still. Mum had laid my clothes at the end of the bed: strange, stiff clothes, for my first day at my new school, and I started to get dressed. I knew I didn't look right. I had no trainers for one thing, only these black shoes with bulbous toes. The jeans were stiff, and too dark. Mum had bought them for a fiver at a market stall.

I tried to forget about my clothes. I read a whole Tintin book. Then I practised the dates of the kings and queens of England. I'd learnt them by heart from the *Guinness Book of Records*. I thought they'd be useful at the new school. I imagined myself telling the whole class these dates and names, getting a prize. Then I looked at my *Child's Book of English Cathedrals*. I knew which king or bishop had built each one.

Mum wanted to walk me to school, but I wouldn't let her. I made her leave me on the corner of the High Street, on the far side of Cannon Park Estate, so nobody would see her kissing me. Then I ran down the road to the school gates, into the playground. The New Crosland Comprehensive was a huge steel-frame building at the end of the High Street. Its whole front was glazed with Perspex panels: big yellow and plum-coloured panes, glowing in the morning light.

I stood at the gates. You could see the three main blocks from the playground: they formed the shape of a C around the open space, with the entrance in the middle. All across the big open space, and on the steps of the main door, were groups of pupils. We were all supposed to line up according to years and classes, but I couldn't see where to go. There were crowds everywhere.

A gang of boys were working their way round the yard. 'Subs!' they shouted. 'Subs for the posse.' They were wearing big jeans, low round the hips, and jackets with the hoods up.

I watched as they surrounded a black boy, bigger than me, but fat and soft-looking. 'Subs,' they screamed. 'Give us your lunch money, you fat cunt! You should be on a diet, in any case.' One of them punched the boy hard, and he staggered back, feeling for the railings. He fell clumsily, his glasses hitting the tarmac. On the ground he tried to protect his rucksack, but the gang started kicking. Their blows made a thudding sound. The leader grabbed the bag and held it upside down. Red and blue exercise books fell out in the sunlight, and the boy's pen rolled across the tarmac towards me. It was an old-fashioned one, the kind that needs ink cartridges, and I slipped it into my anorak pocket. The gang leader didn't notice; he was looking for money. And the others were still kicking the boy on the ground, taking it in turns like a penalty shoot-out.

Then the beating stopped.

'I'm Savage,' the leader of the gang said. 'Remember my face, nappy-head.' The boy said nothing. He was moving with difficulty, trying to sit up. 'You get two quid from your mum, right?'

5

the leader went on, tossing the rucksack aside. 'That's how much we'll take.' And he spat at him. 'Gob on him,' he told the others. 'Go on! Gob on his jacket.' They all spat on the boy's clothes. Then one of the gang, short and ferrety with blond hair, stamped on the fat boy's glasses.

I began to move slowly out of the playground, away from the bright buildings. I was just a few yards from the High Street; I could have been out in seconds. But they had seen me, and someone shoved me from behind. 'Subs!' they were shouting.

Two of the posse were black, the others were white. But the one in charge really had no colour at all: he was very pale, almost translucent, with pock-marked skin. 'I'm Savage,' he said quietly, staring in my face. He had bright blue irises, like pieces of chipped glass set in jelly. 'Give us our subs.'

'What's a sub?' I said.

'Oh! What's a *sub*?' He did a gay voice. '*Cash*, batty-boy. Give us your dinner money.'

'I don't have any.'

He leaned forward to take hold of my bag. 'Hit him!' he said. 'Do it *now*.' Someone kicked me from behind and I fell. Then the leader tipped all my stuff on the tarmac and handed the empty bag to the blond ferret. 'Search the bag, Terence.'

'Give it to me,' I said.

'Shut your face.'

My money was in the back flap. The blond boy found it straightaway.

'Kick him again!' the leader said. 'Lying cunt.'

Two of the boys held me spread-eagled, arms and legs pinned down, while the others began kicking. I must have cried out, because they were imitating me. Then they let go, and immediately I doubled up on the ground, while the whole gang joined in together, hitting as hard as they could.

'Go on,' the leader shouted, 'do it properly.'

They were kicking my back and legs. Tears came to my eyes, and for ages I couldn't breathe, but I didn't cry.

Then a man's voice shouted out: 'Oi, you lot. Time for assembly!'

'Sod that,' the savage said. 'Let's go.'

And the gang ran off.


'He broke your glasses,' I said.

'It's okay. Forget it.' The fat boy turned his face away, searching the ground nearby. My eyes were hot; I was trying not to cry. But he came back towards me.

'Here.' He held out a pudgy hand. 'Stand up. You'll feel better.' So I got to my feet. 'I'm Daniel Johnson,' he told me.

'Merton,' I said, rubbing my face. 'Merton Browne. Look, I got this . . .' I took his pen from my pocket.

Daniel grinned. 'Thanks, man. My mum would kill me . . .' His face was trembling but he was pulling himself up, straightening his clothes. The teacher who had shouted came up to us.

'You boys all right?'

'Yes, sir,' Dan said.

I just nodded.

'You don't want to hang around with those lads,' he told us. He was wearing track-suit bottoms and old, worn-down trainers. 'Come on, let's get your things. You'll be late . . .' And he moved off ahead of us, leaving a tang of BO in the bright air.

# 2

There was a boys' gang and a girls' gang at the New Crosland. They fought for lunch money in the playground, and controlled the classrooms. Paul Savage was best friends with Terence Arkwright – the nervous, ratty boy who had searched my bag – and they hung out with people like Victor, Tatham and Calvin, who were much bigger than them. Tatham was over six foot already, and everyone knew he was the best fighter in the school.

The girls followed Mary McDermot – Gaelic Mary – a thir-teen-year-old redhead with big tits and beefy shoulders. When she passed Dan and me in the corridor, she always gave us a thump on the arm. 'Pass it on,' she said, and the other girls in line behind her did the same, so that we got twelve punches as they marched past. The girls' gang was called the Banshees.

Mary liked to empty my rucksack and confiscate the books. She did it my very first day. 'I'll take this one,' she said, grab-bing Red Rackham's *Treasure*. She ripped the pages out of the hard cover and started tearing them up. Dan and I didn't move. We stood there while she dumped all my stuff on the floor.

'Now piss off, Merlin,' she said, suddenly getting bored, 'or I'll fist-fuck you in front of the class.'

In our first term there was a teacher shortage, and we kept being left on our own. So for a few weeks they doubled us up with an older class, and gave us this Australian supply teacher, Victoria Dent, who later became our form teacher. She specialised in history, but during the early days she took us for Personal, Social and Health Education, which meant sex.

Miss Dent handed out a booklet, *Sex 4 U*, with bright cartoons of kids fooling about. 'Take a look at these books,' she said. 'I'm treating you as adults. I expect you to react appropriately. The important thing is to respect yourselves, and be open to new experiences with your bodies.'

'Oi, miss, this is gross,' Dan said. He held up a picture of a group of lesbians on a big bed. 'They're freaks.'

'Don't be judgemental, Dan. Remember the three Ds: don't judge yourself; don't judge others; don't let others judge you. Your sexual choices are part of who you are – part of your uniqueness as a person.'

Dan and I were sitting against the back wall. Miss Dent was miles away. So I started testing myself on the dates of the kings and queens of England. I wrote them all out on a worksheet. It helped to keep me calm.

'She ought to be using a dildo,' Gaelic Mary pointed out.

'Who?'

'The girl having a wank in the bath, miss. She should use a broomstick or something.'

'Mary's a slapper,' Calvin commented. 'She could fuck a horse.'

'She prefers horses, miss.'

I had put down all the Saxons and Danes: Cnute, Edward the Confessor, Harold Godwin – everyone before the Norman Conquest.

'Hey, miss, there's no pictures of people screwing animals.'

'Yeah. That's true. It's discriminatory. It's excluding people who like dogs.'

'*You're* a dog, miss,' Mary said, 'they should photograph you.'

'That's enough,' Miss Dent said. But Victor had found the pictures of two boys wanking each other off, and everyone started complaining.

'That's fucking Dan,' he said. 'Dan and Merton, right? They suck each other.'

Dan nudged me nervously, but I was working through the Normans and Plantagenets: *Stephen of Blois, 1135 to 1154; The Empress Matilda, 1141; Henry II, 1154 to 1189* . . .

Tatham stood on his chair to make a formal complaint. 'Fucking batty-boys, miss. You teaching us to be faggots, right? I mean, that's not how it is. I'm a fucking yard man. I'm not a fudge packer.'

'Sit down, Tatham. You've made your point.'

But Tatham carried on standing on his chair, pointing at Miss Dent, trying to intimidate her.

I went on with the table of kings. I was doing the Wars of the Roses, which is pretty complicated.

'Settle down, *all* of you,' Miss Dent said. 'Turn to the diagrams at the back of the book.' So everyone had a look at the pictures of a man and woman screwing in cross-section, and the whole class started groaning again.

'Any questions?' Miss Dent shouted.

'Yes, miss. I've got a question.'

'What is it, Calvin?'

'When do you get your period, miss?'

'Don't be silly. That's nothing to do with this class. It's none of your business.'

I got through the Tudors in half a minute, writing automatically. I was getting faster.

'But miss, *miss*!'

Terence had had his hand up for ages. He was sitting quietly at the back, not smiling, but jabbing his hand in the air. He looked very serious.

'Yes, Terry?'

'I just want to know: does your boyfriend give it to you up the arse?'

'That's enough! Any *sensible* questions?'

*James I, 1603 to 1625; Charles I, 1625 to 1649 – then the interregnum . . .*

'But it's a real question, miss. Is it safe, like?' Terry's thin, ferrety face was marked with deep lines. Although he was small, he looked much older than he was.

'Me, miss!'

'Calvin?'

*William of Orange, 1689 to 1702 . . .*

'I want to know: will you give me a blow-job?' Calvin asked. 'I need the experience.' He put on a meek voice. 'I'm – I'm a virgin, see.'

Everyone laughed. Even the well-behaved girls at the front started laughing. And I wrote down Queen Anne's dates.

'Right, that's *it*! You're all on detention.'

'Oh, miss!'

'Remember the three Ds, miss.'

I had reached George IV and Queen Victoria; I was almost up to date.

'Loss of privilege, F2,' Miss Dent yelled. 'No school journey for you.'

*George V, 1910 to 1936; Edward VIII, 1936; then George VI . . .*

'You're all staying in.'

'That's fascist, miss. You can't do that.'

And I reached the end: *Elizabeth II, proclaimed Queen in 1952, crowned in 1953.*

I was lying on top of my duvet. Downstairs Tuck and my mother were arguing. The noise of it came into my reading, like life intruding into a dream, but for ages I ignored them. I was learning about the Vikings, out of this book I'd nicked from a charity shop. It said that if a Viking died in battle he went straight to heaven, so the only thing that mattered was being brave. I thought about that, and I kept reading. I really wanted to be a Viking.

Then later on, when Tuck started beating my mother – when she was shouting *Bastard, bastard*, and he kept belting her – I got up on an impulse, marched to the boiler cupboard, and took the biggest chisel from his toolkit. I prepared myself with a deep breath, called on Odin to protect me, and ran downstairs, straight into the sitting-room, charging towards his thick leg.

'Watch out, Tuck! Merton'sh got a blade.' Mum was kneeling on the floor, pressing a cushion against her lip.

'Watch it, nipper!' He swung his hand to keep the chisel from his thigh, and it fell under the TV. Then he picked me up and bounced me out the way on to the sofa. 'You stay there, mate. Don't fuck with your uncle Tucky.'

'Behave yourself, Merton,' Mum put in, 'there'sh a love. You don't know what's good for you.' There was blood on her T-shirt.

I jumped to my feet, head pounding, squaring up in front of Tuck. 'If I die,' I said, 'I go straight to Valhalla.'

'Merton, *lay* off, lad,' my mother sniffed, still kneeling. 'This is between us. It's grown-up stuff.' Tuck took the chisel from the floor, and placed it out of reach on his shelf of sex videos. But I screamed with the whole strength of my lungs, and charged him again.

'He's a right tearaway, for his age,' Tuck laughed. 'He's getting too old . . .' And he fended me off, pressing my face with his right hand. But I opened my mouth and dug my teeth into the karate-chop edge of his palm. I bit as hard as I could. It was crunchy, as though my teeth cut through a ligament. Tuck roared at me.

'That's the fucking limit.' He stood staring at his hand. 'He's drawn blood, the cunt. That's my working hand, that is.'

'He didn't mean it,' Mum said.

'*Mean* it? I'll fucking kill him.'

'Leave it out, Tucky,' Mum whined. 'He's only young.'

'You spoil him,' he said, 'reading and lying about . . . He's got to learn who's boss in this house.'

I got up and backed away. I wanted to charge him again, but Tuck was moving across the room with giant steps. He grabbed hold of my arms and lifted me up. There was a moment of stillness in my mind. I could see myself, suspended between the floor and ceiling. And I watched as he tossed me against the sitting-room wall like a plate of spaghetti.

Mum and Tuck were standing over me.

'You had us worried for a couple of days there, professor,' Tuck said.

'You did, love,' Mum put in. 'How you feeling?' She had drawn neat brown lines around her eyes, but I could see she'd been crying.

'I've got a headache.'

'They gave you stitches, see.' Mum held a mirror for me. There were four black threads zigzagging past my right eyebrow.

'Regular little Frankenstein.' Tuck attempted a smile, fingering his Arsenal bag. 'We'll get you some pills and that. Painkillers.'

Mum bit her lip, glancing at Tuck. 'You'd better say something,' she told him.

'Well, now, Merton . . . Wait, I bought you something . . .' Opening his football bag, he brought out a giant fruit and nut bar, and pressed it into my hand.

'Say thank you,' Mum said.

It hurt when I spoke. 'What's it for?'

'Just a present.'

'I don't want it.'

'*Take* it,' Tuck said. 'No hard feelings.' So I did. Then he lowered his voice. 'See here, Merton' – he glanced down the ward – 'if they come asking a lot of questions – *you* know: the police, the social – you'll keep it in the family, won't you? Your mum doesn't need the interference, does she?' My mother sniffed and stared at the wall. 'We'll make amends, like. We'll take you to Center Parcs.'

I observed them in silence for a while. Before they came, I had been reading a Sherlock Holmes story, lent to me by this old guy in the next bed, and I was looking for clues. Although it seemed strange, I could see that Mum and Tuck were frightened of me. It made me smile.

'Well, mate?' Tuck said.

'It doesn't matter,' I told him. 'I don't care if they arrest you or not.'

'Don't talk like that,' Mum said.

'You'll do as you're told,' Tuck put in.

'Or what? If you go to jail, that would be fine by me,' I said.

'Now you listen here. What have you been telling them?'

'Nothing,' I said. 'I'm still thinking about it.'

'You threatening me?'

'Yes,' I told him. 'Now fuck off. Both of you. Go on, leave me alone.'

Tuck snatched the bar of chocolate from my hand, and Mum began to cry.

'Little bastard.' He shoved it in his Arsenal bag, and I opened my book.

'It's the pills,' Mum said. 'He's not responsible.'

'Let's get out of here, before I give him one.'

'I'll be back tomorrow,' Mum said.

'Not if you've got any sense,' Tuck told her.

He took her arm, and they walked out along the avenue of beds.


After I came out of hospital I had to stay at home for ages, missing a whole month of school. Mum's friend Mel had found me these books on the legends of ancient Egypt, Greece and Rome, and I read the whole lot about three times over, sitting in my bedroom, or laid out on the sofa downstairs. The whole of that month I read as much as I wanted, because Tuck left me alone. He had become paranoid since our argument in the hospital, worried about the law because of some job he'd pulled. And he was convinced I was going to shop him. He suffered from nightmares, and spent half the day in bed trying to sleep, or lying on the sofa in front of the TV. The fight had gone out of him. He didn't even speak any more. If Mum started hassling him, he just used to walk out the house.


I went back to school after half-term, which was okay because I'd run out of things to read at home. Nobody asked where I'd been, except Dan. Even Miss Dent didn't seem to notice. She was having a bad time, because every time she went out of the classroom, the gangs attacked her. Savage's friend Tatham kept tripping her up whenever she walked past. Then he pretended to help her to her feet. 'Oh, sorry, miss. I didn't see you . . .' He gave her arm a yank which made her wince. One time he pushed her head against a door-frame, and she had to see the doctor. But Tatham never got punished; he always made it look like an accident.

Mary McDermot was worse. In the break once, Miss Dent argued with her about her attendance record, and Mary punched her on the arm. Miss Dent went to the staff-room and cried. The next day she had a huge bruise under her T-shirt. We all saw it.

After that, Mary's gang started calling her Aussie Bitch, or Cunt-face.

'Why aren't you in class, Mary?'

'Oh, *I'm* sorry, Cunt-face. I can't be arsed.'

Miss Dent put on a little laugh. 'You have got a *lot* of growing up to do.'

'Fuck you,' Mary said. She stared for a moment at Miss Dent, pushed her aside, and walked out of the school.

One day, a few weeks after half-term, Tuck packed a few things, got on his motorbike, and roared away. Mum sat on the sofa, shaking her head. She didn't even go to the window to watch. And at the weekend, when I realised he wasn't coming back, I piled up the rest of his clothes and magazines in the garden in front of the house, and set fire to them all. Mum said she didn't care. I burned everything, even his Marvin Gaye records.

After that, we were alone. Coming back from school in the dark, I used to see the curtains drawn across the blue light of the TV. And when I got inside, Mum forced me to hug her, which made me feel sick. 'Come here, love.' I held my breath. 'I want more time with you, Merton; get to know you, like.' She gripped me, exhaling smoke. '*You're* my man, now.' And when I pushed her away, she started bustling about making tea.

\* \* \*

Later, when the days got really short, my mother slowed down. She refused to go outside, lying on the sofa while the house filled with the smell of bath oil and Silk Cut. Then, one day when I came back from school, just before the Christmas holidays, I found the curtains open. The sitting-room was lit up, but there was no one there.

I crept up to the landing.

'Mum?'

I could see the shape of her under the bedclothes, and the orange end of a lighted cigarette. 'Shut the door, there's a love,' she murmured. 'I need my space, like.' But I went up to her. Beside the bed were bottles of prescription pills, ashtrays, a litre of Scotch.

'Are you committing suicide?' I said.

'No, love.'

'I can call an ambulance.'

'Just lying down, love. Honest. Go on, get yourself some tea.'

The next evening my mother was sitting at the kitchen table, slumped over a saucer of stubs. She had been chain-smoking her way through the news. She didn't look up when I came in, but she wasn't really watching TV, either – just shaking her head. When I turned it off, she went on staring at the screen.

'Mum?' I waved my hand in front of her face. 'Mum, are you conscious? I'm on holiday. School's over . . .' She looked grey and dusty – I felt sick just looking at her.

# 3

One day early in the spring term, the posse came up and surrounded Miss Dent in the corridor outside our classroom. Her lesson had just ended, and most of us were still there. We stood about watching. Dan and I were at the back of the crowd.

'Out the way, boys,' she said.

'We only want to ask a few questions, miss.'

'All right.' Miss Dent stood still. 'One quick question.'

'Well, miss – no offence or anything, but why're you so frigid?' Calvin was speaking in his shy voice, and the boys started laughing.

'Calvin, that's not a proper question,' Miss Dent said. 'Out the way, all of you.'

'But, miss, I mean it. Don't you fancy me, or what?' It really sounded like he was upset. 'You're giving me low self-esteem.'

'He's got a lot of issues around women,' Mary added in a confidential whisper. 'He needs *therapy*, miss.'

'And we could get together, me and you,' Calvin went on, ignoring Mary. 'I could help you loosen up, like.' And he moved towards her, still speaking bashfully. 'I got a big cleaver, right.'

'Don't talk like that, or I'll put you on detention.' Miss Dent was trying to back away from the group, but she was surrounded.

'That's fucking typical!' Tatham complained. 'You won't touch him because he's black. It's always the same. You spends nuff time with your boyfriend.'

'Hey, miss, forget Calvin,' Victor said. 'If you really want some action, I'm your man, right?'

'She's not interested in you,' Calvin jeered.

'She fucking is.'

Miss Dent shouted as loud as she could. 'Calvin, Tatham – *all* of you. You've had your last warning!'

'I'll fight you for her,' Calvin yelled at Victor.

'What about Savage, then?' Tatham asked her. 'He's white. You could fuck him, miss.'

'Make way *immediately*!' Miss Dent tried to raise her voice again, but she sounded weak. 'I've got to go. I'm late for a meeting with the head.'

'The "hid"? What's the fucking "hid"?' Terry came up and stood in front of her. 'You never keep order, miss,' he told her. 'You're a fucking useless teacher, do you know that? What do you get paid for?'

But Tatham and Calvin moved in. 'Leave it out, man,' Tatham said. 'Let her go.' And the crowd began to make way.

Miss Dent paused for just a second. She was small; most of the boys were much taller than her. And she was probably no more than twenty-five. She clutched her worksheets against her stomach, about to walk away. Then Savage spoke for the first time.

'Hey, miss,' he said, 'don't listen to them. They're talking shit. One day soon – in the yard, right, after school – you'll get raped.'

For a moment there was silence. Miss Dent said nothing. Dan and I watched as she composed herself, keeping her head up. Her face was pale. Then she fixed her eyes ahead of her, and began to walk away.

There were three things you could do in our school if you wanted to read a book. There was the library, but that was mainly for computer terminals, with a few books full of cartoons and text boxes, and nothing you'd actually want to look at. Secondly, you could find an empty classroom to sit in, except that people used to come in to do drugs, or for blow-jobs. And finally there was a special classroom near the lavatories, where you were supposed to go if you were on detention. Usually there was a teacher in there, marking papers or reading the *Guardian*, and that kept the posse away. So I used to pretend I had been sent out of the class, and sometimes I stayed in there for hours at a time. That was when I decided to learn all the stories from the Old Testament. In three weeks I read the whole way from Adam and Eve to the exile in Babylon, and no one asked me once what I was doing in there.

For a few weeks after the rape threat, Miss Dent started going about with an assistant – a big bloke like a bouncer, from an agency. As long as he was there, Savage kept away, but Miss Dent had already started behaving strangely. Sometimes she couldn't remember what she was going to tell us, and she didn't seem to care if we paid attention or not. She just talked quietly to the people at the front of the class: the Chinese kids, and the posh girls like Deborah and Rose. Sometimes I sat up there too.

Deborah's parents were rich socialists. They had sent Debby to our school to prove their commitment to the New Jerusalem, but she had tutors at home, and she was always going on holiday with Rose to Florence or Rome, to study art. Mary McDermot used to kidnap Debby on the way back from school. One time she tied her up and kept her in her flat on the estate. She cut her hair with paper scissors and wrote 'bitch' in black marker pen right across her forehead. Then she made her walk home without shoes. Even then Debby's father didn't take her away.

Just before the spring half-term, when half the school was on an excursion, Miss Dent sent Dan and me down to the store-room, to bring up boxes of new textbooks. 'Here are the keys.' She handed them to Dan. 'Bring them straight back. I'm trusting you, right?'

We wandered out of the back door into the bright sunshine and across the tarmac, to the storeroom entrance. It was very cold. Dan fumbled with the keys, but when we finally opened the door, he didn't want to go inside. He said the place smelt of damp and piss, which was true, but really he was frightened of the dark. So I went in on my own.

I found our boxes right there in the first section of the store, and tore one open to make sure. The books were brand-new, twenty quid-a-copy A4 paperbacks. Volume One was page after page of social history: petticoats and top hats, children in the factories, Peterloo. The others were all twentieth century – Lenin, Hitler, the miners' strike. But I didn't tell Dan I'd found them. I decided to stay there, just to give him a fright. So I began trawling up and down the room, checking out all these old cardboard boxes full of exam papers and official circulars, GCSE guidelines, Best Practice manuals. There was masses of weird hardware and old equipment, too – broken chairs, ancient computers, a couple of lamps. Everything was shrouded in dust. Dan started calling out, but I ignored him. I kept moseying along through all the stuff, ferreting about. I found more boxes full of books, and I picked out a couple at random – a big hard-back: *A History of Europe: Vol. 1* by H. A. L. Fisher, and a geography book with diagrams of cocoa beans and photographs of black guys loading a ship in Lagos. Each book had a stamp in Gothic script on the inside cover: *Cannon Park Grammar School*, which is what the New Crosland used to be called, with a coat of arms – a harp, a sword, three books inside a shield, held up by a couple of angels. And there was a Latin inscription: *Possunt quia posse videntur.*

'What you doing, fucking nappy?' Dan was fidgeting by the door. 'It's cousin of Dracula in there, man.'

'Wait,' I said, 'I've just got to check something.'

Beyond the stacks of boxes, out of sight from the entrance, there was an iron handrail, and a flight of concrete steps that led down to a basement. I took hold of the railings, and crept downstairs. The whole place smelt of damp paper – the air was thick with it – and the basement was pitch-dark. I stood at the bottom of the stairs, feeling the wall for a light switch.

When the strip-lights came on, I was blinded. I stood at the threshold with my eyes screwed up. Very slowly, I began to make out the size and shape of things: the enormous room with these tall metal cases which ran across it. From where I was standing, all the way to the other side, seven-foot metal stacks were laid out in parallel lines, floor to ceiling, every one of them packed with books. It took me a while to understand what it was all about. I walked up and down, running my hand along the spines, breathing in the smell of damp binding, and my mind began to float. Our library in the main block was full of CD-ROMs and videos. The real library – the old one, all the stuff nobody read any more – had been dumped down there. I'd never seen so many books in one place. They made me nervous. And this library was private: a bunker cut off from the world. Nobody would disturb me if I hid in there.

I crouched down and took a book from the lowest shelf: Jacob Bronowski, *The Ascent of Man*. It was full of pictures of ancient buildings, old works of art, but I didn't read what it said. My heart was thumping, and my mind started racing about. I looked along the shelf. And I was thinking, 'I'll read the whole lot, book by book. They can't stop me. I'll keep coming down here till I know every page by heart.'

By the time Dan and me made it back to class with the books, Miss Dent had gone. Most of the class had left, too: there was just Debby and Rose, waiting at the front for Miss Dent to come back. So Dan and I went out into the sunlight, and started to walk away from the school, keeping to the shadows at the edge of the school yard.

I still had the keys to the storeroom. We wandered around for a while, but when nobody came to see what was happening, I slipped out through the gates, and ran down the High Street to the hardware shop. They weren't supposed to cut keys for pupils at the New Crosland, but I said they were for my mum, and the guy did it anyway. Afterwards I returned the originals to Ms Tooley, the school secretary, who was pleased with me for being so thoughtful. Everybody else had bunked off. The teachers were having a meeting, and I saw some policemen standing about in our classroom, which was sealed off with blue and white tape. So I went home with the new keys in my pocket.

The next day there was a special assembly. Ms Simpson, the head-teacher, was holding the microphone. There was a plain-clothes cop on the platform with her.

'I trusted you,' she told us. 'I have always tried to let you develop in your own way . . .' She looked at her notes and adjusted her glasses. Her hands were shaking. 'We have never subjected you to judgemental attitudes . . . You have been free – free to grow and explore and discover for yourselves . . .' All the teachers were there on the stage, except Miss Dent.

'Where is she?' Dan whispered. 'Where's Miss Dent?'

'Savage did her,' someone said quietly behind us.

Everyone was saying Savage and the boys had burst into Miss Dent's class when Dan and me were in the basement, and marched her down the corridor to an empty classroom. Nobody had been allowed to watch. They covered the little window in the door with a sign: *Silence! Examination in Progress.* Some people said Savage had made her have sex with the posse, one by one, and that now she was in a loony bin. But it was only a rumour. Nobody knew for certain.

'This is now a matter for the police,' Ms Simpson was saying. 'They will be interviewing everyone who was present in the school yesterday. You must be *completely* cooperative. I have been reasonable with you – with all of you, including some young people who I know have – do – have' – she searched her notes – 'have not found it easy to conform to a structured school environment . . . I insist that you respond to this situation as adults . . .'

And she handed the microphone to the copper.

\* \* \*

Our whole class was on detention. They were kept in all morning, while the police interviewed people one by one in Ms Simpson's office. But I didn't show up. It was the first time I decided to spend the day in the storeroom basement. I just moseyed along from the playground after the break, keeping to the side of the school building, and wandered into the little courtyard where the admin buildings were. I waited for footsteps, or a voice to stop me, but there was nobody there. As I reached the storeroom door, I could hear my class scraping chairs and groaning in the assembly hall where they were doing detention. I moved into the shadow of the doorway, took out the key, and slipped inside.

I didn't switch on the lights. Feeling my way past all the boxes, I grabbed the iron handrail, and crept downstairs to the bunker. Then in the darkness I crossed the huge room, right to the other side, and got myself organised by the far wall. There was an old armchair there, and a reading lamp which I set up beside it. The lamp emitted a circle of yellow light, and I looked at the shelves nearby, trying to decide what to read, but it took ages just to work out what all the subjects were. There were literally hundreds of books, dozens of novels I'd never heard of, shelf-loads of history, works of literary criticism, philosophy, religion, anthologies of poetry, science and maths books, dictionaries, books about ancient languages. And every volume had the Grammar School coat of arms on the inside cover.

In the end I picked something called G. M. Trevelyan, *A History of England*, Volume One, and sat down by the light.

At first I read very slowly, breaking off the whole time to look things up in the dictionary. Sometimes the pump in the boiler-room changed gear, or I heard footsteps in the yard upstairs, echoing like little gunshots. But mostly it was silent.

By the afternoon I had started the chapter on the fall of Rome. Trevelyan made it seem real, the way he wrote: eagle banners straining in the wind; legions waiting in ranks for the last bugle; columns of men marching along the straight roads, as they headed for the ships. And after the Romans, nothing but war – war for centuries. The Saxons landed on beaches like pirates, or sailed up the rivers. In fifty years everything was destroyed, towns and temples overgrown, fields returned to wilderness. I sat in silence for a long time, imagining that.

During the Easter holidays, when it was lighter, Mum started to move about again. She went out in the mornings and bought the *Guardian*, spreading the job section on the kitchen table, and spattering it with red felt-tip circles. Then she and her friend Mel put together a CV, emphasising her A levels, and the name of the college where she said she had met my father, before her life collapsed. They invented jobs to fill the gap of the last ten years, and Mel lent her *Bluff Your Way in Office Administration* and *PCs for Dummies*. They sent out a dozen applications every week.

In the mornings Mum got dressed in her interview clothes, and laid the table. 'I'll get something,' she said, gusting blue smoke. 'A proper job – like I used to have. *And* a man. I can feel it. Someone to look after me.' She was looking away, frying bread. 'Someone to make me feel alive.'

'Someone to thump you,' I said.

'Oh, you're too young, love. You couldn't understand.'

Every day of the holidays I ran out across the Cannon Park Estate, along the High Street, through the school yard, down to the bunker. The school was silent. There was nobody to ask me questions, no one to stop me reading all day if I wanted.

I was going to finish the Dark Ages, but I didn't sit down right away. For a while I went stumbling about in the stacks, searching at random. And in the end I pulled out this anthology of poetry – a big old hardback with gold letters on the spine.

It fell open at *The Rubaiyat of Omar Khayyam*. So I sat down and started reading, silently at first, but bit by bit speaking out loud, chanting the strange, rhythmic words.

*Up from Earth's Centre through the Seventh Gate*
*I rose, and on the Throne of Saturn sate;*
*And many a knot unravelled by the Road;*
*But not the Master-knot of Human Fate.*

Page after page it went on, always in the same beat, until it started to give me a buzz. And after I had finished reading it, I decided to memorise the whole poem – to learn every verse – until I had all those spermy, melancholy rhythms buried in my brain. It took forty-five minutes to say it right through. And once I'd learned it, I used to recite it every morning on my way to school.

I started reading things in this old Bible I found, as well – the King James Version, the only one they used to use in school assemblies. I started with the psalms. They made no sense, but I liked reading them. *Thou shalt not be afraid for any terror by night: nor for the arrow that flieth by day; For the pestilence that walketh in darkness: nor for the sickness that destroyeth in the noon-day.* You could see how people could believe in that stuff. You could almost believe it yourself. I read it just to soothe my head, like a tranquilliser.

Apart from that I mainly read *A History of England*, working through the chapters on the Danes and Alfred the Great, Cnute, Edward the Confessor, till finally I got to the Normans and Plantagenets. And I made notes as I read. All the dates of kings and queens I had memorised before I came to the New Crosland started to fit together, and now there was a point to it all – a sort of pattern. It was hard to argue with Trevelyan. He wrote in this very detached, totally confident way that I'd never seen before, and he seemed to understand everything. In a way I could see why they had buried him down there.

# 4

Early on Easter Sunday, while Mum was still asleep, I went to block B of the Cannon Park Estate to visit Dan.

He lived with his mother and grandfather in a small flat that smelt of piss and fried bacon. The old grandfather sat in the armchair, sleeping, or mumbling to himself, while Dan's mother cooked us breakfast. Then she made us sit at the table and stood over us, her arms folded across her huge bosom. And she kept talking all the time. 'You eat up, you boys. You need your food. You're growing so fast I hardly know you.' She had a very strong Jamaican accent; she sounded totally different from Dan.

When we were done, Mrs Johnson roused the old man and made us all go to church.

The chapel was a prefab building, stranded in the courtyard of the Cannon Park Estate between three medium-rise blocks. Dan's mother and her friends looked after it. They planted spring bulbs in the flower-bed, and painted the woodwork. Someone had erected a ten-foot cross on the roof over the door, rigging up a white neon tube around the outline, so that it shone at night. And on Sundays people came from all around to hear the preacher.

I was practically the only white person in there. People smiled and put their hands on my shoulders because I was a guest. Dan's mother told me I had been brought by the Holy Spirit. She left Dan and me jammed in with the grandfather and loads of other people in a pew, while she went to sing in the choir, up by the preacher.

They were Pentecostalists. The singing went on for hours: *Jesus Christ is risen today, Alleluia! Our triumphant holy day,*

*Alleluia!* It was incredibly loud. The rhythm started to get to me, and I couldn't help smiling. When I closed my eyes, I could imagine I was anywhere – in America or Jamaica, or in another age. I was part of something bigger than me. And we were all clapping, swaying in the pews, like everyone in the church was connected. I couldn't sing, because my voice was breaking: it either came out too low, or squeaky and too high. But even so, I liked it.

At the end, Dan's mother sang a solo, making the church judder with her *vibrato*. She was extremely fat, much fatter than Dan, and when she sang her whole body wobbled – boobs, arms, even the flesh on her face. But her voice was incredible: it drilled right into my head, and everyone stood still, listening to her. Then, when she finished, the whole church applauded – everyone except Dan, who was embarrassed.

Mum received a letter from the employment agency. She'd landed a flexi-hour job at the Local Education Authority, working as an assistant in their Equal Opportunities Assessment Office.

'I start right away,' she said, giving me a kiss on the forehead. 'They're expanding. Look . . .' The council motto was written across the top of the letter: *Caring For All Our Communities*. 'A real job,' she said.

Mum had lost loads of weight. She had her dark suit on, and before she went out she stood in the bathroom and sprayed Coco Chanel behind her ears.

She hesitated in the hall. 'Wish me luck, love.'

'Go on,' I said. 'Don't think about it. You'll slay them.'

When we went back to school, Savage declared war. The cops were still investigating the attack on Miss Dent, and he was beginning to think that someone might name him. So the posse increased the pressure. They used to wait at the school gates in the morning while people came in, ambushing anyone who knew what had happened – especially people like Rose or Debby, who maybe thought the police were going to do something about it.

'You talk to the police and I'll cut your fucking face,' Tatham told Rose.

Rose stared at the concrete with her big wide-open eyes, while Terry tipped everything out of her bag. 'I haven't said anything,' she whispered.

'I can't fucking hear you.'

'I haven't said anything,' she repeated.

'If you think the cops will look after you,' Terry added, 'you're out of your fucking mind. They'll be gone in a week. But we'll be here, we're always here. Do you understand?'

Rose nodded.

'I can't hear you.'

'I understand.' She bent down and started picking up her glittery pens.


Dan and I kept away. We usually ran past the school gates down Fisher's Lane, along the side of the yard. Climbing the wall at the back of the school buildings – right where the bunker was – we slipped in through the janitor's door. It was out of bounds, but that way we escaped the posse. Then we would mosey towards the classroom.

But sometimes Mary McDermot was waiting for us in the corridor.

'Where are your books, Merlin?'

'I don't have any.'

'Liar. Punch him.' Tracey Millen hit me in the stomach and I doubled up. '*Where?*'

'Fuck off,' I said.

'Make him piss himself,' Mary chanted. 'Go on. Take him to the bogs. Nappy-head, too.'

They marched Dan and me to the loos.

'Open his bag,' Mary told them. 'Dump his stuff down the toilet.'

Tracey pulled Trevelyan's *History of England* out of the bag. She and Mary started tearing it apart, feeding the creamy pages into the bowl. 'Pull the chain.' The water churned over them. Then my felt-tips and pencils got kicked across the tiles.

'Why don't you eat shit?' Mary asked. 'There: there's some nice fresh crap on the seat. You can eat it, can't you, Merlin? Do you good.'

They had me in a double Nelson. Tracy Millen and this big girl I didn't know held me face-down on the loo seat, right on this shit-smear. The smell made me retch. Then Mary grabbed my testicles through my trousers, and started squeezing. I kicked out, but she gripped tighter.

'Eat shit, Merlin. Go on! Just a little nibble . . . Or I'll ram this thing up your arse.' I couldn't see what she was holding.

'Fuck off!' I said. 'Get off me!' The shit on the loo seat was right up against my face. I couldn't breathe for the stink of it. I tried to kick my legs again, but they were held tight.

'*Temper*, Merlin! It's not good to lose your cool, sweetie. We're only fooling about. Can't you take it?' And she twisted my balls in her fist.

'Ah, Jesus!' I could feel myself turning cold. My head was banging from being pressed down. And I was thinking, *No, no, don't let me lose it*. But I felt a warm area growing across my belly.

'Fucking Nora,' Mary said. 'He's pissed himself, the little bastard.' And she let me fall on the tiles. 'That's not very hygienic, is it? Tidy up, now, there's a good boy.' She threw a roll of loo paper at me. 'Clear it up, you freak!' And all the Banshees copied her, chucking loads of toilet rolls into the cubicle.

I didn't go into class. Dan got my track-suit from the locker room. I put it on, and washed my trousers and shirt in the basins. Then I climbed out the window to the little courtyard, and made it to the bunker. When I had spread my clothes over the pipes, I made a sort of mattress from the panels of a cardboard box, like a homeless man. I lay down, staring up at the knife-edge of light that came through the ventilation system. I was shaking. I just lay there imagining myself shooting everyone in the school, one by one, starting with Mary McDermot.

When everyone had left, when it was dark outside and I couldn't hear a sound, I crept out to buy samosas and chocolate in the High Street. But I didn't go home. I went back to the bunker, and tried to sleep. And when I was feeling better – some time in the early morning, after I'd slept a few hours – I searched for another copy of Trevelyan. I had reached the English Civil War, and I really liked that. I started to picture the hills and forests, the raging streams, war horses steaming in the dawn, towns and castles on fire. It made me feel alive – as though I had suddenly woken up – to learn that the world had been born in violence.

I stayed in the bunker as much as I could that summer term. But I had to come out sometimes, and Mary McDermot always started shouting down the corridors when she saw me. 'Hey, Merlin, got your nappies yet?'

By half-term, everyone knew I had wet myself. Girls came up offering paper tissues. 'Feel like a piss, Merton?'

'Fuck off,' I said. 'I'll fucking kill you.' But I could feel myself going red.

'How will you do that, you prat? You going to piss on me?'

Mum kept her job, and soon we were rich. A freezer appeared at the back of the house, big enough to stand in, and Mum packed it out with steaks and crinkly chips. She started going out at the weekends, tripping across Spenser Close in pneumatic jeans to see her friend Mel. Or she sat waiting in the sitting-room for some new man to come round and take her out to dinner.

One morning, when I came down, there was a red BMW on the pavement outside, and one of Mum's boyfriends was eating breakfast in our kitchen. He glowered over his coffee. 'This is Brett,' Mum said from the stove. 'He's moving in for a while.'

'Great,' I said. '*Hi*, Brett.' He grunted and munched his toast.

'That your car on the drive?'

'Yup.'

'Brand-new,' mum said. 'We can all go out in it.'

'Sure, if you like . . .' Brett waved his toast magnanimously.

'Oh, right,' I said. 'Nice one.'

And when I passed it on my way to school, I scraped my penknife as hard as I could down the whole length.

I was trying to find another book as good as Trevelyan, but for a while I read poetry instead. The truant office sent letters to my mother, but she knew I always went to school, and I told her it was just a mistake on the computer. Nobody knew where I was. Sometimes I stayed in the bunker at night, too. I had taken these blankets and pillows from home, and made myself a sort of bed down there, next to the reading lamp and the armchair.

Dan hardly ever showed up in class, either. We met in the evenings sometimes, or at weekends, but during the school day he just used to walk up and down the corridors, humming to himself, or playing in the computer room. The teachers didn't seem to mind. They all liked Dan. Once I heard one of the supply teachers asking, 'Who's that quiet, *cuddly* boy?' None of the grown-ups were frightened of Dan – that was probably why they never noticed when he wasn't in class.

Brett was still living with us when the summer holidays came. He took Mum on a Gordon's-and-Silk Cut holiday to Boulogne, while I stayed with the neighbours.

Mum's friends Mel and Raiza had this girl, Tess, who lived with them because her real mother's boyfriend kept trying to fuck her. She was almost fourteen, a bit older than me, and she already had big tits. Tess was in the class next to mine, and one of her friends was Emily, who was a member of Mary McDermot's gang. Tess must have known that Gaelic Mary beat me up, but she never said anything about it.

We slept in the same room. Mel thought I was too young for sex, so that I'd leave her alone. But Tess got into my bed on the first night, and told me to kiss her. I didn't want to, so we talked and fooled around instead. She showed me the scars of cigarette burns on her arms and back, where one of her mum's boyfriends had burned her for making too much noise when she was little. Then she stood by the bed, and pulled her T-shirt up over her knickers. 'Punch me,' she said, 'hard as you like. Go on, give me a dead leg.' So I thumped her, not too hard, just to test the muscles of her thigh. 'Do it properly,' she laughed, 'like you're angry.' So I thumped her harder, and she flinched but she didn't move her leg. 'See?' she said. Her legs were hard as a board. She had pale skin which bruised easily. 'You can hit me any time,' she said. 'I like a man with shoulders on him.'

Tess became my girlfriend that summer. I went over to her house when I wasn't in the bunker, to snog her and to read. I'd found Pope's translations of the *Iliad* and *Odyssey* in the stacks, and I lay on her bed reciting passages of that, though she pretended not to listen.

Apart from Homer, I'd dug out a book on the legends of Rome – Anchises and Aeneas, Romulus and Remus, Tarquinius Superbus, Horatius, the founding of the Roman Republic. Sometimes I spent hours in the bunker just reading the dictionary, or *The Encyclopaedia of the Ancient World*. And I started on real Roman history, too: Julius Caesar, the Emperor Augustus. I committed everything to memory. Miss Dent once said we shouldn't learn anything by rote, because it was bad for our imagination. But I liked knowing things – it gave me freedom. Whatever was happening, nobody could ever stop me going inside my head.

*   *   *

When Mum and Brett came back from France, she said the relationship was all washed up. 'He's too bleedin' eager,' she told me. 'Sickly, he is – like a little kid. He doesn't do nothing for me any more.'

So Brett moved out, and a man called Sticker came into our lives. But Mum was dissatisfied. After a fortnight of arguments, Sticker was replaced by Sam Meat, who lived with us for more than a year.

To start with, Meat did a lot of work round the house. He painted the sitting-room canary yellow, and decorated my room with London Underground wallpaper. I quite liked Meaty, except that he was an acid head. The second autumn he was with us, he lost his job. And after that, he started getting fired up all the time, lying on the sofa hallucinating.

I went on truanting. I read about a hundred books – novels, history books, biographies, poems. And after a few months the truant office stopped writing to my mother. Not even the gangs knew where I was. Gaelic Mary and Savage were running the school between them. They used to beat people up at random, and they stole stuff from the storerooms – not just books and pens, but overhead projectors, computer screens, anything they could wheel out. Nobody tried to stop them.

One night, during a bad trip, Meat gave Mum a beating with a chair leg. He thought she was a giant snake. He was shouting, 'Fucking snake-in-the-forest! Fucking serpent!' I came downstairs after a while, but he'd already stopped hitting her. He was holding the broken chair in his fist, and staring at Mum, who was curled up by the door. He couldn't take his eyes off her.

That was the first time I called the police. Meaty was led away, crying and rubbing himself. He thought there were snakes all over the place, and he picked his feet up to avoid them. But for some reason he didn't mind the cops. 'You're justice,' he said as they led him to the van. '*Justice*, see. I respect that. I only want what's right.'

* * *

Mum tried to patch things up with Meat, but by Christmas he was in an institution. And soon afterwards she met Mike Burnes at a party given by Mel and Raiza. I had spent that night with Tess, and when I came home in the morning, Mike and Mum were lying naked on the sofa in the sitting-room, in front of the TV.

'Who the fuck is that?' Mike said, pulling a sheet over himself.

'Leave us in peace, love,' Mum said.

She came to find me later.

'I'm sorry, love.' She tried to give me hug, but I pushed her away. 'I didn't know you were coming home so early. And I wasn't having Mike in my bedroom, was I? Not on day bloody one.' She tied her dressing-gown cord and looked at herself in the mirror, examining the lines round her eyes. 'I'm not a whore, love. I'm not just his for the asking.'

After a week, the house was filled with Mike's gear – Fender Stratocaster with a portable amplifier where he stashed his drugs; a seventies hi-fi system; Bob Dylan songbooks. A Toyota four-by-four stood on the pavement outside.

Mike said he was looking for a job in IT. Just as soon as he got settled he'd be paying rent, covering the bills – keeping the place. Mum offered to fix him up with the Council Maintenance Office, but he wasn't interested. I never saw her so excited, though. He was big and quiet, built like a boxer. 'Mike's pure sex,' Mum told me. And he set to work at once, fixing all the broken appliances in the house. He had *fuck off* tattooed on his wrist, and *I love you* on the upper arm. Mel told Mum he'd served time, but she never found out what his line was, even when she asked him straight out.

'I'm a changed man, my Di.' He cupped her chin. 'Don't you fret.'

In my third year we got a new form teacher, Mr Daly – the one who had seen off the posse on my first day. Daly kept order better than Miss Dent. He used to stand in the middle of the room, chatting and taking questions. 'Call me Andrew,' he said. But the other teachers called him Reg, from some character in *The Life of Brian*. So we called him Reg, too – everyone except Gaelic Mary, who called him Small Cock.

'My job is to make this stuff relevant,' Daly said, jerking his thumb at a GCSE history book. 'How does the system work? Who's running your lives? I want you to *think* about that, D2.'

I liked Daly. I even decided I'd turn up to some of his classes, and I wrote down the titles of the books he kept on the shelf by his desk: *One Dimensional Man, Dialectic of Enlightenment, The Wretched of the Earth* but I couldn't find any of them in the bunker.

# 5

Mike and Mum had a lot of sex to start with. They used to argue; then Mike thumped her; and after that they screwed. I could hear everything through my bedroom wall. Sometimes Mum missed work at the council, because her face was bruised. But she was happy. Even when her boss gave her a formal warning, she still didn't get to work on time. 'He's a real man,' she told me. 'Mike can pay for *all* of us.' And she winked, nodding her head towards his amplifier.

One night he hit her so that half her face was bleeding. Then she locked herself in the bedroom and refused to talk. Mike slammed the front door and roared off in his car. But I didn't get involved. When Mike had been gone for a while, and I reckoned Mum was asleep, I went downstairs, and unscrewed the back of the amplifier. There were three big packets of white powder in there, and I took the biggest to the kitchen. Carefully, without tearing the plastic, I started to peel the masking tape away. I cut out squares of clingfilm, and piled two teaspoons of coke on to each one, twisting them into mini Christmas crackers, and slipping them into my pocket. Then I resealed the bag, patting it back against the woofer, and fastened the board on the amp.

I kept the coke in my pocket for three days, waiting for my chance. Then one morning I saw Savage standing alone in the yard, and I walked right up to him.

'What do you want, nappy-head?'

'Here,' I said. 'I've got something.'

'Piss off.'

His face was washed out in the grey light, and he kept looking

36

away from me, as if I was offensive to him. I took a twist of coke from my jeans pocket and held it for him on my palm. His little blue eyes didn't seem to notice, but he walked me over to the shadow of the school block.

'Try some,' I said. My heart was banging in my chest, but I sounded calm. Savage dipped his little finger in the powder, the way Mike did, and opened his lips to spread it on his gums. The taste made him smile.

'Who says I won't take it off you for nothing, you little cunt?'

I wrapped up the coke, tucking it away. 'You could,' I said. 'But there's more.'

He shrugged. 'What do you want?'

'You keep Mary out of my way,' I told him, 'one whole week. Plus the posse lays off Dan and me.'

'And?'

'In seven days, you get a supply. But if they touch us again – no deal.' He briefly looked me up and down. 'Well?' I said.

'Maybe,' he sniffed. 'Give us that packet.'

'No way,' I said. 'One week.' And I walked away.


The next day I talked to Daly when the class was over.

'I've been looking for those books,' I said.

'Which books?' He was gathering up worksheets, stuffing them into his shoulder-bag.

'Oh, you know: Herbert Marcuse, *One Dimensional Man*. Horkheimer and Adorno – *Dialectic of* – This one . . .' I pointed at the shelf.

Daly stopped what he was doing and looked at me. 'You find them?'

I shook my head. 'They're not in the school library.'

He smiled. 'I should think not. I'll lend you mine if you like.'

Normally Daly was breezy and defensive, but he wasn't taking the piss now. He put his bag down. 'You do a lot of reading?'

'I found these old books,' I said. 'There's a writer called Trevelyan . . .'

Daly bit his lower lip, folding his arms with an ironic smile. 'You reading him?'

'I read him ages ago. *A History of England*. I finished it last year. Now I'm reading about the whole of Europe . . .'

'How did you find Trevelyan?'

'Fit.'

'Relevant?'

'Course. The first part is exactly like nowadays,' I said. 'Gang wars, different races and religions. Nobody's in charge. Then there's all the stuff about kings and parliaments, the common law . . .'

'That's – well that's great. Tremendous . . .'

'You don't like Trevelyan?'

'He's – you know, you're *reading*, and that's terrific. As for Trevelyan . . . What can I say? He's a great scholar – a giant of the old school.' He swiped his hair off his forehead. 'You need to see a man like that in his context. He's an old-fashioned historian: he talks a lot about law and the constitution – political ideology.'

'Is he wrong, then?' I asked. 'I mean, those things did happen, didn't they?'

'I don't know a lot about medieval history,' Daly said with a shrug. He pulled a book from his little library. 'Here, Merton, I'll lend you this. Don't lose it.' I took it carefully. It was Eric Hobsbawm, *The Age of Revolution*. 'It'll give you another perspective,' he said. 'Take a look. We'll talk about it some time.'

Mike was oiling his Black and Decker toolkit. He had laid out the pieces on the kitchen table and was taking them up one by one, checking them over. When he concentrated or was anxious, he had a deep crease across his forehead as though someone had wrapped a cheese-wire round his head and was slowly tightening it.

I was lying in the sitting-room, reading Hobsbawm, trying to ignore Mike. We never talked much, in any case, but he was extra quiet that day because he and Mum had been arguing more than usual. I had heard them in the night. And he'd hit her again. In the morning, I nicked another load of his cocaine: exploiting the exploiter. I thought Hobsbawm would have liked that.

As I read about the Great Terror, I was wondering what the next revolution would be like. Mum and Mike thought they were free already. They weren't worried about conventions, about marriage or obeying the law. But even so they were still trapped, and I wanted to know why. I wanted to know if they would ever be free.

Later, Mum came back from the council office.

'Hello, love.' She touched my hair, keeping her dark glasses on, but she didn't say anything to Mike.

'Here, Di.' He took a step forward, but Mum kept her distance.

'What?'

'I got you a present.'

He offered her a package wrapped in silver paper. Mum put her shopping down and took it in her hands. She started examining the ribbon.

'It's for you,' Mike mumbled. 'Let bygones . . .'

But Mum didn't hear. 'What *is* it, Mike? You know you shouldn't . . .' She pulled the paper away.

'There, see!' His forehead was furrowed.

'Oh, Michael!' She let her arms fall at her sides, holding the present. It was a giant bottle of Chanel Number Nineteen, a blue ribbon round its neck. 'You're a *sly* one.' I got up and moved towards the door. Mum stood there, stroking the ribbon.

'It's your kind, isn't it? Your favourite? I said I'd make up to you.' Mum put her hands up to brush away her hair, and involuntarily touched the puffy part of her face, which made her wince. 'Friends?' Mike asked, and he came up to her.

'Where're you going, Merton, love?' Mum called out.

'Out,' I said.

'Here, sweetheart,' Mike took hold of her. 'Forget him for once.'

I slammed the front door.

Nobody bothered Dan or me that week. Gaelic Mary stared at me as she passed in the corridors, but she didn't say a word.

The next Wednesday, I found Savage in the yard. He was surrounded, but I walked right up to him. 'Well?' he asked.

I showed him the coke.

'Same thing next week,' I said. 'So long as me and Dan are safe. Deal?'

Savage squinted at me. 'Okay,' he said. And he took the packet.

'One other thing,' I added. My heart was thumping.

'What?'

'I want you to beat up Mary McDermot.'

He smiled, his face grey and washed out. 'That would cost more.'

'I'll give you twice the usual amount,' I said.

He stuffed the package into his pocket. 'Tell me something, Merton: are you going to keep supplying us?'

'Sure,' I said. 'Till you leave school, right? It's a good deal.'

'All right. Next week,' Savage said. And he marched off.

During break, the posse went into Mary's class and frogmarched her out. They taped her mouth and carried her to the boys' lavatories. 'Hey, Merton,' Terence shouted. 'Observe the scene.'

So Dan and I went to the loos and stood at the door. The boys bundled Mary into a cubicle. Three of them held her facedown on the floor in front of the toilet. Nobody said anything; it was all planned. Savage was watching from the urinals. Two of the boys began to pull Mary's clothes off – jumper, skirt, tights, shoes and everything, though it was hard to get them off completely. They had to tear her knickers, and Mary was trying to cry out, but Tatham pulled her head up by the hair and held a big knife to her face. 'Give me any excuse,' he said, 'I'll cut you open.'

When she was almost naked, they lifted Mary off the floor, and pushed her head into the toilet bowl. 'It's full of shit, man,' Tatham was saying. 'You drink that, Mary. Go on, *drink*, or I'll cut you.' He pressed the knife into her arse.

Then Mary wet herself. We all saw it. The piss squirted all over her clothes, which the boys had dumped on the cubicle floor. 'That's not nice.' Terry took a step back, and started kicking Mary's legs as hard as he could. 'Next time we'll give you a pasting. You hear me?' Mary nodded inside the toilet bowl. 'Behave, or you'll be sore.'

Tatham put his knife away. Mary had stopped struggling, and the boys left her. For a while I waited there with Dan, just watching while she tried to get dressed. And then she started crying. The loo doors were fixed open. Everyone in the corridor could see her, half-naked, kneeling in her own piss, crying like a child. I couldn't believe it. We stood there watching as she tried to close the cubicle door, until Dan nudged me and walked away. I knew he wouldn't be pleased, even though he hated Mary. But I didn't go with him. A new sensation was taking hold of me, a mixture of anxiety and power, like I was a grown-up. And even though I was feeling sick, I knew that nothing would ever be the same.

Mum and Mike became more sociable. Their friends took the house over on Saturday nights, Mel and Raiza brought cases of Red Stripe, and loads of Mike's clients turned up. Mike could make a couple of thousand pounds on a busy weekend. Then Mike and Raiza would get wired, and start singing Bob Dylan songs and Led Zeppelin. It was impossible to sleep, but it didn't matter because I could take it easy all day, and I liked to stay up in my room, reading, jerking off, swallowing vodka mixes.

In the morning, when everyone was laid out on the sofa, I

used to unscrew Mike's amp and pick up a few ounces for the Savage gang. I took most of my cocaine to the bunker, but I kept a reserve at Mel and Raiza's house, under the floor in Tess's room. They always let me come and go – they kept a latchkey under a flat stone in the front garden. That was my emergency supply, in case Mike got wise.

By the Christmas holidays I was seeing Tess more and more. I spent half my nights with her. Sometimes she gave me a blow-job, mopping my stomach with her bright red hair while I clutched the bars of the bed. And afterwards we just lay there smoking dope. Then she would start telling me some complicated story, but she always got confused, and we were too far gone; neither of us could stop laughing.

'Fuck!' She tried to concentrate. 'You're confusing me. What was I going to say?' She banged her forehead, and took another drag. I always fancied her more when we were both stoned.

'Don't ask *me*. It's your story.'

I started coming on to her, making her smoke more, pulling off her clothes, and after that I couldn't even understand what she was saying. Her words were just noises, and my head was swimming. I had a sensation like my brain was expanding, taking up the whole house. Then Tess' round, elastic mouth stopped talking. She started to smile at me, and her eyebrows went up in surprise as she just stared and stared. That was when I liked her the most. She looked so shocked, so amazed, although absolutely nothing had happened. And we always screwed after that – just before we got too strung-out to move any more, and we could hardly remember who we were. I banged her for ages.

One day after school I went to talk to Daly. Dan was with me, too. He wanted to ask about Miss Dent and the Savage gang.

'Did she go mad, sir? I mean, is she in an asylum or anything?' Dan was always interested in mad people.

'Nothing like that, mate.' Daly sat cross-legged on a desk in the middle of the room. 'Vicky Dent moved back to Australia. The local authority gave her a pay-out. My guess is, she's putting the whole thing down to experience.'

'Yeah, but she doesn't want to teach any more, right? I mean, I bet she's well freaked out – I bet she hears voices – like a Vietnam vet.'

'She's taking a sabbatical. *She'll* be all right.'

But I was wondering about something else.

'Savage, the posse – are they revolutionaries, or reactionaries?' I really wanted to get that straight in my mind.

Daly hesitated, gazing through the high, empty window towards the yard. 'Savage – lads like him: they *can* go either way. You get fascism in those gangs – sexism, racism. But there's always potential for positive change. You could argue they're revolutionaries – anarchists. They see things from the bottom up, don't they? They've got nothing to lose.'

'So you think Savage is a progressive?'

'Jesus,' Dan said. 'You got to be joking. Savage is a psycho. Everyone knows that.'

'I don't get it. Savage doesn't believe in human rights or anything. If he had his way, everyone who annoyed him would get beheaded . . .'

'But his *rage* is real,' Daly said, leaning forward and uncrossing his legs. 'And you've got to see the context. Vicky Dent understood that. She'd never seen anything like the poverty of Waterfield or Cannon Park. There's nothing like that where she came from in Australia.'

Savage left school that summer, so Dan and I were going to lose our protection. But it didn't matter, because Gaelic Mary was leaving, too – all the Banshees were. There was nobody left who could really screw us about. We were going to be free. And I didn't have to steal from Mike any more.

Most of the summer, things were peaceful. When Mike was working, I hung out at home, reading. But sometimes Mum would trap me in the sitting-room, forcing me to hear how great things were. 'He knows how to keep a woman satisfied,' she told me once. 'Mike's a man, Merton. With him, what you see is what you get.' She winked. 'What *I* see, anyway.' I watched the blue smoke rising in a column as she exhaled. 'You should try to get along. Spend time with him. You need a father in your life. And it makes me *secure*, you know?' She stubbed out the cigarette, looking away with a little smile. 'If I rile him – if I give him grief, like – he puts me right. We understand each other, him and me.'

The first term the posse had left school, I used to get in early, going straight to the bunker before anyone had seen me, and just staying there all day. From time to time, if I felt like it, I went to lessons – especially Daly's – but mostly I stayed in my hole, reading poetry or history, making notes, daydreaming, sometimes till ten or eleven at night.

That was when I started studying the New Left classics Daly lent me. They were hard. Sometimes I used to go over the same paragraph again and again without ever understanding it. But I kept reading. Those writers were talking about freedom, progress, revolution, and my thoughts flew out towards the future.

One night, a couple of weeks into the autumn term, Terence and Tatham ambushed me as I was sprinting home from Dan's, along the walkway of block B. They must have been watching from the shadows: they came out of the stair tower, standing with their hoods up, blocking my way.

'Merton, man, how you doing?'

'Hi, Terry.' I leaned against the wall, catching my breath. 'Tatham?' Tatham was looming over me. 'You okay, man?'

'I've got to search you,' he said. So I held out my arms and he patted me all over. Then he stepped back and spat over the railings. 'He's okay.'

'Come with us,' Terry said. 'The boss wants you.'

They led me down the stairwell, out across the Cannon Park atrium, past the neon cross of the little church, towards block A. At the end of the last section of flats, beyond the walkways and towers, was an area of concrete with wheelie bins, and a locked gate to give emergency vehicles access from the road. It was a good area for dealing, or planning burglaries. You could look out over the whole estate, and see who was moving along the walkways or in the atrium.

The boys marched me past the bins, across the concrete, to a row of garages with up-and-over doors. One of them was open. 'In there,' Tatham said.

The posse had turned the garage into their office. They had a carpet in there, a sofa and TV, even a fridge. Savage was marching up and down between a couple of chairs, swinging a baseball bat. Victor and Calvin stood at the far side. There were two Asian guys, too, older than them, who I didn't know.

Terry shoved me into the middle of the room. Then Savage came up with his baseball bat, and started staring at my face. His eyes were bloodshot, and his skin was very pale.

'Hey, Paul,' I said. 'What's up?'

'Shut it. Don't say nothing.'

He took a step back and raised the wooden bat over his shoulder, taking aim. 'Give me one reason I shouldn't smash your face.'

'Don't, man,' I said.

'That's not a reason, cunt.' He shook his head slowly, but he was hesitating, and he let the bat fall to his side.

'I'm not going to kill you,' he said quietly. 'Not now. I want to do some business, right?'

'What sort of business?'

'Same as we used to, only more. We're not pussying, yeah? I'm selling the product on. I need big weights.'

I said nothing. The boys moved in behind Savage, forming a half-circle. Terry had his own baseball bat; he was tapping it on the floor.

'Well?' Savage murmured. 'I can't hear you.'

'I – I'd like to,' I said. 'But I never had a supplier. I just used to take what wouldn't be missed.'

'Well, business is growing,' he said. 'You'll have to get a new man.'

'Can't do it, Paul.' My hands were shaking. 'I'm sorry. There's no way.'

'Don't disappoint me, man.' He raised his club again, aiming at my head.

'I don't have a line,' I said. 'I'm telling the truth. I took small parcels from a dealer I knew, but if he found out he – he'd . . .'

'What?' Savage moved right up to me, resting the bat on my shoulder. His face was two inches from mine. 'If he found out – *what* would he do?' he asked. 'Tell me. I'm interested.'

'I – I don't know.'

'I'll give you another chance,' Savage said. And he spoke very slowly. '*I want to do business with you.*'

'I can give you what you had before,' I said. 'I think I can. You were getting everything I took. But I can't get more.'

'Bullshit. We need twice that. *Three* times.' He walked away. 'Impossible.'

'Hit him,' Savage said, and Terry leapt forward and swung his baseball bat into my stomach. It happened so fast I didn't have time to turn. In three seconds I was on the floor.

'If you were taking a bit,' Savage said, 'you can take *more*. I'm not asking much. What's wrong with you? It's business.'

When I looked up he was watching me. 'Well?'

There was silence. They were all staring. I wiped my palms on my jeans, forcing myself to get up.

'Look,' I said, 'we had a good thing. Why can't we keep it as it was?'

'Because I need a *supply*, you fucker.' He nodded to Terry, who whacked me behind the knees, and I dropped down instantly. 'Don't be so fucking slow, Merton.' Savage began walking round me. 'Think about it. I can get you *any* time. Danny, too. And

Tess. We can cut her tits – bang her. I could fuck her with this.'
He thrust the baseball bat in my face. 'You should think about
that. We can kill Dan's mother if we want. Or yours.'

I started to get up again, but it was difficult to straighten my
legs.

'Hey, Paul,' I said, 'can we talk?'

'I thought we *were* talking.'

'Just us.'

He shrugged. I limped with him to the side of the room.
'Don't take this the wrong way,' I said, 'but do you need the
gear for yourself? Are you strung out?'

'You pissing on me?'

'No, I mean it. If that's what it is, I can get you your own
supply, no problem.'

'It's not for me,' he said. And he shouted: 'It's not for me.
It's business. I'm building up my customer base. Understand?'

'Sure,' Terry said. 'You're the man.'

'Got it?' Savage gazed at me with his pale eyes. 'This gang is
going to service Cannon Park.'

'Okay,' I said. My whole body felt cold.

'Find me the cargo,' he said. 'You've got three days.' He turned
away. 'Get Merton out of here.' And Terry grabbed my arm and
led me away.

# 6

For the rest of the week I avoided the posse. I stayed in the bunker all day, pacing up and down, or lying on the cardboard mattress. Sometimes I tried to read. I looked at the *Communist Manifesto*, which Daly had lent me, and reread the chapters about the 1848 revolutions in Hobsbawm. I was trying to work out what I had to do. All revolutions in the past had turned to terror; but still I thought there had to be some way to change the world. I kept trying to imagine things as they should be, and the future seemed to me like the distant past: a vast wilderness in the ruins of London. I imagined myself running through the forests, escaping from every form of control. And I tried to work out if I was running away from Savage, out on my own, or if the posse was waiting for me on the other side, masters of a new world where everyone would be free.

One evening, Daly kept Dan and me back after class. 'There's something I want you to do for me,' he said. 'From now on, I want you to start turning up for class.'

'We do.'

'No, I mean every day. Regularly.'

'No way.' Dan couldn't help smiling. 'What's the point, man?'

'He's right,' I said. 'I mean, school is part of the system, isn't it?'

Daly shook his head. 'Not if *I'm* teaching.'

Dan looked right at him. 'No offence or nothing,' he said, 'but how come you're not part of the system? You keep saying it runs everything. I mean, you *are* a teacher.'

Daly folded his arms. 'I'm free of the system because I don't buy into it.'

'But why do you want me to come to class?' I said. 'It's a waste of time.'

'I want you to get some GCSEs.'

'You must be joking.'

'Listen, Merton, *think* about it. This is important. They'll give you choice, open up the possibility of A levels, university.'

'But it's all coursework and shit,' Dan said. 'It's for nappy-heads.'

'It's not ideal, Dan, but it can give you a chance to empower yourself.'

'*Inside* the system,' I objected.

Daly took a breath.

'Look, you two boys can achieve something – I really believe that. You ought to be looking to your futures. The world won't change if you don't engage with it.' And he turned to Dan. 'If you try, you can do well, mate – I know you can. You could do vocational A levels – ICT, business. Think about it.'

'I don't know,' Dan said. He was looking at the ground.

'Merton?'

I shrugged.

'You two talk it over,' Daly said. 'It's up to you.' And he went out, heading for the staff-room.

That weekend, Mum and Mike gave a party. Some of Mike's mates had agreed to come in with him, dealing in our neighbourhood. I'd heard them conspiring in the kitchen. They'd stashed the cargo under the floorboards near the freezer, and now they were toasting one another with vodka shots.

I lay on my bed, searching through this book of Romantic poets I'd found in the bunker. They turned up the volume downstairs, and I started to recite *The Rime of the Ancient Mariner*, saying it out loud over the throb of the music. At first I checked in the book that I'd got it right, but after a while I went from memory.

> *The fair breeze blew, the white foam flew*
> *The furrow followed free;*
> *We were the first that ever burst*
> *Into that silent sea.*

Bit by bit as I recited, I started remembering strange things –
events from my childhood, things I hadn't thought about for
years – like I was daydreaming and I couldn't stop.

> *Down dropt the breeze, the sails dropped down,*
> *'Twas sad as sad could be;*
> *And we did speak only to break*
> *The silence of the sea!*

There was a tap on the door, and Tess emerged from the
landing, a mass of red hair over bruised lips. She leaned against
the door to close it.

'I didn't know you were here,' I said. 'I would have come
down.' I closed the book.

'Raiza brought me.' She stood looking about uncertainly and
sat on the bed. Then she drooped down to put her round mouth
next to mine. She smelt wonderfully of vodka and peppermint.

'Are you tired?' I asked, and she nodded.

I watched her lock the door. She pulled her T-shirt over her
head, flinging it on the chair, and stood smiling in her black bra
and black tights.

Downstairs they were shouting. I could hear Mike's voice:
*Bitch! You bitch!* But he was only fooling around.

'Come and lie down,' I said.

Tess peeled off her tights and knickers in a single movement
– they fell in a nylon coil by the Romantic poets, and she slith-
ered under the duvet. For a while I just lay there, penis flooded
with blood, surveying her freckled shoulders, running my hands
through her hair. Although it was pale, her flesh looked raw, as
though she had been skinned. And Coleridge was hammering in
my head:

*All in a hot and copper sky,*
*The bloody Sun, at noon,*
*Right up above the mast did stand,*
*No bigger than the moon.*

'Hold me,' she said.

For a while I squeezed her, unable to remember the next verse. Then I relaxed, and we tried some of the foreplay advice they'd given us in *Sex 4 U*: tongue-clitoris-nipple-ear, tongue-clitoris-nipple-ear, until she started sighing and squirming. Briefly I kissed her mouth, too; for a moment I even wanted to say something. But as soon as I moved on top of her, I shot my load all over her belly.

After that, my head was jammed. We lay in the darkness for ages, Tess searching my face and chest with her hands, and I didn't say anything.

But later, when my tackle had recovered, I made myself screw her, grinding and burning long enough for Tess to start shouting. And when I shot up inside her, I actually called out 'Baby', and she said she loved me.

I carried on humping for another tormented cycle. Tess shuddered and clutched my back, thumping her feet on the mattress. My cock felt like raw leather. And for some reason I kept thinking about Mary McDermot, upside down and naked in the loo.

Afterwards, I turned my back on Tess and curled up like a baby. My mouth had filled with cotton wool, and I pretended to sleep while she kissed my shoulders.

We went downstairs in the early morning. All over the house, the air stank of cigarettes and dope. Mike's CDs were scattered across the floor by the hi-fi, the little amp still humming.

Mike and Mum were asleep: we could hear them snoring above us. I took a screwdriver and pulled up the floorboards by the freezer. There were six bags of coke in there. 'Here,' I said. 'Have some.' I took three bags and opened them up, piling little mounds on Mum's Horoscope mirror. Then I chopped and caressed them into two neat lines, and we snorted the lot.

'It's not doing anything,' Tess complained.

'It takes time. Make some tea.'

I took a load more, peeling the Sellotape from each of Mike's white packets, and dropping a couple of spoonfuls into a freezer bag. The whole operation took ten minutes, and we hid the stash in Tess' coat. It was loads more than I'd ever taken before.

Next I searched Mike's music collection, and put on *Morrison Hotel*. Then Tess and I lay together with our mugs of tea in the reek of the sofa.

After the coke, I fancied her again, but I couldn't get it up. For about an hour my brain went into overdrive. I was possessed with dark, obsessional rhythms, and when the music stopped I went on reciting *The Rime of the Ancient Mariner*, picking up where I had stopped. My memory was clear again, and I said it very passionately, weighing every word. Tess lay there giggling to herself, or covering my mouth with her hand.

When I had finished, we fooled around again till Tess yelped. 'More coke,' she demanded. 'Rub it on my lips. It's like I'm falling through air. I feel – I don't know. I feel free.'

Two days later, Terence and Tatham ambushed me on the way to school.

'Come on, cunt, the boss wants to see you.' They marched me to Savage in his garage.

'Hi, Paul,' I said. Tatham and Calvin stood behind him, with these two Asian guys who were there before.

'Merton, mate,' Savage said. 'How you doing?' He didn't have his baseball bat.

'All right.'

'Haven't seen much of you, man. You been hiding?'

'No way,' I said. 'I've been getting my supply.'

'Nice one.'

'Let's see some result,' one of the Asian guys put in. 'He's *well* late.'

'Who are they?' I asked.

'This is my mate Bhikhu,' Savage said. 'Bhikhu and Tariq. They're advising me on my business expansion.'

'Hi,' I said, but they just stared at me.

'Okay,' Savage said. 'So you got a supplier?'

'Sort of.'

'Excellent. You just have to make the first delivery, right, and things can only get better. You've made the right decision, man.'

'I can get you the stuff,' I said. 'But what do I get in return?'

Savage frowned. 'You get the same as everyone. Protection. That's the deal. You, Dan, Tess. Anyone you want. I'll give you protection.' He smiled. 'Nobody gets hurt.'

'We don't need it,' I said.

He looked like I'd punched him. 'How?'

'We're all right as it is.'

'But you want to *stay* that way. Think *ahead*, man. When you leave school, right, out on the streets. You're going to need to be part of something.'

'It's the way of the future,' Bhikhu put in. 'You got to be organised.'

'I'll talk to the others,' I told Savage. 'I'll come back next week.'

'You don't go anywhere without paying,' Bhikhu said quietly, stepping towards me.

'I've got nothing on me,' I said. 'If you want the drugs, you've got to let me go.'

'He's all right,' Savage told him. 'Let him go. He's supplied me before.'

'He's late. It's not cool.'

'He'll be back.'

So I walked to the door.

'Remember, Merton,' Savage called after me: 'if you're not

with us, you're against us, right.' And he laughed. 'Jesus said that.'

Mike was laid out in the front room watching TV. Around him on the floor was an irregular tide-line of boxes from the Indian takeaway, empty beer cans, DVD cases. He got up when he saw me and tramped into the kitchen.

'I thought you were at bleedin' school.'

'Half-day,' I explained. 'We were sent home to do a project on the local wildlife.'

'Fucking typical.'

'Yes, isn't it?' I watched him crouching in the door of the fridge, anxious and muscle-bound, his forehead creased with concentration. 'Had an argument?'

Mike moved away, slamming the fridge door. 'Bloody tart.'

He resettled himself on the armchair in front of the mute TV, clutching a can of Red Stripe.

'You hit her, then?'

'Fucking right. I sorted her out. And I don't need any judge-mentalism from *you*, you poncy wanker. I've enough on my mind.'

I began to move towards the door. An old, very familiar sensation of anxiety was taking hold of my stomach.

'Where is she?'

'Upstairs in her bleedin' bed. She spends her life there, the lazy cow.' He cast his eyes mistrustfully across the ceiling, before leaning back to take a slug of beer.

'Sometimes I wonder what she wants,' he mused, fingering the remote control. 'I mean, what does she get out of it all? All those men – creeping around when I'm away. It does my nerves.' He shook his head. 'I don't know what it is between us. Really I don't. There are thoughts in my head you wouldn't under-stand.' I wondered for a moment if he was going to cry, but he just stared at the silent TV. Someone was answering questions in front of a glittering cardboard star. 'Sometimes I lose it. I admit that. I can't contain myself. She *asks* for it – don't get me wrong. But I do my nut. I'm out of line. It's a pressure, like – a pressure in my head. *Here.*' He traced his thumbnail along the crease of his forehead. 'Something's pushing from the inside. Jesus, I wish it was different. Sometimes I really wish we could be different, her and me.' He looked at me, his small eyes full of perplexity. 'That's why I hit her, you see: it releases the pressure in my brain.'

On the screen, the contestant was sitting below a sign saying *£1 million*. It flashed on and off over his head. 'Maybe we should go away,' Mike said. 'Sell up, her and me. Go to Spain. We could marry, like, have kids. Have a life.' He finished his beer thoughtfully. 'It's never too late to be what you should be.'

In the bunker I shone the yellow circle of light on the shelves, and pulled out a Latin textbook. Everything was supposed to play its part in history, but it was difficult to see how Latin could be revolutionary or counter-revolutionary. After all, it was just a language. I lay down on my blankets and pillows, staring at the Introduction. But it was hard to concentrate. I had a packet of cocaine the size of an apricot in my jacket pocket. And I wondered about jail – whether they have libraries there, whether you're free to read, or if it's like a school.

Verbs are divided into conjugations, the book said. I started to read about the present tense. Some sixties schoolboy had marked the page, putting a bracket around *amo amas amat*. There was silence in the yard above, and my brain began to relax. *Amo, amas, amat, amamus, amatis, amant.* In my imagination I was running – running as fast as I could from the New Crosland and the estates, out across the suburbs, into the fields and hills beyond London. I was free: I was never coming back. *Amo, amas, amat, amamus, amatis, amant.* In my heart, the revolution had begun: I was sprinting across some primitive wilderness, looking for other people who were free, whoever they were, wherever I found them – searching, searching. And everything was in ruins, the whole system had been destroyed. The rhythm in those strange words gave me courage. I said them out loud: *a*mo-*a*mas-*a*mat-am*a*mus-am*a*tis-*a*mant . . .

'Where's Savage?'

I stood with my back to the wall. Dan was with me, and the boys were in a circle around us in the dark.

'He said to wait,' Terence told us. 'We've got to search you. Stretch out your arms.'

Dan and me let Tatham pat us about. Then someone shouted out, 'The boss,' and Savage burst in.

'Merton, my man.'

'Hi, Paul.' I could see the shape of him in front of me. He kept his hood up in the darkness.

'What have you got?' he said.

I held out the coke.

'Jesus, man!' Tatham squealed.

Savage came close. He opened the pack to taste the powder, spreading it on his gums with an index finger. He was smiling, shaking his head.

'That's a month's supply,' I said.

'Jesus, Merton. How much is here?' He tried some more, still grinning. 'I mean, someone's going to miss this stuff, right?'

'We'll weigh it.' Terry brought out some scales.

'Do I get protection?' I asked.

He laughed. 'For this? You – your weird friends – you can have what you want.'

# 7

Mike and my mother were fighting all the time. Mum was convinced he was cheating on her, but Mike believed the same thing about her; he was constantly looking for evidence against her.

He had started fretting about his merchandise, too, accusing Mum of stealing from him. She definitely was taking stuff – she got wired whenever they argued – but she wasn't freeloading off him like I was. The whole of that year at school I kept Savage supplied. I used to go down in the early mornings when Mum and Mike were asleep, spooning cocaine into freezer bags, and Mike never suspected. He was getting clumsy, and I wasn't the only one who was taking advantage. His hands shook, and when he wasn't wasted, he was always stupid and depressed.

Being at home made me sick; I only went there to nick drugs. But at school I was made. People thought I was part of the Savage family, and I could do anything I wanted. I started to spend a lot of time with Daly. We talked almost every day – about politics and schools, why he'd become a teacher. He said his job was to break down the barriers in society. For example, he wanted everyone to go to university – Dan and me, even people like Savage. He didn't think universities should choose their candidates; it ought to be the other way round. And he believed in pure sexual relationships, too – relationships without commitment, which you could change any time. He used to say, 'We'll never have a free society – a fully *human* society – until all those structures have been broken down: social barriers, academic ones, old-style morality.' It blew my mind the first time he said that. And he put his hand on my shoulder. 'Liberation is being true to yourself, Merton. It's up to *you*.'

About that time, I started wearing these old suits, and a big trench-coat. I had a green suit that I had found in a charity shop, and a grey one with pleated trousers. I dressed like that all the time. I didn't care if nobody wore suits any more. They made me feel like some guy in an old film. And they fitted me pretty well. I had shirts with collars and everything, but I didn't have the right kind of shoes, so I just wore my trainers.

Dan and I made a pact to do our GCSEs, however stupid they were. I had thought about it, and I didn't believe in the exams, whatever Daly said. But if we got to do A levels, it would mean we could hang out at school for two more years. I could keep going to the bunker, and Dan would be able to stay away from the posse, at least in the daytime. Dan wanted to get qualified, in any case. He had this uncle in Jamaica who ran a boat-hire company, and he said Dan could come and work for him if he got a qualification in computer technology. Dan kept showing me this photo of his uncle, standing on a jetty next to an aquamarine fishing boat. He was obsessed with it.

All the subjects depended on coursework. They were designed for kids with computers in their bedrooms, and parents who helped them. We'd already missed too much of the course to do really well, but from then on we did everything we could. Dan studied at home. Sometimes at the weekends or after school, I used to go to his place, and we worked together on the table by the TV. His mum fed us toasted sandwiches, standing over us while we ate, and talking the whole time to the grandfather, even though he never said a word.

When the summer came, we sat with Rose and Debby and the Chinese kids in the assembly room, and Daly invigilated. The papers were a joke. History was all about Hitler and the Cold War. We had to comment on these little snippets of text from the Nazi newspapers and the scripts of propaganda films.

The examiners pretended this was the way historians really work. The most difficult thing was not to say straight out that the whole paper was crap. It was the same with English. I'd read loads of poetry in the bunker, learned it by heart. I knew there were millions of poems the examiners could have chosen – poems which shocked you, made your head explode. But they came up with some piece of garbage by a writer you'd never heard of who was still alive.

I didn't pull any skanks, though. I did it with a straight face: six GCSEs altogether. The whole thing took about a month.

Savage was waiting for me outside the school yard the day the exams finished.

'What's happening, man?'

'Not much,' I said.

He was staring at me. 'There's something I want you to do,' he said. 'Some special work.'

'What kind?'

'Nothing physical. It's not dealing or anything. I want you to be my adviser, yeah? My *consigliere*.'

'Your what?' I smiled, but he didn't notice.

'It's Italian,' he said. 'My *legal* adviser. Like in *The Godfather*.'

'You serious?'

'Why not?'

'Well, I mean, you've got the whole posse. What about Terry?'

'They're ignorant,' he said. 'Terry, too. They can't even read.' He scanned my face. 'Do it,' he said. 'I'd like you to.' And he looked at my green suit. 'Anyway, you look like a *consigliere* – your weird suit and shit. You do it for me.'

'It's an honour,' I told him.

'It's not a big deal.' He looked away. 'I'll pay you.'

'I'll do what I can,' I said. And he punched me on the shoulder.

All that summer, after the GCSEs were over, I hung out with the posse, learning how they operated. Terry, Tatham and the others used to go out at night, working in packs, ambushing people coming home along the aerial walkways of the estate. But they didn't have a proper plan; they just stole mobiles and cash, sometimes jewellery, from whoever they saw, or they went shoplifting on the High Street. It was easy work: the police didn't know the estates; they had no local knowledge because they only ever turned up after someone reported a robbery, and even then they didn't bother to wait around. That's why people wouldn't tell the cops anything – they knew there was no point.

That was the first thing I understood about the future of the posse. When I saw the way the police were working, I told Savage they could easily be put out of action – that we could have the estates to ourselves, if we just raised the temperature a bit. And the first thing I did as *consigliere* was make it harder for the cops to come inside Cannon Park. The boys would hide on the outside corridors, and start throwing stones at police cars near the garages, or by the High Street beyond block B. If the cops parked further away and walked in, a small group of us used to keep them talking in the atrium, while the others smashed their windows and blue lights with crowbars. If the coppers came back in force, we just dispersed all over the estate. There was no way they could track us down. And whenever they tried to question one of the boys, we always gathered around in a big crowd, like a riot was about to begin, and started screaming at them, accusing them of brutality, fascism, racism – whatever we could think of – until they got frightened and left us alone.

After a few weeks, Savage and I started coordinating the posse's robberies. We kept the muggings to certain areas where nobody could see, and we always had somebody keeping guard from the top of the stairwells, or on the outside corridors of the estate. My plan was to bring the estate under the posse's control. I didn't want people to mug just anyone who came along. We started favouring certain people, because they were cooperative, while anyone who challenged us got robbed the whole time. And I got the boys to start stealing from big shops, and from gangs who worked on the other estates. 'Loot the looters!' I told them. We made much more money that way, and people learned that if they showed us respect we'd leave them alone.

As *consigliere* I got twenty per cent of everything we took. Savage got half, and the rest was shared out between the others. I was pretty rich, considering I was still at school – we all were. I could buy whatever books I liked, and I got stuff for Tess, CDs or clothes that she wanted. Savage and I were almost best friends, starting that summer. We used to spend a lot of time together, not just on business. Sometimes Savage would hot-wire a car in one of the streets around Dante Park while I kept watch with Tess and Emily, and we'd all drive out into the countryside. He'd never had any lessons, but he drove pretty well, except that he always went extremely fast and kept the engine revving. I used to sit next to him, scanning the radio for some Drum and Bass, and the girls sat in the back, pretending not to be scared. Then we used to park in some lay-by miles from anywhere, and we all sat there listening to the music and getting stoned.

Once when Savage was out of it, and he'd started fooling around with Em, Tess and I went off into the woods to be on our own. We found a clearing, in a hollow out of sight from the road, and lay on our backs in the warm darkness, staring up into the trees. Half the sky was smudged with the orange light of the suburbs, and we could hear the motorway thundering in the distance. But in the fold of the woods, where we were hidden, there was real darkness, even a sort of peace, and at the top of the sky we could see a few raggedy stars. I told Tess that if she and I could hide in the woods for a whole night, perhaps we could really escape. We imagined living in the trees, eating what we could find, until nobody knew where we were. We talked about starting a family, too – starting our lives again as new people.

But after a few hours, when the drugs began to wear off, we got up and went back to see if Savage was bored of Emily yet, or if he'd set the car on fire. And sometime before the dawn, we drove back to Cannon Park.

If I needed to sleep or just to be on my own for a day, I used to go down to the bunker. I never told anyone where I went – not even Tess. And when I had got some rest, I used to sit propped up with my fountain-pen in my hand.

*There are degrees of liberation*, I wrote. *Number one: sexual liberation. That comes first, because everything follows from it. When the sperm leaves the body, it is liberated – it is* free *sperm. It's not part of a man's life any more.*

Upstairs the boiler started pumping; it made the pipes hum next to my chair.

*Then there is liberation from mental oppression, from the idea of God, moral law, memory . . .* I was getting it down on my stack of notepaper. *Nothing is wrong or right. Nothing is fixed. All judgements depend on the conditions of history. When you have discovered that, you get rid of all social control. It follows naturally. After the revolution, there will be no law or conscience. Our minds will just expand.*

I paused, trying to remember what Daly had said, what I had read in *One Dimensional Man*. I was thinking about the posse, but about ordinary people, too – the people on the estate, Mum and Mike.

*Society has been freed from the memory of God,* I put down; *from the burden of right and wrong. Soon the last vestiges of ancient authority will be thrown aside. But we are still not free. Sometimes I think we are less free than the people in the past – the people who wrote those poems. Something is controlling us. There is less knowledge, less memory, less culture to keep us in bondage, but we still haven't become what we truly are. People are still frightened – even Mike. Even Daly.*

I straightened up, writing with increased energy.

*Marcuse is right,* I scribbled; *this is the subtlest tyranny: the totally permissive, totalitarian state. We seem to do what we want. There are no taboos; no personal responsibility; no need for self-control. And everything's free – education, medicine; we get money for doing nothing. But it's all a trick. That is how they rule us. In exchange for their money, they take our minds. We must become independent, then – we must recover what they have stolen.* And as I wrote that, I remembered Savage again, and the whole question became clear. *The only people who aren't frightened,* I wrote in bold letters; *the only ones who can change anything at all, are people like Savage. The rest is a fraud – everybody else is part of the problem.*

My exam results were good. I got Bs in most of them, even some As. And Dan did well, too. So his mum took us out to the Chinese place on the High Street to celebrate. She said Dan and I could eat whatever we liked, so Dan ordered crispy fried duck with pancakes and plum sauce, and we had about fifty pancakes each. She even let us have beer.

To start with, Mrs Johnson just kept smiling at us, and didn't say much. But gradually she started talking, mainly about what Dan was going to do when he'd finished school. She said the exams had saved his life; that he was going to get out of England and work for his uncle – that everything would be all right. And she wanted to save me, as well. 'I'll ask Dan's uncle to find you work,' she said. 'He'll treat you like family, Merton. My brother's got fingers in a *lot* of pies . . .'

By the time the waitress brought us the hot towels that smelt of air-freshener, Mrs Johnson had sorted everything. Even the fortune cookies made her optimistic about Dan and me. When she began to describe her childhood in Jamaica, Dan rolled his eyes, but I listened. I could imagine the colonial houses and clapboard churches, and all Mrs Johnson's family – the uncles and sisters and old grandparents she kept talking about. She was talking about the way things used to be – the way she remembered them. Probably it wasn't like that in Jamaica any more. Maybe it never was. But she believed it.

Even when she had paid the bill, Mrs Johnson still didn't want to move. She leaned forward and took hold of our hands across the table.

'You keep away from evildoers,' she said, 'both of you. I know the temptations in that so-called school you go to. You avoid the junkies and hoodlums. If you go that way, your life will be a living hell. And as soon as you can, get out – both of you. You listen to me, Dan. You know what the Bible says . . .'

'Oh, Mum, cut it out, will you. We're not at church . . .'

'He doesn't want to hear,' she persisted. 'So I'll tell *you*, Merton. The Lord says, "I have put before you life and death: *therefore choose life*." You *choose* it, boys.'

'Yeah, yeah,' Dan said.

'No: you *choose* it,' she repeated. And she looked right in our eyes.

Mrs Johnson got up and started thanking all the people who worked in the restaurant; she made us shake hands with them all. And then we walked back to the estate, the three of us, Dan fooling about on the pavement, Mrs Johnson humming as she marched ahead.

One evening just after the New Year, Mike was sitting at the kitchen table, a deep crease across his forehead, his stash laid out in front of him.

'Pissing Nora! Look at that.'

'What *is* it, love?'

'It's been interfered with. *Look*! The Sellotape's all messed about.'

Mum looked up from the sofa, but I ignored them both, passing behind Mike to put the kettle on.

'Can't be,' Mum said. 'Nobody knows about it.'

'Except you.' He looked up from the damaged packet, and

the crease disappeared from his forehead. 'I've been blind,' he said. 'Just blind . . . I knew there was a rat in the house.'

'I wouldn't touch your stuff,' Mum said. 'You know that, Mikey.'

'If it wasn't you, who then?'

'How should I know?' she whispered.

Mike went up to her, clenching and unclenching his fists, and I stood watching by the kitchen window. There was steam coming off a saucepan of potatoes.

'What you do with it?'

'Nothing, Mike.'

'You ask for it, Diana. Honest to God you do.'

She put her hand up to stroke his face. 'Don't, love. I never touched it.'

Mike was breathing heavily.

'Maybe it was one of your mates,' Mum said. 'You know – taking a bit on the side.'

'*Mates*, was it?' He grabbed Mum's wrists and yanked her up. 'Let's think about that . . . You accusing my mates, Di?' He twisted her arms in a double Nelson and rammed her face down on the table.

'I didn't mean that.' Her voice was a squeak. 'Just, some-times, when we have a party, you know . . .'

'You think I don't remember what I do?' He was speaking gently into her ear.

'No, Mike.' She gasped as he yanked her arms tighter. 'You'll break my arm.'

'You've got a brass neck.' Mum was looking sideways at me now, breathing heavily. With his free hand, Mike snatched the saucepan and tipped the potatoes on the floor.

'Don't, Mike,' Mum whispered. 'Not my face, love.'

He was weighing the pan in his grip, twisting the handle while he kept Mum pressed down with his other hand. Then he whacked her hard across the cheek.

Mum shouted out. Blood spurted from her nose, and from

the part of her skull above her eye. He released her with a look of disgust and threw the pan down. Then he marched into the sitting-room and came back with the power cable from his amp clenched in his hand. 'You clear this up, Di.' He doubled up the flex, making the wires whistle. 'Now!'

Mum felt her way to the sink. She put a hand out to the tap, but Mike banged the draining board with his improvised whip. 'Don't you do a bleedin' thing till you've cleared up this shit.'

Upstairs, I took some books from my under my bed, and got my trench-coat. I dropped them in my rucksack, checked the stash of coke in the inside pocket, and went downstairs.

There was a lull in the fighting. Mum was on her knees, scooping up the potatoes with her hands. 'I'm sorry, Mike,' she was saying. 'I'm sorry. Believe me, I am.'

There was blood everywhere: on her shirt, all over the lino floor, on her hands. And it had sunk into the powdery potatoes. I hesitated, standing in the doorway. I wondered for a moment if I should say something. But when Mum looked up and I saw her face again, I turned and ran.

It was a deep blue evening. The clouds were flying out across the towers of the Cannon Park Estate. I should have gone straight to the posse, but I really didn't feel like it. So for a while I just kept walking from block to block on the elevated corridors, all over our dense little city. Then I went up on to the roof of B block, wandering up and down, or staring into the distance.

Out to the east, beyond the High Street, was the whole of London. I could make out office buildings and shopping malls a mile away or more – blue luminous cubes linked by fragile threads of street-lights. But on the other side of the estates, in the open country to the north and west where the roads disappeared, there were huge areas of darkness: Dante Park; some gravel pits near the motorway; the thick woodland where old villages lay buried. And immediately below me, spread out around my feet, was the half-lit labyrinth of Cannon Park, its corridors pock-marked with blackness where the lights had been broken. I watched the atrium for a while. The white neon cross stood out in the centre, and all around countless windows shone grey or blue, as the images changed on TV.

Finally I went down and started walking the corridors again. At the junction of C and D, I looked towards the next section of Cannon Park, four blocks in a square. F block had been empty for over a year, scheduled for refurbishment by the council, the doors and windows sealed behind metal shutters. The other three blocks were still inhabited, but it was the worst part of the estate. I peered from the balcony into the grassy area below. Someone had thrown the entire contents of a flat down there: sofa, TV, mattress, an old fridge. And further on, by the bollards which closed the estate off to traffic, tarts and drug-dealers were moving about. An old woman appeared from the car park near the High Street, dragging a suitcase behind her. She started to move across the open space, and as the little crowd made way for her I caught sight of Tess, smoking a cigarette. She must have been there all along, standing by a low wall next to Emily.

They were standing in a pool of light, Em wearing a school-girl uniform with a blazer and short skirt. I leaned right out to see what was going on. I didn't believe Tess screwed people for money – I would have known if she had. But all the same I started wondering who she was waiting for. Of course I knew she had slept with other people. Savage had always fancied her, for one. But I had never asked her about that – about whether he came on to her, or if she fancied him – and suddenly, when I thought of it, I was angry. I wanted to shout out across the empty space. But I forced myself to wait. I knew I shouldn't care if she fucked strangers, or Savage, either – and probably it was better if she did.

When the old woman had gone, a man in a suit came up and started chatting. Em began to laugh. She put her hand on the man's chest, and Tess came forward with a sports bag and showed him what was in it. He took out his wallet, bantering with Em while Tess counted the money. Then Tess handed him the sports bag, and the man said something which made Em laugh again. He took Em by the hand, escorting her to the car park, and I heard them drive away.

When they had gone, Tess stuffed the money in her jeans, said something to the other people who were hanging about, and set off towards the High Street. I wanted to run after her. I thought I could catch her before she got home, take her to the bunker, fuck her down there among the book-stacks. I was so relieved she hadn't gone with the guy in the suit – I was so pleased she was only being the pimp. But she was walking fast, and I was too far away.

After that I wandered around the estate. I went up to Dan's flat, and stopped outside the front door. I could smell toast; probably Dan was eating, as usual. And I waited for a while, wondering what to do. But I knew I couldn't go in. Dan's mum had found out about the posse. She blamed me for getting him into it. She said I was doing the Devil's work – that I had betrayed them both. She was terrified of Dan turning out like his older brother, and I'd never be able to explain that this was different. So in the end I walked away, going across to the other side of the block instead, and looked out towards the High Street. For a while I thought I might go to the bunker, but I didn't feel like it – I was too nervous; I wanted something to happen. And I didn't want to be alone any more, either. So in the end I went back to the atrium, past the electric cross, out to the garages behind block C. It was about midnight.

# 8

The lights were on, and all the boys were there – Tess, too, fidgeting and humming to herself. And Emily had come back from her job. She was asleep on the sofa next to Tess, still dressed as a schoolgirl.

'Where you been, cocksucker?' Savage said. 'We've been making plans without you.' He was walking up and down on his own.

'Hanging out.'

'You let me down. You're my fucking adviser, man.'

Dan let out a little groan.

'What goes on?' I asked.

'Ask *him*,' Dan said. He was sitting at the table with his head in his hands.

'We're doing a job,' Savage said. He drilled me with his pale eyes, then looked away. 'Tell him, Terry.'

Tess started singing. She was smiling to herself, stroking Em's hair.

'We're going to nick a gun,' Terence explained. 'Nice, easy job.'

'Where?'

'Let me have some E,' Tess chanted. 'Give me some E!'

'Shut up, will you?' Savage told her.

'There's this snitch in block B,' Terry said. 'Old cunt called Frank Cooper. He lives on his own.'

'So?'

'He used to be a soldier.'

'And you think he has a gun?'

Terry smiled. 'Army revolver. He gets all this stuff in the post from his regiment. I know; I've nicked cash from him.' He turned to Savage. 'Everyone knows he's got a gun.'

'Course.' Savage said. 'It's a gift: a grass with a gun.'

'How do you know he's a grass?'

'Listen, cunt: my *dad* told me, all right?' Terry turned to Savage. 'We're wasting time,' he said.

'Give me some E,' Tess repeated. 'I feel weird.' She had curled up on the sofa.

Dan pulled his head up. 'What kind of weird?'

'My brain's hot,' Tess told him.

'Give her something,' Savage said. 'She's getting on my nerves.'

'People like that register their guns,' I said. 'The cops will have the serial number – a description.'

'They're not going to waste time on some old cunt's gun,' Terry said.

'What are you saying?' Savage asked me.

'It would be easier to *buy* a gun,' I said. 'Or nick an illegal one.'

Terry jeered. 'We don't need to *buy* anything. Jesus! Besides, we should teach the old wanker a lesson – show him who's in charge.'

I looked at Terry and Savage. Tess was humming on the sofa behind me.

'If we do this,' I said, 'burglary, guns – it'll change things.'

'So let's change them,' Terry shouted. 'We're not kids any more.'

'We need a gun,' Savage agreed. 'We can do much more.'

I hesitated, and they stared at me. 'All right,' I shrugged. 'We get the gun. Why not? It's a simple job.'

But Dan buried his face again. 'No way, man. This is such shit. I bet he doesn't even *have* a gun.'

'What would *you* do, nappy-head?' Terry turned on him.

'He's scared, that's all. He wouldn't do anything,' Tatham said. 'He doesn't want to upset his fucking *uncle*, man . . .' He spat on the ground near Dan. 'Let's go. Leave this pussy with the girls.'

But Savage had been staring at Tess for a while, and he hadn't been listening. 'We're going to get wired,' he announced. And he turned to Terry. 'You know where he lives?'

'He's next to this mate of Dad's.'

'So, let's get mashed,' Savage repeated. He was trembling now, his feet fidgeting, stamping the ground. 'Hey, Tatham! Where's my gear?'

'We should get stoned *after*,' Terry said. 'We need to keep our wits.'

'He's right,' I said.

'Fuck that,' Savage snapped. 'We don't need *wits*. We need to *feel* right. Victor, give us the stuff. I've got to get my head set up.'

Victor started handing out the ecstasy – one pill each, like a ration – and Tess gave Emily a shake. 'Take something,' she said. 'Do you good.'

'Give the girls three,' Savage put in. He was pacing up and down again. 'We'll have a party when we get back.'

I sat on the sofa, but I didn't touch Tess or Emily, although they were right next to me. I was thinking about the job we were going to do.

'Merton, Terence, Tatham,' Savage was saying: 'you come with me to the old cunt's flat. Victor, Calvin, Danny: keep guard on the stairs of B, D and A. Okay?'

'Sure.'

'You going to kill him?' Danny asked.

'Good idea, you fat fuck,' Tatham said. He made a pistol with his fingers and shot Danny.

But Dan ignored him. 'We just give him a fright, yeah? And nick the gun.'

'We'll do it nice and gently,' Savage promised.

'Sure,' Terry said. 'If he's nice, we'll be nice with him. And if not, we'll shoot the bastard.'

Nobody said anything. Savage stopped marching up and down. He pressed his head against the wall and started muttering to himself. Everyone was waiting. 'I know,' he said at last, 'I *know* I must be leader. This gang belongs to me: all of you do. Does anyone say different?'

'No, man,' Victor said, 'You're the king.'

After that, we all started drinking – just a couple of beers at first to get the blood racing, and then some bitter white spirit that Terry had found. I drank it all down. By the second round I was impatient to do the job – my heart was jumping.

'We'll do it now,' Savage said, steadying himself against the door-frame of the garage. 'It's time.'

Everyone got up – except Danny, who just sat where he was, staring at his hands. Then Tatham ordered him to stay with the girls, and I went over to him. 'Come on, Dan,' I said quietly. 'It'll be okay.' So he pushed the table away, put on his glasses, and tramped out on his heavy legs.

The boys were pretty much off their heads, and I wasn't straight – but I knew what I was doing. Halfway across the atrium, Calvin and Victor split off to take up their positions on the staircases of the neighbouring blocks. The rest of us ran on under the electric cross towards block B. Then Danny went ahead, wheezing his way up the stair tower. Savage and I waited in the atrium with Tatham and Terry.

I wasn't afraid. The police were irrelevant. They only ever came in cars, lights flashing along the High Street, or across the waste-land at the back of the estate where Savage had his headquarters. Either way Dan and the others would see them miles away.

It was very cold. The boys all had their hoods up. I was in my big coat, with my suit and everything. Tatham and Terence led the way upstairs and along the top corridor. They brushed past bags of rubbish and empty window-boxes. Savage walked beside me. But when we reached the old man's front door, nobody knew what to do.

Downstairs the alcoholic woman started to shout. A man yelled at her to shut up, and a dog started barking, but nobody came out of their flats. Terry pulled his hood low over his face, pacing up and down the landing. He stopped at each of the walkway lights, carefully smashing the light bulbs, until the whole corridor was pitch-black.

'Knock on the door,' Savage said. 'Tell him it's the police.'

'No,' I said. 'People will come out.'

'Just *knock* then!'

So Tatham banged the door with his fist.

'Harder, man!' The noise echoed in the atrium. We could see someone moving about behind the wobbly glass of the door. 'Come out, you cunt!' Savage shouted. And he added to Tatham, 'Break the glass.'

Tatham smashed the panel in the door. He put his hand in to pull back the latch, but the door wouldn't open. 'It's a deadlock. I cut my fucking hand.'

'Don't bleed on me, man,' Terry said. 'Keep away.'

'Open up!' Savage shouted. 'We'll fucking kill you.'

We could see inside the flat now, through the broken pane. At the back, silhouetted against the far window, was the shape of the old man.

'Open the door, you cunt!'

A light went on somewhere at the back of the flat. We could hear a voice, but there was no movement. 'He's calling the cops,' I said.

'Sod that.' Tatham and Terence were dancing back and forth between the front door and the window. Tatham was holding his wrist, trying to stop it bleeding.

'You've cut your fucking jugular,' Terence said. 'Clumsy cunt.'

'It's not his jugular. That's in your neck.'

'Thanks for the lecture. He's bleeding like a whore.' But he started laughing.

Tatham's T-shirt was glistening with blood. 'It's all right,' he said. 'It's slowing down.'

'Keep it away from me, you fucking freak,' Terry told him. 'I hate blood.'

'Put the phone down!' Savage yelled through the broken window. 'Put it down or we'll kill you.'

'We'll have to take the door off the hinges,' I said. 'We haven't got all night.'

'Let's do it,' Savage snapped. 'Come on. Break it down.'

There was a window-box on the old guy's wall. Terence and Tatham lifted it from its brackets, and began battering it against the hinges of the door. It made an incredible noise.

'Go away!' the man shouted. 'Leave me alone. The police are coming.'

'No they're not, mate,' Terry told him. 'You think they'd come out for you?'

'Go on!' the old man shouted again. 'Clear out of it! Bugger off!' And his voice reminded me of something – an old film, a wartime newsreel I'd seen on TV. 'What if he doesn't have a gun?'

'Let's find out.' Savage was standing aside, waiting for the boys to take another run. 'No harm having a look.'

'What if he *does* have a shooter?' Terence asked. 'That's a bit more fucking relevant.'

He and Tatham charged the door again. It cracked, but it still didn't give way. The wood was splintering near the hinges.

'Get on with it,' Savage said. 'Do it again.'

Every time they rammed the door, the noise echoed from the darkness on the far side of the atrium. Everyone on the estate must have heard, but no one came out.

The next thump forced the deadlock out of its socket, but the door was held in place by a chain. 'Break it some more,' Savage said. 'Knock it down.' So Terence and Tatham moved back and took another run. They sent a new shock wave through the night, then another, pulverising the wood by the hinges, until the whole door fell forward into the flat. Finally they heaved the concrete box into the old man's hall.

We could see him clearly now. He was standing perfectly erect in stripy pyjamas, six foot tall. 'You don't frighten me,' he said.

He was looking straight at us, his bright eyes taking us all in. 'You get out, you little Nazis. Bugger off, you hear me!'

'He's got attitude,' Terence said.

The boys kept giggling, but I was beginning to think more clearly.

'Let's get on with it,' Savage said.

He stepped over the window-box, tramping earth into the carpet.

'You keep your mouth shut, or we'll fucking kill you,' Savage told the old man. 'Where's your gun?'

'I don't have a gun,' he said. 'And if I did, I wouldn't give it to a little Hitler like you.'

Savage moved towards him. 'We know you've got a shooter. If you don't tell us, we'll have to tie you up and search for it. Do yourself a favour. No need to make things unpleasant.' He was speaking quietly, his pale eyes glancing up and down the old man, who was much taller than him.

'Get out of my flat!' the man bellowed.

Savage screamed back at him: 'Give us the *shooter*!' The old guy put his arm up, as though Savage was going to hit him, but Savage turned away, suddenly losing interest.

'Get out, then!' the man said. 'Go on. Hop it!' He was a sergeant-major giving Savage an order. A wisp of military music floated across my mind, and the echo of boots on the parade ground.

'You're beginning to get on my nerves,' Savage told him. 'One more sound and you'll do my nut. You understand what I'm saying?'

'You don't frighten me!' the old man shouted furiously. 'Get out!'

'We should be searching,' I said to Savage.

'Do it, then! Go on. *Search*! I'm staying here.'

In the little sitting-room I switched on a lamp and began turning the old man's possessions over. Terry and Tatham were rummaging through the bathroom and the kitchen. The only other room was the bedroom, where Savage and the old man were facing each other. I began looking at the books and photographs on his shelves. He had a bust of the Duke of Wellington and, piled up on the shelves behind his sofa, a little museum of ceremonial headgear: peaked caps and tam-o'-shanters, a spiked helmet, hats with plumes. I put on a Scotch beret with a red and white band, and for a while I just stood still, unable to move, gazing at the cover of a book. It was called *Forgotten Army*.

Savage was yelling at the old man. '*Tell* me where the gun is.'

'Go to hell.'

'I'll flatten you, you fucking snitch.'

'You don't frighten me,' the old guy repeated, 'coming in here like Al Capone.'

'I won't warn you again,' Savage said.

For a moment there was silence. Then the old man spat at him.

After that, Savage started beating him. I could hear it all from the sitting-room. The old guy was down in a moment, and Savage was kicking him on the floor. *This is how it starts,* I thought. *We have to do this. But afterwards, very soon, everything will be different.*

'You'll fucking kill him,' Terry said, looking out from the kitchen.

'Lay off,' Tatham added. 'You're doing your fucking nut, man. We don't need to kill him.'

'He's a piece of shit,' Savage said, holding back for a moment. He was almost crying. 'He doesn't show me any fucking respect. I was being *nice*, you know what I'm saying? Who does the cunt think he is?'

I stayed where I was. In my mind, a sense of fear began to isolate itself – fear and impatience. 'Has anyone found the gun?' I called out. But nobody was listening. I took off the beret and chucked it on the floor. Then I cleared all the hats, throwing them in a pile. I pulled out the books and started dumping them. Then, at the back of the shelf, I discovered something. There were four narrow cases of red leather, and I carried them over to the light. Inside the first, on satin lining, was a gold disc, two inches across, stamped with the profile of George VI. There was an inscription, too, and a ribbon. It flashed when I held it up.

'Show me.' Savage was in the doorway behind me.

'What have you done to him?' I said.

'He's quiet. What have you found?'

'Bling.' I handed it over. 'I don't know what it is. A campaign medal, I think. He fought in the Far East. Perhaps in Burma . . .'

'Hey, Merton, shut the fuck up.' Savage held up the gold disc. 'What's this worth?'

'Worth?'

'Nicker, cunt. What's it worth?'

I shrugged. 'It's a collector's type of deal. You couldn't get anything for it on the street. There's more, too.' I opened another box.

'I like it,' he said. 'I could do with one of these. Let's see that lot.'

There were five medals altogether, some silver, some gold, each with a different coloured ribbon. They all bore the profile of George VI except one, which had Elizabeth II looking very young. 'This'll do,' Savage said. 'Must be worth a bag of skank.'

'Not on the street,' I told him.

'Terence would know how to do it.'

I put out my hand to take them back. 'Leave them,' I said.

'You what?'

'Leave them here,' I said. 'It's bad karma.'

'*Fuck*, no!' he laughed.

'I'm your *consigliere*, man.'

Savage looked at me in the half-light. 'You're not really a bad person or nothing, Merton,' he said. 'But sometimes you are fucking weird, you know what I'm saying?'

Terry and Tatham appeared behind him. 'Look what I've

found.' Terry said. He was grinning, holding something under his sweatshirt.

'Well, cunt, what you got?'

Terry hesitated, standing back.

'He's got an erection,' Tatham said. They were laughing. 'He wants you to see his dick, man.'

Terry unzipped his sweatshirt, and I saw a gleam of metal in the dim light. He raised it towards us: an oiled barrel, shiny wooden handle. 'The old man's shooter,' he said. 'Here.' He offered the revolver to Savage, holding it in both hands. It was much bigger than I had imagined – as long as my lower arm. I'd never seen a gun like that. It was almost an antique. Savage put the medals down and started to examine it. He didn't know how to open the chamber, so he started thumping it with his palm. 'Hey, Tatham, what you stopped searching for, you thick cunt? Does he have any ammo?'

'Chill the fuck out,' Tatham said. 'I don't know. There's loads of little drawers.'

'Where did you find it?'

'The kitchen.'

'Then go and look. He must have bullets.' Tatham went off. We could hear him pulling out drawers, dumping everything on the floor. Savage was standing in the middle of the room. For a long time he gripped the revolver in his hand, aiming it straight at Terry's forehead. But Terence paid no attention. Then he pointed it at me. 'Die, Merton,' he said with a smile. 'I give you ten seconds . . .' But Tatham came back from the hall.

'Put it down, batty-boy!' He was right behind me. 'You'll kill us both, man. Look, I found the bullets.'

'How many?'

He held out a fistful. 'There's a couple of boxes.'

'Okay,' Savage said calmly, 'we're done.'

'Look at the size of that thing,' Tatham said. 'It's bigger than my cock, man.'

'You want to get your tool out?' Savage aimed at Tatham's balls. 'We can compare.'

'We should go,' I said. 'Is the old man alive?'

'Who knows?'

I picked up the boxes of medals which Savage had dropped. 'Give them here,' he said. 'They're mine.'

'They're worthless,' I told him. 'Easy to trace. Anyone finds that lot with you, and you're nicked.'

'How do you know?'

'Because it's obvious. Ask Terry.' Savage stared at me, holding the gun to my forehead again. I got a cold sensation in my brain. 'They only handed out a few of these, didn't they?' I said. 'There'll be a record. They'll know they belonged to this old guy. If we tried to sell, they'd be on to us right away.'

'I won't sell them, will I?' he said. 'They're for me. I like them. They're my fucking reward.' He took a breath, raising the revolver from my temple, and stuffing it into his trousers.

So I handed them over. 'Just keep them hidden. I'm going to check the old man.'

'What for?'

'See if you committed a murder yet.'

'Don't do it, man,' Tatham said. 'What difference does it make?'

'About thirty years,' I said. 'They still investigate murder.'

'Don't be a cunt, Merton,' he laughed. But he and Terry moved back, out of my way.

The old man was curled up in the foetal position on his bedroom floor. I felt for the pulse in his neck, stretching him out in his blue and red pyjamas. He was still alive. I didn't know how much harm Savage had done. He wasn't bleeding or anything. He was just unconscious, breathing steadily. The room smelt of piss, and when I moved his body my hand got wet from his pyjama trousers. There was a smell of shit, too, and I didn't want to touch him any more. I grabbed a pillow to put under his head. By his bed there was a Second World War photograph, a group of men in a jungle clearing, toothless and pit-eyed in their combat fatigues. There was a little black book, too, and I picked it up with my clean hand: *The Book of Common Prayer*, a green ribbon marking his page. All of a sudden I remembered: *Thou shalt not be afraid for any terror by night: nor for the arrow that flieth by day; For the pestilence that walketh in darkness: nor for the sickness that destroyeth in the noon-day.* I opened the book. I was going to search for the passage. But the boys were fidgeting in the hall.

'Come on, cunt.'

'He's alive,' I said.

'Come *on*, for fuck's sake.'

'Forget it,' Savage said. 'We're going.'

At the end of the open walkway we waited for Danny. In the cold air, I was completely sober. I got a shot of adrenaline when Terry produced the gun, and now my stomach was full of energy. Savage had pocketed the medals, and the other boys had taken a few things from the flat – a couple of silver cups, a radio. But it wasn't until Danny arrived that I was really frightened. He had been on the floor above us, up on the flat roof with the water tanks and aerials.

'I could hear everything,' he hissed. 'You woke the fucking dead, I'm telling you.'

'Let's go. People will start coming out.'

'You're scared,' Savage said.

'We've been here too long,' I told him.

Savage was stroking the butt of the gun, and the others were fooling about. Terry made a kung-fu kick at Tatham, who was stuffing the silver cups in his sweatshirt pockets.

'Come on! *Jesus*!' Dan pulled at my coat. 'Let's go.'

'I'm staying,' Savage told him. 'I'm not running anywhere. This is *our* estate.' He looked out towards the far side of the atrium. The neon cross was standing in mid-air. Here and there you could see the blue light of a TV filling a window. Otherwise the whole complex was dark. 'We own it now,' he said.

But just as he turned, the old man appeared on the balcony.

'Shit!' Savage said. He was almost impressed. 'I thought he was fucking oblivious.'

'He's fucking Dracula,' Dan said. 'I knew it.' He was looking back from the mouth of the stairwell.

'Yeah, he's like the undead.'

'Not for long,' Savage said.

'Give me my *things*!' the man shouted along the walkway. We were about thirty yards away. 'You come back here!'

'Shoot him,' Terence said. 'Look at him. What's he so proud of?'

'Let's go, man. Come *on*, will you!' Danny tugged at my arm again. He thudded down the first flight of stairs.

Savage pulled out the revolver. He waved it at the old man, and tried to fire. 'What's wrong with this fucking gun, man? It doesn't shoot.'

'You have to cock it,' Terry told him. 'My dad showed me. Look.' He guided Savage's thumb to the back trigger. 'Hold it straight, man. Both hands.' The old man was moving unsteadily towards us, clutching the rail. He was having difficulty staying upright.

'Let's *go*, man!' Danny shouted from the landing. 'Don't shoot. It's not worth it.'

'Don't tell me what to do, you pussy.' Savage kept his eyes on the man over the end of the barrel.

Tatham and Terence were standing right by Savage. I was just behind. Then there was a little shout from Savage – a happy grunt, like he'd shot a load – and the gun went off. The sound was huge. It ricocheted around the courtyard. Down below, I saw Victor running across the atrium from the far side of block A where he had been keeping guard.

'Jesus fucking Christ, man!' Tatham was staring at Savage. 'You killed him.'

The old man was lying on the walkway. 'Let's go,' I said. 'Someone's going to call the police.'

'Do what you like, nappy,' Savage said. He was rubbing his wrist. 'This thing should have a health warning. I've broken my fucking arm.'

'Hey, listen to me,' I said. 'I'm your *consigliere*. I keep you out of jail, remember? *Paul?*'

He turned and looked into my face, and his voice was suddenly quiet. 'What are you telling me?'

'Time to go,' I said. 'Put the gun away, come downstairs.'

Savage looked about. His eyes had an expression of pain, of some old, secret injury he had just remembered. 'You all heard Merton,' he told them. 'Do what he says.'

As soon as they moved, the boys were running headlong. They jumped the stairs a flight at a time. Danny tripped and Tatham stamped on him in the dark. Then on the ground floor we met Victor and Calvin. 'The old man's dead,' Tatham told him. 'Big Boy killed him.'

'Shit!' Calvin said. 'What you do that for?'

'It's all right,' Terry put in. 'We've got the shooter.'

'You didn't need to do that.'

'Shut it,' Savage said. 'I don't want to talk about it.'

'Now we split,' I announced. 'Nobody speaks till we meet at the garage tomorrow.'

'Scram,' Savage said. 'Don't open your mouth, you know what I'm saying? I'll fucking kill you.'

But we all hesitated. A siren was sounding in the High Street, and a woman had started to shout at us from the fourth-floor balcony. She was a long way up, and she definitely couldn't see our faces. 'You boys: I know who you are,' she was yelling. 'I seen *all* of you. What you been doing with my Danny? I'll find you. As the Lord lives, I'll search you out.'

'Jesus,' Dan said. He looked away from the building, pulling the hood down over his face. 'It's my mum. She'll go mental when she finds the body.'

'She doesn't know a thing,' Terence said. 'She's bluffing. Go home, just act normal. You haven't done nothing, remember. You was only looking from the tower.'

'He's right,' I said. The sirens were getting closer. 'Now we split. Go on.'

We moved off. I made myself walk normally across the yard, slowly past the electric cross, towards the suburbs. But before I made it to the far side of the atrium, I heard a scream – a long, wailing shriek from block B, that penetrated my brain across the darkness – then a series of short, jabby cries, like an animal, gagging and retching. By the time I reached the bollards on the far side, the police siren had stopped, but Dan's mother was still crying out – praying, perhaps; I couldn't tell. And I didn't turn round. I kept marching on past the garages, as fast as I could, out of the estate, towards the suburbs and the empty, pitch-black countryside.

# 9

Three in the morning. It was silent on the roads – no traffic, no lights in the houses. For ages I tramped through the suburbs, while the panic grew inside me. I was horny; terrified but turned on, an electric charge running through my guts. I kept thinking about Tess – her round mouth, its permanent expression of bewilderment.

I couldn't go home. I thought at first I should go back to the bunker. I wished I could read the way I did when I was little, blocking out the noise in my head. But I knew I'd just lie there wanting to throw up, and thinking about what we'd done. The whole thing disturbed me – it frightened me. Whatever happened now, I was committed – I was never going to leave the posse. And I had this conviction that whatever we did, however many people we killed, even if I went to jail and everything, still nothing was going to change. We had tried to start something – I still believed that: we had assaulted the system. But it would make no difference. And when I left school, even when I was old, it would still be the same. The whole shape of my life was fixed.

For ages I walked about, from the estate into the suburbs beyond Dante Park, then out to the open countryside. Finally I stood in a small lane in the middle of some woods, staring into the darkness. It was the kind of place we used to go joyriding. But it reminded me now of something I had read in Trevelyan – of the centuries of dissolution and war in which history had begun. And I longed so much to be taken away from the present; to step out of the country and walk into the past, as though it was there in front of me, no more than a yard away. But after a while I stopped dreaming. I was still right there on the tarmac, still feeling sick, and I made myself go back.

I circled the fringes of the estate, looking for coppers, but there was nothing going on. So I took a risk, and tramped back to the Savage headquarters.

Tess and Emily had fallen asleep on one of the sofas. They were hugging each other like sisters. I held up a light, and stood watching them.

'Who is it?' Tess turned away, covering her eyes.

'It's me,' I said.

She rolled over, examining me through her fingers. 'You look like shit. What happened?'

'Nothing. Let's not talk about it.'

'Where's Paul?'

I shrugged and moved to the mattress in the corner, still in my big coat. Then I squatted on the floor, and put on my sunglasses. I was staring at Tess's white legs, the breasts under her T-shirt.

'You want some soup?' She sat up on the bed.

'Sure.'

'Go on,' she said, 'talk to me.' She got up and poured soup into a saucepan. 'What are you thinking?'

But I didn't say anything. Em turned over in her sleep. I was wondering about fucking them both.

'Are you stoned?' I asked.

'Not really.'

'Do you have anything left?'

She shook her head as she stirred the soup. 'Paul promised more E.'

'He won't get it tonight.'

I closed my eyes and rolled my head against the wall. I could have fallen asleep if I hadn't been so hungry. 'Do you ever want to do what Em does?' I asked.

'Nah,' she said. 'Not me. I'm a home bird. Here.'

I drank the soup very quickly, and chewed my way through

85

a piece of stodgy pitta. *After this*, I thought, *I'll screw Tess – here, on this shitty little mattress. Then I'll go – I'll get out right away, hide in the bunker before she's caught her breath . . .*

Tess attempted a wide smile, putting her hand out to stroke my hair, but there was a tremor in her stomach when I laid my hand across it. 'Take your glasses off,' she said, reaching for them.

'No, wait – leave them,' I told her. 'I want to look at you like this for a while: like we're strangers.' I watched her lips fall away at the edges. 'I want to fuck a stranger.'

She pushed me away, getting to her feet, and took out a ciga-rette. 'Fuck a stranger, then.'

'No, don't be angry. I just want to have sex. That's all right, isn't it? Can't we have a screw, like Em does, without thinking about it?'

'That's different,' Tess said, blowing smoke towards me.

'But that's what I want,' I said, suddenly clear in my mind. 'I want to be alone – *invisible*; all alone with someone who doesn't know me. I've been thinking about it,' I said, taking hold of the waistband of her jeans. 'We don't have families. That's not the way it is. We have mothers and mothers' boyfriends – half-sisters, half-brothers, aunts, maybe – people who come and go. That's the way it works. If you get close to someone – if you get obsessed . . .' I kept pulling her towards me, but she was resisting. 'We need freedom, Tess. We shouldn't love anyone.'

'You think you're hard,' she said, and her voice was tender again, 'but when you smile, you look just like a little boy.'

I let go and adjusted my sunglasses, keeping my eyes on her. She had an expression of resignation and reluctant desire, like someone was about to hit her. 'Come here,' I said. 'I want to hold you.' And she let me pull her down to the mattress.

I peeled off Tess's T-shirt and unfastened her bra. Her skin was cold. Then I cupped her breasts and nibbled them. They were big breasts, satisfying to bite, or press your head against. I ripped off her leggings and knickers, but she kept looking at me, and I really wanted to hide. I felt as though she could see right inside me. By the time we were naked I didn't even want to fuck her any more. And she started whining: 'Come on. Hold me properly.' I took her wrists, but I felt so depressed. There was a sort of pain in the pit of my stomach. Then I took the sunglasses off and put them on Tess. 'There,' I said. 'That's better. You look great.' She seemed like a stranger after all, and we made out.

The springs creaked. Tess kept the glasses on. Even in the middle of sex I wanted to run away, confronted with that round, nervous mouth. And she kept clutching my back or grabbing my arse, like she'd drown without me.

Even before Tess started crying out, before I shot my load, my mind closed in on itself. And when it was over, I felt worse: frightened, completely alone. I rolled away, closing my eyes.

'I've got to go,' I said.

I started searching about for my shirt and jersey. Suddenly I was freezing.

'Stay,' Tess said. 'Hold me.'

'I need to get away.'

'Five minutes.' She reached out towards me. '*Please.*'

'No,' I said. 'I'll do my head.'

I gathered up my clothes, abandoned in a crooked line across the floor, and started to pull them on. Tess was sprawled naked on the mattress, her cunt exposed to the world. I kept my eyes from her face as I pulled on my trousers. In theory it was so easy: sex as a pure relationship, Daly called it. That was all I wanted: billions of sperms flying to their death while a flash of hope filled the mind. But afterwards everything was darker than before. *Post coitum omne animal triste.* I had read that somewhere in the bunker.

'*Don't go,*' she said. I was jamming on my trainers, and I

hesitated. Then I forced myself to kiss her on the forehead as I buttoned my big coat.

'Come back later,' she said.

'I promise,' I told her. And I slammed the door.

The clouds had cleared, and the moon had risen over the towers of Cannon Park. The tarmac was shining like dark silver. At first I headed home, hugging my coat around me and jogging along. My rigging was aching. But by the time I reached our cul-de-sac, I'd decided I couldn't go home, so I padded back to school, taking the long way round, avoiding the estate.

In the bunker, I sat staring at the paper-stack in its circle of yellow light. Repeatedly, with a shock, I remembered the old man's face. And when I lay down, a little spot of moonlight which had forced its way through the ventilation system, pinpricked my forehead with mercury. Hectic apprehension hammered in my brain. I kept telling myself the boys and me were right – that we belonged to the future. We weren't committing a crime, we were creating a new world.

I slept for a while, and when I woke the whole bunker was pockmarked with grey light. The temperature had risen, too. I could hear the water pump purring on the next floor.

I started thinking about the old man again. I had the feeling there was something I hadn't considered, something which would explain it all; but I was too tired to take down a book, and for about an hour I just lay on the mattress.

Later, when I went to take a piss, it was bright outside. So I got my coat and jumped over the wall into Fisher's Lane. Then I headed for the estate.

I jogged for a while, just trying to get warm, my shadow running in front of me. I wanted to see the place where we'd done the job. I wasn't remorseful, exactly; it was just a matter of seeing how things had turned out, if the cops would do anything.

From the top of the tower in the middle of block C I had almost a complete view of the estate. Below me, the atrium was filled with the shadow of low-rise buildings, cast in a semi-circle. Small silhouetted figures were moving silently towards the High Street. And I could see straight across to the fifth floor of block B, where the old man's flat was. I stared intently. There was nobody there: no cops or crowds of residents, no ambulance crew. Most people were asleep; you could see the curtains drawn all round the estate, the broken windows patched over with cardboard.

I made my way towards B block, keeping to the fourth floor. Probably I should have gone round the back where I didn't know anyone. But when I looked out from the tower, all the doors had been closed, and I didn't pass anybody as I marched round. Then, when I got to B, I was going to go up to the floor above, to get a good look at the old man's flat. But I heard voices and stopped where I was. Mrs Johnson was talking to somebody.

'. . . if you knew these boys, officer, *preying* on my Danny, God forgive them . . .' She must have been standing in the doorway of her flat. I was three doors away, halfway to the stairs. In the background, a male voice was speaking through the static of a police radio. 'We should have gone to live in Jamaica with my brother – that's the truth. I blame myself. This isn't a society, constable – it's a predicament. And now Danny –' Mrs J broke off. 'It was my fault,' she added quietly. 'I stayed because of *him*.'

There was a protest behind her, and I thought of Danny's grandfather, staring into the middle distance from his armchair.

'My brother's a businessman in Jamaica, officer. He could have put Danny through school – a *real* school – with discipline and books.' I began to move back towards the stairs. 'They use the cane in Jamaican schools. Can you believe that?'

'Well, madam, you've been more than helpful.' A copper in uniform appeared on the landing. He was looking away from me, back into the flat. I kept moving away along the walkway.

'You just catch those boys.'

'We'll do our best.'

'You'll do nothing. *I* know. There are boys running up and down all night, banging the doors.'

The policeman was putting his helmet on. I had reached the tower. All I had to do was run down the stairs and I would be out.

I leapt down the first flight, but there was a shout behind me. '*There*! That's one of them. Him on the stairs . . .' Mrs Johnson had come out on to the balcony. 'You talk to *him*,' she told the policeman.

'Wait there, son,' the cop shouted. 'Don't go anywhere.'

I jumped the next flight, and the one below, down to the third floor. There was no way the copper could have caught me – he was far too fat. Then I ran to the back of the block, where it overlooked the car park, and sprinted down the back staircase, past bags of rubbish, into the open space. But just as I broke out, a police car turned in from the High Street and drove straight towards me. Immediately the blue lights started up, and the siren gave a yelp; one of the cops yelled at me to stop. I couldn't get past them, even if I ran for it. And in any case, I wanted to prove I wasn't frightened – that I had nothing to hide – and on an impulse I stopped.

They arrested me in the car park on suspicion of burglary, cautioned me, read me my rights. Then they took me back upstairs. Mrs Johnson was still standing in front of her flat, with the small, fat cop beside her.

'*That's* Merton Browne,' she said at once. 'He'll know about the shot in the night, officer, you mark my words. I have a mother's knowledge. He's always with those boys these days.' Mrs J narrowed her eyes towards me. 'Yes, *you*, Merton,' she said, 'I'm talking to the police this time, and I don't care if you know it. I don't understand what happened to you, but I'll see you punished.'

'All right, Mrs Johnson,' the fat copper said. He had a Welsh accent. 'Perhaps we should have a word with the lad – just him and us, like.'

'You do what you have to do,' she said, skewering me with her little eyes.

The fat copper walked towards me and the other two cops.

'Come with me, son. I want to show you something.'

'I'm not going anywhere. I demand to see a lawyer.'

'There's plenty of time for that. We won't ask you any questions. You don't have to say anything.'

'Then let's go to the police station,' I said. 'This is crap.'

'We'll be down there soon enough,' he sighed. 'This won't take a moment.'

He marched me past the open door of Mrs Johnson's flat, towards the tower at the other end, and we climbed to the fifth floor. 'All right,' he said melodically. 'Over here.'

They had nailed a panel of plywood over the old man's broken door. 'I don't want any foul language,' the cop told me. 'You understand? Keep your mouth shut. This old gentleman's had a hell of a night. It's a miracle he's alive.'

'Then why are we here?' I countered, but my voice broke.

He was examining my face. 'Late night?'

'There's no law against staying up late.' My stomach had given way. I thought I was going to crap myself, but I was glad the old man was alive. I had to stop myself smiling.

'Barrack-room lawyer, is it?' The policeman said, and he grabbed my arm. 'In your suit and all.'

'Let go, or I'll sue you,' I told him. 'This arrest is unlawful. I should be accompanied by a lawyer.'

A policewoman opened the old man's door, her blonde hair in a bun. 'Who's this, Bill?' she said, quite friendly.

'He's under arrest,' he said. 'He was making off, like. I thought he might want to see the scene of the crime, before we take him down to the station.'

They brought me in to the little sitting-room, and the old man was sitting there on the sofa with a bandage round his head. He was propped up on cushions, his possessions laid out around him. He and the WPC had been making an inventory of what was missing. My head froze when I saw him.

The old man looked up, putting his head on one side.

'That's one of them,' he said calmly.

'You sure?'

He briefly looked me over. 'I'd know him anywhere. The coat. That scar on the forehead.'

'Was this the one that hit you?'

'No. That was the pale, scabby-looking lad,' the old man told them. 'The skinhead with skin trouble, like I said. This one was quiet. I think he was in this room, here, before they . . . before I went out.'

'Well, lad?'

'Well *what*?' I said. 'I deny it. I wasn't here. And I demand to see a lawyer. This is ridiculous. It's a breach of my human rights. I've never even *been* here. He's confused. You can't convict me on one person's evidence. I bet there were loads of guys – it was dark.'

'Who told you that?'

'It's obvious. It must have been.'

'Nobody said anything about the dark.'

'Those things don't happen in daylight.'

The old man was shaking his head. 'It's him. I'll swear it.'

'Well, lad?' The cop took out his notebook again. 'Not so smart after all.'

'This is bollocks,' I said.

'I suggest you don't say anything more. You can tell us all about it down the station.'

'I've got to have a shit,' I said.

'Caught short? A bit nervous, are we?'

'He's not going in my place,' the old man told them.

'Come on, son.' The woman copper took my arm. 'I don't need to cuff you, do I?'

'I'll keep an eye on things here, Julie,' the other cop said.

'You can have fun booking this lad. I'll be down to take over in a couple of hours.' And he turned to me. 'You know what you are, lad – as far as we're concerned?'

'What?' Suddenly I felt completely hollow – hollow and tired, as though all my adrenalin had worn off in an instant.

'*Paper*work, lad. Four hours of bloody paperwork.'

And Julie led me out.

# 10

Julie left me in the interview room, a windowless cell with a couple of wooden chairs. I walked up and down, put my sunglasses on, crouched down in the corner. There were public awareness posters on the walls, about carrying knives, and Hate Crime, and a chart made up of red and black columns. The inscription read *Operational Throughput Rates by Category*. I read and reread the words without making sense of them. My mind was stalled. None of the posse had ever been arrested, except Tatham and Calvin for shoplifting a few times, when they were little. When they did burglaries, or muggings at school, nothing ever happened, and after Miss Dent got a pasting, everyone thought Savage would be expelled for sure, but nobody was even suspended.

I stared at the race crime poster, leaned back, closed my eyes. I had made up my mind not to cooperate, but apart from that I had no plan.

Julie came back with a box file of forms, dumping them on the desk. 'Your lawyer's on his way,' she said, ignoring my dark glasses. 'Do you want a coffee while we process you?'

Behind her was the poster with charts. 'What does that mean?' I asked.

'What?'

'The bar-chart.'

She swivelled round. 'That? Stats for the politicians. The Chief Super wants more convictions per thousand of recorded crimes. That's what they call the throughput rate.' She turned back to the forms, blowing a strand of blonde hair from her forehead. 'Sit down and have some coffee.'

My mind began to unfreeze. I was frightened, but I was getting horny. And I was pretty sure Julie fancied me. She kept looking down at me on the floor. When she concentrated on the forms, her mouth made a tight red circle. 'We can do some basic stuff while the lawyer's on his way,' she said. 'If you don't mind, that is. Age, name, address, that kind of thing. Nothing incriminating. All right?'

I shrugged.

'You live on the estate?'

'No.' And I explained. I gave Mum and Mike as my next of kin, Daly as referee. I knew Daly would be on my side.

'How old are you?'

'Sixteen,' I said. 'Seventeen next month. How old are you?'

'None of your business.'

'Go on, tell me.' Her lips became a red circle, but she hesitated. 'Go on, Julie,' I said. 'Go *awn*!'

She smiled and I got up from my corner to take a chair. On the wall opposite the door was a picture of a skinhead. *Don't let him get away with it*, it said. *Race Crime is Hate Crime.*

'Twenty-six,' she said.

'You're fit,' I told her.

'Flattery won't get you anywhere. Occupation?'

'I go to school.'

'A levels?'

I nodded.

'You're hanging out with the wrong crowd.'

'Do you have a boyfriend, Julie?'

'None of your business.'

'What's your name, then – after Julie, I mean.'

'If it's any of your concern, it's *Denton*. Can we get on with these forms?'

'I fancy you, Julie Denton. You've got a fit mouth.'

'Give us a break.'

All the same, she was blushing. I knew she liked me. I wasn't nervous at all by then, but just when I was getting somewhere, the lawyer arrived.

'Merton, this is Benedict Doyle,' Julie said. 'He's been appointed by the Legal Aid Board to represent you.'

The lawyer was wearing a tweed coat, patches at the elbows. 'Benedict,' he said, offering me his hand.

Then a plain-clothes cop came in, and Julie stood up. He was about six foot four, much bigger than the rest of us.

'This is Merton Browne, sir,' Julie told him. 'Arrested in connection with the gun job in Cannon Park last night.'

'Good.' He looked me up and down. 'You the lawyer?' he asked Doyle. 'I'm Detective Constable Peterson. Colin.'

'Good to meet you,' my lawyer said. 'Shall we get down to it?'

'Can you take notes, WPC Denton?'

'Julie,' I murmured.

'Watch your lip,' the new cop told me. He put his huge face right up to mine. 'Keep it zipped. All *right*?'

'All right,' I said. 'Keep your hair on. I only said her name. It's not a state fucking secret.'

'Just watch it,' he repeated. 'You're facing charges of aggravated burglary. You don't need any more trouble.'

The interview went on for hours. The Welsh copper, Bill Simms, came in halfway through. They kept asking about the gun, but I said I knew nothing about that. Benedict intervened sometimes so that they changed the questions a bit. He told me they couldn't make me answer if I didn't want to. All the same, I said quite a lot in the end. I told them I'd been with Tess, and then in my place near the school. I didn't explain where it was, because I didn't want them going down there and finding all my stuff. When they brought out a map of the area, and told me to point to it, I refused. But after that, Benedict got annoyed. He took me aside. 'Don't piss around, lad.' He had big pouches under his eyes. 'We're talking about a serious burglary. Don't be so bloody cocky.'

So after that, I told them there was no place near the school, but that I was on my own, never went near the estate, and they should ask Tess.

Then they started on about the posse. They had a complete description from Mrs Johnson, and they were obsessed with Savage. As the interview went on, I found it easier to say nothing – it was just a matter of practice. And Peterson changed his tone, too. He was more resigned. I was sure they didn't have a case against me. I was certain they'd apologise and let me go.

'I want to make your client an offer,' Peterson told Benedict.

'Go ahead.'

Peterson brought his wooden chair up next to me. He tried to smile. 'You know all these lads,' Peterson said. His breath smelt of coffee.

'And?'

'I'll do you a deal.'

'Give us a break.'

'You haven't heard it.'

'Give him a hearing,' Benedict urged.

I stared at a poster of a woman with a bruised face. *Don't Let Him Get Away With It. Domestic Violence is Hate Crime.*

'Listen,' Peterson said: 'we release you for lack of evidence, let you off with a caution. In return you keep us informed about what's going on.'

'A spy?'

'Keep us in the picture, that's all. Tell us about guns, drugs, gangs. Who's in, who's out.'

'Think about it,' Benedict said. 'You'd save yourself a lot of trouble.'

'It's impossible. I don't know that stuff. And I'm not guilty of anything. They're bluffing.'

'We're not bluffing,' Peterson said with a sigh.

'I'll sue you if you don't release me,' I told him.

'Put a sock in it,' Benedict said.

'No. I'll sue them for wrongful arrest – false imprisonment.'

'Too bad.' Peterson scraped the chair back and walked over

to the door to get his jacket. 'There'll have to be an identity parade. We'll let you know as soon as it's scheduled.'

Benedict began to shuffle papers. He was getting ready to go.

'They won't do anything,' I told him.

'Don't bet on it,' Peterson said.

I looked at Benedict. 'You *could* do time, son,' he put in quietly. 'It's serious enough.'

'Okay,' I said. 'I can't give you the posse, right. But I'll give you something else.'

'*What*?' Peterson came back and stood in front of the statistics poster.

'I'll give you evidence to convict someone of assault.'

'Don't tell me: a copper.'

'No. My mother's boyfriend,' I said. 'Mike Burnes.'

He raised his eyebrows. 'That's a difficult call.'

'Why?'

'Has she reported him?'

'Course not. *I*'m reporting him.'

He shook his head. 'There's not a lot we can do.'

'You could if you wanted.'

'If your mum won't help us, we're on a hiding to nothing. Domestic violence is a tricky one at the best of times. Witnesses disappear, charges are dropped, relations weigh in. Nobody thanks us for intervening.' And he turned to Julie Denton. 'All right,' he said. 'I'm done here. Let's get the lad bailed.'

Mike turned up when Julie had finished my forms, throwing his baseball cap on the table.

'What have you been doing, you little fuck?'

'Where's Mum?' I said.

'She couldn't make it.'

'Why?'

Julie gave Mike a quick once-over, and he shifted on his trainers, his forehead garrotted by the invisible cheese-wire.

'She's under the weather.'

'Bit bruised?'

'She's having a nap, all right?'

'Perhaps you could all come in together next time,' Julie said. 'The three of you. We like to see the whole family . . . It helps with the pre-trial process.'

'Jesus, Merton! What kind of trouble are you in?' He turned to Julie. 'We've been worried sick, his mum and me.'

'Nothing,' I said. 'It's just a mistake.'

He folded his arms. 'What they charging you with?'

'Burglary. Some old guy in Cannon Park.'

'You?' he laughed. 'Can't the pigs get anything fucking right?' He glanced at Julie. 'No offence.'

'None taken,' she said. She was studying my forms.

'Your mum will be gutted,' Mike went on, frowning again. 'Inconsolable.'

'Here are your papers.' Julie passed them across the table. 'You have to sign here, Merton. And you – Mr Browne, is it?'

'Michael Burnes.'

'Mr Burnes. You sign here, and here.'

And she told me quietly, 'Think about what we said. Promise?'

She was all blonde bun and round lips. I started getting an erection as soon as she touched my hand. 'Do you have a card?' I asked.

'You can reach me at the station.'

'But you might be working.'

She smiled, brushing me away with the sheaf of forms. 'You can go. Keep out of trouble. Don't make it worse for yourself.'

In the car Mike's face was criss-crossed with lines. I'd never seen them so clearly.

'You fucking ponce. What did you tell them in there?'

'What do you mean?'

'About *me*. What did you say?'

'Nothing,' I shrugged.

'They looked at me like I was the Yorkshire bloody Ripper.'

'Maybe it's the tattoos.'

'You're getting a sight too lippy.'

'You can let me out here,' I said. 'I want to go to school.'

'You're coming home. We've got to have a little chat, me and you.'

'About Mum?'

'About my bleedin' supply, big-mouth.'

'I think I should arrange an interview with the boys,' I said.

'I'm not dealing with those little wankers.'

'The question is, whether they'll deal with you.'

'That fucking does it.' He pulled the car up on the side of the High Street. A group of primary school girls were moving down the road towards us, twanging the aerials of parked cars.

Mike turned to face me. 'Are you threatening me?' he demanded. There was an involuntary twitching in his cheek.

'I'm just suggesting a business arrangement,' I told him.

'I never laid a hand on you,' he said, knuckling his forehead. 'I should of, when I had the chance.'

'Life is full of regrets.'

'Don't get clever with me. It's not too late. I'll give you a bruising, I swear to God I will.'

I opened the door. 'Thanks for the lift, Mike.'

'Oi, faggot-face! I haven't finished with you.'

I jumped out. The posse of girls were kicking a Coke can across the pavement by the car.

'You fucking stay here!' Mike yelled.

But I was marching down the High Street towards the school.

# 11

The schoolgirls were swarming down the High Street ahead of me, occupying as much of the pavement as possible to drive people into the gutter. A few blocks from the New Crosland they invaded a newsagent, and I followed them inside. The owner, an elderly Asian, stood at the counter reading a copy of the *Daily Telegraph*. He briefly looked up to peer at the girls through his glasses. They were shouting, running up and down the aisles, and they started to ransack the shop, stuffing their pockets with chocolate bars and cans of drinks. One of them strutted past the counter brandishing a copy of *Heat*.

'Come here and pay for that,' the owner said.

'It's mine,' she told him. 'I bought it in Smith's.'

'I'll call the police.'

'Go on then!'

I went to the back of the shop to get water from the fridge. A fat redhead was shoving a Mars Bar inside her tracksuit. She scowled at me, and marched out towards the street.

'And *you*,' the shopkeeper came out from behind the counter, 'you have hidden sweets under your clothes.' He tried to take hold of the redhead, but she squealed, pushing him away.

'Fuck off, you rapist! Paki pervert! You're a child abuser.'

Nobody was looking, so I took what I wanted and started walking out. The girls had surrounded the old man. They were shouting all at once. 'Child abuser! Paki freak!'

'Go,' he said. 'Leave me alone. The police are coming . . .'

But they were enjoying themselves too much. 'Search me, you weirdo! Go on. Put your hand here . . .'

And when they started slapping him, I slipped through the door and ran to school.

The corridors were deserted. I peered through the glass panel in the door of my classroom. People were working in groups; the room hummed with conversation. I saw the back of Daly's head and, by the window, his girlfriend Rachel Neill, who usually taught us English. They were moving between the tables, answering questions.

I had a shower in the changing rooms, put on clean clothes from my locker. For the first time since the burglary I wasn't scared. I made for the café on the other side of the road, and installed myself at a Formica cubicle. The whole place smelt of vinegar and disinfectant, but the waitress was pretty. She brought me eggs and bacon, pouring refills of dusty coffee, and I had a good look at her peachy breasts. 'You're fit,' I told her.

She gave a little shrug. 'I've seen you before.'

'Merton.'

'I'm Anna.' We shook hands. Anna perched her Lycra arse on the next table while I ate. 'You're hungry!' There was a frown across her wide Slavonic face. And she went to get me a second helping of everything.

When she came back, I told her I'd been arrested, and she sighed sympathetically, while my tackle pulsated. Then some other people came in, so I got her to write her mobile number on a paper napkin. 'I'll call,' I said. 'We can go to the movies.' And she shrugged, as though she didn't care.

Alone in the bunker, I paced up and down, trying to make a plan. Julie Denton had said the ID parade would take a few days to organise, and then if they charged me my case wouldn't be heard till June or July. For a while I got depressed, unable to work, certain it was all over. But then, just as suddenly, my mood changed completely, and I was confident: probably there would never be a trial. The case against me depended on the old man's testimony – him, and Mrs Johnson. He might not pick me out in a line-up, and then they'd have to drop the whole thing. In any case, the police, the Youth Court, even prison seemed irrelevant: I told myself it was important to grasp that – and I should even have told them more lies. The whole apparatus of uniforms and procedures was a barbaric survival. It didn't matter. Below the streets and schools, out of sight, a great force was gathering strength. I was convinced the posse had started something. People like the old man would be swept away. I only had to stay alive to watch the world being torn apart. And instead of fear, when I thought of the court case and the cops, I was on fire with anger.

On my stack of paper, I recorded my liberation from fear. *The more they try to defeat us,* I wrote, *the more they keep us down, the better it is. Our anger proves we are right. Now the posse must take control, not just at night; not just because the police have given up. We must control the estates at all times, and by right. There is no authority in the old society; we must create our own.*

They lined us up against the wall. The old man recognised me right away, he didn't even hesitate. And after that they charged me.

From then on, I couldn't be seen with the posse till the court case was over. So all through the Easter holidays, and in the summer term I just worked in the bunker, reading and making notes, preparing for my AS levels, or thinking about the future of the posse. I read masses of stuff while I was waiting for my trial, and the whole time I was developing these long-term plans for the Savage gang: how he could control the estates and build up his power by offering people protection.

I reread Daly's books, starting with *One Dimensional Man* by Herbert Marcuse, which was my favourite. 'Remembrance of the past may give rise to dangerous insights,' Marcuse wrote, 'and the established society seems to be apprehensive of the subversive contents of memory . . .'

I read and reread that passage. I really believed it. History was too radical for system, too full of dangers. The past was the prototype of the future; it contained its secret. Such knowledge could only demonstrate how empty, how worthless, how narrow we had become – 'a spectre of man without memory'. And when I understood that, I went back to Trevelyan and Fisher, and the other historians they had banned. I knew it wouldn't help with my exams, but I didn't care.

I wasn't nicking Mike's stuff any more; the posse had loads of suppliers now. He had started beating Mum again, almost every day. She used to lie on the sofa in the mornings, her face wrapped in scarves, while Mike sat with his back to her, smoking and staring out the kitchen window. He told her to cover herself; he said he couldn't stand her face.

Sometimes, just for a moment as I saw her lying there, I felt some sad, antique emotion rise in my throat. But I made myself wait, took a breath, walked past without a word. I was training myself: I wasn't going to deal with him until I was completely ready.

'Hi, Mike,' I said. 'Fancy a beer?' He scowled at me, and I handed him a Four X from the fridge. 'No point dwelling on things.'

'She puts me up to it,' he explained, frowning at the beer can.

'What can you do?' I started frying eggs.

'I don't mean to. It's wrong, I know, only she –'

'No,' I said. 'There's no such thing as right and wrong. There's only what's right for *you*, Mike.'

He drank the beer. Mum was smoking silently in the next room. After half a can he became philosophical.

'I used to think you were a right cunt,' he told me as I sat down to eat, 'but now I don't know. You're not as stuck-up as you used to be . . .'

'No?'

'Not so judgemental.' He sat back. 'If there's one thing I hate, it's people sitting in judgement. I mean, no one's to blame, are they? You can't help the way you are.' He creased his forehead. 'Me, for instance. I got a temper on me. I got strong feelings. It's not my fault. What can *I* do? It's fate, right? It's the luck of the bleeding draw.'

The night before the trial, just after the AS levels, I slept with Anna the waitress in her bedsit over the High Street. She wouldn't let me screw her, though, because she was a Catholic. She even claimed she was a virgin. So I just sucked her boobs and made her give me a blow-job. She said that wasn't allowed, either, but I told her they should give her a break. How can a blow-job be wrong? She did it pretty well, too. I bet she'd given a few before.

Later I got angry, and I couldn't sleep. I wished I'd made her screw me. I was strong enough, if I'd wanted. I sat on her little armchair trying to read *The Lord of the Flies*, while she lay curled up on the bed. But I couldn't concentrate. For a long time I almost wanted to kill her. And when the dawn came I was too tired to move.

But Anna made me get up. She tried to hug me, staring at me with her green, snaky eyes, but I didn't let her. I was teaching her a lesson for not fucking me.

'Good luck,' she said.

'It'll be okay. They'll never convict me. The whole thing's stupid.'

'I'll say a prayer.'

'Don't bother.'

She frowned. 'I will, all the same.'

So I punched her on the arm and went out.

They were supposed to hear my case at eleven, but they kept us waiting most of the day. Benedict bought sandwiches and water, and started rearranging his appointments for the rest of the week. Then he settled down to work, shuffling papers on his knees, while I looked at the paper.

The old man was sitting at the other end of the corridor, in a chalk-stripe suit and regimental tie. PC Bill Simms and WPC Julie Denton came and went, bringing him lunch and cups of tea. And Mrs Johnson was there, dressed for church: full bosom of evangelical pink, tight across her cleavage, with a gold-coloured brooch. She kept sweating the whole time, and the old guy sat in silence while she gossiped away.

Benedict had given me strict instructions how to look. I had my *consigliere* suit, like always, but I had grown my hair, and had it cut with a parting by an old-fashioned barber in the High Street, so that I looked like a fifties schoolboy. Also I used a trick Daly had told me: I had bought a copy of *the Daily Telegraph*, keeping it with me when they finally called us at three o'clock.

The old man spoke first. Benedict asked him about his glasses, but he told the judge he only needed them for reading, and that otherwise his eyes were okay. 'They're on the top line, madam.' He held himself erect, speaking carefully. 'I'd know that face anywhere,' he said when Benedict asked him. He peered towards me. 'It's the scar on the temple. I noticed it right away.'

Benedict tried to trap him, but he was pretty smart. And he never raised his voice.

Mrs Johnson sang out the oath, grasping the wooden lectern of the witness box. She told the court she had heard me on the night of the burglary. 'I know his voice like my own son's, Your Worship.'

'And how can you be so sure, Mrs Johnson, with all due respect?' Benedict leaned forward, smiling persuasively. 'There was a group of boys, you say. They were on the floor above – a confusion of noise –'

'I know his voice in a crowd.'

'That's not an easy thing, is it?'

But she turned on him. 'Are you doubting my word?' Her breast strained at the gold clasp. 'Who's on trial here? Am I accused?'

'The defence has a duty to cross-examine you, Mrs Johnson,' the judge said. 'Please answer the question.'

'I know his voice because I know this boy very well,' she explained. 'He's a friend of Danny's. He leads my son into all kinds of scrapes.'

'Stick to the facts, please, Mrs Johnson.'

'The facts? Those *are* the facts. He's always with that gang – morning, noon and night. He's good for nothing.'

When I was called, I just said I hadn't been at the burglary. The prosecution guy asked me again and again where I *had* been. I'd talked it all through with Benedict, and it was clear in my mind. It was simply a matter of claiming I was in the school storeroom all night. But when it came to it, I didn't want to say anything that would lead them to the bunker. So I just told him I'd been walking about.

'But you can't say *where*?'

'I could if you showed me a map.'

'Can't you tell the court from memory?'

'I went down the High Street.'

'Did anybody see you?'

'It was late.'

'There must have been people about.'

'I didn't notice. I didn't think it mattered, did I?'

He leaned forward on his lectern. 'Merton, when you spoke to the police, you didn't say you were wandering around, did you?'

I didn't say anything.

'Merton?'

'Please answer,' the judge said.

'Will you repeat the question?'

'When you were interviewed by the police, you didn't tell them that you'd been *wandering around*, did you?'

Benedict looked up at me, and I shrugged.

'Please speak up,' the other lawyer said.

'No.'

'Do you remember what you *did* tell them?'

'I said I was on my own somewhere.'

'Then why can't you explain this to the court now? Why the mystery?'

I didn't say anything.

'In fact you were quite specific, weren't you? You explained exactly where you'd been. *Didn't you?*'

'Yes.'

'The only problem is, that no such place exists.' I looked up at the gallery. 'Merton?'

'No.'

Then he produced a map.

Benedict was rubbing his glasses. In my mind I was suddenly a thousand miles away. I wanted to jump out of the box and run. But I kept quiet. When my mind came back to the court, there was silence all round me. The magistrate was looking down from the bench.

'Merton Browne?'

'*What?*'

'I asked you a question.'

Benedict resettled his glasses. Someone in the public gallery stamped out, slamming the door.

'Well?'

'I wasn't there,' I said.


I had to go back the next day for sentencing.

This time we didn't have to wait. Benedict led me into a little room where the same judge was sitting behind a desk.

'You have been extremely fortunate in the timing of your trial,' she told me. 'I would certainly have handed down a custodial sentence, but for the recent guidelines. In the circumstances, I have little choice but to give you a Community Service Order. I must stress that I do *not* believe that this reflects the gravity of what you have done.'

'I didn't do it,' I reminded her.

'Shut it!' Benedict hissed.

The judge asked him about the terms of the order, and Benedict said I should do something useful, because I wasn't a run-of-the-mill hoodlum. 'In my judgement, Merton is an intelligent young man,' he said. 'He might yet be steered away from a life of crime.'

'Really?' She sounded pretty bored. And after that she sent us out again.

# 12

They put this bald, angry guy in charge of me. I found him waiting in shirtsleeves on the steps of his yellow-brick two-by-two, out beyond the Cannon Park Estate, on the edge of the countryside. He was squinting at me in the sunshine.

'My name is Gibbon,' he said. 'I'm responsible to the court for your compliance.'

'Merton Browne,' I told him.

'I know.' He walked up to examine me. 'You're twenty minutes late. That's a very poor start. You may think this order's a joke, Browne, but let me tell you how it's going to work. If you're late again, even a minute late – or disobedient or cheeky, just once – I'll treat it as a breach. Is that clear? You'll be back in front of a magistrate within twenty-four hours.'

'Don't worry,' I said. 'I'm never cheeky.'

'We'll see.' He backed away.

'What's your first name, then?'

'Mister,' he said as he marched towards the house. '*Mister* Gibbon. But you can call me Sir if you like.' He locked his front door and stood watching me again. 'We're not going to be friends. And your opinion is of no interest whatsoever. Just do the work. Otherwise, you can go back to court. It's your choice.'

Gibbon brought a can of emulsion from the garden shed, and we walked in silence to the Waterfield Estate, his bald head gleaming in the sunlight. My job was to paint over graffiti on the walls and garage doors.

'You're a burglar, then,' he steaméd, as I started slapping

paint about on the wall of the first block. 'I told them not to send me a thief.'

'A case of mistaken identity,' I explained.

'Be quiet.' He took a little book from his coat pocket and found his place.

'You want to send me back?' I asked. 'That's fine by me.'

'Get on with the work.'

'You might get lucky,' I murmured: 'spend a few weeks with a nonce.'

'Be quiet. I'm reading. You've missed those marks by the door.'

I had been celebrating all weekend, and my head and hands wouldn't stop sweating in the heat. The boys had taken me clubbing in an old warehouse behind King's Cross. It was the first time I'd seen Savage in ages. We were drinking vodka, and he kept telling me about the jobs he was planning – all the people he was going to wipe out. He had bought a load of guns from these Russians – modern automatics; nothing like the old man's revolver – and he kept shouting about them through the music. Then for the first time, I explained my strategy to Savage: how we could use the guns to build up a system of protection throughout the estate, getting rid of the rival gangs, the criminals – clearing the place up. I said it would make him rich if we did that, so long as we were disciplined. And he kept punching me on the arm, and slowly nodding his head.

I was sharing a giant spliff with him – rich, hallucinogenic grass from one of his mates in Haig Johnson's gang. 'I'm burning,' Savage screamed. 'I'm fucking burning . . . There's a rage inside me. I could rip the head off a baby, you know what I'm saying? But it's focused, right? I agree with you, man: you're right. I have it all clear in my mind: I know where I'm going.'

'It will work,' I told him, speaking right into his ear through the metal sound. 'You need to protect people. It all follows from that.'

'Speak *up*, mate.'

'We'll get everything we want,' I shouted. 'We'll do it so that nobody can take it from us. And you know, all of that – I mean, the way you feel; that makes sense, too. I feel the same. But we have to *use* it – we must keep to the plan – like athletes in training . . .' We stared at each other. My mind was reeling, my whole body dropping down into the concrete. The sound of the music was unbearable, pounding my skull, and as I looked at Savage, his head was surrounded by a halo of purple light, which flashed with the music.

'Go on,' he shouted. 'I want to know. I want to understand. *Teach* me!'

Savage stopped tugging my arm to take another hit, and he grinned. In my mind everything was merging: the lights and smoke, the noise, Savage's pale face. And it was getting harder to hear him.

'You know how it is with babies?' he was shouting. 'How they scream and scream? They're always fucking screaming. It's unbelievable. But grown-ups – we never scream. And I want to know *why*. Why can't we?' He threw his head back. 'I'm going to scream,' he shouted. 'I'll make the fuckers *listen to me.*'

He was ecstatic. His eyes were alive, and he went on shouting. But the music was so loud, I couldn't hear what he was saying. And suddenly I was clear in my mind. Everything was clear.

'We should find some girls,' I announced.

'Fuck, yes!' Savage yelled. And he grabbed my arm. 'Come on, mate. This is crap. Let's get some women.'

I slapped the paint around, making as much mess as I could. 'You're doing a bad job,' Gibbon barked, and I started to hate him. 'You're one of the worst I've supervised.'

'It's not my *métier*.' My head was thumping, and the smell of the paint made me sick.

'Shape up, or I'll hold you in contempt.'

'Do I get a break?' I said.

'You've only just started.'

'Jesus!'

'In any case, your whole sentence is a break. You ought to be in jail.'

'The law doesn't think so.'

'The law may have given up,' he said, 'but *I* haven't. Keep working. I didn't say you could stop.'

'*You're* not working.'

'I *am* working, you little bastard. I'm spending my day supervising you.'

Savage and I found some girls in the car park, and they led us to a council flat above the Caledonian Road. All the way up the stairs they pulled at our sleeves, whining about drugs, until Paul produced the magic packet from his coat, rolled a spliff, and lit up on an open landing. Then we fell into their flat.

The place was a compost heap, strewn with knickers, T-shirts, Tampax boxes, yoghurt cartons. I sat by the open window, staring out over Islington, or sucking from the bong. When the girls were stoned, Paul kissed the hand of the best of them – a laughing, purple-skinned princess – and raised her to her feet. I watched him lead her to the narrow bed in the next room, where her gold chains rose and fell in the darkness as she undressed.

He had left the monsters for me – three dough-skinned babies in micro skirts. I passed the bong to the girl nearest to me, and gripped her ankle. Her tired eyes watched as I pulled her towards me, until she shivered, maggot-like, and started squeezing my cock. We had nowhere to lie down, so I carried her on to the balcony.

There was a cool breeze out there. Behind the tall window, the other girls were falling asleep. I watched my maggot fidget and stretch. She had small boobs and a mean, ferrety face. 'I'm Tina,' she said, trying to kiss me. She took a lungful from the bong, and lifted her skirt, inviting me to fool around. I hesitated, keeping her at arm's length. But suddenly I was ambushed by desire. I took her small body, turned it away from me, bent her over the balcony. And I fucked her from behind, not even looking at her, but face to face with the scattered, oyster-grey lights of north London, while Tina gripped the railings and cried into the void.

Gibbon's shoulders were stooped and his face was pale, as if he'd spent his life trapped under a stone. While I was working he kept squinting into his little book, holding it close to his face.

'What're you reading?' I asked.

'Sir,' he said.

'What are you reading, *sir*?'

'None of your business. Keep painting.'

My head was throbbing, and I leaned against the wall. 'Bloody Nora. Don't you ever lighten up? I'm not working. I need some water. It's too hot.'

So he handed me a bottle of water without a word, and went back to his little green hardback while I drank.

'What's in the book?' I repeated. 'Tell me. Go on.'

'What difference does it make? Work. In silence. Every time you say something, you stop working.'

'It's my coordination,' I said. 'I can't walk and chew gum at the same time.'

For some reason that interested him. 'Why not?'

'I don't know. I'm a malco.'

He shielded his eyes from the sunlight, still watching with his angry white face. 'I suppose you had a bad childhood,' he said, more to himself than to me. 'No doubt your father walked out when you were two and you've never known any stability, just a series of men coming and going to gratify their sexual appetites with your mother.'

The paint fumes were making me giddy, and I was sweating like a madman.

'To many people that would exonerate your behaviour – explain it anyway. But it doesn't cut it with me. You have your excuses – your reasons – but the real problem is your will. You're too proud to change.'

'Very good,' I said. 'Do I get to psychoanalyse you, then?'

'It's hardly psychoanalysis,' he sniffed. He was searching for his place in the book, and suddenly he got angry again. 'Paint, will you! And no, you *don't* get to psychoanalyse me.'

After I'd fucked the maggot-girl, I flattened my hands against the kitchen wall, and threw up into the sink.

She came in from the balcony, and began to paw me with her weird little hands. I was trying to rinse vomit from the washing-up bowl. 'Here,' she said, 'I'll do it.'

I wandered on to the landing. A dog was barking in the next flat, and someone was shouting at their child. All round the block, windows shone with the grey light of the TV. I wanted to wait for Savage, but he was still getting laid in the bedroom, and I was coming down. So I ran for it, pounding the stairs all the way down to the courtyard where they dumped the rubbish.

I waited about ten minutes. Then Savage came out, shouting for me, and I stared up towards him. He was leaning over the railing, pleading with me not to go. He said it was still early and we could find some other girls. But I didn't feel like hanging around any more. Savage was completely out of it, and I was hardly drunk at all. I wasn't stoned, either. I just wasn't enjoying our night out anymore.

In the end, he went back inside to his black and gold goddess, and I wandered out into the Caledonian Road, heading for King's Cross to get the night bus.

I worked my way along the blind wall of Waterfield Estate. A couple of the boys had come to watch, and I slowed down to keep them happy. But when they got bored and cleared off, I worked pretty fast. There was something about painting over the tags that pleased me; after an hour the whole area looked different.

'We're pretty much done,' I said, stepping back.

'No we're not. There's a fresh crop on the next section.'

'What about your sex life, then?' I was splashing paint across the new wall. 'Single or divorced? Lush, queer, or just frustrated?' Gibbon didn't reply, so I carried on, chattering for my own benefit. 'Do you seek out younger women? Or is it boys?'

'I'm celibate,' he said. 'Not that I'd expect you to know the word.'

'Like a Catholic priest,' I said. 'Unmarried.'

He eyed me again and pulled out his book. But I wanted to go on talking.

'I saw a therapist once,' I said.

'Don't stop painting!' He came up close to keep his eye on me. 'Didn't do any good, I suppose?'

I shook my head.

'Of course not. It's unlikely to help in a case like yours.'

'How can you say that? You hardly know me.'

'I know enough. You don't want to change. I don't blame you, either. Your whole identity depends on your jaunty, foul-mouthed malice. You'd be nobody without your mask. You'd lose your friends, your self-image. Even your income would collapse. Look at you! You think you're smart, but you've already given up.'

I thought about that, painting over a Johnson tag.

'Have *you* had therapy, then?' I asked.

'Will you be *quiet*?'

'Have you, though?'

'Of course not. I'm perfect.'

'Oh, yeah. Classic denial.'

And he smiled – the first time all morning. 'No doubt I have a lot to repress.'

'Childhood sphincter abuse, I should think. Obvious symptoms.'

'If you say so. *Don't stop working!* It's obvious you've never done a day's work in your life.' He squinted at his book, but he wasn't reading.

'Of *course* you don't believe in psychotherapy,' I went on. 'You're in denial.'

He snorted again.

'So what do you think?' I said. 'You think people can't ever change?'

'I didn't say that. That's a different question.'

'What, then? You must have an alternative theory, if Freud is wrong.'

'I suppose so,' he said, but he took up his little book again. 'What difference does it make?'

'It makes a difference to *me*, sir.'

'Enough. Do the work.'

'Oh, come *on*, Mr Gibbon, you can tell me.'

But he was deep in his book again, so I worked in silence. I wondered if I'd hurt his feelings, but it was hard to be sure. When I'd covered a whole new sign, he decided to talk again.

'If you really want to know, my view is very simple,' he said. 'People can change if they want to. It's a matter of willpower. An unfashionable idea, but it happens to be true.'

'So you believe in free will, then?'

'Of course,' he shot back.

'Not me,' I said. 'I don't buy it. We're bound to be the way we are. It's all been explained: historical materialism, production relations, class war. Everything follows from that.'

He peered at me again, an expression of disdainful curiosity on his face as he mopped away the sweat.

'What you call willpower and morality,' I went on, 'they're just constructions – just a trick of the system.'

'If so, they are constructions of every culture that's ever existed. Doesn't that tell you something?'

'Yes: we need a revolution.'

Gibbon smiled. 'You sound absurd. I wonder if you know how absurd you sound . . .' And he changed his tone. 'Stop dawdling. We've got another three blocks to cover.'

After I'd left Savage, I made it to the High Street by about four. Then I stood leaning my head on Anna's doorbell, pounding the door, till she came down in her Mickey Mouse T-shirt and opened up.

'You'll wake the neighbours, you idiot.' She led me up to her flat. 'There: you can sleep on the floor,' she said. 'Use the sleeping bag.' I knelt down in front of her, but she ignored me. 'I'm not kissing you,' she told me. 'You smell like a tramp.' She hugged herself, standing back. 'Hurry up. It's late.'

So I drank three glasses of water, and lay down beside the bed, the room rotating around me.

'Anna!' I said. I reached towards her in the darkness. 'I love you, do you know that?'

'Don't be stupid.'

'No, I mean it. I love your eyes – your bright green, East European eyes . . .'

'Go to sleep,' she yawned. 'I'm working in the morning.'

'But can't we sleep together – just this once? Can't we make a new Anna, a new Merton?' She curled up, and I gulped down more water.

Then I lay still, watching her face pressed against the duvet. The more I looked, the more I wanted to screw her. She had these Catholic convictions, and for some reason that aroused me even more. In her mind there must have been a whole maze – a labyrinth of taboos and commandments in which her desires were imprisoned.

'You'll have to give up your religion,' I told her. 'I mean, all that repression, devils flying about and everything . . .' And I remembered something Daly had said. 'The whole *point* of modernity, the whole point of being modern, is that there are no limits, no restrictions on our experience.'

'Go to sleep.'

'*Why* can't I fuck you? Even if you don't want it?'

'You're out of it,' Anna said. 'Stop talking.'

Gibbon was beginning to relax, but I could tell he got easily depressed. In between our little chats he pored minutely over his book, looking up occasionally to see if I was working. So I painted as well as I could, smothering the graffiti until you couldn't tell it had ever been there. And the more I worked, the more energetic I became. Instead of slopping the paint around, I laid it carefully over the walls, standing back to assess the results.

'It's looking better,' I said.

'It'll take more than paint,' he said. 'We need a social revolution.'

'Oh, fine. I'll see it done.'

But he stood beside me, surveying my work. 'All right. That's enough for today.'

'What are you *doing*?'

'I'm having a wank.'

'You're an animal.'

'You can't blame me.' I was stark naked at the foot of her bed. 'You don't even want sex.'

'Have some self-control, for God's sake.'

'It isn't natural,' I told her. 'You're repressed. You must never repress your sexual need.'

'I'm not a whore, so I must be sick?'

'Yes: a sickness,' I said. 'Self-control is a sickness. I love you. I want to fuck you. The pressure is building up. It can't be helped. You want me to be one of those lonely old fucks with nobody to sleep with, mouth dribbling, swinging my catheter bag . . .'

'You're fucked up,' she said. 'Lie down and stop shouting. Go on! You're out of your head . . .'

'But I *want* you.'

'Well, you can't have me.'

'You've got to be joking.'

'Sleep!' she said. And she covered her head with her pillow.

# 13

On the way back to Gibbon's house we walked in silence. I was wondering about him, and I kept taking deep breaths. My stomach was in turmoil. Gibbon didn't say anything, and when we reached his garden he just stood there surveying me, before he went over to the tool-shed.

'I told them not to send me another thief,' he said, unlocking the door. 'It means I can't take you into the house.'

'I'm really not like that.'

'Only at night, is it? Only with a gun?'

'It wasn't me.'

'Save it. I've heard it before.'

He carried the paint into the little shed, but for some reason I wanted to keep talking.

'Are you always like this?' I said. 'Always angry?'

'Yes, always.'

'No wonder you're celibate.'

'That's enough.'

'No, I mean it. What kind of sex life *could* you have? You probably don't even masturbate much. Once a twice a week, maybe. Saturdays in front of the TV.'

'I said, that's *enough*.'

He came and stood in front of me, staring at my face. He wasn't smiling.

'You're a rage-aholic,' I went on. 'I read about that once. It's like booze, but you get your highs by flipping your lid. Sex substitute.'

'I'm warning you,' he said. His head was shining like polished wood.

'Or what? I bet you like a bit of rough . . .'

That did it. In a second he had thumped me back against the wall of the shed, pressing his arm under my chin. I could hardly breathe.

'Don't you trespass on my private life, you little shit, or I'll knock you out cold.'

'Jesus! Cool it.' I tried to push his arm away from my throat, but he was pretty strong.

'Do you get it?'

'Calm down, man. Can't you take a joke?'

'Do you under*stand*?'

'Yes. All right. Christ! Relax, dude.' He released me reluctantly. 'I guess I hit a nerve.'

'*Just* keep it to yourself.'

'Is that how you deal with all life's little obstacles?' I stretched my neck, feeling for bruises. 'Instant resort to violence?'

He was buttoning his jacket, ignoring me. The top of his head shone like a conker, but his eyes were empty hollows. For a while we were both quiet. Gibbon fixed the padlock on the shed, and I was ready to clear off for the day. By the time we were back at his front door Gibbon had recovered a little; he was trying to act normal, though his hands were shaking.

'Tomorrow at eight-thirty,' he said. 'Day two. We'll finish Waterfield in the morning, then move on to Cannon Park.'

'Whatever.'

'Don't be late.'

But his tone softened, and he steadied himself against the door, fishing the keys from his jacket pocket. 'I'm sorry,' he said grudgingly, looking away. I shrugged, but I didn't say anything, and he immediately changed the subject. 'What will you do tonight?'

'I don't know.'

Gibbon had been pointing his latchkey at my chest, hesitating, but now he opened the door with it. 'I'll see you tomorrow,' he said. 'Get some sleep.' And he added from inside his hall, 'And don't be late, or I'll send you back to court.'

\* \* \*

All that evening in the bunker I reread Daly's books to get my argument with Gibbon straight in my mind. I knew he wouldn't listen, but I wanted to be able to explain things properly. But the next day he wouldn't even talk, and we did nothing but painting. I blacked out the graffiti on the garage doors of Waterfield, and even when I asked him questions straight out, Gibbon hardly said a word. He just stood in the shade, staring at his little book.

Later though, when we were walking home, I did finally get him to talk.

'Go on,' I said, 'tell me: what's in the book? I know it's porn, but I won't tell anyone.'

'Of course it's not porn.'

'Why you so secretive, then?'

'Because you wouldn't be interested.'

'Try me.'

'Very well: I'm rereading Thucydides.' He spoke with a sort of wariness, like I was going to object or something. 'I've been going over it for one of my pupils. It's been a long time.'

I walked on for a moment. 'Thucydides,' I said, after a pause. 'Let's see. Lived 460 to 400 BC. Approximately. Aristocratic historian, exiled for twenty years for screwing up on campaign in the north Aegean. He wrote *The History of the Peloponnesian Wars*. That's what you're reading, right?'

Gibbon squinted at me, his bald head shining in the sunlight. 'Have you read it?' he said.

I shook my head. 'Not all of it. But I want to. It looks good.'

We had reached his garden, and I put down the paint pots. Then he hesitated, and handed me the little volume. 'Have a look, then.'

It was a dual text: Greek on one side, English on the other. I stared at the Greek letters for a while.

'Tell me then, where did you come across Thucydides?' Gibbon was looking towards me but not at me: he seemed to be gazing beyond.

I shrugged. 'In the library at school.'

'Seriously?'

'They have some old books,' I explained. 'Hidden, of course. You have to know where to look.'

'Do you read a lot?'

'Now and then.'

'You're not completely illiterate, then?'

'I can't read Greek,' I said.

'Hmm.' He gave another snort, took the paint and went over to his little shed, and put everything away. When he came back he sounded depressed.

'I used to believe,' he said, 'when I was young and idealistic, that education in itself has a positive effect on moral character. You of course are one of *many* proofs to the contrary.'

'I'm sorry to disappoint you.'

'Oh, I'm way past disappointment.' He came right up to look me in the face. 'But all the same,' he said quietly, 'perhaps next time you have the urge to ruin the life of a blameless old man, you could exercise that precious gift of understanding, and sit down to read Thucydides instead.'

'Nah, not me,' I told him. 'It's like the man said. The philosophers have only interpreted the world in various ways. The point, however, is to *change* it.'

He shook his head. 'That really takes the biscuit. Don't tell me your delinquent behaviour is *revolutionary*.'

'Sure,' I said. 'Why not?'

'Moronic.'

'No it's not.'

But he just bit his lip. 'Same time tomorrow,' he said. 'Be on time.'

On the third day I finished the work. He said I had done more than he expected, and he seemed less depressed. As we walked back to his place I tried to get him to talk about history again, but he only grunted. All the same, he was weighing me up, and when we reached the house he started to talk.

'So, in all the wide world,' he said, 'you seriously think that *you're* one of the oppressed?'

'It's obvious.'

'Tell me something: do you know the meaning of the word egoist?'

'You think I'm imagining it? You don't see the world as I do. You're in a state of false consciousness.'

He smiled at that. 'And I suppose you think there is a way of overthrowing this, this oppression?'

'There must be.'

'Is that what you were doing when you robbed the old man?'

'I don't know.'

'That was stupid.'

'Why?'

'It didn't work, did it?'

'It might have.'

'Stupid,' he repeated. But he seemed to relax. 'At any rate, I'm glad you've admitted your crime. That's progress of a kind.'

'I didn't admit anything.'

'I think you did.'

I couldn't believe he'd tricked me. But Gibbon just smiled.

'Do you want a cup of tea?'

I shrugged.

'Come on. Take off your shoes. No need to tramp paint through the house.'

'You trust me, then?'

'*Trust* you? Should I? I'm offering you a cup of tea.' He glared at me again. 'And if you steal anything – and I mean anything – a button, a safety pin – I'll tell the police you've broken your Community Service Order and you'll be doing time before you can say second-hand video. Not a day too soon. Got it?'

I nodded.

'All right.'

'You're not a fan of the Community Service Order, then?' I took off my shoes and waited while he opened the door.

'Not for burglars. You should be in jail. In the orient you'd be flogged – in pretty much any Muslim country. I can't see what's wrong with that. It *seems* to work. Leave your trainers here.'

Gibbon's house was full of papers, pamphlets, old pictures. There were prints of Roman ruins in the hall, and at the end of the passage, as he led me to the kitchen, a crucifix jammed with dried palms, postcards from Jerusalem, a battered poster of the Acropolis on the wall.

'Don't you believe in rehabilitation, then?' I asked him. 'You should, if you're a Christian, right?'

'That?' he smiled. 'That belongs to Mrs Grant.'

'Your ho?'

'My housekeeper.'

'*Still*, though. Don't you believe in rehabilitation? It's better than punishment.'

'Another brain-dead confusion of the TV age. Punishment and rehabilitation are quite unconnected. As it happens, I believe in both. But rehabilitation depends on the offender. It's your choice. *You're* the only one who can repent of the evil you've done – the harm to that old man, the terror and anxiety you caused him, years wiped off his life, the loss of his most precious possessions.'

'Yeah, yeah . . .' I said. He had led me to his kitchen.

'Other people can point it out to you, help you see, but you're the only one who can repent. It's like giving up drink or drugs: basically a matter of choice and determination.' He filled the kettle. 'A belief in God seems to help. Or a strong marriage. Otherwise the research indicates no particular pattern. Have a seat.' I dumped myself next to his kitchen table, by a pile of political pamphlets, and postcards from Italy.

'On the other hand,' he went on, getting mugs from the cupboard, 'punishment is a *social* affair – a matter for the authorities. The courts inflict punishment to demonstrate society's horror at the crime, and at the person who committed it. Also to prevent the victim and his supporters taking matters into their own hands – for example, by beating you to a pulp. In addition, the punishment should keep people like you off the streets. A punishment which fails to protect the victims from further acts of cruelty is a failure. So, yes, the CSO is a failure.' He dumped teabags in the mugs and waited over the kettle. 'In any case, rehabilitation is no more likely to follow from community service than from jail.'

'Don't you think there's a reason, then?'

'A reason for what?'

'A reason my life is like this. The causes of crime.'

He looked round and fixed me full-on in his gaze, while a jet of steam blurred the window. 'So you *are* admitting it was a crime?'

'I didn't say that.' I avoided his eyes. 'But – you know, I've done other things. There must be a reason, don't you think?'

'A reason? Let's see . . . How about this? You have a corrupt moral character. That is presumably the result of a thoroughly bad upbringing, but has been made worse by an education system which rewards mediocrity, ignorance and fraud, and by a popular culture that promotes sex as a form of entertainment, denigrates learning and self-control, and regards fathers who abandon their children as existential heroes.'

'Still,' I said, when I'd mulled that over for a while, 'if you think about it, none of that's my fault, is it?'

'You were never punished by your parents,' he went on, 'or at school for being cheeky or inattentive, and now, almost without noticing, you have graduated to really dangerous crimes – crimes which make life impossible. You've settled in to a narrow, myopic, malignant, egotistical mode of life. You'll spend the rest of your days in and out of jail, living with third-rate gangsters, wondering who will rescue you and whom to blame . . .' He paused, filling the mugs with boiling water, and let them stand as he turned to face me again.

'Well let me tell you something, Merton Browne: you might reasonably blame your parents, or the destruction of education and morals in the last forty years by the "system", as you call it. But none of that will keep you out of jail for a single day, or redeem an hour of your wasted life. If you want to change anything at all, you'd better look to yourself. You had a bad start: that's true. The damage is done. And it *wasn't* your fault. No. That part wasn't your fault. But nobody will do anything to help you now – you can bet your criminal record on that. The rest is up to you.' And he turned to the fridge. 'Milk?'

'Thanks,' I said.

Gibbon went to take a phone call in another room, and I started looking at all the books and pamphlets scattered about. They were piled up in the hall as well, and along the passageway – political tracts and press cuttings, stacks of periodicals, old news magazines. I picked up a book called *Political Pilgrims*, and started looking at pictures of Soviet concentration camps.

When he came back, he had calmed down. He made me another mug of tea and brought out a huge tin of biscuits. I piled about ten on a plate, and he led me through a door in the hallway. On the other side was the area that used to be the garage, but which was now his study, the largest room in the house. There was a big old-fashioned desk in the middle covered with papers, three filing cabinets against the wall, some office chairs. The computer terminal was plastered with post-cards and post-it stickers, and round the room, in shelves and on the tables, or stacked against the walls, were hundreds and hundreds of books. The old up-and-over door was sealed off with a bookcase, and the other walls were fitted out, floor to ceiling. It was like the bunker, except it was his home. Everything had been chosen deliberately, by a single man. On the far wall the books were in German or French. The section to the right of the door – the first place I looked – was full of Italian and Spanish poetry, Russian below, and dozens of little green and red books: red for Latin authors, green for Greek, just like the ones in the bunker – with grammar books and primers and dictionaries. But most of the wall space was taken up with political works, philosophy, history by the yard.

'You're at the New Crosland, then?' Gibbon sat down in his swivelling chair, watching me as I moseyed around the room.

I nodded.

'It was a grammar school once,' he said.

'I know.'

'I used to teach there.' His voice was subdued, but he pierced me with his small eyes. 'I was head of Classics.'

'*Possunt quia posse videntur.*'

He smiled. 'How did you know that?'

'Old books.'

I was still only halfway round his library, but it was obvious he wanted to talk, so after a while I went to sit opposite him. Then he told me a bit about his work, while I ate my way through his biscuits. He explained that he was a private tutor – that he gave lessons to A level students, setting them up for university entrance in Latin, Greek, history, sometimes English. He had been tutoring people since he left the New Crosland, and he also worked sometimes for the probation service, supervising Community Service Orders – even though he didn't believe in them.

After a while my brain started taking a sabbatical, and I was only half listening. I was floating off like I used to at home, seeing things from the outside. And I started wondering what his pupils were like – and what he would be like as a teacher, since he was always in a bad mood. Then I began thinking about the bunker again, because the one thing that had always defeated me – the books I was actually frightened of – were the little densely printed works of Latin and Greek. I had made a start: I could say the present tense of Latin verbs. I had learned one type of noun, as well. But I didn't know how to put it all together, and in any case there was so much more – boxes and boxes of nouns and adjectives, page after page of verbs in their different tenses, moods, voices. The book I was using had three hundred pages of stuff like that. And then there was Greek. Sometimes when I was stoned I used to stare at Greek texts until my brain started flipping out.

So when he stopped talking for a bit, I began to tell him about the bunker – not too much; just that I'd found these old books that didn't belong to anyone, and that I was reading novels and poems, weird atlases, volumes of history. Then I said I'd always wondered about the Latin and Greek, but he just grunted.

'Do you think I could learn?' I said. 'I mean, if someone taught me properly?'

'Oh, I don't know,' he sighed and looked right past me. 'You're really too late. Our lads used to start at eight or nine. They were reading Virgil and Horace by your age.'

'I could catch up.'

'I don't think so.' He seemed depressed again.

'So if they were all such geniuses,' I said, 'why did you stop teaching them?'

But he was silent behind his shadowy eyes.

'Well? There must have been a reason.'

'The school got merged,' he said briefly. He picked up a glass paperweight. It had a seahorse trapped inside, and he dropped it with a thud on a pile of exam papers. 'The curriculum changed. The world changed. I had to look for a new direction.'

'So now you teach rich kids how to get to posh universities?'

He nodded. 'That's about it.' He shrugged, but his face was red. 'And I teach a few poor kids how to keep out of jail,' he added. 'The ones that will listen.'

'But if I worked hard,' I blurted out.

'If what?'

'If I studied every day,' I said, 'six or seven hours; I don't know – *ten* hours – how long would it take me to learn Latin and Greek? Tell me honestly. What do you think?'

He shrugged, eyeing me with his head on one side. 'At least a year to master the basics. You could be reading in two or three.'

'Will you teach me?' I said.

He paused. 'No. I don't think so.'

'But why not?'

'Because I'm supervising your CSO.'

'Okay. When that's finished – when I've done all the painting and whatever you want – will you give me lessons? Just an hour a week?'

He frowned, biting his lip. 'No.'

'But *why*? Just a few . . .'

'Two reasons. First, you're still breaking the law. Or if you're not, I want some *proof*.'

'How can I prove it?' I said. 'You can't prove a negative.' But he ignored me.

'And second, even if you *were* a reformed character, it's already too late. You couldn't do it. We'd both be wasting our time.'

'How do you know I can't do it if you won't even try?'

'Because it's impossible. You've never done a day's academic work. You're bright, but that's never enough. The brain needs to be trained, disciplined. We could do some history together, maybe, or English; but not classical languages. That really is another world.'

'But I've already started,' I told him. 'I know some things already. Listen: *amo, amas, amat, amamus, amatis, amant. Habeo, habes, habet, habemus, habetis, habent. Dico, dicis, dicit, dicimus, dicitis, dicunt. Audio, audis, audit –*'

'That's enough,' he said, frowning. 'You're giving me a headache.'

'*– audimus, auditis, audiunt,*' I shouted. 'You see: I know them. I can do some nouns, too. Do you want to hear?'

'No.'

'You're frightened.'

'Don't be ridiculous.'

Gibbon wandered over to the book-stacks.

'You think you can't do it.'

'The question is whether *you* can do it,' he said. He was searching for something.

'Well, let me try.'

'I tell you what . . .' He took a book from the shelf. 'We'll make a wager. Read this. If you can learn it all by next week, we'll talk about having lessons. But it'll depend on your behaviour, too. I'm not teaching a sociopath. Do what you can and we'll take it from there, a week at a time. All right?'

I recognised the book from the bunker, *Kennedy's Latin Primer*.

'The grammar schools were schools of Latin grammar,' he went on. 'You probably knew that.'

'No.'

'The basis of the liberal education was a knowledge of Latin morphology. Almost a criminal offence now, of course. So – let's see . . .' He examined the book in the light. 'Do you think you can learn these? Here: the first three declensions of nouns. They give these as examples. Learn by heart how they decline. Recite them to yourself. Try to become fluent. You need to recognise each ending without running through the table.'

'What about history?' I said. 'Give me some light relief.'

'Are you sure?'

'I promise I'll bring it back.'

So he wandered along the shelves. 'Has anyone shown you this?'

It was R.W. Southern, *The Making of the Middle Ages*. 'No,' I said. 'We don't do medieval history. Only the Nazis.'

'It's good. Take a look.' And he gave me one of his cheese-paring smiles, handing me the two books. 'Keep out of trouble. I've got to prepare for my next pupil. She'll be here any minute.'

His pupil arrived as I was going out. I stood watching her neat arse while she got off her scarlet Vespa, collected books from the box on the back, tugged at her chin-strap. Then she came towards me, a heap of black hair falling around her face as she pulled off her helmet.

'Hi,' she said. For a moment her eyes beamed at me while I stood in the doorway: huge, luminous discs, the colour of motor oil. 'Er, may I get past?'

'Say what?'

'I want to go inside,' she said.

'Oh, yeah. I'm sorry.'

I moved out the way, smelling her lemony scent as she called out into the hallway: 'James? *James?*'

Gibbon came shuffling down the hall towards us, putting his arms out to take her books. And he shook her hand rather formally. 'I should introduce you,' he said. 'Miranda, this is Merton. Merton is a new pupil.'

'Hi.' She took my hand, but immediately turned away.

'Hi, Miranda,' I said. She had brand-new blue suede Pumas on her feet, with pink laces. I smiled as I looked at them.

'We should get going.' Gibbon held the door for her. 'How have you been getting on?'

'I finished Book Three,' she told him, unzipping her leather jacket.

She seemed quite calm, almost like she was floating, but she was making me nervous.

'Well done,' he said.

'Well goodbye,' I said. 'I've got to work.'

'Goodbye.' Miranda came back towards the front door, but she still didn't look at my face.

'I'll see you, then,' I went on.

She nodded. 'See you.'

I stepped out in the purple evening. Miranda had started to follow Gibbon down the passage, into the dark house. I watched her narrow hips moving away.

'Nice to meet you,' I called after her. 'I like your pink laces.'

But she didn't reply.

# 14

Mr Collins peered down from the lectern through a pair of rectangular glasses. 'My name is Simon Collins,' he told us, speaking loudly into the mike. 'I am your new headteacher. Following the difficult events of the last few years, Rosamund Simpson has taken early retirement, and . . .' there was a long wolf whistle from one of the boys, 'and – and the school is now moving on. I want to welcome you all at the start of this new term, and – please settle down now – I want to make a few short announcements – thank you – yes, if I may have silence . . .' Some people were still shuffling about at the back of the hall, chatting and fooling around. 'Quieten down, *please*. First of all, I am very pleased to tell you that Andrew Daly has been appointed deputy head. Mr Daly is well known to all of you, and his appointment will greatly strengthen the school's management team.'

Daly looked a bit embarrassed, but Collins turned to give him a smile, and the other teachers clapped.

'And now I am going to say a few quick words about the school's objectives,' Collins went on, 'the way ahead . . . First, I want you to understand that, whatever difficulties the New Crosland has faced, it is my team's job to raise the quality of education that is provided here, to raise the level of performance. Many of you will soon be out in the world, looking for work, finding your feet in life. My responsibility is to ensure that we have done everything possible to prepare you for that . . .' His glasses briefly reflected the strip lights.

'To this end, the staff and I have spent much of the summer developing a new strategy for the school – a working approach based on objective targets and a system of internal reporting which you will learn about, and I hope will *enjoy* as we roll it out during the coming terms . . .' He raised his voice above the din. 'Because quality is not just a matter of concern for the staff. It is a matter for all our stakeholders – for administrators and parents, certainly – but most importantly, for *you* – the students. You must seize the opportunities the school is offering you. It is your lives which are at stake. You will all need skills that prepare you for success in the conditions of the twenty-first century, enable you to meet the challenges of the global market-place. You are our *partners* in this work – our customers.'

There was a loud noise like a fart at the back of the room, and a voice remarked to nobody in particular: 'Oh, shuddup, cunt-face, give us a break . . .'

'You are our customers,' Collins repeated, 'and I may say, some-times also our *teachers*. We certainly learn as much from you as you learn from us. How can we improve the school together? What are the priorities? I cannot address all the points now, even briefly. And I look forward to hearing your ideas, your input. But if I can leave you with just one thought, it is this. In a word, I believe the most important skill the school can provide is a compe-tence in information technology. This is an *information* society. A learning society. You will all need skills which equip you to handle life in a modern, information-based workplace . . .'

The general hubbub was growing now. Collins's voice began to fall, his face streaked with sweat. A group of fourth-form boys started slow hand-clapping.

'I want to wish you the best of luck with the challenges that lie ahead this term,' he concluded, speaking more quickly. 'Most of all, remember this: believe in yourselves; work hard; focus on your future. Because it always, always pays to aim high.'

Immediately after assembly, I caught up with Daly in the Perspex corridor.

'Hey, deputy *head*,' I said. 'You got the power.'

But he half pretended he hadn't heard.

'You'll have to see Mr Collins, Merton. He's been asking about you.' He squeezed my arm. 'No need to look worried. I've filled him in.' And he skipped a few yards along the passage towards the staff-room, leaving his usual trail of BO. 'How's the community service? They using you as cheap labour?'

'Sort of,' I smiled. 'I cleared up the graffiti in Cannon Park and Waterfield. The guy's quite pleased. He's an old teacher.'

'Name?'

'Gibbon.'

'*James* Gibbon?'

I nodded, and Daly stopped in the corridor. He looked at me with an ironic expression.

'There was a James Gibbon who used to work here,' he said. 'I didn't know he'd gone into social work.'

'Why did he leave?'

'Let's just say he didn't get it. The school had to move him along.'

'He told me the new exams were crap and he wouldn't teach them.'

'Well, he certainly had his differences with the modern world.'

'He's given me work to do. Reading and stuff.'

'He can't do *that*,' Daly snapped. 'He's exceeding his powers.'

'No, I asked him. He's given me Latin.'

'What the fuck for?'

'I don't know . . .'

Daly gazed at me with a bewildered look, and I shrugged. 'We need to talk,' he said, tapping his forehead. 'We *really* need to talk. You've been smoking the wrong weeds. Come on. You'll be late for class.'

He moved on and I followed slowly. 'I want to ask you about something,' I said. 'About politics.'

'What about it?'

People were streaming past us now, heading towards their classrooms.

'Well, that old guy – the one in the burglary. I've been thinking about him.'

'Yes?'

'I mean, he's working-class, right? He lives on his pension.'

'He's poor,' Daly agreed. 'What's your point?'

'So according to Marx, isn't someone like that going to be on the side of change?'

'How do you mean?'

'Well, he's bound to be a progressive, right?'

Daly stopped, and for a moment he hesitated. Then he answered in a low voice. 'Listen, Merton,' he said, 'let's get one thing straight. We can talk about politics, you and me, but that's where it ends. Don't expect me to excuse what you did, or be a party to it. I absolutely don't condone it – not for a minute. It's a hundred per cent out of order. You understand?'

'But in *theory*,' I said.

He cast his eyes to the ceiling.

'You're asking about some old guy's *politics*. What can I say? I don't know him, do I? Just because he's working class, that certainly doesn't make him a progressive. It's a matter of culture. There's a lot of bad politics in all classes, mate – there always has been: racism, sexism, social snobbery . . .'

'So it's not really a question of material conditions, then?'

Daly glanced at his watch, putting his arm round me and pushing me in the direction of the classrooms. 'Listen, we'll have to have a chat, you and me – a *proper* chat. I think maybe you should start reading some Gramsci – the Frankfurt School. I'll have a look for something you could tackle – if you're not too busy doing Latin for James Gibbon, that is . . .' And he turned into the staff-room. 'Meantime, keep out of trouble. And don't forget to see Collins.'

I didn't feel like seeing Collins right away, so I bunked off instead. There was a lot to do.

Down in the basement I made a tour of my library. I had

promised Gibbon I'd learn the Latin he'd given me, and I started with that, reciting the different declensions of nouns again and again for about two hours, and learning masses of new words. I wanted to go back to his house with everything clear in my head. I thought maybe if I did that, I could persuade him to teach me – maybe even get Miranda to look at me. Then I started *The Making of the Middle Ages.*

I was concentrating pretty well, but I kept wondering about what Daly had told me, and in the lunch break I went back up into the school and waited for him outside the staff-room. He was in a hurry, but I got him to lend me his copy of Antonio Gramsci, *The Prison Notebooks*, and I escaped back down to the bunker.

After that, until my next appointment with Gibbon, I just kept reading every day, over the weekend and everything. All day long I read like a madman – Southern, loads of Latin, *The Prison Notebooks*. And in the evenings, I went to see Savage.

The way I understood it, Gramsci believed that there could never be a revolution in a western country like Italy or England, because there were too many independent institutions propping up the state. It wasn't just a matter of getting control of the government, like Lenin did; there were all the other centres of power to deal with – families and churches, clubs, universities, army regiments, schools, charities. There was the whole traditional way of life based on thousands of institutions, and people would fight to defend them. Gramsci said these bodies were like the ramparts or ditches defending the capitalist state; that you had to take them over, one by one – you had to undermine them, abolish them, and change the culture completely – before there could be a revolution. He said it would take years, decades even.

That was the first time I really understood what the New Crosland was all about. Everything which seemed so random and useless was actually part of a plan: the schools, the TV, the whole system – everyone in authority was trying to break down the old way of life, to abolish everything that reminded people of the ancient power structures – marriage, Latin grammar, going to church, old soldiers who kept their own guns, difficult exams. Nobody had ever explained it to me before; it was just taken for granted. Even people like Mum and Mike seemed to understand. But I really thought they should teach us this stuff straight out – explain it openly on TV – tell everyone about Gramsci.

All the same, after a few days of reading, I began to wonder if there was a problem. I wanted to know what was going to happen after the revolution was finally over, when every institution had been completely changed – once the schools and families, and everything that's going on were part of the new, revolutionary world, and all the old habits had been rooted out. Because there would still be people with power – there would still be the TV and schools, laws and customs, headteachers. And I just kept wondering, wouldn't we have to go on undermining all of that? Wouldn't we have to break down the new institutions, just like the old ones, and bring about *another* revolution – and another after that, and then another – going on for ever? I didn't understand why it should stop with us – why everyone was going to be happy and free just because they'd abolished grammar schools and families with fathers. We should abolish comprehensives, too – abolish all schools, all families.

Savage and I met almost every night to plan the protection system for the estates. I kept drilling the boys about it, getting them to explain in their own way why we had to be disciplined – why we couldn't just do whatever came into our heads, pushing people around, that everyone had to work within the plan. And they were getting it. Savage understood; even Terry was going along with me. We were still waiting for the Russian guns, but everything else was in place. And I started to believe that we could really achieve something. I thought we could create a permanent change – protect the weak, punish the powerful, remake the whole place.

In the second week of term, the same evening that the Russian guns were being delivered to the posse, I finally went to see Mr Collins in his office. A group of pupils were already standing around outside the door. Then Collins came out, blinking behind his glasses, and they followed him into the study.

I tried to look at Gibbon's Latin primer while I waited. I had pretty much learnt what he told me. I could recite all the nouns, block by block. But he wanted me to jump about, as well, forming and decoding the endings at random.

I was staring at the book when the others trailed out, and I shoved it in my suit pocket.

'Merton Browne,' Collins called out. 'Good. You can come in now. Have a seat.' I sat across the desk from him. 'I did ask you to come and see me last week,' he said.

'Oh, I'm sorry,' I told him. 'I must have misunderstood.'

He looked at me blankly. 'Well, never mind that. You're here now.' And opening a green file, he pulled out some papers. 'Yes. Here we are. I was interested by this.' He was spreading my court order on the desk in front of him. 'The report from your defence lawyer, Benedict Doyle . . .' He peered at a passage he had marked. 'He found you an interesting and alert young man.'

'He was okay,' I said.

'And how is your community service work?'

'Fine,' I shrugged.

'Who's supervising you?'

'James Gibbon. He used to work here, when it was a grammar school.'

'Interesting.' He made a note. 'I'm glad that's going well. You also have to report weekly to me. That's one of the terms of the order.'

'I know.'

'I don't see why it need be an unpleasant experience for either of us. Just a regular part of the schooling process.' He smiled. 'Let's say every Monday morning after assembly?'

'Okay,' I said.

'I want you to think about your situation, too, Merton. It should be a conscious objective for you to learn from what has happened – to develop new skills-for-life through the rehabilitation process.'

His eyes darted around behind thick lenses; he never looked at my face.

'How do you mean?' I said.

'I want you to improve your interpersonal skills – your communication skills with other pupils and with your teachers – with the adult world generally.'

'You want me to be nice to people.'

'You could put it like that. And I think you should make it your particular mission to improve your feeling-management skills.'

I stared at him. 'And how are you going to monitor *that*?'

'I think it will be a matter for *you* to monitor, Merton. It's a self-evaluating process. That's a key skill in itself.' I thought he had stopped, so I got up. It was getting late, and I had to get to the garage. But Collins went on talking, his pillar-box mouth in a half-smile. 'There's another requirement in the court order, which I can't evaluate sitting in this chair. The court is concerned about the male group networks in your life.'

'The what?'

'Sit down, please. This is important. I really don't think you've fulfilled your potential, Merton. I have the sense – and your lawyer confirms it – that there's more you could do. It would mean breaking away from your present companions, striking out on your own. You have some unsavoury friends, Merton. You know it and I know it. The rumour is that you are still associated with a number of extremely dangerous young men.' His mouth fidgeted when he told me this, and he took off his glasses, holding them over the desk. 'I really do urge you to take a different path in life – *straightaway*, Merton.'

'Like what?' I said. I perched on the chair.

'Well, for instance there are university courses,' he went on; 'courses which really might interest you. I would like you to think about that. You've got three terms before your final A levels. Your AS grades were good' – he glanced at his notes again – '*well* above average. Most useful results. But your social interaction – your behaviour . . . You know better than I do: it's time to make a fresh start. You must start to be punctual and gain a proper attendance record. Just don't allow yourself to fall behind. Most well-paid jobs these days depend on some exposure to tertiary education or training. It pays to aim high, Merton. Really it does.'

'I'll remember that,' I said.

And he peered back at me.

'One thing, sir.' I started to get up, but I was hesitating.

'Yes?'

'Can I work on my own a bit? I mean, can I read on my own, or do I have to go to classes?'

He smiled. 'Of course you must go to classes. That's the essence of the schooling process. You can study at home in the evenings.'

'But what if I work better on my own?'

'In what way?'

'Well, for instance, I do a lot of reading. But you can never read in class. You're not meant to, and anyway it's too noisy. There's so much shit – so much stuff going on . . .'

He started to clean his glasses, rubbing them with a special cloth he kept in his intray, and resettled them on his little nose. 'What you need above all is to socialise in a healthy environment,' he explained. 'School is not just a matter of study, Merton. You must learn to interact with others. To relate.'

'What if the lessons are crap?'

'That's not appropriate. It's not the attitude I want to hear from you.' He had a troubled, almost kindly expression.

'But seriously,' I said, 'what if it's a waste of time? I mean, I learn more in five minutes on my own than in a week of classes. They're useless.'

'Learning isn't just a mental activity. We train the whole personality – your life skills, communication . . .'

'But can't I read sometimes?'

He leaned over the paperwork, scanning the court order. 'Not during lesson hours. The terms don't allow it. In any case, I'd be against that. You've got to improve your performance in the context of a learning environment . . .'

My brain reeled, and I stood up. It was almost five o'clock. I was already late for Savage. Collins looked at me in surprise. Behind his head a great expanse of dark blue stretched out beyond the wide windows, in the direction of the country.

'This is a waste of time,' I said. 'I've got to go. I have an appointment.'

'We haven't finished our talk. Sit down.'

'No, it's important. I've got to get out,' I told him. 'I'm sorry. There's a lot to do.'

'I'm asking you to *stay*.'

'Well, fuck that.'

'This will go on your file. Are you aware of that?'

'Fuck my file.' I could see a group of boys moving across the yard outside, pretending to fight.

'You will carry such antics with you always,' Collins said, taking up his pen. 'Your projects and achievements will be damaged by these outbursts. Future employment, university entrance, your Home Office records . . .'

'I know.'

'Do you really want to do that to yourself?'

'I don't believe in any of that.' I opened the door.

'You sadden me,' he said.

'You sadden *me*,' I told him.

Savage embraced me, handing me a carrot-shaped reefer. Everyone was celebrating because the Russian guns had finally arrived. There was a wooden crate full of weapons at the back of the garage: assault rifles, automatic pistols, even grenades. And Savage had been guarding them. Nobody was allowed to use the new stuff till he and I had given the orders.

Tess was there, on the sofa at the end of the room, rubbing cream into Emily's back. She smiled at me, but I felt depressed seeing her, and I ignored them both. I took a drag from Savage's spliff.

'Okay,' Savage was saying. 'Everyone listen. This is the day. We're putting the plan into action. It's starting tonight. Merton's going to tell you what you have to do, so you all pay attention and don't fuck around.'

So I started to explain.

'Paul and I have divided the territory,' I said. 'Terry and Tatham will move in on block A. Paul will do B and C, with Victor. Calvin and Dan are going to work on D and E. Then, when Cannon Park is covered, we move over to Waterfield.'

'What about you?' Terry said. 'What are you doing? You give the fucking orders in your wanky suit, but you never *do* anything.'

'I keep out of sight,' I said. 'I've got a record, remember? I'll be somewhere else, getting you all an alibi.'

'It won't take long,' Savage said. 'By Saturday we'll have it all. Both shit-hole estates under our control.'

'There's another thing,' I said, turning to Savage. 'I want us to do a job on my mother's boyfriend. He's getting above himself. He's dealing on the estates all the time, and he's a pain in the arse.'

'Mike the man – we'll run him out,' Savage said. 'We'll do it tonight, when we've wrapped up the estates. He won't argue with us.'

'We'll grease him,' Tatham put in.

'No,' I said. 'All we do is confiscate his cargo, right, and his suppliers will kill him for us. An invisible crime, right? We're not involved.'

'That's neat,' Terry admitted.

'Does everyone understand how this works?' I asked. 'Tatham, Calvin – *somebody* – tell me: what are we offering? When you knock on someone's door, what are you saying to them?'

'We tell them to give us money, right? Ten pounds a week.'

'But it's not money for nothing,' I said. 'We've been over this. You've got to get people to trust you. How do you do that?'

'Fuck that,' Terry said. 'We just take the money. If they don't pay, we make them.'

'No way.'

'Why not, faggot?'

'Because that's never going to work. It only works if we give them something in return. It's a deal, right? From now on, starting tonight, we have a monopoly of force in this place.'

'What the fuck does that mean?'

'It means we're the only people on the estate who can use guns. And we start to do what the police used to do: we keep the place decent.'

'Fuck decent!' Tatham said.

'No, fuck you,' I told him. 'That's the way it works.'

'He's right,' Savage put in. 'Listen to him. This is what we're doing. You don't like it, you can fuck yourself.'

'I promise you'll get into it,' I told them. 'It'll make you rich; it will get you miles more respect than just pushing people around. Think about it. We stop the kids doing graffiti, or shoving dog-shit through letter-boxes. We drive out the pimps and dealers. We get control by keeping order. And everyone's paying us, just a little each week, but it adds up. Ten pounds a week from a thousand flats – two thousand with Waterfield. That's twenty thousand a week, a million a year – a real business. You can get loads of drugs for that sort of money – loads of guns. And nobody's telling the cops, because they *like* us – we're doing them a favour.'

'He's right,' Savage said. 'I like this fucking plan.'

'But you've got to present it like you're really *protecting* people,' I explained. 'You say, The pigs are nowhere, the place is a fuck-tip. So we'll do the job, right? We're the ones with power.'

'Respect,' Savage said. He had taken out a rifle, and was running his finger along the barrel. Then he grinned, pointing it at Calvin, who stared straight back at him without blinking. 'Let's get some fucking respect.'

Savage put down the gun and took a drag from the spliff. He smiled uneasily.

'Merton's got it,' he said. 'There's no law on the estates. *We'll* be the fucking law. We'll keep order, you know what I'm saying? If someone pisses in the stairwells, if they steal, or rob some old guy – we teach them a lesson. Out in the open where everyone can see. We give them a beating – we'll make them scream.'

'*Sharia* law,' Calvin said, and Emily started giggling. 'Fucking seen. My brother's a Muslim. He converted in jail.'

'Yeah, whatever!' Savage said, waving the reefer.

But Terry interrupted. 'Not that, man. We get into that stuff, and we can't fuck the girls, right? Besides, I don't believe in God. I'm an atheist. No disrespect or nothing, but I just don't believe in all that praying and shit.'

'We're just going to run the estates, that's all,' Savage said. 'We're going to make people behave.' And he turned to me. 'You organise it, Merton. You make it happen. I want to rule this place. You're the best, you know?' He gripped my arm in his hand. 'You fucking understand things.'

# 15

At seven, when it was getting dark, and the boys had gone out in pairs on to the estate, I left Em and Tess watching TV on the sofa, and ran to Gibbon's house. I had brought my books from the bunker: the Latin book he had lent me, R.W. Southern, and a great bundle of disordered notes – everything I had written in the last two years thrown together, with the names of all the kings and wars from the Dark Ages to Disraeli and Marx and the Factory Acts. I wanted to make sense of it once and for all. I wanted to see how it worked from Gramsci's point of view – from the point of view of Savage and me. I was going to talk to Gibbon about it.

But as soon as I got to his street, I came to a halt. The scarlet Vespa was standing on Gibbon's driveway. For a while I waited in the dusk at the edge of the lawn. I was stinking: scabby from the bunker and the garage. And although I had been thinking about Miranda quite a lot, now that she was virtually standing in front of me, I couldn't make up my mind whether to go in and see her, or run right back to the garage and spend the night with Tess.

In the end I marched across the grass, taking deep breaths, and pressed the bell.

An ancient woman answered the door.

'Mrs Grant?' I said.

'Yes?'

'I've come to see Mr Gibbon.'

'You from the social?' Her face puckered as she looked me up and down, a map of sand-coloured contours.

'I'm a pupil of his.'

'Wait,' she croaked, and slammed the door.

I moseyed away from the house to stare into the darkness of the fields. On the other side of the road, orange lights stretched towards London. The whole city was emitting grimy radiation beyond the horizon. But I started looking in the other direction, over the garden fence, where there was an orchard, a paddock with a horse, and some woods. And in the distance, all I could see was a vast darkness. When I had come in the daylight, I had seen the square tower of a church half a mile away, a footbridge across the motorway. Of course there were houses all over the place. But that night I couldn't see any lights, and I started to imagine the fields going on for miles, divided by streams and hedges, and somewhere in the distance, beyond a wilderness of hills and moors, the dark ocean. Then I wondered what the land had been like before the suburbs were built – before railways or tarmac roads, when the Romans were there, or the first Saxon tribes.

But the crone had come back, peeping through the half-open door. 'He'll see you later,' she called out. 'You'll have to wait. Come in out of the cold.'

We shuffled past the prints of Roman ruins, and she told me to sit in the kitchen. 'He's working,' she explained. '*Private* pupil.'

I hadn't eaten all day, but Mrs Grant wasn't going to offer me anything, so I got a glass of water, and started revising Latin nouns. After a while a door opened somewhere. I heard Gibbon's voice asking a question, and Miranda replying. I took a deep breath, trying to calm myself. I was still looking at the Latin book, forcing myself to concentrate.

Then for a long time Miranda just stood in the doorway, a grey velvet bag under her arm, talking to the witch, while I observed from the side. I could smell myself, too: dried BO and damp dust. Miranda just smelt of lemons; the air was heavy with them. Suddenly I had to get away. Rising from the table I moved towards the back door and grasped the handle, carefully turning it. But Gibbon was behind me.

'Leaving already, Merton?'

'Of course not.' I tugged at the door.

'It's locked,' he said. 'Shall I open a window?'

'Thank you. I need some air . . .'

'You two have met, haven't you?'

'Ha! I didn't see you.' Miranda smiled, hesitating. She was having a good look at my green suit, but then she turned to Gibbon. 'I should really go,' she said. 'I'm meeting someone in an hour.'

'See if you can polish off Book Four,' he told her. 'Just the grammar and vocab. Then we'll read it together for style.'

'What are you reading?' I asked.

'The *Aeneid*. Dido's suicide.' She turned towards me, and for a moment I looked right in her eyes.

'Stay for a few minutes,' Gibbon urged. 'Have some tea.'

Miranda sat down slowly, examining her mobile. Then she turned on me. 'Are you doing Latin?'

'Well – not exactly,' I began, moving towards her. 'The thing is . . .' I was slipping in behind the kitchen table, directly opposite her, but just as I sat down I knocked over my glass of water. It ran out over the pamphlets and old prints. The old woman ran up with kitchen paper, tutting over a postcard of the Colosseum. 'I'm sorry,' I said.

'I'll do it, Mrs Grant.' Miranda took the paper.

'Let me.'

'No. Look: it's done.' She mopped expertly around postcards of Rome, and put the paper in the bin. 'Well, *are* you?' she insisted.

'Not exactly,' I said.

'What, then?' There was a V between her eyebrows.

'We're just finding out,' I explained. 'I'd like to do Latin . . .'

'So why don't you?' She sat down, laid her arms across the table in front of her.

'I don't know if it's my scene,' I shrugged. 'There's a lot of other things I'm interested in. I could do loads of stuff . . .'

But Miranda looked down. She had started to examine her mobile again, and she dropped it into her velvet bag with a shrug.

'We might do some history,' I added. 'Or English. I haven't decided.'

Gibbon didn't say anything. He was disappearing towards his study, chatting with the crone. And Miranda started looking away, searching the room for something. Her lips had an expression of sceptical bemusement. Then she bent over her tea, pushing back a clump of glossy hair. She was making me nervous. I really just wanted to kiss her. It would have made everything easier.

'So' I said, 'do you go to school?'

'Not any more.' She started to get up. 'Tutors mostly.'

'Which school was it?'

'St Margaret's.' She pointed towards the country. 'Five miles that way.'

'So Mr Gibbon isn't teaching you everything?' I asked.

'Only Greek, Latin and history. I see another tutor for French and Italian. He comes to my house. And I do English with this post-graduate guy.'

'You sure you're doing enough subjects?'

'A levels aren't what they used to be,' she said lightly, going over to the sink. 'You have to do loads, to make up for grade inflation. Everyone says so. What about you?' She put her head on one side. 'Do you go to school?'

'I go to the New Crosland,' I said. 'I mean, from time to time I do.'

'I've got a friend there: Debby Hughes.' Miranda looked right at me for a moment, as though knowing Debby was a great achievement. Then she started washing her mug. 'She's my oldest friend,' she said. 'But I know it's a big school. Debby hates it. She says it's a jungle.'

'She's right,' I said. 'The place is a war zone. Well, Debby. *Debby*. She's actually in my class.' I was trying to remember whether I had said a single word to Debby in five whole years. 'We do English together.'

'No way,' Miranda said.

'So, tell me: who are you meeting? Boyfriend?'

'Hmm . . .' she sang.

'What does that mean?'

She put the mug aside, still looking away from me. 'It means, *Hmmm.*' She hesitated. 'I don't know if you'd call him a boyfriend.'

'You're not *sure?*'

'We're thinking about it.'

I was watching her from behind, breathing in the lemon scent. She had a great arse, and she was wearing her trainers with the long pink laces. I got up and moved towards her. 'So, can I ask you a question?' I asked.

Miranda turned to face me. 'All right. If I can ask one, too.'

'Fine.'

'Go on, then. You first.'

'What's your phone number?' I said. 'Your mobile.'

She boggled her eyes at me, but she was half smiling. 'What kind of question is that?'

'A very practical one.'

'So you mean, since I don't really have a boyfriend, can you have my number?'

'Can I have it in *any* case?' I asked. 'We don't have to have sex or anything – not right away.'

'Oh, thanks for letting me know!'

'Though obviously, if you *insisted* . . .'

She didn't say anything, but she was looking towards her bag.

'No, really,' I said. 'I mean it. I'd just like to see you.'

'Yes?'

'Sure. Why not? After all, if I don't get your number now, how will I ever get it? You'll be here sometimes but I won't know when, and we'll miss each other, so it just won't happen. Weeks will go by, months – God knows – and your exams will come and I won't have seen you. The critical moment will pass for ever . . .'

The edges of her lips twitched in surprise, but she was frowning too.

'How could I *not* want to see you?' I was saying. 'Be reasonable. I bet you have millions of men following you about . . .'

Miranda gave a quick laugh.

'Go *on*,' I said. 'How about it?'

She swung her bag over her shoulder and picked up the crash-helmet. She was still sort of smiling, but she didn't come any closer.

'Is that your usual chat-up line?' she asked.

'Oh, no. Not at all.' Suddenly I was depressed. 'I'm not usually so subtle. I mean normally I come right out and just say what I'm thinking. But I thought, since you're an intellectual and everything, I should take my time, get to know you, feel my way . . . Go on, then. Give me your number.'

'No,' she said.

'You've *got* to be joking.'

'God, listen to *you*! Now you have to answer my question.'

'Okay.'

'All right. Tell me honestly: how did you meet James?'

'How did I meet *who*?' I could feel my heart contracting. 'Oh, you mean Gibbon.'

'Of course I mean Gibbon. Don't prevaricate.'

'Why do you want to know that? That's a waste of a question.'

'Go on.'

'I – well, all right, if you insist . . . It's not that interesting. We did some work together.'

'*Ob*viously,' she sighed. 'But what kind of work?'

'Oh, you know, social work. It was a project – that was it. A sort of project to improve the estates.'

'Tell me more.'

'Well that's it,' I said. 'What more can I say? We did a bit of cleaning up, and then I started being his pupil.'

She was still looking at me with her serious, V-shaped eyebrows.

'That's hopeless. That's not a proper answer.'

'Yes it is,' I said. 'I think it's a very good answer.'

She was shaking her head, but I knew she was thinking about it. She was just about to say something else, and I almost put out my hand towards her. I was desperate to touch her face.

But just at that moment her phone exploded, rattling out a trumpet fanfare, and she started ransacking her velvet bag. She turned away, cupping the tiny gadget in her hand. 'Hi – Nathan?' And she seemed to forget all about me, wandering out towards the front door.

Gibbon met me in the doorway of his garage study. 'Has Miranda gone?'

'She's on the phone,' I said. My tackle was throbbing, and I was about to shit myself.

'Nice girl,' Gibbon said. 'Very mature for her age – but girls often are, aren't they? She's only just starting her A levels, and already far better educated than most undergraduates. She's had some advantages, of course. Her mother's French, so she's bilingual. Gives her a tremendous advantage in the Classics.'

'Handy,' I said. 'Where's the loo?'

'Down there . . .' He pointed, and I flew along the hallway. 'If you want, we can do some work together,' he called out. 'I just had a cancellation.'

# 16

I crouched on the toilet seat, curved over like a shrimp, staring at the floor between my knees. Drops of sweat were running down my forehead. I thought I was going to throw up as I crapped. But when the crisis passed, I stripped to the waist, soaping my armpits and face in the basin.

The whole operation took for ever. By the time I came out, Miranda was driving away. I could hear the carmine Vespa straining and turning on the road outside. Gibbon was breaking eggs into a bowl in the kitchen, and I sat down without a word. When I'd consumed a whole plate of cheese omelette, my brain began to stir.

After that, I felt less sick. We went to the study and I rattled off the Latin nouns, which made Gibbon laugh because I got them all right. Then he showed me a whole lot of new things to learn: the forms of adjectives, masses of vocabulary. We spent an hour practising, and reading these Latin sentences he wrote for me.

When the lesson was over, I asked Gibbon about Gramsci, and for a while he got pretty excited. He poured himself a big glass of whisky and started talking about his angry youth, and what a huge deal Gramsci had been for him in those days. He was very emphatic. He kept booming away in his deep, burbling voice, and I was thinking what a weird father he would have been, if he'd had children of his own.

That was the first time he told me he had been in the Communist Party, when he was young. 'I was a slow learner,' he said, biting his lip. 'I didn't resign till sixty-eight.'

He gazed beyond me the way he always did, but I didn't say

anything. Then after a while he got up and started collecting books from the shelves, political books, books by people I'd never heard of.

'It was only after I'd left the Party that I read Gramsci with much attention. He was rather despised in CP circles. The whole tradition seems astonishingly naive, of course, looking back – but still, he was on to something. More than anyone else, perhaps even more than Trotsky, he was the master spirit of the long march through the institutions.'

So I tried to explain what I had been wondering about.

'What do you think?' I said. 'Let's say that all the institutions have been taken over – the schools, TV, the social, the estates and everything. Even so, there'll still be a power structure, won't there?'

'Of course.'

'So, if Gramsci is right,' I said, 'there'd have to be *another* revolution after that – and another and another . . .'

'. . . and so on ad infinitum. Unless you believe in miracles.'

'So then, *what*? What's the answer?' I was thinking about the boys taking over the estates, the kind of society we were going to build.

'I don't know,' he said, smiling thinly. 'Perhaps you're asking the wrong question. Who says society can be perfected?'

'But things can get better, can't they?'

'It's possible,' he said. 'But they can easily get worse, can't they?' And he looked at me. 'What about you, then, Merton? Are you getting better or worse? You keeping out of trouble?'

'Yes,' I said.

'Look at me when you say that.'

'I *am* looking at you. Jesus. I'm not in any trouble.'

'Good,' he said. 'I'd like proof, remember?'

'Proof?'

'I want to teach you, Merton. I'd like to help. But I'm not wasting my time with a criminal. You're clever enough. You decide for yourself.' And he took another slug of his drink. 'Here, have a look at these.'

He handed me two books: a textbook which could have come from the bunker, and something called *The Waning of the Middle Ages*. 'I want to set you an essay,' he said. 'How about it? Have you ever written an essay before?'

I said not really. We mainly did projects at school, downloading text from the internet. So he told me about planning an essay, and then we talked about the Middle Ages.

'See if you can explain how the constitution developed in the reigns of Henry the third and Edward the first,' he said. 'Make it an essay. That means setting out your arguments and *developing* them, *probing* them – putting them to the test. Have a go. We can talk about it on Thursday.'

'Is this part of the CSO?'

'Why not? I'll sign it off, if you do good work. It's more useful to you than sweeping the streets. You might even learn something about living in a free society.'

'Because of Edward the first?'

He smiled. 'Certainly because of him. And because you're examining an argument based on arguments grounded in historical reality – getting to grips with the complexities of life, the ambiguities – not just imposing some abstract theory.'

By midnight, all the boys had returned to the garage. They were fired up, laughing and fooling about.

'Piece of cake,' Tatham announced. 'I got like four hundred quid.'

'That's nothing. I made eight, easy. One Polish guy gave me all the money in his wallet. He thought I was robbing him, right? I said, no, mate, you keep it, but he didn't understand. He was trying to close the door. He just kept shoving notes in my hand – everything he's earned in a fucking month. He thought I was going to kill him. You should have seen his face.'

'We saw your mum's man, too,' Savage said. 'Paid him a friendly visit. I told him right out he wasn't dealing on the estates any more. I explained the situation.'

'Did you confiscate his cargo?' I said.

'Nah,' Savage said, waving his hand magnanimously. 'I let him off with a warning. He understood. I told him to watch himself.'

'He'll be well vex with you,' Calvin told me. 'You should carry a gun, man.'

'I'll be all right,' I said. 'He never touches me; only my mum.' And suddenly I felt elated. 'It's done, then. Tomorrow we can start on Waterfield.'

'Only one thing,' Savage went on.

'What?'

'That old army fuck, remember? The one who snitched you.'

'Frank Cooper,' I said automatically. 'What about him?'

'He wouldn't pay.'

'No?'

Savage shook his head.

'How did you leave it?'

'I told him we'd be back,' he said. 'I explained he should think extremely fucking seriously about what he was doing.'

'Fuck him,' Terry said. 'We should hit him now – make an example of him.'

'He'll come round,' I said. 'He'll change his mind when he sees how things are.'

'Bollocks.' Terry brought his pale face close to mine. 'You never want to get rough, do you, Merton? You're all talk and no muscle.'

'He'll pay,' I repeated. 'It's okay.'

'What do *you* say, Paul?' Terry asked.

'Merton's the *consigliere*,' Savage said. 'We're following his plan.'

'*I* should be *consigliere*,' Terry said. 'I know more about it.'

'Shut it, Terence,' Savage told him. 'That's up to me.'

I didn't go home that week, or the weekend. I thought I should give Mike a few days to calm down. So I slept in the bunker at night, and read during the days about Simon de Montfort and Henry III for Gibbon, or fantasised about Miranda, with just a few breaks for Latin verbs, and the occasional, therapeutic bout of masturbation.

The harder I worked, the more I thought about Miranda. I was getting obsessed. I kept remembering the way she just said *Hmm* and stared at me, when I asked about her poncy boyfriend. Probably if she had just given me her number, I would have almost forgotten about her. But as it was, she made me nervous. I decided I would definitely chat her up again – that I'd see her again when I had loads of money from the Savage racket, and do something she couldn't ignore, like offer to buy her a sports car or something.

The essay was difficult. For a long time there was no order in my thoughts at all. I no longer really believed all the stuff in Daly's books, but I didn't know how to start again. I read and reread Gibbon's books about the Middle Ages, and crawled over parts of Trevelyan, too. I had started to wonder if these old-fashioned historians were right after all; if history worked in the exact opposite way to what Daly believed. I wanted to know how it would be if medieval people really *had* been religious, for example – if it wasn't just ideology and false consciousness, but they actually bought all that stuff about self-sacrifice and the will of God, really believed in heaven and eternal life. And I decided to try and write my essay from the medieval point of view.

So I argued that most people in the Middle Ages – even kings and nobles – believed they were enmeshed in a matrix of divine law; that that was what they meant by freedom. Freedom came from serving God, and God wanted you to serve your neighbour and do your duty according to your rank in society. Monks and nuns were free if they kept their vows – if they lived in poverty and chastity – because then they were free from their own desires. And I argued that all the stuff about hierarchy and feudalism was part of it, too, because it meant that everyone had a role to play.

In the end I wrote for ages: I filled ten sides. Then I ran to Gibbon's house and shoved the whole thing through the letter-box.

On Monday morning, after assembly, I had to see Collins. I waited outside his study with my pockets full of Latin adjectives, just practising by going back and forth between different cases, trying to catch myself out: *omnis omne, omnem omne, onmis omnis* . . . I paced up and down reciting them, and he caught me talking to myself.

When I'd closed the door he told me to sit down.

'Well, Merton . . . Things are going well with Mr Gibbon, I see.' He had my file in front of him, 'So, congratulations on that. But *here* – yes: your attendance record . . . This isn't good. We really *must* have an improvement. I even have a complaint from your, er, stepfather, Mr Burnes . . .'

'You're not serious?'

'I – I'm afraid so. He has written to me himself.'

'Mike Burnes is not my stepfather,' I said.

'He's named as next-of-kin for the purposes of this legal order.'

'He's a psycho,' I explained, trying to be calm. 'It doesn't make any difference what he thinks. He's stoned most of the time. And he beats my mother.'

'Well, let's not, er . . .' Collins slipped the paper back into its place. 'We can't really . . . I mean, despite our previous chats, you haven't been attending lessons.'

'I've been working,' I told him. 'I've got a lot to do.' I was too angry to explain, and I virtually jumped off my chair, but he motioned me to sit down again.

'We've been through this before. You have to meet your attendance targets, or you'll be in breach of the court order.'

'Jesus. I don't even have to be in school. I'm seventeen.'

'But the court decided that since you are in school – which was your decision, remember – you *must* attend regularly.'

'*Fuck* Mike.'

'That language doesn't take us anywhere.'

'It's just, I really don't need this. I've got a lot of studying to do. Reading. Essays. Plus, I'm learning Latin.' And immediately I regretted saying that.

'Latin?' He raised an eyebrow. 'You're not doing an A level in Latin. I admire your enterprise, Merton, but you must stay focused.'

I had got to my feet again, but I didn't leave right away. For a while we just stayed where we were, staring at each other. Outside in the yard, by the school gates, a group of girls were fooling around, punching one another.

'I won't take any action at this stage,' Collins said, closing the file. 'But I need clear evidence of your performance outcomes over the next fortnight. I have to report to the court, Merton.'

I turned to go. I thought I would go calmly out of the room. I really didn't want to say anything else, and I was desperate to get away and deal with Mike. But all the same I stopped at the door, forcing myself to stay calm.

'Look, Mr Collins, I'm doing everything in the court order. I'm seeing Mr Gibbon. I'm going down to the police station next week to talk to DC Peterson. Can't you just give me a break with the lessons? I mean, nobody learns anything. It's fucked up. I mean, it's really useless . . .'

'I won't hear it, Merton. It's my job to keep you within the terms of the order. It's out of my hands, it's not negotiable.' He watched me with his questioning, ambivalent eyes, and I hesitated.

'It isn't education, is it?' I said. I was really just thinking out loud.

'*What* isn't?' He dropped the file into the out-tray, ringing the bell for Rachel Tooley, the school secretary.

'This – the curriculum. Nobody *knows* anything.'

'That's not fair.'

'No, it's true. We did GCSE history, right?'

He opened my file again. 'You got an A.'

'Right. It was all about the Nazis. That's practically the whole course. But all you do in the exam is look at these little extracts and pretend that you can *discover* something from them. It's a joke.'

Collins pressed the bell for Ms Tooley again.

'This isn't getting us anywhere,' he said. 'I want to see your attendance record up to at least eighty per cent . . .' Ms Tooley had come in behind me. I could smell her scent.

'Mr Collins?'

'Thank you very much. I've finished with Merton's file.' He blinked at me once more. 'Keep to the terms laid down, Merton. If you don't do that, there's nothing anyone can do to help you.'

'I know,' I said.

'Come on, then,' Rachel Tooley told me. 'I've got an errand for you.'

I followed her back to her office. She was wearing a chalk-stripe skirt that hugged her thighs, and I could see her black bra straps through her shirt.

'Wait here a second,' she told me, slapping my file on her desk. A dozen ginger coils sprang out in every direction from a tortoiseshell clasp at the back of her head. 'I've got to get something from the archives.'

Alone in the office, I hunted in my file for Mike's letter. He didn't write much. I had seen him writing a note to Mum once, after one of their sessions; he had gripped his pencil in his fist, his tongue mimicking the shapes of the letters. But he had written to Collins, all right. I found his note at the back of my records. *I thought you should now, Merton truantted from School to day and is spending the afternoon with his drug deeler gang. Yours sinserely Michael Burnes, step father.*

I stuffed the note in my pocket, dropped the file on the desk, and ran. Ms Tooley called after me as I banged through the double doors at the end of the passage, but I charged down the orange corridors till I reached the playground, sprinted across the sunlit cement, burst out of the gates. Daly could have seen me from his classroom window. Collins could see me too, if he looked. I didn't even think about it. I ran out across the road, through the Cannon Park Estate, into the suburbs, the quickest way home.

The moron was sitting with his back to the door, watching TV, with the volume turned up high. Mum was Hoovering two yards away with belligerent urgency.

'What the fuck is this?' I had his little note in my fist.

'Merton!' Mum stopped Hoovering.

'What're *you* doing here?' Mike grunted. He cast his tiny eyes over me. 'You should be at school.'

I stood in silence for a moment. *Complete the saying,* the game show host was saying: *Too many cooks spoil the – what?*

'What's this?' I repeated.

'Leave it out, Merton, love,' my mother said. 'He's had ever such a day.'

'Who? This ape?'

'Merton!'

'This cretin? He's had a bad day? How was that? Couldn't find the remote? Finished his Strong Brew?'

'You've got a lip,' he rumbled. 'You know what she means. It's your bleeding fault. I should have taught you a lesson when you was small enough.'

'It's fucking well time I taught *you* a lesson, you walrus. Look the fuck at you!'

'No, love!' Mum ran to intervene. She dropped the Hoover to stand between us. The TV bellowed: *More haste, less – what?* Then I pulled the plug.

There was an obliterative silence. Mike didn't move at first. He had been deactivated, paralysed in his pool of litter.

'That wasn't very bright,' he said.

'What is this note?' I asked again. 'How did the thought enter your blockhead that you would send this drivel to the school? How? How the fuck can you call yourself a *step*father? A *step* fucking father? You're not even married. You think because you fuck my mother and punch her every week you have some sort of power over my life? *Do* you? What constitutes a stepfather, then? One fuck? Would that count? Living together for a week, an hour? *What*?'

'You're getting above yourself, no mistake.'

'No, shit-face, *you* are totally out of line. You're finished.' The blood was pounding in my head. 'You are *fucking* finished.'

I had planned a little speech, as I sprinted across the atrium of Cannon Park, but when it came to it, I was pretty much on Mike's level.

He rose slowly from the sofa, turning his creased face towards me. 'And what do you mean by that, exactly?'

'You can't live here any more,' I said.

'Merton!' Mum shrieked. 'Don't listen to him, Mike. He's not himself.'

'Little bastard.'

'You can't live, you can't deal, you can't beat her up. If you lay a finger on her or me, I'll have you killed. I swear I will.'

Without a word Mike moved forward keeping his eyes on me and lunged halfway across the room to grab a wooden chair. 'Don't, Mikey,' Mum said. 'Leave it out. He doesn't mean it. He's upset.'

'He *will* be.'

'I do mean it,' I said. 'What do you think you're going to achieve, you thick bastard? Try to think for once in your life.'

My head had almost cleared, but my body was immobilised. I was still gripping Mike's note in my hand, and I didn't take up a weapon. I just stood in front of him while he smashed the chair against the floor to create a cudgel.

Mum was wailing by the window, her voice low and steady. 'No, Mike, no, love, don't do that, love. He's only a lad.'

Mike was half a foot taller than me, probably twice my weight. I had seen people fighting, and I knew what you're supposed to do when you take on someone bigger than you, but I still didn't make any of the right moves.

The first blow landed on my ribcage, then another on the side of my face. My ear rang with the impact of it. In an instant I remembered the time Tuck had thrown me across the room. Mum's reasoning began to shift. 'He asks for it,' she admitted quietly; 'he's got a lip on him, cheeky bugger.'

I tried to dodge the next blow, putting out my hand as a shield, but Mike thumped me on the side of the head again, and I fell heavily across the doorway next to the sofa. A splash of blood reached the carpet before me, and my face was sticky when I put my hand to it. Mike's blow had reopened the scar across my forehead. I don't think I lost consciousness; I just lay there for a moment, stunned by the pain. Then I tried to get up. But each time I started to rise, he beat me across the back with the chair-stump, or pounded my legs. Mum was out of sight, but I could hear her talking the whole time: 'It's bound to happen, like: he's pushed you too far.'

Unable to stand up, I crawled behind the sofa, and for a moment I was out of Mike's range. At the far end, just out of reach, was his Stratocaster and portable amp, and next to them the blue toolkit containing nails and chisels, screwdrivers, a four-pound hammer. I crawled towards them, reached out and took hold of the hammerhead. I was still face-down with no room to move, my back throbbing. But Mike was clearing some space. He dragged the table away from the middle of the room, then lifted the sofa, pulling it right over towards him. Mum screamed again, and on an impulse I jumped up, clutching the massive hammerhead. Mike was only a few feet from me, approaching with his club, bent over like a caveman. 'Merton, no!' Mum shouted. 'Don't, love!' I threw the hammer as hard as I could at the crease of his forehead.

But Mike was ready. He shifted his big frame to the left, and the hammer flew past his saucer face. It spun across the room, over the upturned sofa, travelling towards the TV. 'Oh, God!' Mum said, and we all watched as the iron head struck the glass. Mike briefly covered his face, and there was a massive explosion. The three of us stood gazing at the cloud of dust and tiny glass particles within the hollow machine. The hammer was lodged a foot inside the tube.

'Jesus fucking Christ,' Mike mused. And I edged towards the door. 'That is unfuckingbelievable.'

'Now he's done it,' Mum said. Neither of them could take their eyes off the shattered screen. 'What'll we do now, Mikey?' she asked, and for the first time she began to cry real tears. 'What are we going to do?'

I had reached the hall before Mike turned back.

'Little rat's running away,' he said. And he threw the chair leg through the doorway at my head, but I ducked and got to the front door. 'You'll fucking pay for this!' he screamed. 'You'll fucking live to regret it!' But I had grabbed the latch and was sprinting away.

# 17

They kept me waiting half the afternoon in casualty, opposite a man with plum-coloured skin and motionless eyes. He hardly stirred all the time I was there, gazing directly at the wall beside me under the buzz of his personal stereo. Beyond him, towards the duty nurse's office, stretched a neon limbo of alcoholics, incontinents, prescription junkies. Nobody spoke. Every few minutes, one of the orderlies called the next patient by number. I took out the book Gibbon had lent me, *The Waning of the Middle Ages*, and started to read.

In the end a doctor took me to a consulting room and sewed me up. He asked what I was reading, and I tried to explain while he worked on my face. He was very young – hardly much older than me. When he was done, he gave me a whole load of painkillers and sleeping pills, and told me to take it easy for a while. And I persuaded him to give me a note to get me out of school for three weeks.

I wondered about going to see Paul in the garage, but I thought the boys would go on the rampage when they saw what Mike had done, and I wanted time to think everything through. So I broke into the school, took clean clothes from my locker, and bedded down in the bunker.

It was the first hard frost of the year, but the hot-water pump wasn't working, and I couldn't sleep for ages because of the cold. Also my head was thumping, although I took more painkillers than I was supposed to. Then I had strange dreams. In the middle of the night I woke up, terrified and freezing. At first I didn't remember where I was. But all at once it came back to me, and I started thinking about Miranda again – her face, her arse – everything I could remember about her. After that, I started to feel anxious. I lay awake for about three hours, with a sensation in my head like I was being hit with a rubber truncheon, obsessing about her. I was trying to work out how I could keep everything together in the posse and still work on Miranda.

Eventually I calmed down. The first thing I had to decide was how to deal with Mike. I thought it would be hard to control him if we just cut him off; that he could turn informer and use the police against us. So in the end, I made up my mind to wait till we were ready, and bring him to justice in our own way. The whole thing depended on covering the estates with our protection. It was clearer than ever. And I started thinking about the old man again. I wanted to give him his stuff back – to tell him we had found the people who robbed him, prove that we would give him better security than the police. I even thought Gibbon would see that that we were doing good if we protected people like that – maybe even Miranda. And finally, when it was all clear, I fell asleep. I didn't wake up till late in the afternoon.

Savage was strutting up and down the garage, a Russian handgun stuffed into the front of his baggy jeans. Tatham and Dan were sprawled at opposite ends of the sofa. The others were cleaning their weapons under the light. Terry scowled at me as I came in, but nobody said anything about the bandage, and I sat in the shadows.

It was quiet in there. Everyone was focused. The boys were going out that night on to Cannon Park and Waterfield, to see the people who had refused to pay the first time, or who hadn't been at home. We had planned it all; everyone had a list of flat numbers. We were going to raise the pressure. Only I had to explain about the old man.

I came up to Paul and stood in the light.

'Jesus, what happened to you, man? Who did that?'

'It's not so bad.'

'Fucking Mike Burnes,' he said.

I shrugged.

'He's got a nerve.' Savage screwed up his eyes to examine the bandage. 'That's serious damage, that is.'

Terry had come up. 'We should have finished him,' he said, glancing at Savage. 'We made a mistake, leaving him to run around. *You* made a mistake, Merton.'

'Maybe,' I said. 'We'll deal with Mike when we're ready – when he doesn't expect it. There's loads to do before that.' And I lowered my voice. 'I've been thinking about Frank Cooper, Pauly.'

'What about him?'

'I want to talk to him myself.'

'But you said you couldn't go out, man. Your *record*, remember?' Terry said.

'This is different. I want to win him over. I think we should give him back his medals.' I moved round to face Savage. 'His gun, too, Pauly. Then we'll get money from him. How about it?'

Terry laughed right out. 'No *way*, you cunt. You're going way too far. We're not giving that wanker *any*thing. He put the pigs on us, remember?'

'It's a matter of showing we're real.'

'You what?' Terry shook his head. 'You see, mate?' he said to Savage. 'What did I tell you?'

'What's he saying?' Calvin said.

'He's giving up. He wants to give the old cunt his medals. *And* the shooter.'

'Only to show we're for real,' I said. 'To build trust.'

'We're real because if he doesn't pay we fucking kill him,' Terry said. He imitated me: '*It's a matter of showing* – shit!'

'This is the plan. We agreed, right? We need to do it properly. If we're just another load of criminals, it's not going to work.'

But Terry spat on the ground in front of me. 'You're obsessed with those fucking medals, man. Who gives a shit? I'll *fight* you for them.' He started punching the air like a boxer. 'Go on: you fight me.'

'Shut the fuck up, Terence,' Savage said. 'I'm trying to think.'

But Terry kept wheeling around me, throwing out his fists. Then, when I ignored him, he went to get the old man's revolver and the three boxes with the medals in them, and put them on the table where everyone could see them.

Savage had withdrawn into the shadows. 'I decide who does what. The rest of you can shut the fuck up.' He was shaking his head. 'I do what I like.' And he hesitated, looking at Terry again. 'So you can tell me, man: what would you do if you were *consigliere*? Just tell me. I want to know.'

'It's fucking simple.' Terry raised his voice. 'I been over it a hundred times with my dad's mates. Either we get people to do what we tell them, to show us respect, or we're just pussies fooling around. Merton wants to be nice to everyone, right. What's the point of that, man? Tell me.'

'He's right,' Tatham said. 'If we never act hard, nobody will pay.'

'We start with that old cunt,' Terry said. 'Everyone knows about him, because of the court and everything. He's proud. He goes about like he's fucking special. So we bring him down. We just kill him, out in the open. After that, the whole place will know we're serious. No one will talk to the cops, then: they'll fucking talk to *us*, Pauly. What do you say? Decide, man.'

Tatham and Calvin were lining up beside Terry. Savage watched them in silence for a while. Then he turned to me. 'Well?'

'Listen,' I said. 'We're starting an empire – a business. It only works if we give something in return for the money people pay, right? We're moving out across the estates offering security – not crime; not more burglaries and shootings – protection.

Protection for the old freaks, for the welfare wankers who never get off their arse, the illegal immigrants, mothers with too many kids – for everyone who can't go out at night – who's frightened all the time. You're offering them security – and it will make us rich. It will make *you* rich, Pauly – give you power. If you bring off this protection scam, you'll be made. You'll have the cash to deal in the big league.'

Terry had moved into the light next to Paul. 'We know how to fucking do it,' he said quietly.

I stared back at his strange, old-looking face. 'But there's more than one way,' I went on. 'You can do it the short-term way. That means you get money from people but you don't protect them. It means they don't get a good deal, and after a while they stop paying. Then, because they're not paying, you start getting tough – you'll be breaking bones to get the money. That's what Terry wants, right? But it's not clever. The cops will be in. Someone always ends up calling the cops. You'll spend your whole time trying to stop people informing on us, trying to keep the estates under control. So you never achieve real power, and the whole idea is a failure. Just as you're getting it together, the whole thing fucks up.'

'So. What's the other way, batty-boy?' Tatham asked.

'He talks too much.'

'Shut up,' Savage said. 'I want to hear.'

'The other way is the way Paul and I agreed,' I said. 'We thought it out. It will work much better if you do it our way.'

'Which is *what*?' Calvin said.

'You give people what you promise. You offer them protection, and you give it to them. You take their money, and you clean up the streets. You get the whores and junkies out of their doorways. Get the rubbish out of the yards. You stop the little kids doing graffiti, you come down on them, teach them a lesson. You drive the other gangs out. You balance violence with discipline. That way you keep the business to yourselves. You get paid, you deal drugs – all on your own terms. You won't need to break any heads, and the cops will leave you alone. More money, less hassle. You tell me.'

Savage came up and stared right in my face.

'You've always got words,' he said very quietly, like he didn't want the others to hear. 'You can talk. But would you ever kill someone, Merton? If you had to, could you do it? If you won't kill, you're only dreaming.'

I didn't say anything.

'We can vote on it,' Tatham said. 'Terry or Merton – we can vote for who will be *consigliere*.'

'We don't fucking vote.' Savage wheeled round. 'That's shit. I'm leader and I choose the *consigliere*. It's nothing to do with you.'

'But he wants to start giving away your *stuff*, man,' Terry told him. 'He's not even helping you any more.'

'That's right,' Tatham put in.

'So what's *your* plan,' Savage demanded, suddenly turning on Terry, 'if you're so fucking smart? What would your *dad* say, then?'

'It's not my dad,' Terry shot back. 'I got my own plans.'

'Let's *hear* them.'

Terry hesitated. 'I already said,' he began. 'It's not the way Merton is saying. It's not going to be like that. We take the streets – we organise this protection skank like we agreed, and we run our drugs out of here, and the whores. We get the money coming in. But we don't need to be the fucking dustmen. We're not going to be slaves, you know what I'm saying? We're the guys with the power. We've got guns – fucking machineguns. Then Savage goes to talk to Haig Johnson and his crew, and he says: Here's the whole fucking neighbourhood wrapped up. We don't need any favours from you, but we'll do a partnership. And in return – in return for making them partners in Cannon Park – they introduce us to their contacts in the West End. In the rich parts of town. That's my fucking plan, see? You don't need to listen to this faggot any more.'

'That's right, man,' Calvin said. 'We do it with the guns.'

'You'd never pull it off,' I said. 'You'll end up in a war.'

'Then we'll win,' Terry said.

'Never.'

'Why, arsehole?'

'You're talking like you're invisible,' I said. 'You start using machineguns, the whole fucking police force will be after you. Ask your dad. They haven't gone away, you know.'

'Fuck the pigs! They're frightened of us already.'

'And even if the cops don't react, the Russian gangs will.'

'Let's vote,' Tatham repeated. 'It's the best way.'

'You shut the fuck up,' Savage said. And he raised his gun at Tatham's face. 'Shut up or I'll kill you.'

'Hey, Paul, take it easy,' Calvin said. 'He's your mate.'

'Fucking shut it!' Savage shouted. 'Everyone! You're doing my nut.' He went on holding the gun to Tatham's head, and slowly he moved in a circle around him. Everyone stepped back. Then Terry turned to me. He had this big, ironic smile on his face.

'Okay, Merton,' he said. 'What do *you* say? Tell us, *consigliere*. Does Savage shoot? Is that what you advise? Do we shoot, or do we vote?'

And Savage looked at me, still holding his gun to Tatham's head. 'It's up to Savage,' I said. 'He's the boss.'

'Yeah, but what's your *advice*, man?'

'We don't start killing each other,' I said. 'That's not it. If we do it my way, everyone gains. You, too, Terry. Think about it. You can have what you want. Loads of girls – a beemer.'

'I don't want a fucking beemer,' he said. He tried to sound like he didn't care. 'I want a *jeep*, you cunt.'

But Savage shouted: 'Jesus! What's wrong with you all? I told you to shut the fuck up. I'm *thinking*.'

Everyone waited in silence. Savage kept his gun aimed at Tatham for a while. Then very slowly he moved it on, till it was pointing at Terry's forehead. And when Terry didn't move, he aimed it at me. He kept it there while he addressed the posse.

'You all fucking listen,' he said. 'This is my *consigliere*, right. Merton. He's still the man. He gets twenty per cent, like we agreed.' He paused. I stared back into Paul's eyes. And finally he took his gun from my face. 'But we're not doing his plan any more,' he added quietly. 'Not now.' And he turned to the others. 'We're going to have some action on this fucking estate. We're going to clean up. We'll do it like Terry says. We'll rub out the old man. You can give him back his stuff if you want,' he said to me. 'If it makes you happy – soften him up, right. I don't care about that. But it's only a loan. When we're ready, we're going to kill him. You understand?' I nodded. Then Savage raised his voice. 'And another thing,' he said. 'If anyone tries to have a fucking vote again, I'll fucking shoot them.'

I picked up the medals and the revolver, putting the gun in my coat pocket. I even took a box of bullets. Terry was watching me. 'What you doing, *consigliere*?' he said. 'What will you do with that stuff, man?'

'I don't know,' I said. 'I'm going to borrow it.'

'You got to be careful what you do,' Terry pointed out, 'who you speak to.' And he turned to face Savage. 'You should watch him, Paul. He knows everything about us.'

'Leave him alone,' Savage said. 'He's all right.'

Danny came up and stood beside me. He had his hood up, ready to go out. 'You stay,' I told him. 'You shouldn't come with me.'

But Dan was nervous. 'Let's go,' he mumbled. 'I got to get home.'

'You go with the pussy,' Terry said. 'This gang will be better without you.'

'I'll be back,' I said. 'I'll come and see you, Paul – tomorrow – I don't know. We'll talk.'

'I'll see you, man,' Savage said.

And Dan and I went out.

\* \* \*

We marched to the atrium in silence. It was very cold. The electric cross was burning in the middle of space, three hundred yards from the garage. By the church we stood together, Dan hoodied up, and me in my big coat with the old man's pistol against my side.

'What you going to do *now*?' Dan said. 'We're both fucked.'

I hugged my coat closer to me. 'I'll think of something.'

Neither of us moved for a while. The drunk old woman was somewhere in the darkness nearby. We could hear her muttering to herself, like she was carrying on a conversation with a whole head-full of devils.

'You should go home,' I told Dan.

'Why?' he said, and he was suddenly angry. 'What's at home?' He spat on the ground. 'We're on our own, isn't it? Admit it: we've got no protection.'

'No,' I said. 'You'll have to be careful.'

'I've got my gun. Haig's been teaching me how to use it.'

'Keep in with him,' I told him. But Dan only shrugged. 'How's the boat business?'

'It's cool,' he said. 'Better than this shit-hole posse. I'm going in the summer, anyway,' he added. 'My uncle's asked me. As soon as the exams are finished.' And he sounded almost happy. 'Fuck Savage,' he added. 'I'll see you later, man.' And he tramped off towards block B, disappearing into the shadows of the staircase on the far side of the yard.

I wandered about for a long time, trying to decide what to do. If the boys were going to get serious, I thought I should stay with them, advising Savage. At least I would have influence if I did that. At least I'd make money. And in a way Terry was right – we couldn't have a protection system without terror. All power in the world depended in the end on physical force. That was obvious from the whole of history. Everything depended on who was willing to use it. And I thought about Tess. I wondered if I could still see her when I wanted – if she would want to be with me if I wasn't *consigliere* any more.

I circled around the whole of Cannon Park, till I came back to where I'd started. I was standing right there by the garage, near the bollards at the entrance to the estate, staring at the door. And I made up my mind to go in. I was going to say, *I was wrong: I agree with you; let's do whatever it takes.*

But I hesitated. The gun was pulling my coat pocket down, so I stuck it into the belt at the small of my back. And I walked away from the garage, slowly at first, back towards the suburbs. I didn't go to the bunker straightaway, or to Gibbon's house. I couldn't take the gun, in any case. I had to get rid of it. So in the end I marched to Tess's house. There was nobody around, and I put the revolver and the boxes of bullets in the space under Tess's bedroom floor where we used to hide the drugs. Then I shut the house up, made my way to Dante Park, and ran towards Gibbon's place.

The Vespa was squatting on the driveway, and for a while I hesitated. I didn't think I could talk to Miranda the way I was. But I was too tired to go back to school, so in the end I went up and rang the bell. And when Mrs Grant came, she let me in without a word, squinting reproachfully at my bandage, and told me to wait in the kitchen.

There was the usual pile of postcards and papers on the kitchen table, and loads of books: poetry, literary criticism, *Pride and Prejudice* in a beaten-up paperback, which I opened. Miranda had written her name inside the cover, with a little heart underneath and the date. I put the pages against my nose and breathed in, and I thought I could smell lemons, very far away. Then I picked up a book of T. S. Eliot, turning to the first poem Miranda had marked, and started reading 'The Love Song of J. Alfred Prufrock'.

There was a chunk of Italian verse at the top. Miranda had marked in the margin, *Inferno, Canto XXVII, l.* 61, in her neat italics. I read straight through the first stanza of the poem, under my breath. Then I cleared my throat and tried again. I didn't realise at first that it really was a song. So I read louder, rapping it. But the rhythm wasn't right, because the words slowed down and speeded up, as though they were heavy towards the middle of the lines, but suddenly light at the end. And each time that happened I could feel myself being mesmerised: my heart slowed, my breathing almost stopped; it was like I was being drugged. And finally I let the poem have its own rhythm.

> Let us go, through certain half-deserted streets,
> The muttering retreats
> Of restless nights in one-night cheap hotels
> And sawdust restaurants with oyster-shells

For a while I kept rereading the same lines, fixed in my chair. Then I went on. By the time I heard voices in the corridor I had read the whole poem, and I could barely move. A thousand strange thoughts gripped my heart.

They were talking about Horace. I heard Miranda's voice rising and falling in the darkness, and I watched the door, unable to move. I didn't know if I was relieved or frightened. She was saying something about the dative of possession which made Gibbon laugh. Then they burst into the room.

'God! What happened to you?' There was a catch in Miranda's voice as she looked at my forehead.

'Nothing.'

'Strange kind of nothing,' she said. Her skin was creamy under the black hair.

'Someone attacked me.'

Gibbon sighed. 'Has Mrs Grant seen you?'

'She told me to wait.'

'You should keep that wound clean,' Miranda said.

'It's okay. They cleaned it last night at the hospital.'

'But it should have a new dressing. I can do it.'

'You don't need to,' I said.

'I *know*,' she sang. And began searching about for TCP and cotton wool.

'I'll make some tea,' Gibbon said.

I watched Miranda, breathing in her scent. She came to sit on the chair next to me.

'Just a second,' I said, 'before you do that. I brought something.' I reached for my coat, pulled out the plastic bag, and passed it to Gibbon. 'Take a look; it's all there.' He took out the red boxes, laying them on the kitchen table. Then he opened the biggest.

'What's that?' Miranda asked.

'They're campaign medals,' I said. 'From the Burma front. You know: General Slim; the Forgotten Army.'

Gibbon smiled. 'Where did you find them?'

'They were still in circulation.'

He was looking at my stitches. 'You went to some trouble.'

'No, it wasn't that.' I put my hand to my forehead.

'Don't touch it,' Miranda snapped.

'Well . . .' He opened the boxes and laid them out, blue ribbons, silver discs, the head of George VI. 'They will make one old man extremely happy. Two old men, I should say.'

'Okay, I'm ready,' Miranda said. 'You'd better lie down so I can get at you.'

'Let's go to the sitting-room,' Gibbon said. 'Go on. I'll bring the tea.'

By the time she had washed my forehead I was ready for sex, but I didn't come on to her right away. She was putting a new dressing on the stitches, and I didn't even look at her much. There was something fragile about her – she was always jumpy and restless; I half wanted just to give her a hug.

'I read your man Eliot,' I said.

'Which one?'

'Prufrock.'

She stopped what she was doing. 'What did you think?'

'I don't know,' I said. 'It's very good – not just good; it's shocking. It blew my mind.' She smiled, so I carried on. 'What I really want to know is, where does that come from – where does he get that?'

'*There's* a question,' she said. 'He's got it – almost like Dante or Shakespeare . . . Not as broad in his emotional register, not as generous or humane; he's a modern, after all. But everything Eliot says is true to his experience, and unbelievably strong. When I first read it, I could hardly believe any human being could write like that.' And for the first time she looked straight into my eyes. 'Do you think that's stupid?'

I shook my head, keeping my eyes on her. But just as I started to put out my hand to touch her, she stood up, surveying my forehead with a frown, and dropped the cotton wool in the hot water bowl. Then Gibbon came back in. 'There,' Miranda said. 'The bandage is done.' I had an erection, of course, impossible to hide, but she pretended not to notice.

'Anything else?' she asked.

'What do you mean?'

'Do you any have other wounds, or is it just the head?'

'Only bruises,' I told her. In fact my body was throbbing from the battering Mike had given me. I hadn't really noticed till I lay down. My back was aching where he'd hit me with the chair leg. 'Nothing that needs cleaning.'

'You should have a Diazepam or something.'

'I've got Valium,' Gibbon said, and he went out again.

'And food,' she called after him. 'Merton should eat.' She looked me up and down. She must have seen my boner. 'Where will you spend the night?'

'I don't know.'

'Where's home?'

'Home isn't a good idea,' I said.

'Here, then?'

'I've got a place at school,' I explained. 'I can spend the night there. I often do.'

'No,' she said. 'You need lots of sleep. I'm sure you can stay here. Mrs Grant will keep an eye on you.'

'Are you mad? The woman's a vampire.'

'She's not so bad.' Miranda smiled, picking up the bowl and moving to the door. 'She only drinks the blood of virgins. You'll probably be all right.'

Mrs Grant made the bed for me in Gibbon's spare room, drawing the curtains and putting a new bar of Imperial Leather by the basin. Then she heated up a chicken casserole, and I lay propped on the sofa, drugged up with Valium.

Later I started to doze off, while Miranda and Gibbon had a tutorial on English poetry. First they read something in Latin together. Then Miranda recited one of the poems she had marked in her Eliot book, 'La Figlia Che Piange', and I listened through my darkening mind to her sharp, clear voice with the crack in it. As the drugs took effect, I started falling asleep in the warmth. I heard fragments of their conversation – Greek poets, Troubadours, the Metaphysicals, the whole tradition from Homer to Eliot. For a moment I wanted to lift my head and say something – take hold of Miranda's hands – kiss them. But I could feel myself falling away, down and down, until her bright voice was swallowed up in the rhythm of my own breathing, and I couldn't hear a word.

# 18

I woke up at noon in Gibbon's spare room, surrounded with brown wallpaper and black and white prints of Roman ruins. My back was throbbing, and I had been sweating like a madman all night.

The crone scrambled eggs, while I drank pints of water. Then Gibbon handed me a card Miranda had left: *Asia*, 1946, by Matisse. *I never gave you my number*, she wrote. *I'm around if you want a drink. Hope you're feeling better. Rest. Love, Miranda xo*. There was a landline number, and her address. I stared at the 'love', instinctively smelling the card for lemons, and slipped it in my pocket.

I had forgotten the essay I had left with Gibbon, but he had it in his study, spattered with red ink.

'This was good,' he said, leafing through. 'Too long, of course. You need practice – that's understandable. Your spelling is – erratic. And nobody has ever explained the use of the apostrophe to you. Amazing, really. Still, we can rectify that in about fifteen seconds. There are a few infelicities. But your prose . . . very readable: sinewy, fluent. Also a sort of polemical *élan*, which is unusual.' He handed it over.

'You've got no idea how pupils these days so often have the *same opinions*. Very tedious opinions, too. But this is different. At least you have tried to enter the mind of medieval man. And I'd say your argument, your use of information, marks you out. You do it well. I'd like to see more.' He looked up at me. 'How do you feel about that?'

'Fine,' I said. 'It's better than what they want us to do at school.'

He smiled. 'How you feeling?'

'Better. Fine.'

'Want to see a doctor?'

'No way.'

'All right.' And he leaned back in his revolving chair. 'Before we talk about this essay of yours . . . I've got a couple of suggestions. First, stay here as long as you want. That room is usually free. Very occasionally an old friend comes for a few days, but subject to that, it's yours.'

'Thanks. Thank you. If it's really okay, I'd like to stay. Not always, but usually. Is that all right?'

'It's fine,' he said. 'There are some old clothes in there – suits, shirts. I used to be your sort of weight, believe it or not. Take a look. You're welcome to adopt them.'

'Cool.' He had very weird clothes, and I smiled. 'I'll get my stuff from home when I can.'

'What else? Oh, yes: remind me to give you a set of keys.'

I waited, scanning the little green and red hardbacks on the bookshelves behind him. 'Second,' he said, 'I'd like you to think about applying for university.'

'No way.' I laughed. 'Never happen.'

'Well – let's talk about it. There's a couple of weeks to decide about this year's application. Don't dismiss the idea.'

I was shaking my head and looking at him, but he pressed his lips together and built an arch with his fingertips.

'Third, Merton, I have contacted Frank Cooper.' He looked at me sideways. 'I told him about the medals, and he's agreed to see you.'

'Shit!'

'I – acted on my own initiative. It's up to you, of course. I can't make you see him.'

'Jesus.'

'What had you planned to do with them? You were going to return them, I suppose?'

'Well, I thought I'd get one of his neighbours to give them to him. I've got this friend who lives in the same block.'

'He was pretty hard to persuade, but I told him a little about you, and – anyway, he's willing to see you. If you have the – I mean, if you can face it.'

My stomach turned over. 'When?'

'We could go this afternoon. You look a little pale. Are you all right?'

'I'm fine.'

'How about it?'

My mouth had dried out. 'All right,' I said. 'We'll go together?'

'That's what I suggested.'

'Is that it?'

'One other thing. It really is none of my business.'

'What?'

'You got Miranda's note?'

I pulled it out.

'If I were you,' he said, 'I'd give her a call.'

'Why?'

'No reason. Just a hunch.' He gave me his brief, thin-as-a-knife-edge smile. 'Male intuition.'


The old man was barricaded in his flat. It took him about ten minutes to move his boxes out the way. Then he peeped at us with dark, apprehensive eyes, keeping the door on the chain.

I didn't want to grovel or anything, so I just said hello like we hadn't met before. He hesitated, but he let us in, examining my bandage before bringing us into his little room with all the books of military history, his hats and photographs. Gibbon gestured at me to put the medals on the table, while the old guy went to make tea.

He came back with a tray. He had even bought biscuits – expensive ones with chocolate, laid out on a plate.

'Go on,' he said quietly, passing them to me. He didn't look me in the eye. 'Help yourself.' So I took a couple.

'Merton has brought you something, Mr Cooper,' Gibbon told him in a loud voice. 'As I told you. Here, on the table.'

I unwrapped the plastic to reveal the boxes. They were knocked about a bit, and the old guy stared for a while, moving slowly towards them, before picking up the first. For several minutes he didn't speak. He had to examine the medals, one at a time, holding them by the window before laying each one back on the silk lining of its box.

'Merton tracked them down,' Gibbon bellowed. 'He wasn't sure if they were all still there.'

'They're all here,' the old man said. 'All present and correct.'

'Good,' I said, normal volume. 'I'm pleased.'

'These are most of what I have left,' the old guy said, still looking away from us. He put them down for a moment and poured the tea. 'Some of my pals had to sell their medals. They fetch a lot of money.' He handed me a cup. 'Not me, though. I was buggered if I was going to lose them.'

I looked at my shoes in silence. Then the old man asked how I got hold of the medals, so I admitted I knew the boys who'd done the job.

He looked into my eyes for the first time when I said that.

'So *were* you with them on the night, lad? Did I remember right? Tell me: yes or no?'

'Go on,' Gibbon said, *sotto voce*. 'Get it off your chest.'

I looked at the old man's mantlepiece, his hats behind the settee, photo albums, badges, bits of shrapnel. 'I didn't want them to take the medals,' I said. 'I told them it was bad luck.'

The old guy nodded. 'Who fired at me?'

'The gang leader,' I said. 'Savage. The police know about him.'

'Him and another lad were round here last night, asking for money,' he said. 'I told them to eff off. The cheek of it. They were doing the whole block. Protection money, they said. Bloody mafia. I almost took a shot at them with my rifle. But it's not worth going to jail for the likes of them. I'll keep my powder dry.'

'You've got another gun?'

'They didn't know about that, did they?' he chuckled.

'They'll be back,' I said.

'You tell them to lay off. I'll shoot them. I swear to God, if the police won't protect me, I'll protect myself.'

'I'm not involved any more,' I explained. 'We've fallen out. They took your revolver, too.'

He looked down at the medals. '*That* was a bad business.' He was about to post a chocolate biscuit into his mouth, but held it in the air. 'I had no licence for that. They keep changing the bloody law. No one's allowed a gun these days unless they're a hoodlum. Not even a service revolver. Unbelievable!' He took a bite. 'I was given it by *him*.' He pointed at one of the photos. The old man was there in his jungle uniform, haunted and gentle-looking, very young, with an officer and a few other soldiers standing in front of a bungalow. 'Colonel Edwards, that is. I saved his life, you see; got mentioned in dispatches. Then, after the war, he gave me his service revolver, and I gave him my old helmet. As a keepsake, he said, so we wouldn't forget one another.' And he blew on his tea. 'I wasn't going to let them take that away from me.'

We talked about the Burma campaign, Frank Cooper's own brigade, General Slim.

'I didn't know they teach that at school,' the old man said.

'They don't,' Gibbon smiled. 'This one does his own reading.'

'I do some reading myself,' Frank Cooper said. 'About the war and that. I like to read the background.'

'And Wellington,' I pointed out. 'You've got a book on the Peninsular War.'

But he was losing the plot.

'I want Merton to try for university,' Gibbon yelled. 'I think he would benefit.' He kept shouting at Frank Cooper, even though he could hear quite well.

'They're all going nowadays,' Cooper said, with a little smile.

'Load of cobblers. But if it gets you out of this place, it's worth a try.'

He was tired. He gathered up the medals and put them out of sight in his bedroom. I promised I'd come back to see him again, and we shook on it.

It was dusk when we left. Out on the walkway we could hear Frank scraping furniture along the hall to re-fix the ramparts, and I was thinking about the protection racket I had started. 'He ought to move house,' I told Gibbon. 'Things can only get worse.'

'He's stuck,' Gibbon said. 'He's not a priority. He ought to be a refugee.'

'He will be,' I said.

Gibbon and I went down to the atrium. He shook my hand, and marched off towards the suburbs, wearing his woolly hat like a gnome. I thought I'd go and see Dan, or maybe get back to the bunker, but when I went into the stairwell again, the posse were waiting for me. Calvin and Tatham had been watching the whole time from the walkway of block C, diagonally opposite Frank Cooper's flat, with Victor posted near the foot of the stairs, and some other guys by the church. They closed in as soon as Gibbon had gone, trapping me at the bottom of the tower. They all had their hoods up.

'Hey, Merton, we got a message for you.'

Tatham gave me a push, but I'd had enough of being pushed about, and I shoved him against the brick wall.

'Don't fucking touch me, Tatham.'

'Oh yeah? Or what?'

'Just – don't. I'm not in the mood.' They jeered under their hoods, but he kept his hands off.

Then Calvin moved towards me. 'Savage says you betrayed him, man.'

'How?'

'He's been waiting for you. You said you'd come.'

'I was busy.'

'He knows what you're doing. We're watching you, man. You took that stuff to the old guy.'

'So what?'

'You shouldn't have done that. He won't like it. That old fuck is a grass. He talks to the police.'

'No he doesn't,' I said.

But Tatham interrupted. 'I'm warning you, man. You got to stay away from these blocks. You're banned. Savage says so. You don't get another warning.'

'I've got friends here,' I said. 'I've got to come and go. It's nothing to do with him.'

'It is *now*, girl-face,' Tatham said. 'You got a fucking lip. It's a good thing for you . . .' He nursed the back of his head where I'd knocked him against the wall. 'It's lucky you were a friend of Savage. Otherwise you wouldn't be getting a fucking warning.'

'It's true, man. He's vex with you,' Calvin said. 'Terry, too.'

'I need to get in and out of the estate,' I said. 'I don't stop breathing just because of Terry. He doesn't own the fucking streets.'

'He does,' Victor said. '*Will* do. Him and Savage. They're serious. They're getting into the big league. They're not pissing around with school kids any more.'

'What are they planning?' I asked.

They consulted each other with nervy looks. 'It's none of your business, man.'

'I'll find out anyway,' I said. 'It makes no difference.'

'Haig Johnson and Bhikhu,' Tatham said. 'They've made a deal with them. They're going to make this place Paul's territory. Exclusive. Nobody moves here unless he lets them.'

'Including faggots like you,' Calvin added.

'Within a month, man . . .'

'Less than that.'

'. . . we'll be the only people working here.'

'And here's little Danny,' Victor cried out, pointing into the atrium.

'Hey, nappy-head!'

'How's it going in the women's gang, Danny?'

Dan stood at the entrance, looking round. Then he moved in and stood at my side. His face was sweating, and he was wheezing slightly. 'Isn't that nice?' Tatham said. 'Two lesbians together.'

'What about Dan?' I asked. 'He lives here. He's got to come and go.'

'He's got permission from the big man. His brother protects him, right? So long as he performs.'

'That's part of the deal – despite he left with you, like a pussy.'

'But you don't have any protection, Merton,' Tatham pointed out. 'You got nothing, if you think about it. You don't have family. You don't have a gang. You don't have a body, neither. Look at you! What a pussy. You're fucked!'

'Just keep away,' Calvin said. 'It's better for everyone.'

I didn't say anything for a while, and they weren't sure how to break away. Then Tatham said, 'What's your answer, man?'

'I don't promise anything,' I said. 'Tell Terry that. I don't make any promises. There are things I have to do here. He can leave me alone.'

'You're fucking thick,' Tatham said. 'Terry's going to talk to your mum's boyfriend. Think about that, man. He's going to be best mates with him.'

'With Mike?' I moved away towards the stairs. 'Just tell him he doesn't control me.'

'Yeah, I believe you. He can have your mum beaten up any time he likes.' Tatham spat on the ground in front of me.

'Come on. There's no point talking,' Victor put in.

The boys began to back away, out into the atrium. But Tatham stayed behind. 'What have you got then, big mouth?' he asked me.

'If he leaves me alone, I'll leave him alone,' I said. 'If not, I'll fucking destroy him.'

'Oh, fucking brilliant. I'll tell him that.'

'Do,' I said. 'Tell him to back off.'

I had no plan. There was nothing I could do. But the boys couldn't be sure, and I sounded like I meant it, so they went away swearing and shouting, mooching along past the electric cross, towards block A.

I went upstairs with Dan.

'You better not come in,' he told me. 'Nothing personal. Only my mum thinks you're brother of Beelzebub.'

'How did she know that?'

'Don't joke, man. She's done her fucking nut.' And he wiped his glasses on his sweatshirt. 'What are we going to do?'

'You talk to Haig. Get protection for you and your mother.'

'No way, man!'

'You've got to,' I said. 'Go and speak to him.'

'Never happen. Haig hates our fucking mother – he won't protect her. He wants her out of here. He hates the church, all the hymns and shit. He parks down there.' He pointed to the High Street, on the other side of the block. 'With Tariq or Bhikhu, and they hoon her out. They turn the volume up so loud the walls are shaking in our flat. Then they ring the police and complain about her. They say she goes out bothering people, knocking on doors. They want her out of the block, man.'

'*Does* she knock on doors?'

'Yeah. It's her Mission of Deliverance shit. She's preaching the Word.'

'All the same,' I said, 'talk to Haig. Tell him you're in trouble. He'll help you.'

'Yeah, yeah.'

Dan's face was still quite young – he could have been fourteen or something, except that his body was so big and overweight.

'Promise you'll do it,' I said. 'And tell him about Savage. That's not a great fucking partner. Savage will fuck him over when he can.'

'Nah. He's not frightened of Savage, man. He can rub Savage out.'

'Just the same,' I said, 'you tell him what Savage is like. Tell him about Terry. He shouldn't trust them.'

By the time I got to school it was after seven. Some of the fourth years were still hanging out, shouting and fooling about in the yard. I tramped down the side of the main building into the staff car park, listened out for voices from the admin block, crept round the back of the bunker and let myself in.

For a long time I lay on the cardboard mattress, staring into the dark. I had some dope left over from the great days of the posse – a few fragments of compressed grass, mixed with fluff from the bottom of my coat pocket, and a couple of roly papers. So after a while I lit up.

Gradually my mind started floating. Mike, Savage, Terry – everything moved around me in a sort of dance. Then I started thinking about Dan. He was going to get away – he'd be working in Jamaica by the summer – and until then, Haig would protect him on the estates. His mother, the old grandfather watching TV – that was different – I knew they'd never leave. But I thought if Dan was getting out, I should do the same. Only I didn't know how.

I was meant to be planning another essay for Gibbon, all about Edward III, and I took out Trevelyan again and tried to read, but I couldn't concentrate. I was very tired. I kept remembering what Daly used to say about false consciousness: that we're all trapped; that no one can see the truth because we're deceived by the machinery of power. He always said the cure was revolution. But I was thinking, what if revolution makes no difference – what if things never really change from how they have always been, from what we can read about in history?

Then I thought, perhaps in that case there *is* no false consciousness – not the way Daly believed. Perhaps the way people used to think – about God and art, the moral law – was right: maybe it gave them knowledge of the human soul which we have never known. And I started to imagine how it would be if, instead of changing the world, I could transform my own mind – if I could find some way of thinking, some way of being that made things right. And when I imagined that, my heart felt relieved – quite physically altered, as if some pressure that had been inside me all my life had been taken away.

# 19

I found Mum in the Nelson Mandela Ward. She had a tube in her nose, and her left cheek had swollen like a pumpkin, forcing the eye shut. Mike had often given her bruises, but this time she was grotesque. Her nose was blocked and she breathed with difficulty, her mouth hanging open. There were lacerations on her forehead.

As soon as she saw me, she started talking, but her voice was quiet. 'I've learned my lesson, love. No need to give me a lecture. Here – hold my hand.'

I sat beside her. She hadn't had a bath, and her hair, when she moved her head, wafted nicotine and cooking fat.

'What lesson is that?'

'*He's* no good, Merton. He says he loves me, but he's a no-good bugger. I've had enough.' She looked away. 'I've had it with him, I'll tell you that for nothing.' She wasn't tearful. Behind the puffy aubergine face she was calm, peering at me through her good eye. 'Oh, God, I wasted my time with that one. I gave him the best years of my life: handed them over – my thirties, my fertile years. And now –' She turned her head, and the mouth twitched in a kind of smile. 'Jesus, I could do with a fag,' she wheezed. 'They won't let me smoke in here, bloody Nazis. It would do me the world of good.'

'What were you arguing about?'

'Oh, the usual. He's always jealous. Look at me, love. I'm a wreck. I look like the Titanic *after* it sank, and he thinks I'm off with God knows who. Fat chance. He's paranoid, that's what. He's off his bloody trolley. I told him that.' She chuckled. 'That's what got him going.'

'Will you prosecute him?'

She waved her hand. 'What's the point? He'll give us hell. If he stays away, that's enough for me.' She closed her eyes. 'They're making me go home,' she added. 'They need the bed.'

I avoided her face, and stared at her swollen hands. They were blood-coloured, as though they had a birthmark across them.

'I don't want to go back, Merton. Not on my own. Come with me, won't you, love? I need the company.'

'Is Mel around?'

'Oh, Mel. She's got her own troubles. Things aren't the same with Raiza and her.' She peered at me again with her open eye. 'Merton, love,' she began, but I interrupted.

'I think I'm going to be sick,' I told her.

I tried to throw up, but there was nothing in my stomach. Then I drank a lot of water and washed my face. For a while I leaned against the basin, trying to think. I had made up my mind not to live with Mum. I was going to stay where I was, with Gibbon. I couldn't go home again.

When I got back to her ward, Mum was sitting up on the bed. A nurse had come round and taken the tube out of her nose. Her face was trembling, as though she had been crying.

'I thought you weren't coming back,' she said.

'I had to get out . . .'

'I thought you'd buggered off.'

I half wanted to hold her hand, but I couldn't touch her. Everything about her was disgusting.

'Come home with me,' she said. 'Why don't you, love? He's gone. He was no good. I see that, honest I do. I know you were right.' The tears were flowing freely now from the little creases round her swollen eyes. I watched her from the foot of the bed. 'We'll live quietly. Just the two of us – like when you were little. We'll keep to ourselves.'

'I'll take you home and help you with your stuff,' I said. 'But I'm not moving back in.'

She started to wail. 'If you don't – if you won't help me now, love –'

'Shut it,' I said. 'Keep it zipped.'

'I know it's my fault . . .' She took her eyes off me, staring across the ward. 'I'll never get those years back. He stole them from me, the bastard. He took the best years of my life.'

'I'll call a cab,' I told her.

When I got back she was waiting in the armchair at the end of her ward, eyes peeping out between the pillows of purple flesh.

'Let's go,' she croaked. 'Get me outside. I'm dying for a fag.'

I took her bag and helped her up, keeping my eyes from her face, and she leaned on my arm like an old woman. All the way down the corridors there was a hospital smell of piss and dirty sheets. But when we got out into the cold air outside, I realised it was coming from her.

'I'm depressed,' she told me. 'The doctor said so. He's given me pills . . .'

'Good.'

'. . . but they don't work. *Nothing* works. It's all sixes and sevens in my head.'

'Keep taking them,' I said. 'They don't work right away.'

'Here, I need to catch my breath.' We stopped before we got into the cab, and Mum lit a cigarette, smiling as the traffic ground past.

'Bless you,' she said. She sucked in the smoke, starting to shake her head. 'Bloody marvellous.' And she added, 'I don't want to see that bastard again, love, I can tell you. Not ever.'

'It's all right. He's gone.'

'But then . . . I can't say how I'll be on my own.'

'You'll be all right.'

'It's *hard*, Merton.'

\* \* \*

Outside our house was the remains of a bonfire: solidified ashes, burnt pages, a brown-edged gutted mattress. 'What's all that?' I asked.

'You know what he's like,' she said. 'I tried to stop him. Truly.'

The sitting-room had been destroyed, furniture overturned, bookcases torn down. Even Mike's hi-fi was smashed to pieces. The only thing that had survived was the Stratocaster. I put the cushions on the sofa, and Mum took her usual place, gazing through the window into the cul-de-sac.

'They'll want to see me in this state,' she whispered, turning her back on the light. 'Noseys. Draw the curtains, won't you?'

So before I went upstairs, I covered the windows and gave her a cup of tea.

My bedroom walls were bare – the prints and posters I'd had in there since I started at the New Crosland were all torn down, leaving bright patches on the London Underground wallpaper. And the cupboard was empty. All my clothes had gone.

Next door things were the same. Mum and Mike must have started fighting in their bedroom: there was blood on the bed, and a brown trail led across the landing to the bathroom floor. Mike had taken a hammer to the bedroom, too. The mirror, and all Mum's perfume bottles had been smashed, the china objects on her chest of drawers. Her clothes were scattered on the floor.

I sat on the edge of the bed, and picked up a few things. For a while I didn't know what to do. Then I roused myself, and started trying to sort things out.

When I came down again an hour later, Mum was smoking a joint.

'What happened?' I asked. 'The place is a tip . . .'

'Mike,' she said, shaking her head. 'He took against it. I'm sorry, love. He had a clear-out.' She took a long drag. 'Don't be mad, love. I saved some of your stuff. I put it in a case when he wasn't looking.'

*   *   *

I went and found the suitcase full of my things, and got my coat.

'Don't leave,' she said. 'Just when things are calmer, like. Don't leave me, love.'

I had another look at her swollen face as I lifted the suitcase. 'Look at you,' I said. 'You look like an old woman.' She started to shake, clutching herself, and let out a little howl. 'You cry,' I told her, 'but it's true.'

'You're heartless.'

'You know I'm right.'

'Don't leave me. *Don't*, love.'

'Jesus!'

'Help me, won't you? Help me to *see*.'

'You'll see,' I said: 'Mike will be back in a month.'

'Never.'

'He'll be sending you flowers in a week, ringing every hour. In a month he'll be living here again.'

'No, love, I swear.'

'But it doesn't matter. I won't be here to see it.'

She was crying now.

'Give us a kiss, then. A goodbye kiss.' And when I went up to her she clutched me to herself. 'You've always been a cold one,' she said. She had her eyes shut tight. 'Go on, then. You take off. I don't care.'

# 20

'Your essay on Edward the third,' Gibbon said, shaking his head with a smile: 'Good. *Excellent*, I should say.' He leaned forward as he leafed through my spidery script. 'Well-informed, with a clear progression of argument . . . Believe me, you'll need to keep this up, more than this, if you're going to try for Cambridge.'

I looked at him across the chaos of his desk. 'Who said anything about Cambridge?'

'You need to *expand*, Merton. I can't explain, exactly, only perhaps *show* you what I mean.' He bit his lip. 'Knowledge is vital, of course, and you have understood that. But you have the chance to win something greater – to grow: to gain an education.'

'Not me,' I repeated.

'Why not?'

'I – Jesus! It's not going to happen. Let's forget it.'

'I don't see that.' He pierced me with his angry little eyes, and I shrugged.

'Places like that are part of the system,' I said. 'It's for posh kids with contacts and loads of money. I know how it works. Targets, and crap statistics – and people like Collins filling in forms. I'm not buying into that.'

'You have a point,' he said, leaning back and putting his hands together like he was being specially brilliant. 'Things have got pretty bureaucratic. But even so, a good university would provide a refuge for you, wouldn't it? At the very least you would have three years to read in peace. Think about that. No need to hide. Forget about the *system*. Try to think about the *meaning* of education, its real purpose.'

'Which is what?' I said. 'Sending people out to work in merchant banks?'

'No.' He shook his head back and forth. 'Absolutely not.'

For a moment he was roused, and I thought I was going to get a whole sermon. But he just leaned back again, beaming at me in his new conspiratorial way. 'Well,' he said, 'let's forget it for now.' And tossing the essay aside he got to his feet. 'That's enough for the day. We'll talk about Edward the Third tomorrow . . . Let's have a glass of wine.'

There were a couple of cardboard boxes by the filing cabinets where he started to peer about. 'The parents of one of my pupils gave me this,' he said. 'Six bottles of champagne, six of claret, and a case of white burgundy.' He produced a red bottle, holding it up to the light. 'Very generous. Their son made it to Brasenose, and they thought I swung it. But they did all the work: they moved to Normandy, and he applied to Oxford from a French school. Of course they took him.'

'There,' I said. 'I *told* you it was a con.'

But he ignored me, fussing about with glasses. He pulled the cork, dumped a giant packet of crisps in a bowl. It was only five-thirty, but he was shutting up for the day.

I swilled the red liquid around my glass; it shone under the spotlights. And when he settled down, Gibbon started explaining the difference between claret and burgundy, giving me a little lecture on the history of Bordeaux and the English wine trade, going back to the Plantagenets. I hadn't had anything to eat except the crisps, and the wine was sending fumes to my brain. But I kept listening; I wanted to understand. I didn't mind how much he told me – he could go on all night if he wanted. But at the back of my mind there was a sort of reservation, a refusal to be drawn any further. I kept thinking about university – in my mind it was a sort of giant New Crosland, with all the phoney crap going on, but with grown-ups instead of children. And I imagined all the students going to parties and hanging out together, and just being so nonchalant and annoying. I knew I'd hate it.

After a while Gibbon changed the subject. He pulled out three volumes from the bookcase – huge illustrated books on architecture and painting – and just rambled on. He showed me Greek temples with wide open colonnades, Roman ones with solid walls, the gigantic vaults of Caracalla's baths. Then he talked about the fall of the Roman Empire and the rise of the Latin Church, illustrating what he said with pictures of ancient churches. He seemed to know everything. I only had to prompt him, and he would set off on any subject, with a sort of calmness and large perspective, as though everything mattered, but nothing mattered personally to him.

While he explained things, I started looking at the honey-coloured battlements of King's College, Cambridge, in one of the books he had opened. I stared at it as I drank my wine, and I was beginning to get pretty drunk. In every way that building was the opposite of the New Crosland: it was covered with plant-life and angels and mythical beings. When we had drunk most of the bottle, I asked him about Cambridge, but for a while he just sat in silence, his eyes peering gloomily towards me, as though there was too much to say, and he didn't know where to start.

Then he gave a big sigh. 'Our universities are being destroyed.' But he was silent again.

'Well?' I said. 'An hour ago you were telling me to go to one.'

'Oh, that's different.' He waved me aside. 'You should go while you can. They won't collapse overnight.' And his eyes looked through me again. 'There are two moronic superstitions at work, when it comes to the universities,' he went on.

I thought I could hear an engine buzzing outside, and my heart expanded. But I leaned forward, trying to concentrate on Gibbon. 'On the one hand,' he said, 'there's old-fashioned utilitarian philistinism: the universities exist to produce young people for the job market, and keep the Treasury stuffed with cash. Of course it's nonsense, but everyone goes along with it. *Funding*, you see.'

The doorbell rang. There was panic inside me, a desire to fly away. 'What's moronic superstition number two?' I said. I was trying to concentrate, but my head was rotating.

'Number two is worse. Apparently the universities exist to provide more *equal outcomes*: they must act as a means of re-distributing opportunity – whatever that means. Unlike dogma number one, which at least leaves open the possibility that someone *might* go to university for the right reasons, number two is essentially totalitarian. Taken seriously, it completely destroys the conditions needed for education.'

'Is that what you told them at school?'

'I never lied,' he said wistfully, and he was about to say more, but a musical voice called out in the hall.

'Hi!' Miranda sang. 'Don't get up.' But Gibbon was already running towards her. 'I won't interrupt. I'm just dropping off my essay.' She handed him a typed manuscript.

'We'll go over it tomorrow,' Gibbon told her.

'See you then,' she said. But as she turned to leave, she came face to face with me. For a second, neither of us said anything.

'How's your head?'

'Better,' I said. 'It's fine. I –'

We spoke at the same time.

'I brought this,' she said, 'in case you were here. Sorry it's not wrapped up.'

I jumped up and took the paper bag from her. I had a sense of the space around me closing in – a sort of pressure in the atmosphere.

'Open it.'

Miranda was blushing, standing in front of me.

I looked inside. It was a stiff brown paperback: *The Complete Poems of T. S. Eliot*. And I was staring at it, moving backwards towards the wall.

'Is it okay?' she laughed. 'You look a bit freaked . . .'

'You shouldn't,' I said. 'I mean – it's . . .'

'You were saying how much you admired him.'

I hesitated. 'Yes. That's – I like him a lot . . .'

'Well, here he is – in all his depressive brilliance.'

I kept the book shut. It was very hot and my head was burning. Miranda kept looking at me with her puzzled eyebrows.

'I thought maybe we could read him together some time.'

'I – I don't know.' I was up against the wall now. An unmistakable sensation of fear and claustrophobia had taken hold of my stomach.

'Shall I write in the front?' She put her hand out for the book.

'If you want,' I said. I let her take it, but for some reason I was irritated – not just surprised, but angry. Suddenly I wanted to be down in the bunker, alone in the darkness. And I understood what kind of relationship I would have with her, if we were together – that she would have the power to observe every corner and secret passage of my mind, even though she was younger than me; that I would be opened up, laid out in front of her.

'You know, you shouldn't have,' I repeated, 'I mean, Jesus, I read masses of stuff. I've got loads of books.'

She looked up, surprised, and gave a little shrug.

'Keep it anyway,' she said. 'It's not important.' She stood back, thinking for a moment. Then she rapidly wrote something in the book, and handed it back.

After that she ignored me. I wished I could have got away. Gibbon was frowning, and he started talking to her, giving her all his attention. I took another gulp of wine and looked at what she had written.

> *To Merton –*
> *Only at nightfall, aethereal rumours*
> *Revive for a moment a broken Coriolanus . . .*
> *Miranda*

Gibbon was fussing over her like she was about to break in two. He gave her a glass of wine and made her sit down. I went on observing from the edge of the room, watching her. They started discussing some French playwright I'd never even heard of, and I could feel my anger growing all the time. I wished I'd never met her.

I kept drinking, watching Miranda. She looked too perfect, too together: the tight jeans and hippy jacket, the neat little Pumas. I hated her.

'Anyway,' she was saying, putting down the wine. 'I've barged in. I'm sorry. I ought to go.' So Gibbon followed her out into the hall. She glanced at me as she left the study, and I tried to smile, but neither of us spoke. Then I heard the front door shut.

'That wasn't kind,' Gibbon told me.

'What?'

'Couldn't you bring yourself to say thank you?'

'So what?' My head was really rocking now, I was so hot and furious.

'What's the matter with you?'

'What's the matter with *you*?' I said. 'Her, too – what are you on? She doesn't know me. She doesn't have a clue.'

'You obviously don't want her to.'

'Why should I?'

'Is it that painful?'

'You don't know what you're talking about.'

Gibbon shuffled some papers on his desk and switched off the light.

'Mrs Grant has made a shepherd's pie,' he said. 'Do you want some? It'll do you good.'

But I went to the door, ready to go upstairs. I was filled with energy again; I was suddenly clear in my mind. 'I don't want to be done good,' I said. 'I don't want to be straightened out, or educated, or tied to Miranda. I want to be what I am – I just want to stay as I am.'

'Suit yourself,' he said.

'I don't want Cambridge, either,' I added. 'I don't need new friends. I'm on my own, right? That's the way it is. It's the only way.'

Gibbon watched me without moving. 'If you say so,' he said. 'Fucking right,' I told him. And I ran upstairs.

I went to get my coat. I didn't know what I was going to do. I took Miranda's card – *Asia*, 1946 – slipped it inside the cover of the *Complete Eliot*, shoving it in my coat pocket. And I ran out of the house.

Out on the streets it was cold, and I started jogging along, heading for the estates. The road was marked out by street-lights emitting orange light. They stretched out ahead of me all the way to Dante Park, an area of pitch-black before the towers and illuminated walkways of the estates. I thought maybe I would find Tess or Emily. I wanted to get my head clear by seeing them again.

I left the suburbs and sprinted across the park. Then I stood waiting by the railings, a hundred yards from the garage, trying to see if the boys were around, or if the place was full of cops. But there was nobody on the approach roads, and the atrium was almost empty. The silver cross shone out in the middle of the air, directly ahead of me. On each side of it, and in the background, were the muted lights of three blocks. Drum music was playing somewhere nearby. Otherwise I couldn't hear a thing.

I walked on to the estate, making my way round by the upper walkways. Then I turned away from the church, away from Dan's flat and the old man, towards block D and the second section of the estate, coming to a stop on the corner.

From the top floor I could see the dealers and tarts, moving about as usual on the little patch of grassland by the bollards. Tess and Emily were there, too – I saw them right away. And all at once, for the first time in ages, I knew what I wanted. I ran down the back stairs to the ground floor.

*   *   *

'Hi, Merton,' Em said.

Tess was shivering, fidgeting her hands about. Her hair seemed less red than it used to be. 'You got some stuff?' she sniffed.

'Nothing.'

'Bastard,' they said together.

'Where've you been?' Em examined me nervously.

'Around.' I said. 'How's business?'

'No one tonight.' Tess was really shaking in the cold.

'You should keep away,' Em told me. 'Paul's not happy.'

'I'm not bothering him.'

'He says you betrayed him,' Tess put in.

'He won't touch me,' I said. And I went up and put out a hand towards her. 'Anyway, it doesn't matter about Paul. I came to see you.'

For a moment, Tess stopped rubbing herself.

'Thanks,' she shivered, briefly looking up at me. Then I took hold of her belt-buckle and pulled her towards me, starting to touch her face with my other hand. Her pupils were tiny, despite the dark, and her skin had sunk – there was no life in it.

'Do you want to come home?' she said. She quickly captured my fingers in her hand, and pressed them carefully. 'Mel's bunked off. Raiza, too. They started fighting. I don't know where they've gone. I've got the place to myself.'

'What about me?' Em said.

'Come, too,' Tess told her. 'There's nothing happening here.'

At Tess's house I went upstairs and checked the old man's revolver under her bedroom floor. Then I had a shower and put on some clothes of Raiza's.

When I went down again, the girls were smoking a giant spliff.

'You know Mike's trying to get back with your mum?' Tess said.

'I don't care,' I told her.

'He comes round with roses the whole time – from the cash

and carry – piles of them wrapped in plastic. Then he lies outside the front door, shouting through the letter-box.'

'Let's not talk about it,' I said. 'I've left. I'm on my own.'

'Mel says your mum is going to let him in. She says she's bound to. She gets pissed and starts crying whenever she comes round here . . .'

I went up to her and put my hand hard over her mouth. There was a rapid look of fear in her eyes, as if I was going to thump her. But I only rocked her head back and forth, and pushed her down on the sofa. She looked up at me with her grey face.

'What do you want to do?' she asked.

'I don't know,' I said. 'Just don't say anything.'

Em came up to us, pulling off her coat. She had closed the curtains and was starting to giggle. 'I won't say anything, either,' she said. 'Not a word.' And she leaned over the sofa next to Tess.

'I've got an idea,' Tess announced.

She whispered something to Em, and started to search through a stack of Mel's CDs. And she put on Ella Fitzgerald. Meanwhile Em lit candles and dimmed the lights. Then she went to get her soccer bag from the hall, and pulled out a riding whip, whistling it through the air.

'Watch,' Tess said. 'Don't move.'

I sat on the sofa and took a long drag of the reefer. Em and Tess started their act, dancing back and forth in front of me. Em was moving like a snake, wriggling out of her white school shirt with its stripy tie. Then she took hold of Tess's T-shirt, slowly pulling it off. 'Hold me,' she told her. And they danced together in their bras.

I sat smoking, my mind filled with the sound of Ella Fitzgerald singing down a tunnel of white noise, and I began to calm down. All thoughts of Gibbon and Cambridge, Miranda, grew dark and lost their force. For a long time I was at peace. The house, the candlelight, even the girls with their weird dancing all seemed so comforting. And as I watched the girls they started to kiss each other: necks, ears, stomachs, lips. The blood surged through me, melting my fingers and feet. Everything was growing spongy and gentle, everything was giving way. And the girls were beautiful by that time, really wonderful. But I made myself wait. They were still in their bras and stockings, their bodies rubbing against each other, bending, rocking, spinning smoothly to the music. For ages I just gazed at them.

Then on an impulse I lunged forward, grabbed Tess violently by the wrist, and marched her upstairs. I pushed her down on the double bed, making her lie flat with her eyes closed, while I pulled off Raiza's tracksuit. Em brought the music machine and the candles upstairs, and lit some incense. Then Tess and I screwed like we used to when we were children, while Ella Fitzgerald sang 'Summertime', and Em stroked my hair, or ran her fingers up and down my back.

Later Tess lay on the mattress, quietly humming and laughing, smoking another joint. Em started caressing me again. 'I'll give you a blow-job,' she said. 'Just lie down.'

But everything started to change. It wasn't working any more. By midnight I was getting edgy. All sorts of thoughts were coming back to me – remorseless, bitter thoughts. Nothing made sense. I smoked some more, but I was beginning to panic. And I was so tired, too – not physically tired, but tired in my mind – and I couldn't remember why I had gone looking for Tess and Em in the first place, or what I was going to do next.

I became anxious about a million things. I started to worry about Dan, about the old man – what the posse would do to them. I sat up in fright. I imagined Mike breaking down the door of my mother's house. Then I saw myself alone in the bunker – but I was old, much too old to be at school. I was trapped in there because I wasn't allowed on the streets.

The girls fell asleep, but my mind kept racing. In the end, at about five in the morning, I had another shower and put my suit back on. Tess woke as I was going down the stairs.

'What are you doing?' she whispered.

'I don't know. I want to get some drugs.'

'We'll go tomorrow.'

'No, I want to get out. I'll see you later.' And I opened the front door.

My coat was heavy. I had the *Complete Eliot* bulging in the pocket. Tess was saying something at the top of the stairs, but I couldn't hear. It was very cold outside; it pricked my eyes. I pulled up my collar, and started running.

# 21

I didn't even look at Mum's house, although it was right opposite Mel and Raiza's place. I just ran off through the darkness, keeping away from the estates, and getting to school the long way, along the High Street. But instead of going down to the bunker, I waited outside Anna's café until she came to open up.

I thought maybe I'd feel better when I saw her, but Anna was angry with me because I hadn't rung, and although she kept standing over me, leaning her arse against the next table, I couldn't make myself chat her up. I was scared. I kept shaking, my hands and my feet trembling from the grass. And my imagination had cast a sort of twilight around me. I took her hand but said nothing, and in the end she pulled away. 'You're stoned, for God's sake,' she said in a bored voice. 'Have some breakfast.'

I began to feel less terrified when I had eaten, and after a while I pulled T. S. Eliot from my coat pocket, and opened it for the first time. For a couple of hours, sitting in the brown and orange café, I recited Prufrock silently to myself again and again, going over those brief, tight, compulsive rhythms till I almost knew them by heart. It didn't make me feel any better, though. As the dope wore off, I just felt more exposed – as though a whole layer of rubber armour had been taken from me. Eventually I couldn't even read. I was sitting in the café with my head on the table, my whole body trembling inside. So I left some money for Anna, and went away.

In the bunker I lay down on the cardboard mattress. The more sober I became, the worse I felt. I remembered all sorts of things – memories from childhood, from my first days at the

New Crosland, the burglary, meeting Gibbon. Thoughts crowded my mind, but they all seemed so senseless. Then I started thinking about Miranda. Always before, when I had fantasised about her, I had imagined trying to get her attention, forcing her to notice me. I had always pictured her turning away, not looking at me, driving off on her red bike. But now it was the other way round, and I had actually run away from her. I lay in the dust without moving, the reek of books all around me, trying to work out why I had done that. I was full of random, frustrated feelings. My emotions were rising in my throat, choking me, shaking me. I wanted to talk to Miranda – to explain things, to tell her everything. I wanted to know what she really thought; if there was somebody there inside her, if she was real, if she would actually answer me.

I closed my eyes, trying to stay in control, putting my hands to my face. But there was so much pressure in my stomach, in my whole body, and when I turned on my side and sat up, leaning against the hot-water pipes, I started to cry. It ambushed me; I couldn't stop it. I never expected anything like that. I cried for about an hour.

I didn't think I could see her feeling the way I did. Even after I stopped crying I was still confused. Eventually I fell asleep, and then, in the late afternoon, I wrote Miranda a letter. I didn't want to say too much at first; I didn't know how she was going to react. So to start with I just thanked her for Eliot, and said I'd been reading him all morning. Then I told her I was sorry I hadn't said anything when she gave it to me, but that was probably because I was taken by surprise, and also because I really wanted to say so much to her – much more than I had said to anyone, and there seemed no way of doing that.

Then I came right out with it. 'I have this idea I could tell you anything,' I wrote; 'that whatever I said, you'd understand, even if I hardly understood it myself. Do you believe that? I have to see you again. It's very urgent. We must go away; I want to take you somewhere – Greece, Italy – somewhere far away.'

Miranda lived in a little town, on a street of Victorian semis. It wasn't in the country, exactly, but there were some fields nearby; you could see them at the end of her road. The cab driver waited for me by Miranda's front door. I was just going to post my letter and get away, so that she could read it on her own. But I had to go into the porch to put it through the door, and there was this little girl standing there, watching me from the other side of the glass.

'Who are you?' she said.

'I'm a friend of your sister's,' I told her.

'Which one?'

'Is someone at the door?' a woman's voice called out. She had a French accent.

'I'm just delivering a letter,' I told the girl. 'Can you give this to Miranda?'

She nodded, watching me carefully. I handed it to her.

'Who ease it, Liam?' the French woman asked.

Then a young boy arrived. 'How do you do?' he said. He offered me his hand. 'I'm Liam Vaughan.'

'Merton,' I told him.

'He's called Merton,' the little girl sang out.

'*Merton?*' Then Mrs Vaughan came padding along to join us. She was wearing an apron, and she had a knife in her hand. 'What do you want?' she asked abruptly.

'I – I'm sorry to disturb you,' I said. 'I'm just delivering a letter for Miranda. I've got to go. The taxi's waiting.'

'I'll see she gets it,' the mother said. And she closed the door.

I told the taxi driver to leave me in the next street. I didn't have enough money for the return journey, and it wasn't so far. Now that I knew the way, I could easily walk back to Gibbon's. But I didn't go anywhere at first. As soon as I stood alone on the pavement, I wished I hadn't delivered the letter. There was a storm in my mind. I was certain Miranda would think I was an idiot. For ages I wandered about the town, regretting everything. I began thinking of ways I could hide from her, and Gibbon too. After an hour I could hardly even keep walking. My whole body was heavy; I just felt so useless. I stood like that for a long time by the war memorial, totally depressed. But when the clock struck ten, I decided to go back.

The lights had gone off at the front, so I made my way in the darkness along the garden path, through a wooden door that led to a little yard with the dustbins. The kitchen was almost dark, and I peered inside. There was nobody there except a black cat with a white face, which miaowed at me. Someone was playing the violin in another room. I moved towards the shadows at the back of the garden and stood under a tree to survey the house. There was a man working at a computer at an upstairs window. And in the room above him, in a dormer window, I caught sight of Miranda, standing in her nightshirt by a chest of drawers.

The violin stopped, and after a while the father got up from his computer and went away. I picked up a handful of gravel, and started throwing it at Miranda's window. But she didn't look out and I wasn't sure if I was hitting the glass. So after a while I came into the open, standing in the middle of the lawn, and went on throwing pebbles as hard as I could. In the end I ran out of stones, and she still hadn't looked. So I just started shouting, 'Miranda! Miranda!' and finally she opened the window.

'Jesus, Merton, what are you doing?'

'I came to see you,' I said. 'Didn't you get my letter? We're going away together.'

'I can't hear you.'

'We're going to run away.'

She shook her head.

'Come downstairs,' I urged.

'Stop shouting,' she whispered. 'Wait by the kitchen.'

'What are you doing?' Miranda demanded. 'I thought you left hours ago.'

'I waited,' I said. 'I wanted to see you.' She looked at me through the kitchen window. I could hardly see her in the dark.

'I read your letter,' she said, and her voice was calm, but she sounded very cautious.

'So, do think I'm an idiot?'

'Of course not.'

'I've been thinking I probably I shouldn't have said all that.'

'Was it true?'

'What do you think?'

'How should I know?'

'It's true . . . look, this is a bit weird. Can't you turn on a light?'

'No. Papa will see.'

'Let me in, then.'

'It's locked. Anyway, I think this is rather good. You're so unruly and erratic. We'll talk through the window.' She opened it as much as she could, and crouched on the ledge.

'Give me your hand,' I told her.

'No. I'm trying to think. What are you doing here?'

'Like I said in the letter: we're going away together.'

She shook her head with her V-shaped frown, but I could see her blushing in the dark. 'Don't be in such a hurry.'

'Don't you want to come?'

'What kind of question is that? I can't just go away, even if I wanted to – which I don't.'

'That's natural,' I said. 'You're thinking it over.'

'No I'm not.'

'Yes you are. It's obvious. You keep looking down.'

'So?'

'It's a sign. If you were trying to remember you'd look up.

But you're thinking about the future, so you're looking down.'

'That's ridiculous. You know perfectly well I can't come with you. I've got loads of exams. I've got my piano grade eight next month . . .'

'Never mind all that.'

'Besides,' she said, 'I hardly know you.'

'Well *exactly*. This is your chance. Go on, give me your hand.'

So she sighed, putting her hand through the open window.

I pressed it in mine, feeling the size of each of her fingers. 'I've wanted to do this for a long time,' I said. 'Only at first I didn't realise, and later on it seemed impossible. But it doesn't seem so difficult now.'

'I liked your letter,' she said quietly, still looking down. 'I mean, it was the most completely unexpected thing that's ever happened. I thought you hated me.'

'So,' I said, suddenly feeling sick again. 'What about you?'

'I – I don't know,' she said slowly. 'What you wrote – I liked reading it, but it confuses me, too.'

I squeezed her hand. 'I wish I could touch your face,' I said.

'I do – I do have feelings for you,' she went on. 'But it's all been so sudden. A day ago you virtually refused to talk to me.'

'I know.'

'Couldn't we just be friends for a while?'

I didn't say anything, and she looked up. Then she laughed. 'Look at you, with your weird clothes –'

'Don't you like my suit?'

'And I know you committed some crime. It's obvious. That's how you met James. But we've never even *talked* about that, even though I asked you. Think about it from my point of view, Merton. I mean – where did you come from? You frighten me, you know.'

'I frighten *you*? That's nothing. How do you think I feel? I feel positively sick. I feel terrible when I'm with you. Did you know that?'

'Er, no. But thank you.'

'No, I mean it. Don't I make *you* sick?'

'Not at all,' she said.

'Not even slightly?'

'Well,' she smiled, 'perhaps a bit queasy.'

'I should hope so.' I started to put her hand to my lips.

'Merton, wait,' she said. 'Let me have my hand back.'

So I let go, but then, just for a moment before she pulled it inside, she took my hand and squeezed it as hard as she could. 'We can talk tomorrow,' she announced. 'In the daytime. Okay?'

'All right,' I said. 'I won't go away. I'll sleep in the garden.'

'Don't even *say* it. Go home, for God's sake. Ring me tomorrow. Wait. I know, come back on Saturday. Everyone will be at Liam's concert.'

'Saturday?'

'In the afternoon.'

'Okay,' I said.

'But ring,' she said.

And I watched as she locked the window, and disappeared in the dark.

# 22

On Saturday afternoon I went back to Miranda's house, carrying a bunch of red tulips. She opened the door herself, and stood in front of me. She was smiling cautiously, like she didn't know exactly who I was, and for a moment we waited without moving. Then she had a quick nervous breakdown about the flowers, saying how beautiful they were. She had this short red skirt on, thick stockings, knee boots. I kissed her on the cheek, but we immediately took hold of each other, standing in the hall while I smelt her hair and squeezed her arse as hard as I could, trying not to drop the tulips. Finally we fell on to a big, low sofa in the sitting-room, surrounded by musical manuscripts, and I kissed her for the first time. She went bright red, and she would have gone on kissing for hours, but I pulled away to examine her face. Then I twisted her hair in my hands, and pinned her wrists to the cushion above her head.

I thought we'd definitely have sex right away, but after a while Miranda said we should go for a walk before it got dark. And in the end she rolled on to the floor with a thud, standing up to pull me to my feet.

We walked across the fields beyond her house, down to the river. It was a bright day, very cold, and the sun was already near the horizon. For half an hour everything was green and golden, the surface of the river shining at us, as though there was a huge light under the water.

'What are you doing in the summer?' Miranda said, turning to me. 'After the exams?'

'I don't know.'

She looked down at the gravel path. 'I thought we could go away somewhere,' she suggested. 'To Devon, maybe.'

'What's in Devon?'

'The sea. It's very wild – you'd like it. I have an uncle who lives there. There's a cottage he lets us use.' She looked me in the eyes.

'Devon?' I said. 'Why not?' And she smiled and took my hand. 'Did you know,' I asked her, 'that your eyes are very beautiful, very big, and are basically the colour of engine oil?'

'Thank you. That's – that's very poetic.'

'So can we go home now and have sex?' I asked, but she ignored me.

'We'll go away in the summer,' she said slowly, like she was planning it all. 'Until then, we're still getting to know each other. We'll take it slowly.'

'Really?' I said. 'You know that's pretty risky. You might meet someone else, fall in love with them. Think of the regrets in later life.'

'I might get to know *you* better,' she answered.

'Exactly. You might hate me in a month's time.'

'I might. But at least I'll *know* you.' And she stepped away to look at me. 'Okay,' she said. 'Tell me about it. Tell me about your secret life of crime.'

After that we talked about things. I described the bunker to her, the posse, and how Gibbon had started teaching me. I didn't confess the burglary completely; I just said I used to be involved in a gang, and we did some bad things, but now I had left. It made me feel strange, though; I wished I hadn't told her. We kissed again when the sun was going down, but this time I didn't feel so crazy about her. She knew too much about me, and I wanted to get away.

When we got back to the house, Miranda made tea and we sat at the wooden table with our mugs and a pile of biscuits. There were books all over the house – even in the kitchen – and I started pulling out these little volumes of Spanish poetry.

'Can you read this?' I said.

So she took the book over to the window, and started reading this strange, rhythmic poem, all in Spanish. As her voice rose and fell, I began to think of a thousand things. I didn't understand a word, but still it got to me. After a while she showed me the translation in another book, and then we read together, choosing poems randomly, rummaging through different books – Pablo Neruda, Paz, Lorca, St John of the Cross.

'. . . *in darkness by the secret stair,*' Miranda said, '*burning with Love's desire, oh happy adventure! Oh night more loving than the dawn . . . on my flowering breast He fell in deep slumber, and I caressed Him, cooled by the breath of cedars . . .*'

'*Oh girl among the roses,*' I replied: '*oh pressure of doves, oh jail of fish and rose-bushes – your soul is a bottle of thirsting salt . . .*'

'Yes,' Miranda said. 'A bottle of salt.' She pushed a thick rope of hair away from her face. 'This is my favourite Neruda poem. Listen. *And it was in that age, poetry arrived – in search of me. I do not know, I do not know where it came from . . . – I don't know how or when . . . They were not voices – they were not words, nor silence – but from a street I was summoned – from the branches of night . . . or returning alone – there I was, without a face. And it touched me.*'

'There,' I said, 'they're talking about the same thing. They are called in secret; hijacked by some strange desire – by some impulse that makes no sense . . .'

'It's like love,' Miranda said. 'It makes no sense, but you have to accept it.'

'But what if it leads nowhere? Then you'd feel like an idiot, wouldn't you, listening to voices.'

She put the book down and took my hands across the table.

'Promise me something?' she said.

'Perhaps.'

'Promise you won't sabotage yourself.'

'What do you mean?'

'I mean, what are you going to do when you can't go to your bunker any more?'

'I'm going to Devon with you, remember?'

'No. After that. Your whole life.'

I shrugged. 'There's always drug-dealing.'

'Very funny, Merton.' And she dropped my hands.

I didn't tell Miranda, but I started thinking about Cambridge after that. For the next two weeks we kept seeing each other at Gibbon's place, or I went over to Miranda's house. We used to go for walks, and if it was raining we sat in the café at the bookshop near her street. I got her to explain things to me – the way the colleges worked at Cambridge, the whole admissions system, the sort of people who went there. She had friends who were already at Oxford, and she used to spend weekends with them, so she described what they talked about and the kind of life they had. But I didn't want her to think I was getting too interested, so most of the time we talked about other things.

One Saturday, Miranda drove us out into the countryside in her mother's clapped-out Mini. She wanted to show me these old villages in the woods north of the motorway, and she had made a picnic – sandwiches, apples, bars of chocolate, even a bottle of wine. We found a field next to a churchyard where we could sit near some oak trees, and we spent the whole afternoon there in the cold sunshine. I thought she would definitely let me screw her then – there was nobody around, and she kept kissing my forehead, or holding hands. I had an erection for about five hours. But she still said she wanted to get to know me more, and in the end all we did was lie by the trees next to a barbed wire fence, talking all afternoon.

There were some cows in the next meadow, but our field was completely wild, as though the grass had been left to grow all year. The air under the trees stank of damp earth, and all sorts of big flies flew around us, landing on our faces or eating the food. Miranda asked me to tell her more about my childhood, about the New Crosland and the posse. She tried to get me to speak about Cambridge, too – to turn my mind to something new. But I didn't feel like it. Instead, I kept looking at the little houses on the other side of the graveyard, the church tower, the triangle of village green, and all the copper-coloured trees on the hills beyond. I didn't tell Miranda, but I was imagining what it would be like to live with her in a place like that, what kind of life we would have. And even though it was impossible, I felt as though I had always been looking for that meadow, that churchyard; that I had been there before, a long time ago, and had half-remembered it all my life; so that now, finding it again, I would never want to leave.

When it started getting dark and we had finished the wine – just before we went back to the car – we started kissing. I kept biting Miranda's lips and pressing her stomach and breasts, and she was clutching my hair, quietly saying my name again and again. I didn't want to go anywhere. I just wanted to stay in the field, holding her and looking at her face. Nothing mattered apart from that. I didn't care what happened in the rest of the world.


Back in the bunker, trying to do some work for Gibbon, I couldn't stop thinking about Miranda. But I didn't go to see her the next day. All of Sunday I concentrated on writing another essay, this time about the English Civil Wars. I wanted to see if I could do something which was good enough for Cambridge, and right from the start, when I started planning it, I tried to argue the exact opposite of what we were supposed to believe: that the civil war was not produced by class war or material forces, but most of all by the power of ideas – by doctrines, beliefs, the imagination. I talked about religion, the dream of political freedom, the king's sacred duty. And in my notes it was all ridiculously clear. For a moment, before I started writing, the pattern of those events assumed a quite clear shape at the horizon of my mind – looming and solid, like a vast cathedral. But when I tried to explain it in the essay, my ideas burst out in every direction, and all I had produced by the evening was fifteen pages of digressions about Anglicanism and Parliament, reaching no conclusion. I was embarrassed, but it was too late to start again.

I slept in the bunker that night, waking with a shock early on Monday morning, thinking about Cambridge. It was in my head already – obsessively, as though I had been dreaming about it all night. The image of King's College Chapel was fixed in my imagination, and I saw myself standing there – on the meadows nearby, by a river, gazing towards the chapel.

Before anyone had come to school, I gathered my essay together and ran to Gibbon's house. But I had left my key behind. I had to wait in the mist until Mrs Grant came down. Then, when Gibbon appeared, he was still in his dressing-gown, scratchy and hung-over, rubbing his head.

'I want to apply for Cambridge,' I said.

He snorted, pulling the fridge door open, ignoring me. The light of it made him wince.

'Here, I've written an essay.'

'Later, *later*.'

'I thought you'd be pleased.'

'*Timing*,' he sighed.

'Is it too late?'

He hugged himself, searching the shining interior. 'Probably.'

He concentrated on his coffee and toast for the next ten minutes, sitting hunched over the papers.

'This is rubbish,' he said finally, chucking the newspaper on the floor. 'Perfect rubbish. I don't know why I bother to get it. All right. What's caused this belated enthusiasm for university?'

'Here.' I pushed the essay towards him on the table, and he read the title, giving another snort.

'I've been thinking it over,' I said. 'I want to try.'

'Well, it's probably a waste of time,' he said, going to the kettle.

'Even so. It can't do any harm.'

'*Can't* it? I don't see why not.' And he went off with his mug of coffee, slamming a door upstairs. I could hear the bath filling.

'These forms are getting more grotesque by the year.' Gibbon spread the papers on his desk in front of us. 'They want to know where your parents went to school, how much they earn, how many houses they have . . . We're living in a Maoist state.'

'What if I don't know?'

'I suppose that's all right. They can't check the information, anyway. It's pure fraudulence. Let's get it over with.'

The forms were son of Collins: everything had its box.

'They want to know how well the New Crosland does in public exams. You'll have to ask Daly or Collins that one.'

'I'll talk to Ms Tooley,' I said.

'And the league tables. All that. Here, you see?'

'I'll do it today.'

'The form needs to be handed in – well,' – he looked at his watch – 'tomorrow, if you can manage it. Wednesday by five-thirty otherwise. I've got appointments all day tomorrow *and* Wednesday,' he said. 'Otherwise I'd offer to take you there myself. You'll have to go in person. The post won't deliver in time.'

'That's okay.'

'And you'll have to finish filling it in. Give it some time. Here – pay attention: these sections – social background for our political commissars.'

I ran back to school avoiding the estates, and flew across the yard. The mist had cleared. I marched along the bright Perspex corridors.

In the admin block I could hear Ms Tooley tapping on the computer. The doors were all open – the door to Mr Collins' office and to hers – but I made it right down the passage before he called out after me.

'Merton. Come here, please.'

'Can I just hand this in?'

'No. I have addressed you directly. Come in and close the door.'

So I went in, carrying the form.

'May I see that?'

'It's nothing.'

He held out his hand and I gave it to him. Then he sat down, reading it through. He didn't speak at first.

'Well, this is – interesting, I must say . . . It, er, pays to aim *high*, Merton. I commend your ambition.' He let out a little hiss of air. '*Cambridge*! I can't argue with that.' Then he thumped his hand on the form and suddenly stopped smiling. 'But why are you producing the form at this late stage? There's been no consultation with the school staff – I must say I find it all highly irregular . . .'

'I was going to discuss it as soon as . . .' I shrugged.

'Well?'

'As soon as I'd filled it in. I don't know. I just wanted to think about it.'

'I see.'

He flicked the form over again, looking it up and down.

'There are a few preliminary difficulties. For example, you're still in breach of your Community Service Order. This morning you were absent from assembly. I understand there may be good reasons – family reasons . . .' He looked at the scar on my forehead.

'It's okay,' I told him. 'I'm fine.'

'Would you like to seek counselling inside the school system?'

'No, thank you.'

'You should think about it. Many people find it enormously valuable . . .' The form was right there on the desk in front of him. I could have snatched it and run. But I waited.

'I'm okay,' I said.

'If you accepted some help, it would be much easier for us to guide you – to find you a place at the right university.' He was sweating: the side of his face, under the arms of his glasses, was watery and bright.

'Would it help with the application?'

'It will demonstrate that you are trying to overcome a difficult background.'

'I'll talk to Ms Tooley about it.'

'Good.'

'Can I have the form back?' I asked.

'I'll need to read it over.'

'It has to be in by Wednesday night.'

He leaned forward, gazing at me.

'I should explain something to you, Merton, about the school's strategy for higher education. How can I put it?' He cleared his throat. 'When it comes to higher education applications – colleges, universities – we aim to keep a degree of overall control. We want to ensure the maximum number of successful candidates in each category.'

'I understand.'

He sat back, dropping my form on the desk.

'You don't want me to apply to Cambridge.'

He shook his head. 'I would never say that.'

'In case I don't get in?'

'It's not a question of personal esteem. But I do think there are other courses you would benefit from much more.'

'Like?'

'Well, you say you want to study history. Would it perhaps be more realistic to try for a course with stronger *practical* application?' He smiled his weak smile. 'I prefer to guide our candidates towards vocational subjects. You could consider media studies, for example – very exciting, very current. Or business science. There's advertising, communication studies, business decision analysis, public service sciences . . . I'll put your data on the computer, and see what it suggests. Meanwhile, you give it some thought, too. I recommend you set up a personalised search engine – an intelligent agent, dedicated to your preferences . . .'

I stood up, and Collins adjusted his specs. 'If you approach this application cooperatively, Merton, I'll see what I can do about the breaches in your Community Service Order. I'll discuss your ideas with Mr Daly, too. He's taken charge of university admissions. We'll think it through. Now you should rejoin your class.'

# 23

The freckles had exploded on Ms Tooley's face. I stood watching from the door while she surveyed her nails and straightened her skirt, checking her reflection on the blank computer screen.

'Hello, Rachel,' I said.

'What is it?' she snapped. She blushed from her shoulders upwards.

'Do you think I could have a headache pill?'

'Shouldn't you be in class?'

'It's a free period.'

'Sit down,' she sighed. 'I'll get you something.'

As soon as she was out of the room, I started rummaging through the stationery cupboards. There were boxes of paper-work, circulars from the ministry. In the second cupboard I found the school's confidential correspondence with social workers, doctors and parents. And in the drawers in Ms Tooley's desk I discovered her letters and photographs, the school insurance documents, petty cash.

'What the hell are you doing?'

'Nothing.'

'What do mean, nothing?'

'I'm not stealing anything.'

'You shouldn't be looking in there.'

The freckles had dispersed. Her face was pale stone. I got up from the rotating chair.

'You're no better than the other kids in this dump,' she said, throwing down the pills she had brought me. 'Get pissed, get stoned, lie, *steal . . .*'

'I wasn't stealing,' I interrupted. 'I was looking for the university application forms. I need one.'

'Well, why didn't you *say* so, idiot?' She opened a box I hadn't searched. 'How many do you want?' She handed me a sheaf of papers.

'Thank you. And I needed these.' I stooped to pick up the pills. 'I wasn't lying.'

'Take them and go.'

Her face was filled with blood again, her shoulders, too. Even her forehead was pink, and her nipples reasserted themselves through her pullover.

'Thank you.' I didn't move. 'I —'

'Just go.'

'You're wonderful,' I told her.

'Cut it out.'

'No. I really think, in another life, we might have been happy together.'

'Go, before I file a report against you.'

'You wouldn't do that.'

'Don't kid yourself.'


I didn't go far. I sat in an empty classroom on the second floor and filled in the application, stashing the spares in my coat pocket. I gave them Gibbon's address for all correspondence. Then I hid the completed form in a textbook, and carried it back to Ms Tooley's office. Mr Collins had gone, but she wasn't alone. Danny was sitting in the office, with the First Aid box open on the desk. One of his eyes was weeping. He was hunched over her desk, mumbling and swearing, and Ms Tooley kept asking what had happened. His mouth and forehead were bleeding.

'You ought to go home,' Rachel she told him. 'I can arrange a doctor's appointment, but it won't be today.'

'I don't need a fucking appointment,' Danny wailed. 'There's nothing wrong. I just want to get away from this shit.'

'This will hurt,' she told him. The office filled with the smell of TCP.

'Hey, Dan. What's happening?'

'Fuck you. *Shit* that hurts.'

'You're friends, aren't you?' Ms Tooley asked.

'*Were*,' Dan said.

'Could you take Dan home, Merton? Make sure he gets back safely. I've rung his mother, but there's no answer.'

'Will you do me a favour,' I said, 'if I take Danny home?'

'*What?*'

'This has to be signed by Collins.' I gave her the form. 'Reg Daly, too. They both have to see it.'

'I'll put it with the others.'

'Only, Collins doesn't want me to apply for this university.'

She glanced at the paper. 'Well I'm not surprised. Cambridge, Merton?'

'Why not?'

'We've never done that before.'

'Could you get him to sign it? Maybe when he's not sure what he's signing.'

'That would be dishonest.'

'Only if it was deliberate.'

She smiled, but checked herself. 'Why should I help?'

'Because we're made for each other. We're going to fly to the Bahamas . . .'

'Try again.' Her face flushed, and she pushed a strand of ginger frizz behind her ear.

'You know this school is a shit-hole.'

'So?'

'So, what difference does it make if you help me out? It's not against the law to apply to a decent university.'

'Are you sure?' She squeezed her lower lip and sighed. 'Go on then. Give Dan a hand. I'll see what I can do.'

*　*　*

224

At first Dan wouldn't talk to me. He was ashamed because his own brother had got him beaten up. He walked along the edge of the yard in the shadow, and put his hood up. Then he started to explain.

Victor and Terry had grabbed him on his way to school, marched him to the garage, tied him to a chair. They'd yelled at him, punched him, hit him with truncheons.

'They're jumping,' he said; 'they're going mad.'

'Why?'

'I don't know. Something went wrong. They kept asking if I was dealing on block D. I said, I'm not fucking dealing. I never dealt – they know that. But some of their weapons got stolen, their new machineguns. They think it was me and you. They think we're trying to do some deal of our own.'

We were walking along the High Street, and Danny was moving faster. He kept his hood up all the way.

'Who's they?' I asked.

'*Them*. The boys. Savage, Terry – all of them. They're going to start wasting all the people who don't pay them. They're wrapping up the estates.'

'Here comes the Revolution,' I said.

'The Emancipation. That's what they call it. My brother's helping them. They're going to run the estate for him. It's all subcontracted to The Cannon Park Safety Committee.'

'What the fuck is that?'

'That's the posse, man. That's what I'm telling you. It's the new name for the posse.'

We walked across the atrium to B block. There was nobody on the walkways. Most of the windows on the ground floor had been boarded up, the pot plants smashed, soil scattered about. Somebody had laid a pile of turds in the stairwell, right by the rubbish chute.

On the fourth floor, where Dan's mother lived, the old alcoholic woman was standing on the narrow corridor ahead of us, swollen shopping bags in her hands.

'You going to fuck *her*, man?' Danny said. 'She's your kind of woman.'

'Could do,' I said. 'You can learn a lot from an older woman. Someone with experience.'

'Go on, then. Ask her for a blow-job. I dare you.'

'Excuse me,' I said to the old woman. 'My friend has a question for you.'

'Shut the fuck up,' Dan whispered, pulling at my arm. 'Don't let her near me, man.'

'He's a little shy, but he was wondering if you would be kind enough to commit an act of fellatio with him . . .'

'Fuck you, Merton!' Dan pulled me away. But he smiled for the first time.

'What're *you* doing here?' Dan's mother stood in the door, blocking my way.

'They told him to bring me,' Dan whispered.

'I just came by,' I said. 'I'll be going.'

'What kind of trouble are you in, Daniel Johnson? Look at your face, child. Did you do this, Merton?'

'Savage,' Dan said.

'This *is* Savage – far as I'm concerned.'

'No, Mum . . .'

She stepped back from the threshold. 'You come in here, Daniel. I'm going to clean up those wounds.'

'I should go,' I repeated.

But Mrs Johnson looked at me again. 'You didn't have nothing to do with this?'

I shook my head.

'You want a cup of tea?' I could see the dark little room behind her. 'You come in,' she said. 'I'll fix you a cup. We'll say a prayer together.'

'*Mum*!' Dan protested, and he turned to me. 'She's so fucking embarrassing.'

'Don't use that language, Daniel. You're as bad as your brother.'

'I – I'd better get back to school,' I said.

'You come *in*,' she insisted. So I stepped into their room. 'Father,' she announced. Her accent was much stronger when she talked to him: she pronounced it *fader*. 'This is Daniel's friend Merton. You remember him – tell me you do.' Dan's grandfather turned his thin face in my direction, rested his eyes on me without altering his expression, and looked back at the blank TV.

I sat while she made a fuss about Dan's wounds. There on the table, and on the shelf above the electric fire, were the old photographs I remembered – family photos from Jamaica, children in their Sunday best on veranda chairs, or bays of bright water with whitewashed churches. And there was Dan's uncle, dressed in shorts and a tropical shirt with his boat – the same photo Dan used to carry around.

The old man began to snore in his armchair, and Dan's mother started humming in competition. 'Here,' she said, handing me a cup. 'Welcome to the real world, Merton. You have been living in the shadow of death, and now – you drink up.'

'Don't start preaching, Mum,' Danny said. 'It makes me throw up.'

'You curb your mouth.' She was smiling, and the musical hum was entering her speech. 'You ought to know better, Daniel. Hmm. If it wasn't for that church down there, I wouldn't have a sane bone in my body.'

'Who says you do?'

'I'll ignore him,' she smiled. 'I *pray*, Merton. I pray that he won't go the way of his brother Haig. The devil has that boy by the throat. His spirit is turned. But God is protecting Dan: he's getting away from this land . . .'

'Has Haig been bothering you?' Dan asked.

'I don't pay any attention,' Mrs Johnson said. 'I let him fool about, but it doesn't get to me in here.' She pointed at her huge bosom. 'I have serenity in my spirit. And I pray for Haig. *Pray for those who persecute you*.' She took a biscuit, dunking it in her tea. 'He sits out there smoking his ganja – he and his friend

227

– making a noise to rouse the dead, and then he complains to the police. Says I'm knocking on people's doors. So the police come and investigate *me*.'

'Why does he say that?'

'What?'

'*Do* you go knocking on doors?'

'Only as the Lord directs,' she smiled. 'I preach the gospel. But I don't bother people. It all comes from above, Merton. I'm one of the apostles of the Lord.'

'One of the twelve apostles?'

'Yes,' she said. 'One of the elect.' And she took a sip of tea.

Danny groaned, covering his ears in the corner, but his mother was relaxing.

'We try to live good lives, Merton. Clean, orderly lives. We live well in the midst of ignorance and cruelty. We are *in* the world but not *of* the world.'

She leaned over to take hold of my hands, and her eyes were shining. 'Thank you for bringing my son home. I got a message from the school, but I couldn't go out. I was worried. I prayed. And the Lord sent you. Thank you for hearing his voice.'

'That's okay,' I said.

'But if you have heard him once, you should make a place for him in your heart,' she said.

'Don't try to convert my *friends*,' Danny wailed. 'It's fucked up, man.'

'Listen to him! I have raised scorpions.'

'It's okay, Dan,' I said, 'I'm interested in religion.'

'You know our church?' she went on.

'Sure. You took me there a few times when we were little.'

'God be praised. I had forgotten. Do you remember the paintings in there? The choir? Come back one day. Come inside. You'll be welcome.'

By the time I made it back to school it was half-past six. Most people had cleared out, but there were lights on in the offices upstairs. I tried to make it to Ms Tooley's room without being seen, but Daly came out of the staff-room as I was sliding past.

'Merton!' His trainers squeaked on the lino as he took my shoulder. 'What's going on, mate?'

'Not much.'

'You put in a university application,' he said.

'Yes.'

'Thanks for telling me.'

I took a step back. 'I was going to,' I said. 'It's happened a bit suddenly.'

'You've been taking advice from James Gibbon?'

I shrugged, but he was staring me out.

'Well?'

'Sort of,' I admitted. 'He wanted me to have a go.'

'*Cambridge?*'

'He says it's a good place to do history.' I started to move away, edging towards the stairs.

Daly moved closer to me, folding his arms. 'You think so?'

'Why not?'

'Well, let's just say it's not something the school's just going to rubber-stamp. This kind of thing has to be thought through – processed.' He was silhouetted against the Perspex panel, still moving from one foot to the other. 'It's a bit more complicated than you think. You know I'm Deputy Head.'

'Yes,' I said.

'I'm in charge of uni applications.'

'So?'

'So I've pulled it.'

For a moment I said nothing. I could feel the blood beating in my head, and I was clenching my fists.

'What're you talking about?'

'Pulled it. It won't be sent. Not for now, in any case . . .'

I leaned against the wall. Daly went on talking, with this very calm voice, like what he was saying would be obvious to anyone. 'It's a matter of fairness, really. I'm not letting you have some advantage over other kids in the school. If you want to apply for a place in higher education, you can talk it over with me, like everyone else.'

I didn't panic. I still had the second form, the one I had left with Ms Tooley. I waited for him to finish talking. Through the doors at the end of the hallway I could see the pitch-black sky. Daly had his head on one side.

'You need to think about other places,' he was saying. 'There's more to university than bloody Brideshead. And wherever you apply, there'll have to be a report from the school, so I've prepared a couple of letters – one from me, one from Mr Collins. They give the basic background – that you're in breach of your court order for a serious offence involving firearms; that you're a habitual truant, with known criminal associates.' He was moving again, jogging from trainer to trainer, dancing on the lino.

'Since when did you care about that?'

'Like I say, it's a matter of fairness. Loads of kids turn up for classes. I'm not having you rewarded for funking it.'

The bell rang. All at once the corridor started to fill with pupils from the late classes. A crowd of fourth-formers were pushing past us, moving towards the dark yard.

'Hi, Sukhnam,' Daly called out. 'Hey, Darren, mate.'

'Hi, sir.'

'Listen, Merton,' he turned to me again. 'You have the same chance as anyone. If you want to make a serious application through the school, let me know. The rest is a daydream.'

And he walked away.

The application had to be in by five-thirty the next day. In an empty classroom, I took out the spare forms and started filling them in – three whole sets, this time, just to be safe. I tried to remember what I'd written before. They wanted to know what *interests* I had, what my parents did. I said my father was dead, my mother unemployed. I knew I should have pretended I liked rock-climbing or dancing or something, and I couldn't decide, so I left half the personal section blank. Also I didn't know all the stuff they needed about the school – the league tables, measures of social exclusion, racial profiles, all that totalitarian crap.

The next morning I sat at Miss Tooley's desk, the forms spread out in front of me. She had been squirting herself with scent, rearranging her hair and doing her make-up, so that the whole place smelt of her.

'We need the school's GCSE results,' I said. 'And the average results for this category of school.'

She searched on the computer and printed something out. 'Here,' she pointed at the figures, leaning over me. 'At the top. And you need to say something about your hobbies.'

'I don't have any.'

'Well, you can't leave it blank. I'm sure you can think of something.'

'What do most people say?'

'Music. Sport. Drama.'

So I wrote a few harmless lies. And I told them I wanted to travel when I could afford it.

'Okay,' she said. 'I'll see if I can get Mr Collins to sign.'

Collins was in a meeting, so I had to wait for ages while Rachel took notes and poured coffee for them. I started riffling through my personal file. I found the letter Daly had written, and I dropped it unread into the shredding machine; then I did the same to the court order documents, and various papers from social workers about my truancy rate, and my days with the gang. Finally I destroyed all the notes Collins had written about me.

When she came back she was blushing. Her whole neck and shoulders were red – even her forehead.

'I had to interrupt the meeting,' she said. 'They would have gone on all day.'

'Did he sign?'

She smiled. 'I put the form among other papers. He didn't even look.'

'I love you,' I said.

'I could lose my job.'

I took her hand and kissed it.

'Stop it, you idiot,' she said. 'You're in my way. You have three hours to get Mr Daly to sign his part of the form, and take the wretched thing to Cambridge.' She pushed me away. 'Personally, I'd say it couldn't be done.'

'Daly's a problem,' I admitted.

'Won't sign?'

I shook my head.

'Well, I'm out of ideas. You'll have to sort it out. Go! *That* way. I have work to do.' And she held the door for me.

I ran the whole way from the New Crosland, across Cannon Park B and C. The old woman told me Gibbon was teaching, and couldn't be disturbed. I was sweating and panting. 'I *promise* he'll want to see me,' I told her. 'I have to be in Cambridge by five-thirty. If not, everything's fucked.'

'Don't use that language,' she said calmly.

'It's important,' I repeated. 'I promise he'll want to know.'

'I'll ask him.' And padding in her slippers across the kitchen, she disappeared into the stuffy hall.

There was a long silence. I could hear the clicking of the kitchen clock, then the old woman's croaky voice, and Gibbon replying. A door banged.

'Come on,' she told me, peering back in. 'Don't keep him waiting.'

'I'm not your form teacher,' Gibbon pointed out.

'Can't you pretend?'

'No.'

The guy he'd been teaching got up and offered me his hand. 'Toby,' he said. 'Pleased to meet you.'

232

'Merton.'

'You going up to Cambridge?' He was beaming at me, hypnotically friendly.

'Yes. Tonight.'

'Wow! They must have loved you.'

'Why?'

'Merton's *going*, not going *up*,' Gibbon explained, glancing through the form. 'Not yet, anyway. He still has to make the application.'

'Go on,' I said. '*Say* you're my teacher. That's true, isn't it? Daly isn't going to sign.'

'I really can't mislead them.'

His pen hovered about the form. I was sweating again. Toby and I looked at Gibbon.

'It's a white lie,' Toby said.

'We are scholars,' Gibbon said. 'We are committed to truth.'

'That's too exacting in the circumstances,' Toby said. 'You'd lie to the Gestapo . . .'

'We haven't quite reached that stage.'

'All the same. What you want is just.'

'And there's not much time,' I put in.

'It's an emergency.'

'You're both against me?'

'*Yes*,' we said together.

'Oh, what the hell?' Gibbon sighed. He scribbled something in the box. 'I'm saying *Tutor*. Let's just hope they don't look too carefully.' And he handed me the form. 'Go on, then. You've got two hours.'

# 24

It was incredibly cold. I wished I'd brought my coat, but there wasn't time to go back for it. So I ran to the Underground and marched up and down the platform to keep the blood moving, while someone made unintelligible announcements over the PA system.

On the train, a couple of fourteen-year-old heroes started playing football up and down the carriage with a can of Special Brew. When they finally went through the connecting doors to the next compartment, we were already halfway to Liverpool Street. Then the train stopped in a tunnel, rumbling and rattling, for about ten minutes.

I had taken a book from Gibbon's library, *Pagan Mysteries in the Renaissance*, which I kept trying to read, but my stomach was shaking and I couldn't concentrate. I wanted to know everything at once. The book was about the esoteric meaning of art, and I had this idea there must be a single key – one secret from the Greeks or Romans that explained it all. But the writer was talking about dozens of artists and philosophers, and the implications of each idea ran out in every direction, baffling my mind. Half the footnotes were in Greek or Latin, and before the train started moving again, I started to panic. *Perhaps Daly is right,* I thought. *I'll never fit in at Cambridge, even if they take me. I'm not educated. I'll never catch up.*

By the time the train lurched into Liverpool Street, it was already after four. I fretted about under the vast canopy of glass and steel, looking for Cambridge on the notice-board. Then I had to run the length of the station to get to the right platform – the last one, out on its own – where a filthy-looking train was waiting to leave at 4.10.

Everything inside was screwed up. There were sandwich boxes and crisp packets all over the floor, and a stench of beer. I marched through the train, looking for somewhere to sit, and by the time I found a place, I was feeling sick. I sat pressing my hand to my forehead, clutching the application, trying to remember why I was there.

When the doors slammed and the train began to move, I felt better. I couldn't think about the Neo-Platonists any more, so I stared out the windows instead, towards the ginger-brick warehouses and crooked tenements of north London. We passed a thousand lighted windows: street-level kitchens, bedsits with giant TVs, blue lighted tower blocks looming in the mist. Then at the edge of the city, allotments of black earth started flipping by, and on the far side of a motorway, a network of semis in cul-de-sacs, like the one my mother lived in.

I pressed my face against the glass and peered into the half-light. You couldn't see the sun. Down on the horizon the sky was tobacco-coloured like old wallpaper, and when we reached the countryside, the whole earth was flecked with frost. After that I couldn't take my eyes off the land. The fields were so flat and desolate. There were just a few houses, marooned at the end of long tracks.

Later the train stopped. The heating went off, and nobody said a word. We just waited in the middle of some fields. It was almost dark outside. Little birds like starlings flew together and shot apart above the open country. The brakes hissed. A Land Rover drove up to one of the lonely houses. And I just sat there staring out, till the whole country was pitch-black.

We had to change trains at a prairie station. 'Your train has been cancelled,' the guard told me when I asked what was happening.

'How can they cancel it? Look, there it is, sitting on the line.'

'You're being upgraded,' he said, 'to the fifteen twenty-three.'

'But that was hours ago.'

'It's running late.'

'So what time will it get to Cambridge?'

'Seventeen eighteen.'

'Fucking hell. That's too late.'

'Don't abuse members of staff,' he said. 'Customers who abuse members of staff are liable to a fine of up to five hundred pounds.' He started to waddle off.

'I wasn't abusing you,' I said calmly. 'I was abusing the late train. And I'm not a customer. I'm a fucking *passenger*! Jesus!'

As I tramped up and down, it started to rain. The other passengers shuffled about with briefcases and newspapers, or spoke into their mobile phones. I tried to read the *Pagan* book, but I couldn't stand still, and there wasn't enough light, so I went to the edge of the platform and took deep breaths to calm myself down.

Our new train was better than the first, except that it was full and there was nowhere to sit. When we finally got to Cambridge it was twenty past five. I had money, but there was a queue for taxis, so I decided to walk. I asked a woman in a headscarf which way to go, and she pointed down this long Victorian street towards a big church. Then I started walking, but it was obvious it was going to take for ever, and I broke into a run.

The rain had turned to hail. All along the pavement I had to dodge people with shopping trolleys and prams, till in the end I started running on the road towards the huge church. After that there was some open land on the right, and ahead of me a street of shops and offices with Christmas lights strung out between them.

'Where's C— College?' I shouted. 'Does anyone know where C— College is?'

A couple of undergraduates in long overcoats were walking towards me, sharing a big umbrella. 'What do you want to do?' one of them asked. '*Bomb* it?'

'I need to deliver something.'

He put his head on one side to examine me. But his friend started to explain.

'Straight up here,' he pointed, 'past Emmanuel – that's the classical façade on the right – left at the traffic lights, past the NCP car park, through the brutalist shopping centre, out on to the Market Square. C's directly opposite. Gargoyles, Victorian Renaissance flourishes. You can't miss it.'

'How long will it take?'

'Ten minutes. Fifteen?'

'Thanks,' I said. 'I'll run.'

'Wait,' his friend said. 'Here, take this.' He handed me a card. 'Come to our party.'

'Thank you,' I said, grabbing the invitation without looking. I started to run.

'Dress is *fin de siècle*,' he called out, 'but you look lovely as you are!'

I sprinted the entire road.

'Left at Emma!' they shouted after me.

It hailed all the way across town, and I couldn't look up. When I got to the market, the stall-holders were stripping the place down to metal skeletons. A clock struck a quarter to six.

Nobody had warned me about the porters.

'I'm looking for the Admissions Office,' I gasped.

A couple of men in pinstriped trousers were reading the *Daily Mirror* by an electric fire. One of them examined the clock above the door. 'They closed at half past.'

I wiped the water from my face. 'Could I just go and see – I could leave these papers there.'

'Are you a member?'

'What?'

'Of the college, sir – are you a member of C— College?'

'No.'

'The quads are closed. You can't go in.'

'I've just run all the way from the station to deliver this application,' I said. 'Please let me go to the office and see for myself.'

'Come back in the morning.'

'I can't. Please, you've got to help me. It won't take a second.'

The two men looked at each other, then at me. One of them heaved himself out of his chair.

'All right, son. Right out the door, through the next arch, right again – *don't* walk on the grass – through the arch by the chapel, and take the first staircase on your left: Staircase D. The Admissions Office is on the ground floor.'

'Thanks,' I said. 'Thank you.'

'No running,' he repeated, 'and *keep off the grass.*'

I took the first quad at a sprint, cut across the lawn to the arch by the chapel, turned left as the porter had said, ran up and down searching for Staircase D. Finally I tripped on the step, falling on to a women in a raincoat who was rattling a bunch of keys. She fell back against the door.

'I'm sorry,' I said. 'Are you all right?'

She brushed herself down, stepping away from me. Above the door a sign said *Ms P Fanon: Admissions Office.*

'What are you doing?' she asked.

'The Admissions Office . . .' I pulled out my application.

'Yes?'

'I need to hand this in . . .'

'We're closed,' she said.

'Are you Ms Fanon?'

'Yes.'

'Could I – I know I'm late, but – could I just leave this here?'

'I've locked up. You'd better leave it with the porters.'

'But it's the deadline,' I said. 'It has to be today. Tomorrow it'll be too late.'

'It already *is* too late.'

'Look, I know I'm fifteen minutes late, but just this once, could you . . .'

'It's really too much. Is this an application for *this* year? We tell the schools to send everything in good time. What's the point of this last-minute chaos? What purpose does it serve?' She turned on a light and looked at me.

'*Honestly* . . .' She let out a long breath. 'I'm running late as it is. Which school are you from?'

'The New Crosland,' I said. 'Cannon Park. It's a comp.'

She hummed. 'I don't think I know that one.'

'It was a grammar school once,' I added, just to keep the conversation going. 'It hasn't sent anyone to Cambridge recently. Not since nineteen sixty-four.'

She paused, key in hand. 'I *see*. So you're breaking the mould, are you?'

'If the mould will break . . .'

I moved round to make out her face, but she turned back to the door. She was fumbling her key in the lock.

'Is that a good thing?'

'It's a very good thing,' she said simply. 'I even think it entitles you to have the form in on time.'

'*I* think so,' I told her. 'But I'm biased.'

She gave me a brief smile as the door opened. 'Go on, then. Hand me your documents. I'll make sure they're processed with the others in the morning.'

'Thank you. That's very nice of you. Really.'

She went inside the office. There were neat piles of papers all over the floor. 'What's your surname?'

'Browne.'

'Browne. B. Broadhead, Brody, Brooke, there it goes: *Browne*. All right.'

'That's it?'

'That's it. Now, Mr Browne, I really do have to be going.'

'Thank you,' I said again.

'No, no. Don't mention it. Goodnight.' And she ushered me out, snapped the door shut, and scuttled into the night.

It was disgustingly cold and my clothes were wet, but the hail had stopped, and there were lights on all over the quad. I could smell fried onions and disinfectant, and some kind of stew. All at once I felt a sort of elation. I even began to relax. In the next entrance, after the Admissions Office, was the staircase to the main hall. A whole lot of undergraduates started coming through the quads into the inner courtyard, and I made my way with them to the main building.

There were mortarboard portraits on the walls, and in a passage to the right a long bank of pigeon-holes leading to the bar, where undergraduates were drinking and playing snooker. I moseyed up the stairs. People were queuing for dinner on one side, and on the other, almost hidden in the dark, was the entrance to the college library. So I went up to have a look.

Nobody asked for my ID. I stood inside the door, inhaling the smell of leather and wood polish. Low green lamps shone down on the tables where undergraduates were studying. There were ladders for climbing the stacks, tall stained-glass windows, a balcony like a minstrels' gallery over the far end of the room. It was very quiet. I went in and sat on a leather armchair. Nobody bothered me. So after a while I took out *Pagan Mysteries*. It fell open at a passage about divine madness – about the intoxication of the mind with supernatural love – and I read for half an hour or more. I even got up a few times and checked out the different stacks – law books, philosophy, strange old leather books in Latin. But in the end a librarian started clearing up near where I was, and there was a girl who kept staring down at me from the gallery, so I got up, shoved the book in my pocket, and marched to the door.

Out on the streets, I looked at the strange shape of the buildings in the darkness: C— College, encrusted with gargoyles and fabulous animals, and the other colleges, which seemed even older and more worn-down. I gazed for a long time at Trinity – a Tudor fortress set back from the street – and wandered along Bridge Street to the river. Then, without knowing how the buildings fitted together, I went on towards the open countryside, trying to get away from the traffic, and doubled back along the meadows and watercourses behind the town. I was walking on a dirt track, pock-marked with puddles. Most of the time it was too dark to see beyond the next tree, but I could make out the silhouette of colleges on the other side of the meadows, and the illuminated windows of a great hall. Then I came to an open space. There across the little stream, next to a plain classical building, was King's College Chapel, yellow in the floodlights. It was unmistakable. I knew it at once. The stained-glass was burning like a lantern.

I climbed the railings of a footbridge and dropped into the college grounds. My heart was racing, the blood drummed in my head. But there was nobody about, only some ducks in the long grass. And after a while I carried on down the path in the direction of the chapel. A boys' choir started singing, and when I reached the last courtyard I hid in the shadow of a doorway, two hundred yards from the gatehouse. I stood there for ages, listening to their high, weightless voices, and staring at the coloured windows.

Later it started raining again. I left the college through the main gate, and started to wander through the medieval streets. Near the Market Square I found the graveyard of an ancient church. I stood gazing at the gravestones, the high voices of the children still audible from across the road. Then I walked away from the centre of town along an old brick wall that bulged from the pressure of tree roots. There were more colleges after that, and somewhere beyond them, at the edge of town, an open space like a deer-park, enclosed with railings. Everywhere I went, bricks and stone were eaten away by the darkness.

After a while I started thinking about Miranda. The more I thought of her, the more the whole city spun around me. I leaned my head against the swollen wall, trying to impose order on my mind. And then for ages I just went on wandering through the streets, thinking about her, staring into the courtyards and alley-ways, or up at lighted windows, until I was drunk with the whole place.

# 25

Miranda went to France with her family for a couple of weeks, and all the time she was away, I worked in the bunker, or back in Gibbon's house, doing essays for him, reading his history books, practising Latin.

Miranda was annoyed with me because I never rang her when she was in France. And the night she got back, she went straight to this party in a nightclub with Rose and Debby. So I had to go and find her there, after I'd finished at Gibbon's place.

Barlowe's was just off the High Street, not far from the estates. By the time I got there it was almost ten-thirty, and there was a crowd outside, queuing in micro-minis and psychedelic trainers along the pavement, but I couldn't see Debby or Rose.

I went to the top of the queue.

'Get in line.' The bouncer was twice my size. He had a gold stud in his right ear.

'I don't want to stay,' I shouted over the noise. 'I just want to get hold of someone.'

'Yeah, yeah.'

'It's an emergency.'

'Join the queue.'

'Get back, wanker!' A couple of girls in the queue came in against me. They'd been flirting with the bouncer.

'I'll fucking sue,' I said. 'I need to talk to her. Her mother just died.'

'I've heard it before, mate.'

'I can't believe you're saying this,' I shouted. 'I *have* to reach her.'

'Shove off.'

I stared at the rivet in his lardy ear, then looked back at the queue. It went on for a block and a half; I would have been out there till midnight. Blue lights shone from the basement behind him, and the music was pounding like rounds of artillery. It made my stomach tremble.

'All right, let me go in accompanied,' I said. 'I just need to hand her a note – ten seconds will do it.'

The girls had fallen silent. One of them was staring at me, sucking the end of her thumb. Her legs were beetroot-coloured from the cold. 'Let him in,' she told the bouncer. 'He can go in front of us.'

The big man unfolded his arms. 'Wait,' he growled, and took out his mobile.

We all waited. Then a black guy appeared from below, about six foot four, in a purple suit with an orange shirt. 'Vincent, mate, this bloke's looking for someone. Take him down, give him one minute – he finds the person, he speaks to her, he comes up. Stay with him.'

'He hasn't paid?'

'Says it's an emergency. He's not going to hang around.'

'All right, you.' Vincent took my arm. 'Keep close.'

And turning his head towards the underworld, he led me down.


There were people everywhere, pressed against the bar on the far side of the room, or moving about on the dance floor – girls in soccer shirts and string vests, circling each other, their eyes closed. Everyone was smiling. My head was crushed with the sound, and it was impossible to talk. Even breathing was hard; I felt like I was going to drown. I had my big coat on, too, and I was sweating before I reached the bar.

They weren't in the first room. I looked at every face, Vincent at my shoulder all the time. At the end of the bar there was an arch in the wall, and another dance floor beyond leading to a second room where people were moving like machines. The girls were stamping, throwing their heads back, hard nipples against wet shirts. The boys punched out their arms like pistons.

Vincent and I pushed across the dance floor to the loos.

'She's not here, joker-man,' he shouted in my ear. But I slipped away, bashing through the door of the girls' toilets.

A blonde with long fingernails was preparing a line of coke on a metal shelf.

'Miranda,' I shouted.

'Piss off, you,' someone said.

Vincent burst in.

'She's not here,' I told him.

'Fucking right.' He pinned me against the wall. 'You're out of here! No one gives me the run around.' He grabbed my shoulders, ramming me through the door in front of him. Then he made me walk along the side of the dance floor, back towards the entrance.

We had to get past a corner by the fire exit, but we were blocked by these people who weren't really dancing, just shuffling about, bellowing at one another. Vincent started to steer me through, but they didn't make way. I was trying to squeeze past, and everyone was laughing, ignoring me. It was unbearably hot and the noise was bursting my brain. I started to push hard. But then right there, as I scrambled towards the door, I saw Miranda. She was standing with about half a dozen others: Rose, Debby, and some people I'd never met before. She didn't see me, though. 'That's her,' I told Vincent, but he couldn't hear.

I stood watching while Miranda bopped about gently, and I pushed forward. I was only a couple of feet from her. 'Miranda,' I said. She was looking down. I manoeuvred one of her friends aside. I was almost touching her. 'Miranda . . .'

'Merton!' She frowned, but instantly smiled.

'I found you,' I said. My words were swallowed in metal noise.

Vincent had come up behind me. He pointed at the fire exit. 'Out!' he said.

'Hello, Merton,' Rose shouted. 'You made it.'

I gave Rose a kiss. 'This is Vincent,' I explained. 'Vincent, Rose.'

'He's my friend,' she told him, pointing at me. 'Can't he stay?'

'He's out of here,' Vincent said. 'We're over capacity.'

The noise was intensifying, and the crowd seemed to have grown. Everyone on the dance floor was spinning and leaping, punching the air. 'I'm going,' I told Vincent. But I turned to Miranda. 'Come with me. I'll meet you outside.'

'We only just *got* here,' she shouted in my ear.

'I'll hang around,' I told her. 'I'll go to your house and wait there.'

'No,' she said. 'Wait.'

And I crashed through the fire doors.


'Everyone's away,' she explained as she unlocked the front door. 'They're staying in France till next week.'

She went to the kitchen to make herb tea, but I didn't follow her. For a while I sat fidgeting on a deep sofa in the sitting-room, but I jumped up and started moseying about, looking at the different sized violins, the piano which took up half the room, the musical manuscripts. There was a postcard of the Pope on the mantlepiece, next to a big wooden crucifix. And I started checking out the books.

When Miranda came back, she sat on an armchair miles away from me while we both drank tea. I had been desperate and agitated the whole time I was trying to find her in Barlowe's, but now I had her to myself, she really just made me nervous. She was so calm, so unhurried. It didn't seem natural. For a long time I just watched her from across the room.

In the end I went over and knelt on the floor in front of Miranda, and took hold of her legs. I leaned towards her, hugging her knees to my chest.

'When I was in Cambridge, I kept thinking about you,' I said. 'When you were away, too – all the last two weeks. It felt like you were inside me – in my blood. Does that sound stupid?'

'It's not stupid.' She stretched out her hand and started running her fingers through my hair. 'Are you frightened?'

I nodded.

'So am I,' she said. 'In France, when you didn't call, I felt sick. I couldn't sleep. I thought you were dumping me. I didn't know what you were doing.'

'I'm sorry,' I said.

'There's nothing we can do, then,' Miranda declared, putting her hands round my head. 'We're stuck with each other. It's too bad.'

I stayed with Miranda for the next few days, and we had the place to ourselves. We were both meant to be working, but to start with, for most of Friday morning we just lay in the sitting-room, and I told her everything I had wanted to say: loads of things I had never told anybody. After about an hour, Miranda started to give me this long, remorseless hug. Her skin had changed – her face was deep red, and her whole body felt soft, like I could put my finger through her. I started to undo the belt of her jeans while she just lay there, grasping my hair. It was the nearest she came to letting me have sex with her. But she pulled away, kissed me again, and got up. And after that, she worked in the kitchen, out of sight, so that we wouldn't distract each other.

In the afternoon we went for a walk along the river, and that night we talked again, lying together on the sofa for hours.

I spent the rest of Friday curled up under a reading lamp in the sitting-room, working through her father's old books of literary criticism. On Saturday morning, I discovered T. S. Eliot's essays on poetry, and George Steiner. And Saturday was the day Miranda finished *Middlemarch*. Afterwards, she lay on the sofa for ages, staring at the ceiling in a sort of trance, with the book clutched to her stomach.

\*   \*   \*

'Tell me about your father,' Miranda said.

'I don't know anything about him,' I said. 'Literally not one thing. He left when I was a zygote.'

She was lying on the sofa, her head on my chest. I could smell her lemony hair, and I started to imagine alternative childhoods for myself, out of books and films, or from her own weird family – strange, secure worlds like hers. But I told her about something different.

'I used to have this recurring dream.'

'Yes?'

'I was running away from home,' I said, 'along the streets near our house. It was definitely home, except that the roads were much longer, and my feet and body were heavy, that way you get in dreams, so that it was hard to move. At the corner of our street I looked back, and Mum's boyfriend Meat was coming after me, so I ran on, getting heavier and slower till in the end he was bound to catch me. But he only ever took hold of me when I'd run the whole length of Dante Avenue, and just before he put out his hand to grab me, I could always see these enormous blue and green fields, with the woods beyond. There it all was: a wilderness of silver grass, wild flowers, strange animals out of Africa. I could see it perfectly. The field was half a yard away, and all I had to do was jump – take one more step – and I would cross to the other side and get away. But every time it was the same. I stood there paralysed, staring towards the wilderness. So Meat would always reach out and grab me from behind.'

'Then?'

'That's it. I woke up.'

'So it's obvious.' Miranda took my hand, half climbing on top of me. 'All you have to do is jump. You just have to step out over the line . . .'

'Yes.'

'. . . and you'll be free . . .'

'That's all,' she whispered.

\* \* \*

247

Miranda's dad was into psychology. I sat in his study reading this essay which Jung had written after he argued with Freud. It was all about primitive man. Jung didn't believe that sex was the motor of the human mind. He said there were more urgent needs: existential needs, like survival in war, hunting, belonging to a society, dealing with death. Our minds had evolved to manage all that. And he said that getting your end away wouldn't make you happy by itself, because you might still be terrified of death, or living a life without meaning. After that I started to read some very strange things he had written about alchemy.

'Have you ever seen a shrink?' I asked Miranda.

She shook her head. 'You?'

'At primary school. But she was a moron. She kept asking about sex.'

'Dad says we should all see an analyst.'

'Does he?'

'He did for years. He has this theory that you have to be aware of what's inside you – all the bad memories of childhood. You have to know yourself. Otherwise you never grow up. You just project your early experiences on to the world and carry on like a child, blaming other people for everything.'

'What if you can't see a therapist?'

'Then it's just what Aristotle said: happiness depends on upbringing.'

'So I'm fucked,' I pointed out. 'No point even trying . . .'

'That's true,' she smiled. 'No point at all.'

# 26

On Sunday morning I woke early and lay in the sitting-room reading Jung. Then Miranda came down and made breakfast, and at eleven she took me to this big Catholic church at the other end of the village.

Loads of people were turning up, getting out of their cars or shuffling along the street. They swarmed through the church doors. Miranda crossed herself with holy water, and took me to find a seat, right behind a family with children in identical blue coats. Someone rang a bell for the deacon and priest to come in, and the choir began to sing. The deacon was swinging a thurible – the whole place started to smell of incense – and the priest bowed at the altar and walked round it, wafting it with smoke.

I hadn't been to a Catholic church before – only the Pentecostalist hut in Cannon Park. There were some prayers and readings from the Bible. Then everyone stood up for the priest to read the Gospel. It was the story of a man who found treasure buried in a field, and sold everything he owned in order to buy it. We all sat down, and the priest started to preach. He was saying we should all be like that man: strip the junk from our lives, get rid of the chattering voices in our minds, so that we could possess the field with its treasure, which meant the soul. 'We strive for worthless things,' he said, 'but we fail to see the treasure God has placed within us. We are surrounded with opulence, but there is no contentment. We are trapped in a state of longing and agitation, and we postpone the moment of real understanding – the moment of Christ's entry into the world – his penetration of our hearts . . .'

My mind tuned out. I was watching Miranda's profile and

I had a powerful desire to push her down on the bench and screw her right there. All the same, I was thinking about what the priest was saying: that you can break out of the system by clearing the junk from your mind. For a moment it all seemed possible; it was so peaceful. I could almost imagine a world outside. But the priest stopped talking, and we had to listen to this bossy woman reading a whole lot of notices, and I completely lost it.

As we walked back, I saw a headline in the local paper about a riot. So when we got to the house, I turned on the little TV in the kitchen, while Miranda started cooking lunch, and tried to get some news. Eventually I found a local bulletin. There on the screen was the Cannon Park Estate: the towers and the atrium seen from the direction of the High Street, the whole place surrounded with cops.

'What's going on?' Miranda said.

'That's my neighbourhood,' I told her. 'My friend Dan lives there.' I pointed to B block.

The reporter was interviewing Colin Peterson. There were loads of residents milling about in the background. Some kids were making faces at the camera.

'I know that copper,' I told Miranda. 'He's the one who charged me with burglary.'

Peterson was explaining why the police were staying outside the estate, instead of going in. *We have a hostage situation*, he said. *We are in negotiations with the Cannon Park Safety Committee for the release of a number of hostages.*

'That's the boys,' I said. 'The posse. They've really done it. They've taken over.'

I picked up the phone and tried Danny's number but there was nobody at home.

'That's a good sign,' Miranda said. 'It means he got out.'

'I should really see for myself,' I told her. 'I ought to go over there.'

'No way.' Miranda stood across the kitchen door.

'No, I should. I won't be long. I'll be fine . . .'

'Just think for a minute, Merton. What are you saying? There's no point going. The place is full of cops – look at them all. There's nothing you can do.'

'What about Dan?'

'He's not there.'

'Or the old man?'

'It's not your responsibility. He'll be all right.' And she made me sit down.

We kept the TV on while we ate. The news woman said the riot had started the day before, following an attempt by the police to arrest a local youth. She didn't say who it was, or where the hostages were being kept, and the camera didn't show anything beyond the barricades at the entrance of the estate, and a side-view of Dan's block. I tried the Johnsons' number a few more times, but there was still no answer.

'Let's go for a walk,' Miranda said. She turned off the TV. 'Let's go down to the river.'

'I ought to be there,' I said again. 'I should make sure about Dan.'

'No,' she said. 'Absolutely no way. That's all over. You have to choose, Merton. You've got to decide what you want. If you got in trouble again it would ruin everything. Think about James. He believes in you – do you know that? You are the only pupil he's not cynical about.'

'I promise I won't get into trouble,' I said. 'I just need to find out what's going on, see if Dan's there, his mother, the old guy. Then I'll come back.'

'Even if they *are* there, there's nothing you can do.'

'I'll talk to the police,' I said. 'That's all. I won't get involved.'

'You promise?'

'I swear. I'll just tell them what I know.'

'Come back right away.'

'I'll be a couple of hours.'

Just before I reached the suburbs, not far from Gibbon's house, I stopped to catch my breath on a pedestrian bridge over a main road. I could see the towers of Cannon Park from there, perhaps half a mile away in the dusk, but it was impossible to make out what was happening inside. The lights and traffic were mostly on the far side of the estate, along the High Street. On my side there was only the darkness of Dante Park, and the block of garages that the posse used.

I carried on running through the suburbs, past Gibbon's street, into the park. When I was a few hundred yards from the garages, I came to a stop. I thought I could hear something: a pounding like African drums, throbbing and thudding quite rhythmically. It seemed to come from the estate, but at first I couldn't see what was happening. There was a group of coppers in riot gear lined up across the emergency access next to the garages. Behind them, white vans with grilling over the windows were parked in the middle of the street. A load of journalists with cameras and sound equipment were waiting by the railings, with people from the houses around the park who had come to see what was happening.

The police had cut the approach road completely. Nobody could get past. They were kitted out with shields and helmets, but they were just staring into the darkness, like they were waiting for something. The journalists were trying to see, too; everyone in the crowd was peering into the estate, fascinated by the noise. It was coming from the middle of the atrium: a sound like a whole little army beating on doors, railings, dustbin lids – twenty drummers or more. And there was shouting, too – chanting, almost like a song – with a leader asking questions, and the crowd yelling back, though it was impossible to hear what they were saying.

I stood there a while, just behind the crowd, concentrating

on the voices. I was trying to decide how I could get inside. Then I walked away from the police vans and the crowd, along the length of the garages. The garages blocked the view into the atrium, but at the far end, just next to Savage's old headquarters, there was a space that was used for rubbish. We used to get over the wall there when we were kids sometimes, dropping into the estate without being seen. I waited for a rise in the sound, and when the crowd was really screaming I ran across the road into the dark alleyway, pushing my way through the pile of garbage bags till I reached the wall. Then I struggled up, using the bins for support, and balanced on top of the wall.

I could see part of the police line from there, stretched out at the other end of the garages. Nobody was looking my way, and almost at once I let myself down, just a few yards from the entrance to the first staircase of block C, and ran inside.

From the top floor I could see the whole atrium. I stood staring down, while the grey sky started to turn red over the countryside. Below me in the atrium, a crowd had gathered in front of the church; they were chanting, the drummers beating their bin-lids in unison. The boys had lit fires around the church, and the faces of the crowd glowed in the orange light – boys and girls, some very young, their mouths open as they shouted. A few were carrying sticks, but I didn't see any guns. Here and there I could make out smaller groups moving in the half darkness at the edge of the estate. And right in the middle I saw Savage for the first time. He was standing on the roof of the church next to the bright neon cross, shouting at the crowd.

Savage was screaming, jabbing his arm in the air, and the crowd roared out in reply. From that distance I could hear the words. Each time he reached a climax, the crowd repeated his words. 'Take what's OURS,' he yelled, and the whole atrium screamed back: 'Take it, take it . . .'

The speech went on, the sound of it rising and falling. 'Kill the informers!' Savage shouted. 'Purge them!'

The crowd shouted back: 'Kill them, kill them!'

'*We* are the police,' he told them. '*We* are the masters now! We are the *law*. Kill the pigs!'

'Kill the pigs!' they shouted. 'Kill the pigs!'

The drumming rose, and the crowd began to yell different slogans. A police helicopter was flying overhead, and when it came in low, hovering above the church, their voices were drowned out.

I looked across to block B, trying to form a plan, but it was impossible to see what was happening there. Dan's walkway was completely dark, and the old man's above it. I couldn't even make out if their doors had been broken down. Below their flats, at the entrance points of the block, I could see the reflection of blue lights. Squads of policemen in body armour were formed up around the two end towers. Everywhere else, on the roofs and in the atrium, the posse was in control.

I started running towards Danny's place. I thought I could search for him and Frank, and get them out of the estate. But I came to a stop at the stairwell in the middle of C. A guy in a long coat was standing guard, holding a Kalashnikov. I didn't spot him till I was very close. He was in the shadows, out of sight from police cameras and the helicopter, staring towards the cops. But he turned as I approached.

'Who are you?' He raised his gun and stood across the corridor. There was a smell of piss mixed with ganja from the flat behind him; the door had been smashed in, and some people were lying about in there.

'I need to see the hostages,' I told him.

'No way.' He kept the rifle trained on my chest.

'Savage sent me,' I said. 'He wants to know what's going on.'

The guy briefly examined me.

'They're inside, like he told us.' He indicated the flats behind him. 'We had to give the fat woman a beating. She was out of order. The others are all right. They'll run well.'

The drumming had started again, louder than before. The guy lowered his gun, peering out towards the police lines.

'When does it start, then?' he asked me.

'What?'

'The *hunt*, man. What's Savage going to do? We've been waiting all day.'

'The hunt?' I repeated.

The guy frowned at me, and for a moment I was silent. But I forced myself to speak.

'Yes – sure. The hunt,' I said. 'Nobody knows. Savage is still deciding.' I sounded calm, but my heart was thumping. 'He's still talking to the cops.'

But the guy started aiming his gun at my chest again.

'Who are you, anyway?' he asked. 'You're not from Savage.'

'Fuck you,' I said. 'He sent me.' But I started to back away.

'Don't move,' the guy told me. 'I'm going to check you out.'

He looked away to call someone from the room behind him, and I kept moving. Then in the darkness of an open doorway I turned and started running as fast as I could.

I got out through the little alleyway by the garages, and ran the perimeter of the whole estate, making my way round through the suburbs, until I reached the High Street.

As soon as I got to the shops, everything seemed almost normal. All down the High Street, people were shopping under Christmas lights. Santa was ringing a bell in the supermarket car park. You could only see the police and the TV vans once you were near to Cannon Park. The cops were set up in the area between the High Street and Dan's block: surveillance equipment, mobile offices, a whole little village of Portakabins. Loads of coppers in crash helmets and body armour were waiting by the bollards, carrying plastic shields.

A woman police officer was drinking coffee beside one of the parked cars. 'I'm looking for a friend in Cannon Park,' I told her.

She pointed at a big Portakabin directly behind the Johnsons' place. 'Incident Headquarters,' she said.

I pushed through the TV cameramen into the Portakabin, but there was a queue, and nobody would talk to me. Even when I banged my fist on the wall, they just told me to wait my turn. So I ran out again, stepped over the blue and white tape, and stood at the ground floor of block B, next to a line of coppers.

'Are you going to rescue the hostages?' I demanded.

'Who are you?' The nearest cop turned to block my view.

'My friend's missing.'

'There's nothing you can do,' he said. 'It's all in hand. Here, out the road.'

Back in the Portakabin the queue had gone down, and I gave a statement to this other woman cop who seemed half asleep. I explained about Dan and his mother, and the old man. I told her where the boys were keeping the hostages in block C, but she said they already knew that. Then she checked the names I gave her on the safe list, but none of them were there: not Dan, his mother, the old man, or Dan's grandfather.

'It doesn't mean they're in any danger,' the copper told me, 'just that they haven't registered with us yet.'

'Where are they then?'

She arched her eyebrows and gave a shrug. 'Could be anywhere.'

'No,' I said. 'They're inside. I know it. We've got to do something.'

'Leave it to us. Here, sign this. It's your statement.'

I hesitated. 'What are you going to do with it?'

'It'll go on file.'

'Bloody brilliant.' I took the pen. 'You should be moving in,' I told her.

'Look, it's under control,' she said. 'There's a lot of tension on this estate. Poverty, race issues, a lot of complex background . . . We don't just go in with tanks.'

'Do you know where DC Peterson is?'

'You can't talk to him.'

'He knows me.'

'Sign the statement.'

'Not unless you tell me where he is.'

'I don't know,' she sighed. 'Probably in the control unit.'

The control unit was a lorry parked behind Dan's flat. A plain-clothes copper told me to wait for Peterson on the steps. Then he disappeared inside, and nobody came out for ages. After about ten minutes, I went back to the police lines to see if anything was happening inside the estate. Savage had finished his speech. The boys were no longer gathered round the church. They had wandered off in groups, each to their own place in one of the three blocks. But there was still no movement on the walkways; the hostages were being kept inside. I was trying to work out what Savage was doing – what I would have advised him to do, if I was still *consigliere* – or what Terry would do.

Finally, I went to the door of the control unit and walked in.

As soon as I was inside, I was blocked by a guy in riot gear. He took me by the shoulders and started pushing me out of the cabin. But I had a quick look at everything. Peterson was sitting at a little table wearing headphones, and the plain-clothes man was talking into a radio. Then, just as the door closed, I heard Savage's voice on the speaker.

Peterson came out a couple of minutes later.

'Well?' he said. 'What do you want?'

'You told me I should come if I had information.'

'Let's hear it.' He looked up briefly. 'What do you know about this?'

'I know what weapons they have; most of their names – even where they're keeping the hostages. I know what they're going to do with them.'

'We know most of that,' he said. But he corrected himself. 'I mean, of course we'd be glad to have a statement.'

'You should be getting them out.'

'And how exactly would we do that? Send in the army? We're

in the middle of negotiations. We're building up trust. It takes time.'

'Has Savage told you his demands?'

'I couldn't discuss that, even if I wanted to. We're in touch. It's under control.' He was about to go back into his Portakabin, but he paused on the top step and came down to my level again. 'Tell me, then,' he said, 'what do *you* think he wants? You know him.'

'He never planned this,' I said. 'Savage wanted to take over quietly, so you lot would hardly notice. But now he's trapped. He can't just walk out and get arrested. But he can never win a gun battle, either – not with the police.'

'So what does he do next?' Peterson said. 'How will he handle it?'

'I don't know. He'll drag things out as long as possible,' I said, 'pretending to negotiate. That's what he's doing now, right?' Peterson nodded. 'He ought to be demanding that the police move out of the estate, too, because they were being provocative – because the police are violent, people on the estates don't trust the police – all that.'

'Then what?'

'If he was sensible, he'd do everything he could to make it look like you were the bad guys: shoot at you only at night, from inside the estate, when nobody can get a photo. Then on TV it's a David and Goliath thing: you're the only people with guns, and it's the cops against a bunch of unarmed kids. Also whenever he speaks to the media, he'll try and sound like he's a real community leader – a man with grievances, an angry guy who only wants justice. Everyone buys into that.'

'What about the hostages?' he said.

'If he's smart he'll keep them safe,' I began. But as soon as I heard myself, I knew I didn't believe it. I thought about Savage and Terry. I imagined them arguing, trying to work out what to do – and all at once the whole thing became clear. 'Listen,' I said. 'What if he starts killing people?'

'There's no sign of that.'

'But if he does?'

'We have our plans.'

'Will you let me in?' I asked him. 'Now – right away. I think I can talk to him.'

'Absolutely no bloody way. You keep out of it.' Peterson put his hands on my shoulders. 'Go home, son. Don't even think about it. He'll come right. We're wearing him down.'

And he went back inside his Portakabin.

# 27

I found the key to Mel's house under the stone and ran upstairs. The gun was still there, under the floorboards in Tess's bedroom. I checked it over, loaded it, dropped a dozen bullets into my coat pocket. Then when I had locked the house, I went across the close to my mother's place, directly opposite, and peered into the lighted sitting-room through a gap in the curtains. Mike's stuff was everywhere, but there was nobody at home. I stood for a minute on the grass, my face hard up against the window, while I tried to steady my mind. I was gripping the butt of the revolver deep in my pocket. Then I drew it out, stepped back, and carefully took aim at Mike's amplifier, his Stratocaster, his brand-new silver trainers, the TV. But I didn't fire. I waited, forcing myself to focus, until my mind became calm. Then I turned away, stuffed the gun in my pocket, and started running towards the estates.

I got in to Cannon Park over the low wall by the garages. The police had moved back ten yards. They were lined up on the road now, clear of the bollards, and I dropped down well out of sight.

From the top walkway of block C I looked out over the rooftops and the towers. Down below, I could see the Savage army dispersing across the estate. They were spread out in little groups like infantry, with their big coats or hooded track-suits. For a minute the atrium was almost quiet, and I started running, heading towards B. Then suddenly there was a great roar, and the boys started thumping out a rhythm all over the estate, beating on hollow doors, on railings, plastic bins: tok-tok-TOK, tok-tok-TOK, tok-tok-*TOK*.

I was expecting to meet the guy with the Kalashnikov at the

staircase, but two other guards had taken over. They were staring intently towards block B, and I came up behind them unobserved. Beyond them, and on the other floors as well, small groups of soldiers had started to move, marching away from us along the walkways towards B block. Some were holding up burning torches, others trailed their sticks along the railings, making a sound like a giant football rattle. And at the stair-tower on the next corner, I saw some of the hostages for the first time – half a dozen figures, indistinct in the half-light, emerging on to the next corridor. They were moving as fast as they could to get away from the soldiers.

'You see them?' One of the guards was laughing. 'The bastards are running – they're shitting themselves.'

The drumming was growing louder, and a great howl began again. The crowd roared as the hostages were driven away from us along the corridor, like animals in a real hunt, quite slowly at first, then faster and faster.

'I've got to get through,' I said.

The laughing man turned to me. 'What do you want?'

'It's urgent. Out the way.'

I was holding the revolver in my hand, and when I raised it he moved aside. I pushed past, running towards the stair-tower. But the hostages were already half a block away, spread out along the narrow walkway, and I was separated from them by the hunt. I stood for a second in the tower, unable to decide what to do. Then I ran upstairs as fast as I could, out on to the flat roof.

The hostages had almost reached block A, still limping and jogging along the fourth-floor corridor. There was a fat woman who took up half the passage. A small man kept trying to push past her. She looked like Dan's mother, but it was impossible to be sure. Behind them, half a corridor away, their pursuers started breaking into a run. Most of the crowd watched from the ground; they moved in a mass around the perimeter of the atrium, keeping pace with the hunt.

By the time the fugitives were struggling along the walkway of A, the boys were closing in. They were beating the railings with their sticks, shouting at anyone who fell behind, and the hostages were panicking. One man ran ahead, then turned back, looking for an open flat. The others pushed past him. Even the fat woman was trying to run. Then a roar went up as the first of them made it to the stairwell in the middle of block A. There was only one stairway left after that, right at the end of the block, and they were already in sight of it. From that point on they had nowhere to go except up to the roof, or down into the atrium, where the whole army was waiting for them. One of the fugitives tried to double back, looking for a route of escape, but the boys charged him, raising their sticks, and he ran on again. The screaming rose all over the estate. Then the hostages started to enter the last tower.

For a while they were out of sight, and the crowd was waiting. Then one by one they started to appear on the tarmac at the foot of the tower, twenty yards from the garages. They were very far away from me – diagonally opposite where I was standing. I was looking as hard as I could, searching for Dan or the old man. But I couldn't see either of them. The fat woman emerged again; she fell as she ran into the open, and the others moved quickly around her large body. Nobody tried to help her.

After that, the courtyard filled once more with a constant drumbeat. The fugitives were surrounded now, trapped between the army in the atrium, and the boys who had chased them down the tower. Then the army surged forward with a great roar, and the hostages disappeared completely.

Nobody fired a shot. It was all done with clubs and sticks. There was a sort of rhythm to it too, the crowd chanting as they beat the prisoners. I backed away from the edge of the roof and leaned against the wall of the stair-tower. I thought I was going to throw up. But when the roaring increased, I made myself go back, gazing out over the whole estate for a sign of Dan or the old man. And that was when I saw Savage again. He was still standing on top of the church, unarmed, watching the whole scene with his arms folded. He stood like that for a long time.

Finally the shouting subsided. The crowd was beginning to disperse. Some of the hostages were still alive; I could see them moving on the ground. But the fat woman wasn't moving at all. I ran down the tower to the next floor, out on to the corridor where the old man lived, making my way in the darkness. I expected to find the place deserted, his flat burnt-out or looted, but there was a guard with a rifle lying sniper-style on the ground.

'What's going on?' I said aggressively, standing behind him. I pointed my revolver at his body.

'There's an old fuck with a gun,' the guard replied without looking up. He had his rifle trained on a barricade outside Frank's flat. 'I can't leave him.'

'It's all right, I know about that,' I said. 'You can go now.'

The guard turned to look at me. He had a lighted reefer on the ground beside him. 'Who are you, then?'

'I've been told to take over,' I told him. 'The boss wants you down there. There's loads of stuff to do.'

He hesitated. 'You sure?'

'Course I'm fucking sure,' I said. 'You were supposed to be there ages ago.'

'Piss!' He began to struggle backwards with his stuff. 'I wish they'd make up their fucking minds.' He started feeling his way unsteadily towards the stairs. 'I'm out of it, anyway,' he added, waving but not looking back. 'Shoot him if you can.'

The light-bulbs had been broken all along the walkway and it was pitch-dark. I called out Frank's name, but there was no reply. So I started walking towards his flat. Halfway along the corridor I heard his voice. 'Stop there,' he said. 'I'll shoot if you move another inch.'

'Frank?' I stood still. My head was thumping with the sound of drums. 'It's Merton,' I said. 'Merton Browne, remember? I brought your medals.'

He paused. 'What are you doing here?'

'I've come to get you out,' I said.

'Put your hands where I can see them.'

I walked towards his barricade keeping my hands over my head. Then Frank lowered his gun, giving me a quick look of recognition.

'The police are just below,' I said. 'There's nobody watching you. This is your chance.'

But he shook his head. 'I'm staying,' he said. 'They'll only arrest me. Anyway, I'm not letting the Nazis get my flat.'

'Forget the flat. They're killing people.'

'I'll kill a hundred of them before they touch me,' he said, 'easy as you like.'

'Listen, Frank, I'll come with you. We'll dump the gun. Nobody's going to charge you with that. You won't get another chance.'

'I don't want one,' he said. 'I know what I'm doing.'

He started aiming his gun into the atrium, searching about for something. The hunt had dispersed by now. A small crowd was gathered beneath Savage, still standing on the roof of the church.

'You should get out, lad, before they get back.'

'Come with me,' I said. 'We'll go together.'

But just as I said that, a burst of fire rang out across the open space, and I ducked down.

'What was that?' the old man asked.

We both lay there while the echo rang out, looking into the atrium.

'I think it's Savage,' I told him. 'I can't see him.'

A guy on a walkway below us started shouting. 'Is he hurt, yeah? Is the big man hurt?'

Then I saw Savage laid out flat on the church roof, and there was movement around him. A few people had climbed up there, crouching by his body. Someone passed up a torch. And there was a murmur, a sort of muffled cry.

'He's dead,' someone shouted. 'Savage is dead. They've killed him.'

After that there was noise everywhere, shouting from the darkness all round the atrium. Frank started searching the corridors through the sights of his gun. And he gave a little cry.

'Look,' he said. 'There: on the balcony, do you see?' He pointed. 'On the top floor. It's your pal.'

I looked towards the next block. Danny was standing at the midpoint, holding a rifle. He seemed to be alone on the corridor. For just a second he looked towards us, and I saw his face. Then there was a shout and he pulled back into the shadows. Someone in the crowd below had spotted him; a group of boys started running towards the staircases.

My stomach contracted, and I gripped the railings.

'We must do something,' I said. 'We've got to divert them.'

'Let me,' Frank said. 'I know how. I'll keep them pinned down. You get out.'

'No,' I told him. 'We're all getting out; the three of us. Come on, don't argue.' I pulled the barricade away from the door, and made him stand up.

Then I leaned out into the darkness and started shouting. 'Hey, you thick bastards,' I yelled. 'I killed Savage. Move and I'll shoot you.' A gun went off somewhere below me and I pulled back. But I shouted again from the darkness. 'Who's next? Who wants to die?'

My voice echoed in the darkness. In the atrium there was almost silence. I couldn't see Dan. He had disappeared somewhere along the corridor. Frank and I started to move towards the tower. The army was running for the stairs nearest Dan. Then from the end of the old man's corridor I caught sight of him again, still a long way off, jogging in our direction along the fifth floor. I saw him as he emerged from the stairwell in the middle of C. A large group had started up the stairs behind him.

'Dan!' I screamed. 'Danny! Move for God's sake!'

Two of the soldiers were already on the walkway behind him.

'Dan!' I yelled.

'It's all right,' the old man said. 'He can still make it. We'll meet him at the corner.'

We moved into the tower and started to go down. Dan was

still heading towards us, no more than fifty yards away, but the fastest runners had almost overtaken him. We watched as he tried to shake them off. He started punching them, kicking out. Someone grabbed hold of his jacket. He tried to break free, but the others caught up and he was surrounded.

Danny went on struggling while they took the gun from him. Then a great howl, high and long, rose from the yard. The boys had him pinned against the railings. Five of them were tackling him, holding his legs together to keep him still. The noise from below came in waves, a crescendo of animal cries as they lifted him. I could see he wasn't struggling any more.

'What are they doing?' I asked. 'Where are they taking him?'

The boys bundled Dan towards the stairwell. For a while they were out of sight. Then they appeared on the roof, carrying him by his arms and legs, and they brought him to the front where the whole crowd could see. There was an incredible roar from the atrium – an explosion of joy – and the boys on the roof started to swing Dan's body like a sack, back and forth over the edge. The whole crowd started chanting. 'Down, down, *down* . . .'

'For God's sake!' the old man said.

The boys on the roof swung Dan's body out and in, out and in, over the drop, in time to the yelling. He swung higher each time, and the crowd kept shouting. 'Down, *down*, down, *down!*' Then they heaved Dan out one more time, higher than before, and released him in the empty air. There was silence everywhere. We watched as his body seemed to pause for an instant; then he started to fall. And at once the whole army cried out again, shrieking from every corridor, every tower and rooftop.

For a minute or more I hardly noticed what was happening around me. I kept staring at Dan's body on the ground. Frank put his hand on my shoulder. He said something, but I didn't move. Then he gave me a shake. 'Come on. Follow me.' I went with him the way he indicated, almost without thinking, down to the first floor.

The police lines were right there, a few yards away. Frank was leading me out. And I would probably have gone with him, out to safety, without looking back, except that something started happening in the atrium. A sort of gasp went through the crowd – it lasted several seconds; then the drumming started again – drumming and shouting. We looked out from the entrance of the stairwell. People were lighting torches in the atrium. And right at the centre I saw a pale, fragile-looking face peering out from the platform of the church – a smirking face, lit up in the firelight, proudly looking about. And the crowd let out a high-pitched howl.

'He's still alive,' I said. 'There: it's Savage.'

I stepped out from the shadow of the tower. I wasn't aware of anything except Savage's face on top of the church, and a sort of coldness inside me that went from my heart right up to my head. All at once, I knew what I needed to do.

'I'm going,' I said to Frank.

'Where, lad?'

My eyes were fixed the whole time on Savage, and there was complete clarity in my mind. 'Go out to the police,' I told him. 'Dump the gun and get out.'

'What are you going to do?' he repeated.

'I'm going to make things right,' I said.

I watched Frank retreating into the darkness of the stair-tower. Then, almost as soon as he had gone, everything started to change. Someone began to shout through a megaphone at the other end of B block, and all at once there was movement at all corners of the estate. The coppers by the garages on the far side began surging into the atrium, behind their plastic shields, towards the area where the hostages had been left. And the police started moving on my side of the yard, too. I could hear shouted orders, a whistle, the sound of boots on the tarmac.

I started running towards Savage. He was right in front of me, standing on the roof by the dark cross, and I was screaming out, pushing through the crowd. I kept shouting that I had to get past, but nobody would make way. Behind me, the cops were forming up at the edge of the open space. And Savage was yelling orders. 'Kill the pigs,' he screamed. 'Make them pay!'

The crowd was still pressing in beneath him, but gradually people started to move away, shoving past me – a great number of boys, and young, hooded girls, charging towards the police lines, screaming abuse. I could hear someone shouting through the megaphone. 'Get back! Move back or we fire!' Then immediately on the word *fire*, from along the dark walkways and empty flats all around the estate, Savage's snipers started shooting into the police lines.

The sound was unbelievable. The crowd was screaming, pretending to be hit, yelling out, 'Pig murderers! Fascist pigs!' There were sirens on the High Street, the droning of the helicopter over the estate. And every fifteen or twenty seconds another shot was fired from the darkness of the walkways. I watched as an ambulance tried to get through to the atrium. Then the boys started using Molotov cocktails. There was an explosion against the wall of B block – right inside the police lines – and another in the path of the ambulance. A crowd of journalists had broken in behind the cops and started filming.

Everything was happening at the perimeter of the estate: all the police and journalists were there, the whole of the Savage army. Where I was standing, out in the atrium near the church, there was open space, even a sort of calm. I started to look about in the half-light. I thought probably Savage would have run out with the rest – that I had missed my chance – and I went right up to the door of the church.

But Savage was still there. He had climbed down from the roof, and he was all alone now, gazing out across the battle. When he saw me underneath the church, he stood perfectly still, five yards from me.

'Merton,' he said calmly, 'you came back.'

I nodded. 'There's still something I have to do.'

I was gripping Frank's revolver in my pocket, but I didn't bring it out right away.

'What is it?' he said. 'What do you want?' He was grinning, elated. I'd never seen him look so alive. 'You going to come back in?'

'No, Paul.'

'Oh, wait a minute.' He shook his head. 'Don't tell me. You're upset about your mate Danny.'

I took out the gun and aimed it at his face. I wanted to say something, but my mind had become dark, like there was too much blood inside me. I couldn't speak.

For a moment, Savage was almost surprised, but he shrugged, smiling again.

'Go ahead,' he said. 'If that's what you want. I'm easy to kill.' And he took a step towards me. 'Go on. Pull the trigger.'

'Stay where you are,' I said.

'No, mate,' he said. 'You make me.'

He came another step closer, and immediately I raised the barrel, firing a shot over his head. The force of it knocked me backwards, but Savage hardly flinched.

'If you're going to be a killer, Merton,' he said, 'you'll have to do better than that.'

Then suddenly, in my mind, the whole thing seemed so simple. I took the gun in both hands, and levelled it at his chest. 'This is for Dan,' I said. I cocked the back trigger. My thoughts were absolutely clear. I felt so confident, so free of doubt – as though no other thought would ever occupy my heart. The need to kill Paul resolved everything, brought everything to fulfilment. And for the first time, I knew in my heart that he was afraid, too. I looked into his eyes, and I was reminded of something – of some old memory, like the fear and sadness of childhood. I was certain I could see it in him.

Then Savage ran towards me and I took aim. I squeezed the trigger. But instantly three shots rang out in quick succession from the block behind us. Both of us dropped down, and I rolled over to find out who was firing: but all I could see was the riot. Then I looked towards Savage. He was lying on the tarmac two yards away, still staring at me, looking right through me, smiling to himself. We stared at each other for a long time before I spoke. 'Paul?' I said. I crawled over and gave his head a shake, but he didn't move. My mind began to stir. The sound of the battle bore in on me again: the crowd screaming, the police megaphone, the helicopter and sirens. I let the old man's gun fall to the ground. Then, very cautiously, I lifted Savage's head and shoulders. There was blood all around him: a black puddle still spreading rapidly. And there was a wound in his back the size of a fist.

I let him down again and looked up at block B. Someone was watching from the top floor, just beside the stairs, and I gazed back. For a second there was a face, perhaps a rifle, a glimpse of paleness on the balcony – then nothing. And I knew it was Frank Cooper.

I got to my feet, kicked the revolver towards Savage's body, and started to run. I was heading for the corner of C block – the only part of the estate where there was no crowd, no police line – sprinting as fast as I could. Then I scrambled over the wall, falling down on to the bins and rubbish bags next to the garages.

Out on the street, and all across Dante Park, the crowd of spectators had grown. I moved away, crossing the road where it was dark, and just kept running. I didn't stop till I reached the far side of the open land. Then I stood gazing at the estates. The police had retreated twenty yards or more, regrouping at the bollards. Two cars were on fire. In the atrium beyond the garages, the Savage army was setting fire to the church, and block B was burning with vast ginger flames. The whole place was alight – the little hut, the flats on the far side. And I could see the outline of the cross, blazing in the middle of the yard. For over a minute I watched it burn, distinct in the darkness, till at last it lurched forward, hesitated, and collapsed into the wreck of the church.

# 28

I went the long way back to school, skirting the red glow of the estates. It was almost midnight, and the whole place was deserted, shop windows shuttered, no cars on the road. The school itself was completely silent. I climbed into the courtyard at the back, and broke in through the loo window. Everything smelt of disinfectant. In the locker rooms I showered in the dark, standing for ages under the shower head, and washing my clothes by stamping on them. Then I put on a track-suit, stuffed my wet clothes in a bag, and let myself in to the bunker.

I lay on the cardboard mattress with the lights off. There was a great storm in my head, and I imagined that if only I could lie there long enough it would start to clear. But the noise of it kept rising. For a long time, I thought about Savage. It was obvious that he had won, even though he was dead. He had outwitted the police, beaten Daly and Collins and all the frauds who thought they knew what he needed but understood nothing about him. Probably his little empire would be over in a month, but he had not been afraid to do what was in his heart, and everyone would admire him, even if they couldn't admit it. And the strange thing was, I was the one who felt guilty and afraid, endlessly confused, while he had never doubted himself for a second.

Eventually I tried to sleep, but I kept panicking about the old man firing his gun while his block of flats went up in flames, and Dan dropping down into the atrium. Then I remembered Dan's photo of his uncle, standing in his shorts by the aquamarine fishing boat, and after that I just lay there without moving.

I woke up a few hours later, and there was light in the bunker, but I was still terrified. I started searching about for drugs. I wanted something to calm me down. But there was nothing left. I needed to eat, too, but that would mean going outside, so instead I drank water from the basin, and tried to sleep again. Then, as I was lying there half asleep, I started to remember this holiday we went on when I was little, Mum and Sticker and me. The three of us drove up to Scotland in Sticker's Triumph, but it broke down on the road through Glencoe. It was raining, with clouds banked up against the hills, and a tunnel of grey light leading down towards the sea. Stick and Mum were arguing, and I was leaning my head against the window looking up at the cliffs and the sky. The whole world was black as a mine shaft. And all the time that Sticker was yelling at my mother, I just kept staring out. Then I started to get this feeling of floating away, of my mind soaring up into the great solid sky above me until I wasn't even in the car any more.

After that, for the rest of the holiday, I had this feeling – a conviction almost – that nobody could touch me any more. Sticker went walking every day in the hills, while Mum and I sat in the B&B, or wandered along the seashore. And I started to form the idea that I was indestructible – that I could disappear from the world into a secret chamber of my mind whenever I liked. For some reason it made me feel strange, remembering that – sad, even. I had a sense of being overcome by millions of regrets.

On the second morning I was really starving. For the whole of that day I kept having these sharp, very precise memories of childhood, and my mind was floating, almost like I was stoned. I became determined to remember everything: to check my memory and make it work, as though things would become clear to me if I could only remember well enough. So I recited pieces of poetry just to test myself, or looked about in the stacks for books that might help me.

On the third night, I slept much better. I even had a dream about Miranda, and in the morning I wanted to go outside. I really needed to eat, too. But I had to make a decision: I wanted to get clear in my mind. So I sat up by the reading light.

*Everything they have taught us is wrong,* I scribbled on the yellow paper. *Not just wrong: point by point the opposite of the truth. They force us to live without memory, without a soul – and for years I have been reading what they buried down here, to discover the truth for myself. But I have always been alone.*

*Now I must decide,* I wrote in big letters. I paused, sitting up straight. *As long as I am alone, I will not find what I am looking for.*

It was very bright outside. I walked slowly at first, feeling weak, a few hundred yards down the High Street, then out to the suburbs, all the way to Gibbon's place. Everything seemed new: the countryside, the sky, everything in the streets looked brighter than usual, heavy with colour. It was as though I'd never really looked at anything properly before.

Gibbon opened the door, but he just stared at me. He wasn't smiling.

'You've got a lot of explaining to do. Where the hell have you been?'

'Thinking.'

'Good God. The police have been on the phone . . . There was a riot.'

'I know.'

'I thought you were caught up in it.'

'No way.' I shook my head. 'I mean – not exactly.'

'Well, were you or not?'

'I went there,' I said. 'I saw what was happening.'

He faced me full on. 'Did you commit any crime?'

I shook my head.

'*Think*: it's important.'

'No,' I said. 'I tried to save the old man, but I don't know

273

what happened. Dan is dead. And his mother. I managed to get out.'

He watched me carefully, but his voice changed.

'I didn't realise. I'm sorry. Why didn't you phone?'

'I'm – I didn't know what to do. I can't really explain. I came as soon as I could – as soon as I could think straight. You see, I want to get away. I've worked it out. I mustn't stay here.'

He took a letter from the desk and gave it to me. It was from Miss Fanon in the Admissions Office. She said I had an interview at four o'clock that day, and various tests and another interview the next morning.

'We can still try, can't we?' I said. 'We've got time.'

'*We?*' he repeated. 'That beats everything.'

'I can work in the car.'

Gibbon sighed. 'At this point, they're not even expecting you.'

'I'll call,' I said. 'I'll explain what happened.'

There was a long pause. Gibbon was still frowning, but he pulled his little diary out of the pile of papers on his desk.

'No,' he said. 'I'll ring. I'll see what they say. You might as well get changed. Have a bath and pack some things. If we're going, we'll need to spend the night there.'

'Thank you,' I said.

'And you'd better have some breakfast,' he added. 'You look as pale as a piece of cod.'


I put out one of my suits, and started running a bath. Then I lay stretched out with my eyes closed in the grey water, steaming and dozing off. When Gibbon banged on the door I was almost asleep. 'They've agreed to see you,' he yelled. 'Sometime towards the end of the day.' He sounded resigned. 'You'll be told the details when you register. We'd better get a move on.'

I had a shave and started getting dressed, and Gibbon came up with the post. There was another letter from C— College, with its red stamp on the envelope, telling me about the arrangements for staying overnight, and a postcard from my mother, which Miss Tooley had forwarded. I propped the card on the mirror while I tied this two-tone knitted tie I had found.

*Dear Merton*, she said, *How are you? I've got some wonderful news. Mike and I have decided to get married.* I dropped the ends of my tie, staring at the card. Then I picked it up and sat down on the bed. *We really feel it's time*, Mum had written, *after so long, to properly settle down like a real couple. And Mike is so well these days, you wouldn't know him. He saw the doctor and he's a changed man, I swear love. We both feel so different. Please come and see us. Let bygones be bygones. The wedding is in the town hall, next Thursday at six. Then we're going to Spain! Come and support us!!! All our love, Mum and Mike.*

For a few minutes I just sat on the bed. Gibbon was calling me, and the house had started to smell of toast and fried eggs. So I put the card on the little table and finished dressing. Then, when I was almost ready, I read it through again, and looked at the picture. It was from some animal charity: a cat staring at the camera in a red bow-tie. For some reason it made me think of Miranda. I really wished I had called her.

There were no proper shoes I could wear – only my trainers – so I jammed them on. But I looked pretty good: green suit, white shirt, wool tie. There was a pile of old notes on the floor by my bed, but there wasn't time to sort them out, so I just grabbed them all and took them down to breakfast.

# 29

All the way to the M11 we sat in silence. I stared at the suburbs and looked up at the sky over the countryside. Then, when we reached the motorway, Gibbon speeded up, and the road made a thumping noise under the car. He was still angry with me, but I tried to get him talking. I wanted to explain what I had thought about in the bunker, why I wanted to do this interview and everything, but I couldn't put it into words. So I asked him about Cambridge, instead: how it was paid for, who was really in charge. But he wouldn't get into that. He told me I should be thinking about the interview, and he started asking me history questions, like an exam.

We parked on the Backs, behind the water-meadows and over-grown gardens. It was only two, but the sky was low and it was almost dark already.

'What will they ask first?' I said. Suddenly I was light-headed.

'There's really no saying. They want to see if you'll be fun to teach – if you have a passion for the subject.' I was leaning against the car. 'Don't worry. Try to clear your head.'

We walked over Clare Bridge, through the weird, silent quads, into the streets beyond. Gibbon started saying something about the architecture, but I wasn't paying attention. It was incredibly cold. I was only wearing my green suit and a scarf. He kept pointing out the gargoyles on the side of C— College, but by the time we reached the porters' lodge I was feeling sick.

'In here.' He held the door for me. 'I'm not allowed beyond this point.'

'Let's walk around for a while,' I said. My hands were starting to shake. 'I want to see the other colleges.'

'Later,' he said. 'You'd better sign in.'

I stood in the doorway, and he backed away. He had his woolly hat on, pulled down over his head.

'Do you think they'll ask about the Dark Ages?' I said.

'Could do.'

'Or the Fall of Rome?'

'Very possibly.' He smiled.

'What should I think about?'

'Try to relax.'

'I can't remember anything.'

'You'll be fine.'

He stepped forward and gripped my shoulders. I didn't mind. I let him do it. Then he gave me a hug.

By the time I signed my name on the register, and checked the details on my form and everything, there wasn't much time. They sent me through the quad to the main building.

I had to wait with other candidates in a panelled room at the top of the stairs. The interviews were almost over for the day, so there were only a few people in there: a girl with hip-hop plaits, and a couple of spindly guys – one spotty and tall, the other thin-lipped in a midnight-blue shirt, looking Byronic by the window. Sitting down in the corner, I pulled my notes from the plastic bag, and tried to read, but I was distracted by people laughing downstairs. The room was very hot.

'Can I open a window?' I said.

The plaited girl smiled but said nothing, so I went across to sort it out, but I thumped my shin on a little table, and almost fell over. 'Shit!'

'You all right?'

'I'll do it,' Byron said.

'Are they on time?' I asked, hopping back to my chair.

'Seem to be,' the spotty one said in a nasal voice.

I sat down to read again, but nothing made sense. The pages were completely out of order. I should have sorted them in the car. So I sat there staring into space, until the cold air gusted into the room. Then without warning I remembered Dan falling into the atrium, and I really thought I was going to throw up.

I forced myself to concentrate, taking deep breaths. For ten minutes I went over the top page of my notes again and again. But the spidery writing, when I deciphered it, recorded only random thoughts on the history of Europe: the dates of church councils, of popes and emperors; some stuff about Gothic symbolism and the old Catholic Mass. I really couldn't remember why I'd written it. I suppose originally in the bunker, at the climax of some reading binge, there had been an argument there – a great synthesis of art, politics and religion. But now it only made me feel I had forgotten everything.

A woman came out. 'Peter Glover,' she said, smiling. 'Sorry to keep you. I'm Dr Templeton. We're ready to see you now.'

Byron got up and followed her through the panelled door, just as the last candidate came out – a big guy with a mop of blond hair, crooked tie, shirt untucked. In the room beyond I could see four dons sitting along a table.

The mop-head hit his leg against the table, exactly the way I had, and started rubbing his shin. 'Fucking hell!'

'How did it go?' the girl asked.

'Bloody awful.' He limped to the door.

There was silence in our little room while I tried to read my notes again, but things really started to deteriorate. Instead of words and arguments, I just kept thinking about Dan. So I stuffed the notes in my pocket and got up.

'Where are you going?' the girl with plaits said.

'Outside.'

'Hurry, you'll miss your slot.'

\* \* \*

In the courtyard I stared into the sky.

'It's going to snow,' someone said. I looked round and saw the mop-haired man, buttoning his coat by the door.

'Yes?'

'Are you Merton?'

'Yes.'

'Then you'd better go. They're looking for you.'

'Oh.'

'Nervous?'

I nodded.

'What do you want to read?'

'Modern History.'

'Me too. But I screwed up. You can have my place.'

'Thanks,' I said.

'Good luck.'

'What did they ask you?'

'Oh, E. H. Carr, mostly. You know. *What is History?* Are there any facts, or is it all bullshit and ideology? Then we got on to rationalism in politics – Oakeshott, and all that. Cowling on Mill – you know . . .'

'Oh?'

'Templeton's a bit utilitarian, but some of the others are all right.' And he added, nodding towards the entrance, 'You shouldn't keep them waiting. They forget all their right-on relativism when it comes to dinner time.'

I didn't tell him I'd never heard of Oakeshott. I just laughed and flew inside.

'Merton Browne?' The door opened inwards, and I was face to face with her narrow smile. 'I'm Dr Templeton. Do come in. I thought we'd lost you again. Are you all right?'

'I went for some air.'

'Not feeling well?'

'I'm okay,' I said.

The room was panelled, like the other, but whitewashed, with

279

bookcases along the far wall behind the dons. There were three slim volumes laid out on the table, with bookmarks in them, like they were suddenly going to whip them out and make me read or something.

'This is Professor Fisher,' Dr Templeton said.

Fisher nodded and smiled.

'Professor Ffrench and Dr Langland.'

'Hi,' I said.

'John Klimov.'

'How do you do,' he said.

'And Mr Smart will join us for this part of the interview. He's doing a survey on admissions procedures. Admissions and – and *transparency*, isn't it?' she asked lightly. 'For the government.' She smiled briefly, and took her place.

Mr Smart had a chair set back behind the others. On his lap were a clipboard and a stack of forms. He looked up to give me a rapid, lizard-like nod.

There was a pause while they examined their papers. Then they exchanged glances, and one of the men – Dr Langland – leaned back in his chair, and placed his fingertips in his pudgy cheek.

'Mr Browne,' he said, 'Merton. What would you say is the *point* of a university?'

They all sat behind their thick table, staring at me – all except Mr Smart, who silently marked his forms. It was the kind of annoying question Gibbon would have asked, and in fact we had talked about it. Dr Langland raised an eyebrow. Outside the window, the first few flakes of snow started to float by in silence.

'Originally, do you mean? Or nowadays?' I leant forward.

'Is the answer dependent on the passage of time?' Professor Ffrench asked.

'I suppose not.' I could feel my face turning red.

'I didn't say it *wasn't*.' Ffrench's bald head shone in the overhead lights. 'I was just asking.'

I dropped back in my plastic chair and at that moment I caught sight of my green suit. Nobody else was wearing a suit – nobody except Professor Fisher. I felt like a prat.

'What do you think, Merton?' Dr Templeton urged.

'I don't know . . .'

I watched the snow beginning to swirl outside the window-panes, trying to remember what I had read in the bunker. 'At least – well, originally, anyway –' but my mind refused to move. A sound like the humming of a pump began in my brain. 'You know, in the Middle Ages . . .'

'Yes?'

'. . . universities were sort of monasteries . . .' For some reason that was the first thing I thought of, but it didn't seem right. There was a look of pity on Templeton's face. 'I mean, *universitas* means a corporation, doesn't it? A body with its own laws and culture, in which people live a professed life together . . .'

'But *what* life?' John Klimov put in. 'And *who* lives it?'

Mr Smart adjusted his glasses. 'They were poor scholars,' I stammered. 'Poor men, living the life of a community devoted to learning – officially, anyway; to the pursuit of knowledge – and, you know – truth . . .'

'And what was their conception of truth . . . ?' John Klimov smiled. He rested his head on his hand at the end of the table, gazing towards me with electric eyes. 'Where did it arise from?'

'They were Christians in those days,' I said. 'I suppose they thought truth was part of that world view.'

'Yes?'

'But they read Aristotle and Plato, too. They were concerned with logic, the examination of sources . . . They were trying to work out what had to be true, and what was false.'

'Why?'

'Because they wanted to know. It says in the Bible, "The truth will set you free".'

'But what I'm getting at,' Klimov said, as if I was being extremely stupid, 'what I'm driving at is, wasn't the truth these scholars were searching for merely part of the ideological apparatus of their age? Or do you think there is an *objective* truth – something independent of culture or belief?'

That threw me again. It was pure Daly, and my heart retreated. But though I was quiet for another minute, my brain was beginning to move.

'You can connect science and culture with the interests of the ruling class,' I said. 'As though society is a sort of machine – a machine that makes culture.' The humming in my mind rose to a higher pitch. I was trying to think of the names of writers Daly had shown me, the ones who did that kind of analysis. 'But – well,' I made myself go on, 'that's not really right, is it? After all, if you do that, you're assuming that culture is the product of something more fundamental – a product of production and material conditions. But *why*? What if culture is most alive precisely when it's *independent* of material forces – when it escapes from the machinery of power? I mean, a culture involves a certain way of seeing the world . . .' And suddenly I remembered something I had read at Miranda's house. 'Culture is the incarnation of a religious world view,' I said, 'of an ideology. It has to do with shared meaning.'

There was a murmur along the bench, and Langland nodded, but I was depressed. I hated the sound of my voice.

'You speak about "truth" and "knowledge" as though they exist independently of social or political considerations,' Klimov repeated. 'Do you think that's realistic?'

'Why not?' I said. 'What about *your* work – academic work? Don't people do that because they want to know the truth?'

Professor Ffrench and Dr Langland caught each other's eyes, looking along the table. Ffrench watched me with this dead serious look in his eyes, as if he was deciding whether to send me to jail. John Klimov stared back at me, too, raising an eyebrow. Behind him, the man from the Department for Education and Skills made a note.

'What do you think, Merton?' Dr Templeton asked. 'Is it

possible to achieve knowledge despite the distorting effects of power?'

'It must be. You have to work for it. You have to try . . . But I don't even mean just knowledge, in any case.'

'What, then?'

'I don't know. *Judgement* – understanding . . .'

'But what is the *object*? What is the mind being asked to consider?' Dr Templeton asked.

'Anything which helps us understand the world,' I said. 'Not how to mend a car, or something stupid like how many pages there are on that shelf of books. But a knowledge of things which matter – which help you to understand . . .'

'Yes, I thought so,' Professor Fisher declared. 'Merton is a Newmanite.' He picked up one of the books on the table, and started flicking through.

'So, there is a certain pattern of knowledge which acts as a signal of status in society. That's all you're saying,' Klimov shrugged. 'That's all Newman's saying, too. It's just a matter of parroting the right lines.'

'Not only that,' I said. 'I don't think so. There can be a way of seeing things which people share. Isn't that what a culture is?'

'You mean *taste*,' Klimov said. 'Prejudice. But who is the judge of that?'

'People who get it – who understand.'

'So it's a circle?'

I hesitated. 'Yes.'

'A social circle. A club?'

'A culture,' I said.

'A conspiracy against those who do not belong . . .' He leaned back, watching me.

'A sort of language,' I said, 'a way of life. Is language a conspiracy?'

'So would you agree that knowledge is a function of social power?'

I shrugged. 'There might be a university with no powers at

all,' I said. 'It's just a community – a shared life. There's no reason why that should bring power. The opposite, in fact.'

'Why?'

'Because power might depend on stupid ideas – on business management or media studies –'.

'Are you saying that what goes on at a university has no bearing on social power?'

'I don't know. But it's not the *point*, is it?'

'What do you think the merchant banks and the civil service would say to that?' he smiled. 'They recruit here every year.'

'Who cares what they think? That's nothing to do with it.'

'Well, Merton, that's certainly a strong view . . .' Professor Fisher put in. He had opened his book and taken out the marker. 'We were discussing this very point earlier. Between us we occupied three rather different camps.' He gave Klimov a dry smile. 'There is C.P. Snow's famous attack on British universities in the nineteen sixties. He argued that they really *should* be concerned with increasing economic growth. Then there's something quite recent from the government, which we've been asked to comment on . . . And of course John Henry Newman, *The Idea of a University*, which advances a strongly anti-utilitarian view. Let's see . . . If I may?'

'Of course,' Templeton said.

Fisher leaned forward and started to read. '"Education implies an action upon our mental nature,"' he read, '"and the formation of a character . . . it is an acquired illumination, a habit, an inward endowment . . . and since cultivation of the mind is surely worth seeking for its own sake, we are thus brought to the conclusion that there is a Knowledge which is desirable, though nothing come of it, as being of itself a treasure, and a sufficient remuneration of years of labour . . ."'

'Pure rhetoric,' Klimov sighed, shaking his head. 'Where does that take you?'

'No,' I said. 'I think he's right. I agree with that. Why else does anybody read? We're looking for something. Only, we don't know what it is until we find it. Probably nobody believes that any more,' I went on, looking at Klimov. 'Everything has to be measured, evaluated – like you're running a factory: quality assurance, targets, skills for the modern workplace . . . But you can't measure the real thing, can you?'

Fisher was looking side-on at Langland. 'I think I know what you mean . . .' he said: 'Leading-edge services, top-down driven . . . You've come across this sort of language?'

'Our headteacher is an expert,' I said: 'The education process offers challenges as well as opportunities . . . The future will require a learning society, driving problem-solving and key skill acquisition through the higher education sector, the schooling process, and access to information technology for life . . .'

Mr Smart folded his arms and stared at me.

'It's all about generating values,' I went on, 'allocating resources, managing outcomes . . . They're all looking at education from the outside – counting the number of students, the number of A grades, the pass rate, the drop-out rate . . . But it's all rubbish. The only thing that matters is what's going on inside your mind, in your character, and that's private, almost hidden – it's impossible to measure . . .'

But after that I didn't want to say any more, and I just stopped talking.

The room was quiet. Klimov scowled. Smart wrote something on his clipboard. The others glanced sideways at one another. Outside, the courtyard was full of snow. You could see the thick flakes falling and floating in the corridor of light cast by the window.

Dr Templeton was getting to her feet. 'We're running over time,' she said. 'I'm afraid we'll have to leave it there.'

I got up and she guided me to the door. Langland had gone over to Klimov. They started talking together like old friends.

'Is that it?' I asked her.

'You'll have your history interview tomorrow,' she said. 'And the written papers.' She held the door for me. 'I'll see you in the morning, Merton.'

I wandered into the icy darkness outside. A pock-marked blanket of snow had settled on the gargoyles and stone balconies. Then I found Gibbon, and he took me to a Greek restaurant in a narrow lane, where we sat on wooden benches and drank cold retsina from tumblers. I started to cram pitta bread in my mouth, staring at the olive shoulders of the waitress until she caught me in her gaze.

Gibbon didn't ask much about the interview. He was full of sad thoughts about his own days at Cambridge, so I let him talk, and after supper he led me back through the muffled streets to the tower in the college where we had our rooms.

I had to see Klimov in the morning, just the two of us. We argued again, but in the end it wasn't so bad. He mainly wanted to know what I'd read, so I talked about Trevelyan and Hobsbawm. Then I gave him all the arguments from Daly's New Left classics, before pulling them apart.

The written exams were in the afternoon. They didn't ask anything I hadn't thought about before, and quite soon I was thumping out my ideas, almost as though I was writing an essay for Gibbon. In the special paper I answered a question on religion in the English Civil War. And for a while as I wrote, I was elated. Everything was in harmony – the shape of my argument, the evidence I used. It just came pouring through my pen, years of impulses and digressions in the bunker fixed and laid out on the page in three straight hours.

# 30

After the exams, I left a message for Miranda. Then Gibbon and I got our stuff and walked to the Backs.

We hardly talked the whole way back. I just listened to the rhythm of the road under the car. The snow was melting already, and the flat pale ground was broken by sooty pimples all the way to the horizon.

After Ilford, we took the M25 halfway round London. It was dark by the time we drove past Cannon Park, along the High Street. We were heading out towards Gibbon's place, but I wasn't sure. It was the day of Mum's wedding, and I started thinking about her. She and Mike were probably still in the Town Hall; or maybe they were already on their way to the airport. And when I thought of that I suddenly wanted to be on my own. So I asked Gibbon to leave me near Dante Park, so that I could go home. I said I had to collect some things, and I'd ring him later. But he got out of the car and offered me his hand.

'I'm very proud of you,' he said.

'I don't think it was such a huge success . . .' I looked down at his shoes. I didn't want to let him down all at once, but I thought he'd have to know. 'It didn't go too well.'

'You're pessimistic. That's natural.'

'No, I mean it. I said the wrong things. Klimov hated me.'

'Even if he did, that isn't the point. It's a collegiate decision.'

'Well – whatever. It wasn't a great success.'

'Howbeit,' he said, 'whether you got in or not, I'm proud of you.' And he gave my arm a squeeze.

\* \* \*

The house was freakily tidy. Everything had been put away. It was cold in there, too. They'd packed everything up, turned off the heating, and gone. It was so quiet I thought at first I was going to find a dead body or something. For a long time I just sat on the sofa, gazing at the neat stacks of videos and music books, the big blank screen of the TV, all the electric plugs switched off, the coffee table completely clear. On the shelf above the telly there was a new photo of Mum and Mike, grinning and holding hands.

In the end I made myself go upstairs. I wanted to see if I could find any of my things, any books or clothes from childhood – to see if anything was left. But the silence was creepy, and after a while I turned on the TV in my mother's bedroom while I searched about.

Outside on the landing I opened my suitcase, and gradually I started packing a few things: Tintin books, *The Child's Book of Cathedrals*, a few clothes – things that my mother had hidden from Mike.

In the next room, the local news came on:

'. . . *community leaders were today regretting the loss of life on the estate, and there is a widespread sense of anger towards the police, who are believed by many to have overreacted to a situation already made fragile by years of ethnic tensions, poor public services, and high levels of poverty . . .*'

I stood at the door to see what was going on. They were showing the burnt-out shell of block B, Cannon Park Estate. A lot of coppers were standing about in riot gear, but things seemed to be calmer.

'*With me now,*' the reporter said, '*I have a key figure in the Cannon Park Community Organisation. Terence Arkwright is the leader of the Estate Task Force. Mr Arkwright . . .*'

I stared at the screen. There was Terry, looking very grave. Calvin and Tatham were flanking him, all wearing a sort of uniform: combat jackets with some sort of badge on the shoulder.

'*The important thing is to keep order,*' Terry explained. '*There's a lot of drug dealers, child abusers, burglars here. The Task Force keeps people in line.*'

'*Can I ask you about the loss of life on the estate, during the riots?*' the woman asked.

'*At the end of the day it's the system, the police,*' Terry said. '*The police are violent with our youth, and we have a right to protect ourselves . . .*'

I hesitated, staring at him. Then I switched off the TV and started searching round the house again. I didn't know what I was looking for exactly, but I took my time. I hardly found anything else though – just a chart of dates I had copied from the *Guinness Book of Records*, lying at the back of a cupboard. Then I closed all the upstairs doors and turned off the lights.

Downstairs I stood in the hall, trying to decide what to do. I stared back into the empty sitting-room one more time. Then I went outside and locked the door. And when I had dropped the keys through the letter-box, I picked up my case and marched away.

I carried my suitcase across the close, over Dante Park, all the way to Gibbon's house. But I didn't go inside. I left it behind the garden shed, and set off again, to the bridge over the main road, towards the town where Miranda lived.

She came to the door herself. There was the sound of a violin, and some voices – her mother on the phone, children arguing. Miranda stepped into the porch and closed the door behind her. For a moment we just stood there, looking at each other. But I took her hand, and after that she put her arms round me, and we stood there for ages while I felt Miranda's heartbeat.

'God I've been worried about you,' she said.

'I'm sorry,' I began. 'I'm sorry I didn't come back.'

'You should have rung.'

'I was hiding,' I said. 'I kept away from everybody.'

'But you should have trusted me.'

'I know.'

'I watched it on TV,' she said. 'I thought you were dead.' She stood back to look at me, and I took her face between my hands. 'I rang the police and everything,' she said. 'Then finally I got your message.' She was almost crying.

'I'm really sorry,' I said. 'I want to tell you about it. I want to explain everything – as much as I can.'

'How can I trust you?' she sighed.

'It's okay,' I said. 'We'll do it slowly, remember. Let's go somewhere. Let's go for a drive.'

She shook her head.

'Yes, come with me.'

'I don't want to drive around.'

'No, somewhere peaceful,' I said. 'I know. We'll go to that church.'

She boggled her huge eyes at me. 'What church?'

'The one you took me to.'

'Why do want to go *there* all of sudden?'

'I just do. I don't know why. It's peaceful. We can talk. Nobody will bother us.'

She put her head on one side, watching me. 'Oh God,' she said at last. 'Wait there. I'll get the keys.'

She drove us in her mother's mini to the other end of the town. Then we ran through the cold from the car park to the church steps, only coming to a stop in the silence at the back, where Miranda crossed herself with holy water. Far away at the main altar an old woman was bowing before the tabernacle. Another figure, dressed in a sari, knelt at a side chapel, and a couple of men were going about picking up papers from the pews.

Miranda and I walked to the crossing. We sat in silence, a couple of feet apart, near a picture of Mary Magdalene. The blood was hammering in my temples. The old woman touched the floor with her forehead. At each side altar a little bank of candles was burning for a saint.

After ten minutes my pulse had slowed down. It was very dense in there, clogged with images, but I was calm. Miranda closed her eyes, and I thought she must be praying. I didn't pray, though. We didn't talk, either, in the end. There was just the silence of the church, and in my head some stray, disordered thoughts. And then, without warning, I had this sensation in my heart, just for a second. It was a kind of longing, an almost physical tremor, and at once I wanted to get up and fly into the sanctuary. But I didn't move. I started remembering things, surveying them in my mind with a sort of detachment. I remembered Dan and his mother, the riot, then Klimov and the snow in Cambridge. And as I sat there, I felt I was going back in time. It was no more than impressions: memories of childhood, anxieties about things that had happened long ago, or about things that never happened, but were known only through a sort of deficit in the heart, like my father.

A man appeared and started snuffing out the candles. Someone rang a bell. The woman in the sari got up, genuflecting towards the tabernacle. Miranda did the same, and for some reason I wanted to copy her. 'I don't want to go,' I said.

The bell rang again. 'They're closing up,' she said. 'Give me your hand.' And she led me out.

# 31

I spent two days in Paddington Green Police Station with Benedict Doyle, DC Peterson and this guy from Special Branch, telling them pretty much everything I knew about the riot, the murder of Dan and the others. I had to explain exactly what I had done – that I had kept the old man's gun and everything.

At first I was frightened they would grill me about Frank Cooper, whether he had killed Savage or not, and I was ready to deny it. But they just said Savage had been killed by a bullet from an unknown gun, perhaps by one of his own posse. And they said the old man had got out safely before block B collapsed, but that he was ill, and they weren't questioning him.

As for the rest, they already knew most of it. They had been filming the whole time from the helicopter, including a shot of me approaching Savage by the church. But Benedict made a plea bargain: they said they wouldn't prosecute me for having the revolver, so long as I talked. So I explained everything, going right back to when I was fourteen and I started nicking Mike's cocaine.

When the cops had finished, and I was free to go, Miranda and I went to stay with her uncle, miles away from everything, on the coast of Devon.

Miranda had been to his house loads of times, but that didn't stop us getting lost. She drove her mother's old Mini, three hours of Messerschmidt-blast on the motorway, followed by an evening arguing over the map in tiny villages. When we arrived at the hamlet it was already the middle of the night, and there was another mile to go through the woods. The uncle had a cottage he let to tourists: a little Gothic chalet on its own in the trees above the sea, logs piled up in the porch. We got there after two, dropping down in one of the bedrooms without undressing, and fell asleep.

The next day Miranda and I went for a walk in the cold, wandering through the woods to the seashore. The coast was broken up by bays and estuaries. On the other side of the river was an old mill-house standing in a water-meadow with horses. Miranda led me up a path from the beach to the top of the cliff, and we marched along, a hundred feet above the rocks, heading for the next village. To the south there was the flat, soapy grey-ness of the Channel, and on the other side dark woods that covered the hills, without a house anywhere. We walked for hours.

Wherever we went, it was very quiet. At night there were owls, and some other shrieking birds, and at dawn the seagulls. Occasionally we heard gunshots in the distance, or the engine of a fishing boat crossing the bay. But most of the time the whole country was silent. For more than a week I didn't read a word. We still hadn't even had sex, either. Miranda said we weren't ready – that sex implied a lifetime's commitment, and we really had to get to know each other. So we just kept tramping through the woods, holding hands, staring at the sea. And Miranda told me a lot about her life and her family, which wasn't the way I had imagined it, considering the way it looked from the outside.

Miranda's whole family came down to spend Christmas at her uncle's house, and on Christmas Eve we went to midnight Mass in a village miles away. Then one day before the New Year, when they had all gone back to London, Gibbon turned up in his Honda.

'I decided I'd descend on you,' he said. 'See how you're managing.' He shook my hand, and gave Miranda a kiss on the cheek. 'I've got some mail for you, and a few – a few bits and pieces.'

'How's Terry's Republic?'

'Oh, prospering,' he smiled. 'They'll have full diplomatic recognition soon, I should think. What do they call it? A *Police-Community Liaison Committee*. Arkwright's in charge. Here, Merton,' he handed me a pile of letters: 'Have a look at these.'

The first three letters had the C— College postmark on them. I sliced the envelopes with a knife, and went outside into the wind. But when I read the first letter it didn't make sense, so I took the other two, checked the dates, compared them with the first. They were each from a different person – one from Klimov, one from Dr Templeton, and the last from Miss Fanon the admissions secretary. They all said slightly different things.

'I don't understand,' I said, going back inside. 'What's an exhibition?'

'A kind of scholarship,' Gibbon said. 'They give you a couple of hundred pounds, and you get a decent room.'

'But, why?'

'I don't know,' he smiled. 'They must have liked you.'

'Jesus.'

'Merton . . .' Miranda was staring at me. 'That's fantastic. You're in.'

'I can't be . . .'

'It must be true,' Gibbon smiled. 'It's in the local papers.'

Miranda put her arms round me, and Gibbon read out a cutting from the *Cannon Park Chronicle*: *'LOCAL BOY'S SCHOLARSHIP TO CAMBRIDGE. Merton Browne, a pupil at the award-winning New Crosland Comprehensive in Cannon Park, has gained a prestigious scholarship to C— College, Cambridge*. Bla-bla, let's see. Yes: our headmaster speaks. *Simon Collins, headteacher at the New Crosland, spoke of the school's pride in Merton's achievement. "It's a proud day for the school," Mr Collins told the* Chronicle. *"Merton has always been one of our star pupils, and his acceptance by Cambridge is a welcome sign that the ancient universities are moving away from a narrow focus on the privileged to foster the development of a modern knowledge-based society . . ."'*

Miranda laughed.

'Your friend Daly gets a quote, too.' Gibbon was frowning at the paper. 'Here: *Andrew Daly, Deputy Head of the New Crosland, described as a close personal friend of Mr Browne, also spoke of his satisfaction at the result. "Merton's achievement, and others like it, disprove claims that education is in crisis in this country," Mr Daly commented . . . "We have widened access, increased opportunity . . ."* on it goes.'

But Gibbon broke off suddenly. 'I've got a present for you,' he announced. 'Outside.' And he took me to his car. 'Here, take this.' He pulled a small cardboard box from the back seat of the Honda. 'This is just a sample, you understand. The rest are at home.'

I carried the box to the kitchen and cut it open. It had been neatly packed, red leather hardbacks, six of them, individually preserved in bubblewrap. I tore the plastic off the first. '*The Cambridge History of Europe.*'

'I thought you should have this,' Gibbon said. 'Something post nineteen sixty-four.'

I unwrapped all six volumes, I recognised them from Gibbon's study.

'They're beautiful,' Miranda said.

'I – I'm . . . *Thank* you.' I stood looking at them. 'I don't know what to say.'

'It was a pleasure.'

For a moment I thought he was going to hug me again. 'I'm glad,' he said. 'Let's go for a walk. I want to see your new kingdom.'

In the middle of January there was a storm in the Channel. For two days while the wind pounded the cottage, Miranda and I hid in the sitting-room, eating bacon sandwiches and chocolate-chip cookies, reading Shakespeare's history plays.

The gale blew so hard on the second night that neither us could sleep. And on the third day, very early in the morning, we put on our coats and went outside. The rain had stopped, but the storm wasn't over yet. We crawled against the wind to the edge of the wood above the cliffs. Then, at the summit, we tried to stand up straight, looking into the distance, our eyelids pummelled by the violent air.

The southern horizon had been absorbed by clouds. You couldn't make out where the sea ended or the sky began. There was just a single mass between the frantic mercury waves at our feet, and the storm clouds parting and re-forming overhead. We stood there for ages while the sun rose, and the sky became brighter. And as long as I stared into the wind, I felt strange and elated, unencumbered. And I imagined Miranda and me flying out, right into the heart of the storm, towards the bright sun on the other side of the clouds, while England disappeared behind us.

## Acknowledgements

I owe a huge debt to my family and friends for their encouragement throughout the writing of this book. I am especially grateful to Clare Clark for her generous and perfectly timed assistance; Jonathan Foreman for his tremendous enthusiasm from the outset; and Barnaby Jameson for his legal expertise.

I also want to thank my altogether outstanding agent, Clare Alexander, for her wise guidance on countless matters; Matthew Hamilton, also at Gillon Aitken, for his perceptive editorial advice; and Jocasta Brownlee, my superb editor at Sceptre, along with all her team.

Finally and above all, my heartfelt thanks go to my wife Caroline, without whose close involvement at every stage this book would never have been possible, and to whom it is dedicated with all my love.